Lady and the Gent

Also by
Rebecca Connolly

An Arrangement of Sorts

Married to the Marquess

Secrets of a Spinster

The Dangers of Doing Good

The Burdens of a Bachelor

A Bride Worth Taking

A Wager Worth Making

A Gerrard Family Christmas

More romance from
Phase Publishing

by
Emily Daniels
A Song for a Soldier

by
Laura Beers
A Peculiar Courtship

by
Grace Donovan
Saint's Ride

The Lady and the Gent

Rebecca Connolly

Phase Publishing, LLC
Seattle

Cover art by Tugboat Design
http://www.tugboatdesign.net

Phase Publishing, LLC first paperback edition
February 2018

ISBN 978-1-943048-49-6
Library of Congress Control Number 2018930690
Cataloging-in-Publication Data on file.

*A*cknowledgements

To her majesty, Queen Elizabeth II, for the strength she possesses, the character she maintains, and the grace she exudes in everything. The world is only more fortunate for having her in it, and I am so very grateful for her impeccable example of dignity and class. God save the Queen!

And for Aidan Turner, who was instrumental in the inspiration of this book. You are perfectly free to contact me to discuss the matter at your leisure. I am sure we could work something out.

Want to hear about future releases and upcoming events for Rebecca Connolly?

Sign up for the monthly Wit and Whimsy at:

www.rebeccaconnolly.com

Chapter One
London, 1824

"Margaret, stop looking at that man."

Margaret Easton jerked guiltily and looked up at her mother in shock, and not a little embarrassment.

Her mother did not return her look, but kept her gaze fixed squarely ahead of her, chin held high, auburn hair coifed to perfection. She did not look her age, but she held all of the airs of it. "It is hardly proper to stare at any man, let alone a common one. Do not encourage him."

"Yes, Mama," she murmured obediently, lowering her eyes, then covertly sliding them to the window again.

Truth be told, Margaret could see very little that was common about this man. For one, she saw him every week, sometimes multiple times, sometimes daily, and each was a pleasant surprise to her. She could not remember the first time it happened, as she usually stared out of her carriage window in fascination and wonder. But she remembered when it happened again. And again. And she remembered her trip to the milliner the first day he had smiled at her. She could not remember what she had purchased on that day, but she recalled that smile.

She remembered the first day he had touched her hand. A Thursday just like this one, crowded and busy and destined to be miserable, and then to find him there to help her from the coach, as perfectly as a gentleman with all the efficiency of a footman. He fairly towered over her slight height, but the gentleness of his hold had stolen her breath and her sense.

She'd berated herself for her idiocy on that day, and what a simpleton he must think her for her lack of appropriate response or conversation. When she had seen him the very next day, and he'd smiled, she'd forgotten all about scolding herself and given herself up to the delight of being impudent and flirtatious for once.

It had become a little game to them, though neither had ever spoken a word beyond polite pleasantries. If she saw him while riding in her carriage, as she had now, she would stare. He would stare. And one of them would smile first. Some days it was him. Most days it was her.

Every now and again, rather than moments of blatant staring, she would find him at hand to assist her or her mother from their carriage. He would incline his head properly, or lift his hat, or bow, always so polite, murmuring a "Good morning" or "Here you go, miss" or "madam" if her mother were with her. And his eyes would dance, as if their meeting were scandalous and secretive, though the streets would teem about them. Those moments were precious indeed.

Encourage him? How could she encourage a man she did not see for more than ten seconds at a time and rarely more than once in the same day?

But ten seconds seemed more than enough. Every sight of him stayed with her, and replayed over and over in her mind with accompanying breathlessness and swoons.

She could not help but to be curious about him. What was his trade or his employ? He had been seen on Bond Street, High Street, Kensington Street, and in Trafalgar. She had seen him in Cheapside and in Mayfair, and once or twice she could have sworn she saw him near the theater, but he had not seen her. Always he appeared busy and engaged, but never too much to meet her eyes. The places he seemed to be were so varied and vast, and his attire so different, it was impossible to determine his profession. If indeed he had one. It had crossed her mind once or twice that he could have been a peddler of stolen goods or a gypsy without home or means.

He did have that sort of dark complexion that could pass for a Romani gypsy, but not entirely so. Perhaps half of his descent? He was dreadfully handsome, but not in the way that polite females should think. His was a more rough and virile sort of attractiveness, the sort that made the heart quicken and the palms sweat. And her breath caught and her head swam, her stomach clenched and the very hairs on her head tingled in odd anticipation…

It was hardly a proper series of sensations to feel, but that seemed inconsequential.

He was entirely unlike any man of her acquaintance. Oh, she'd met a good many attractive, respectable men, and any of them ought to have done for her. But compared with her ideals of a husband, and the all-too-tempting picture her mystery man presented, they all felt rather… tame.

He, on the other hand, was captivating. He seemed a rather adventurous sort. A highwayman or a pirate, perhaps, though she had never seen him near the docks. She imagined him doing all sorts of daring and impossible things, and was doing so with an increasing frequency that would have alarmed her mother had she any idea.

No girl of twenty-two would do anything so very scandalous as to ogle a strange man and wonder just how expansive his chest and shoulders actually were. Or if the muscles beneath his rough clothing were as defined as the drawings in the medical atlas she found in her father's library. Or if his teeth were as perfect as his smile seemed to indicate. Or if…

Well, there were a great many things she wondered behind her innocent façade as she stared. She knew full well there would never be answers for such things, as they would never be introduced or associate in any way. Wondering was safe, as was imagining. Despite her mother's warnings, Margaret was not the sort of girl to behave in any manner but what she was expected to. She was the picture of a meek, obedient, biddable daughter.

Externally, at any rate.

Still, she rather enjoyed looking at him, despite the brazen nature of it all. Why he should look back at her was a mystery, as she was in her third Season without any more suitors than she'd had in her first. Her cousin Helen thought it might be due to her lack of corset, but Margaret did not think so. Surely there were other females who were opposed to the cinching of such monstrosities in favor of a more natural figure. Margaret's own mother, a paragon of virtue and propriety and high society, did not favor them, nor outré finery of any kind. Margaret had never been forced to parade with the Society misses for want of a husband, nor to spend outlandish funds for gowns of too much regalia and not enough substance.

She was well aware this made her unusual in Society, but her parents were not at all concerned about that. She had been born when they were a bit older than was generally considered normal, and they had been abroad for so many years that England was no longer home. But they had decided to raise her as a well-bred English lady, and so they returned. Even now, they often spoke of their longing to return to Europe.

Margaret suspected they would take her away and have her marry an Italian before she turned twenty-three just so they could travel once more.

She loved her parents, and they truly loved her. But she also loved England, proudly and passionately. And she was alone in that sentiment.

She sighed as she rested her elbow on the edge of the carriage.

Why could her parents not see the loveliness of England? Why could they not wish to regain their own heritage? It was strong and rich, and their fortune reflected that. Years in France and Italy and touring the great European cities had given the entire family an unconventional view of the world, but for Margaret, it had always been England.

And England had *him*. For whatever that was worth.

"Don't sigh so, my dear," her mother said with a gentle pat to her knee. "A visit to Aunt Ada is not very pleasant, but she does have the best tea cakes."

They giggled together for a moment, and then she returned her gaze to the streets. She wondered where the man had gone, with his dark, laughing eyes, and his dark stubble that seemed to never wax nor wane. It became him rather well, which surprised her, as she always considered facial hair to be a bad idea and the mark of a future recluse, not to mention altogether unattractive.

No, indeed, this man, whoever he was, was not common.

And her mother had no idea just how often she stared.

Margaret allowed herself another small sigh. Aunt Ada was

4

certainly not a pleasant woman, and visiting her was never an event she took pleasure in. But she was their only relation in London, and as her father was to inherit her grand fortune upon her demise, which would probably never occur, they were duty bound to make weekly visits. It made no sense to Margaret, as her father did not need any fortune at all, considering the substantial one he already had. It was not spoken of, being a vulgar topic, but they would never want for money. Which made their push for her to get married a bit odd, but that was what one did with unmarried daughters in Society, she supposed.

She tried to imagine that Aunt Ada was lonely, but that was not likely, considering the string of companions they had attempted to encourage her to entertain. Not one had lasted more than two days.

It did not help that the old woman chose to live in the busiest neighborhood in London rather than in the family home, which stood vacant and waiting for its future owners, who were forbidden to tread its threshold before Aunt Ada was "six feet under ground and colder than stone."

The streets were always teeming with horses and carriages, and with the coaching station so near, the noise from approaching coaches and departing coaches and drivers and stable hands shouting and well-wishers calling out their farewells or greetings was so overwhelming that Margaret usually developed quite the headache before the day was out. Or perhaps that was merely the ghastly and absurdly potent potpourri of Aunt Ada's sitting room.

Whichever it was, it made Thursday the worst day of the week.

Except, of course, for a certain ten seconds.

It was as if he knew that Thursdays were dreadful. She could not have predicted any other day more than a few hours in advance, but her Thursdays ran like clockwork, and every Thursday, for ten seconds, she could forget it was Thursday at all. On Thursdays, her carriage would approach Aunt Ada's, and so crowded were the London streets these days that the footmen could hardly manage to get down, thus it had become custom for Margaret to open her own door. But the most recent Thursdays, he was nearby, and he would do it for her.

What a pity she never saw him on the ride home from Aunt

Ada's. That was when she could have used it most. After doing battle with the dragon, she often found herself in need of pleasant memories or delightful oblivion. That was when she relived her moments with him, and it took the edge off of her misery.

They were earlier than usual to arrive at Aunt Ada's, which meant she would not have the pleasure of thanking him for opening her door for her. Only a ten second look today.

What a pity ten seconds did not feel longer.

The carriage slowed and Margaret sat at the edge of her seat, waiting for it to stop so she might take the handle. The less time in the streets, the better.

"Let the servants, Margaret," her mother reminded her gently. "After all, they must feel useful."

Margaret looked back at her incredulously. "Mama, the street is teeming today. The servants cannot get the door without much jostling about. It is no trouble to open it myself."

Her mother frowned, creasing her unwrinkled brow unnaturally. "Yes, but…"

"Allow me."

Margaret froze as the door opened and slowly turned herself back around to see the man whose voice she daily craved to hear. He did not meet her eyes as he stood holding the door open, but kept his eyes obediently downcast, as befitted his low station.

She wished he would not be so proper.

She swallowed and glanced back at her mother, who nodded impatiently. Forcing herself to remain calm and unaffected, and wishing she had worn a finer gown, Margaret moved to the door and prepared to step out.

A hand was suddenly before her. "If you will permit me, miss," he murmured softly, his harsh accent fainter than she expected. He raised his eyes to meet hers at last. "The streets are crowded today."

"Thank you, sir," she replied, unable to resist smiling at the warmth in his gaze. She put her hand in his, and even through her glove, she felt his touch like fire. It was not enough. She stepped down and adjusted her skirt with her free hand. "You came after me today," she added quietly, so her mother hadn't a hope of hearing it. She glanced up enough to graze his features again, daring him to deny that he had.

He hummed a small laugh that seemed to hum through her as well. "Ten seconds was not enough today. Not nearly enough."

His hold on her hand tightened briefly, but then he released her and offered it to her mother. "Might I assist you, madam?"

"Thank you," her mother said primly, but with kindness. "The streets are very crowded this morning, are they not?"

"Indeed they are, madam. Careful now." He helped her down carefully, then closed the door after her, whistling at the driver and gesturing away.

"For your kindness," her mother said, offering a few coins.

Margaret chanced a glance up at him again, and saw amusement in his handsome features.

He shook his head. "Not at all, madam. It was my pleasure. Good day to you, madam, miss." He tipped his hat, met Margaret's gaze for one brief, intense moment, and then turned and disappeared into the crowd.

"Pleasant fellow, I daresay," her mother commented fondly. "It does make the trial of these visits more bearable." Then she cleared her throat and turned towards the house. "Now, to Aunt Ada. Do not worry if she insults your dress, my dear. You know how she despises simplicity. I, on the other hand, adore it, and you look remarkably fetching. Onward, now."

Margaret let her mother precede her, then followed, turning her head slightly with a faint sigh in the direction he had disappeared, hoping for a glimpse of that strong back and dark head.

As if the sound had carried, a head, taller than most of the rest, turned, and laughing, dark eyes met hers. Her breath caught, and he grinned the most devilish grin she had ever seen in her entire life.

And then he winked.

And Lord help her, she grinned back.

"Margaret, what would you think about an Austrian for your husband, hmm?" her mother suddenly mused, paying her no mind as she fussed with her lace gloves. "Austrians are so elegant."

"Yes, Mama," she replied automatically, brought back to her present. "Very elegant."

But hardly so enticing.

"Stop smiling, Gent. You look like a cat."

Rafe Thornton only grinned more broadly as he walked into the small, incongruous office in the quietest section of Cheapside that was ever known to man. Only the washer women, the thatcher brothers, and the seven children of the half lame baker ever traversed this particular alley regularly.

Rumors of smallpox infestations tended to keep people at bay.

Rafe tossed his old cap at the clerk in the corner, a wiry bespectacled chap who had answered to every name they called him from Simon to Rufus, leaving his real name as unknown as anyone else in the building's was. The lad caught it deftly, raised a brow at the cloud of dust from it, and hung it alongside the several others on the wall, in varying states, fashions, and sizes.

"Alley cats always smile, Rogue," Rafe replied cheekily, now addressing his grumbling colleague and turning to face him. "Don't you notice?"

The equally grumbling face glowered deeply, the lines forming resembling the tattered curls on its owner's head so perfectly that he nearly laughed. "I tend to kick the cats that cross my path. Something about their screeching rings rather pleasantly to my ears."

Rafe winced and turned down the hall. "Charming. Are we talking about felines or females? You hate so many creatures, and speak so abstractly, I struggle to follow."

"That's because you're an idiot."

"Avoiding the question."

"Felines and females are all the same to me," Rogue quipped with a dismissive wave of his hand. "Too much trouble and never worth the effort."

"Why do we call you Rogue again?" Rafe asked as they sank into chairs in the quiet room at the back of the building, propping their feet up on desks in a mirrored fashion.

Rogue shrugged and smirked. "It suits me."

That drew a snort from him. "The term 'rogue' seems to indicate a certain level of charm. You have none."

"I have."

He barked a laugh and folded his hands behind his head. "Charm is a quality of attractiveness, Rogue, not a quantity of coin. Didn't they teach you that in your vast university education?"

Rogue's dark brows snapped down over his eerily blue eyes. "You have no idea what sort of education I have, Gent."

He shrugged casually. "That's what you think."

The room was silent for a moment. "You saw her again, didn't you?"

Rafe glanced over at him in surprise. "Who?"

The look of derision was both poignant and effective, and he grinned at the sight. "Now you insult me. Your addictive little bit of skirt."

"She's not my anything," Rafe informed him, not willing to rise to the baiting.

"That she knows of."

That, at least, was true.

"I'm not an idiot, despite your opinions," Rogue stated, folding his arms and watching him steadily. "Once you were content when you saw her just once a week. Now you are seeing her almost daily, and more, if I'm not mistaken. Tell me, how does this rearrangement of your assignment work for you?"

Rafe shrugged. "Rather well. I see her, I get my information, I remain innocuous and blend in…"

Rogue made a noise of disbelief. "With the way you gawk at her, you blend in as well as a cat in a henhouse."

He sighed and shook his head. "Again with the cat references. Is there something you need to get off of your chest, Rogue? Is your aunt bothering you again?"

"Leave your lover out of this," Rogue snapped, smiling at Rafe's squawk of a laugh at that implication. He sobered and tilted his head at him. "You do realize this isn't going to proceed well, right? You have to speak with the girl before you can properly court her. This doesn't count as courting, though it has extended these many months."

"It's not courting," he protested, dropping his arms awkwardly, drumming his fingers on his desk. "It's… It's…"

"Seduction by flirtation," Rogue stated rather simply.

Rafe frowned. He didn't think his behavior with the incomparable, sweet, surprisingly bold Margaret Easton was anything of the sort. He didn't know anything about her, but what his sources could provide. Which was actually a great deal as far as facts went, but it was nothing at all that meant anything to him. She had a fortune, her parents preferred the Continent, and she had never had a suitor worth any kind of salt.

She was innocent, she was sheltered, and she was eager. He could see it in her eyes, she enjoyed the excitement he provided. She craved something she did not even comprehend, some adventure just lurking beyond the horizon.

She was the very picture of his most secret fantasies.

And she *was* his.

But Rogue wouldn't know any of that.

"I will have you know that I am a gentleman," Rafe informed his colleague with the dismissive sniff of Society he had perfected so well. "By pedigree and by behavior. And by my name, as you well know. The Gentleman of the Streets, thank you very much."

Rogue snorted and rolled his eyes. "The beauty of being a spy, Gent, is you don't have to be a gentleman."

They'd had this argument too many times, and it never got old. "The beauty of being a spy, Rogue, is that I can be whomever I want."

"A dandy."

"A nice man," he said with a shake of his head.

Rogue wrinkled up his nose. "Ugh. I'm talking to the Eagle, you need a holiday. You're losing your touch."

"You never had touch."

"They call me Rogue, you idiot."

"It's ironic," he said with a shrug. He slid his feet off of the desk and rose. "Well, as fun as bantering with you is, I have things to do."

Rogue tried for mild surprise. "Oh, are you going to send another note about an insulted debutante? London is not safe without you protecting their reputations, you know."

Rafe grumbled under his breath, knowing this was Rogue's

favorite jab at him. He had never understood why Rafe had taken an interest in Society, and he never would. "I'll have you know I saved her from ruin."

"Oh, what a hero," he mock swooned. "She marries your friend and then she's off your conscience, right? Or are you going to start writing for the gossip column now?"

"Cheers, Rogue. Give my best to the bottom dwellers." He went to leave the room only to find the way blocked by a tall, middle-aged man with piercing eyes and a slow smile, which was absent today.

"Off somewhere?" he asked in his low tones.

Rafe nodded politely. "Cap. Just off to write reports."

"It can wait."

That brought him up short. Cap was second in command just behind the Eagle, and reports could never wait.

Rogue scrambled to his feet. "What is it?"

Cap shook his dark golden head and held out a bottle. "Trace."

That sobered them all.

Rafe thought back quickly, dates and times having little meaning to him these days. Had it really been three years? The recollection cut across him like a knife, swift and sharp. He moved to the sideboard and pulled out three glasses, handing them to the others.

Cap silently poured for them, then capped the bottle.

As one they all raised their glasses.

"Trace," they murmured almost reverently, mourning still their friend and colleague.

And then they drank.

"Any word on…?" Rafe prodded quietly.

Cap swallowed harshly and shook his head, his jaw tightening. "None. Weaver says they won't stop looking, but…"

"There *has* to be something," Rogue muttered, shaking his head, sounding more passionate about this than anything else in his life.

"Eagle thinks so too, but…" Cap shrugged, heaved a sigh that did not fit his nature and cleared his throat, then handed his glass back. "Right. As you were. Get those reports in, Gent, no more dawdling after your muslin miss until you find the gap in the money."

Rafe groaned as Rogue laughed. "Money trails are Rogue's business!"

Cap raised a brow. "Rogue has slippery fingers like nobody else. I wouldn't trust him with tuppence. You do it." A very faint smile appeared, likely the first since his wife had passed last year. "Miss Easton won't know that we're keeping you from her anyway." He cocked his head knowingly and turned from the room.

Rogue's laughs turned to full out guffaws as Rafe gaped after the man he respected so much, now joining in his torment.

It just wasn't fair.

Some men had no idea what to do with hearts.

And some didn't have them at all.

Chapter Two

"What do you mean you're leaving?"

It was much to her mother's credit that she looked so composed and remarkably unaffected by Margaret's outburst, and only calmly sipped her tea as she had been doing all afternoon.

"For heaven's sake, child," Aunt Ada snapped, raising an overly wrinkled hand to her powdered brow, "do moderate your tone. One would think you were raised by gypsies rather than my own nephew."

Margaret gave her great aunt as close to a withering glance as she dared, which was not seen, as the aged woman was bemoaning her approaching megrim.

It had all happened so suddenly, everything as per their usual visits with Aunt Ada, down to the sickening potpourri and the tedious conversation that swirled the same tiresome topics. Margaret was never really invested in these outings and very rarely participated, aside from the mindless and noncommittal answers she could safely offer at any time. It had served her well the last three years, and the ability to listen without truly listening was truly a gift where Aunt Ada was concerned.

But her ears had perked up sharply when her mother had said the words "Europe" and "leaving" within a single breath of each other, and as she was brought back to the conversation at hand, she had intelligence enough to piece together the shocking truth that her parents intended to leave England for the Continent. Again.

Her mother set her cup aside and gave Margaret the smile that told her she was still a child in her eyes. "Surely it cannot be such a surprise, darling. You've heard your father and I suggest any number of countries from which we could secure you a husband. Only minutes ago, you and I agreed upon Austria as an option."

Margaret gaped and shook her head. "I never agreed to anything. I only conceded that Austrians are elegant, and I could name a few that would be exceptions there. I didn't know…"

Her mother sighed and offered a pitying look. "You've had three Seasons, Margaret. That is long enough for Britain's finest bachelors to try for you. None have."

Margaret felt her cheeks flush and she raised one of her lace-gloved hands to her face. "You needn't make me sound so frightful."

"You are," Aunt Ada croaked as she rattled her teacup. "You've grown plump, and those eyebrows of yours are frightfully out of sorts. Too round in the face, and your lips are much too full. You must use powder to calm your complexion and a bit of lip paint to soften those monstrosities. No wonder no man can abide you, child, you hardly look the part."

Though she was beyond accustomed to her great-aunt's severity and criticism, this time it stung.

Her mother sniffed softly, but made no defense for her, as usual. "There are hardly any suitable candidates for you, my love. Certainly none that your father would agree to, even if they had shown an interest. No, no, our best chances for you lie in Europe, and we are certain to find some fine man for you there. How do you feel about Prussians?"

Margaret felt her throat closing up and barely choked out, "Hairy," which made her mother chuckle.

"Oh, they are not," she scolded. "And even if they were, it is better for them to have hair than not."

"Mama, please," Margaret begged quietly, suddenly realizing that she held tea in her hands and that it was quite cold. She set it aside and folded her hands as primly as she could while they shook. "Please, let me have this Season," she pleaded. "I've just spoken with Rosalind Arden this week, and we had settled ourselves with ideas for similar social gatherings, and you know how important it is to have friends in such endeavors."

"I do indeed," her mother said, nodding so sagely it was unsettling, "and if Rosalind Arden would pay any attention to that dashing Captain Riverton, she would have quite the match herself."

Margaret rolled her eyes. "She says he's too confident by half."

"And why is that to be faulted?" her mother shot back. "A man with his pedigree and history in battle has earned his confidence."

A faint growl started in Margaret's throat. "Captain Riverton is not the issue, Mama."

"He ought to be," Aunt Ada muttered as she shifted her voluminous skirts. "And if your waist were the size it ought to be, child, you might *have* his issue as well."

Now Margaret's cheeks flamed in earnest and she raised her other hand to them as well. "Aunt!"

The old woman shrugged, her gaudy jewelry jangling against her skin. "If you will not put forth the efforts to secure what Britain offers, Margaret Mary Christianne, you cannot be fastidious about the rest of the world. Your parents are quite right, Europe is the place to get you a husband." She reached for her tea and somehow shook the cup enough to rattle it but not spill a drop. "Might be the only place at your age."

"I am but twenty-two!" Margaret protested.

"I had three children by your age," her great-aunt snapped. "Much good that did me. Had any been worth the effort, they would have provided me with proper heirs and then I would not have to squander my considerable fortune upon such a hopeless case as yourself."

"Now, Ada," her mother placated, her voice as calm as the spring morning, "Margaret is unique, but hardly hopeless."

Well, *that* was a flattering description.

"Mama," Margaret whispered, her hands falling into her lap. "Please."

The blue eyes so similar to hers turned to meet her and she saw the concern behind the smile. "Darling, you may have your Season, of course. You are to remain with a chaperone that we will hire for you, and she will help you to make the most of this final London Season. And should you find a man suitable for you here, so be it. But should the previous patterns follow, we will have a list of eligible and willing candidates on the Continent. I've already written to the Contessa Olivario, and you know she has impeccable taste."

Margaret's eyes widened and she swallowed with difficulty. The contessa did have impeccable taste... in horses. Her taste in men ranged from the dandy to the peacock, and the variety within was only in the shade of waistcoats and lavishness of cravats. They had limited intelligence and lacked interest in anything of substance. None of her selections would do at all.

And she highly doubted her parents' would be any better.

"Don't look so forlorn, dear," her mother said with a placating smile. "It is only a preliminary trip, we will not be gone for long. Just enough to get an idea of prospects, and then, after your Season, we will take you and all go together."

Preliminary trip or not, this was the absolute worst thing she could have heard. Her parents would be looking for husbands everywhere, and no matter what her mother said, they would return with candidates and plans for her.

"When will you depart?" she whispered, her lips barely moving.

Her mother smiled and sipped her tea again. "In a week, I believe. Pass the crumpets, darling, I think I will have another."

Aunt Ada snorted and clinked her teacup and saucer once more. "Oh, really, Millicent, it's no wonder the child is chubby, the way you carry on with your diet."

The two traded words for a while as Margaret sat in her stupor, slowly losing feeling in her extremities.

Marriage to a European would mean leaving England, perhaps forever. She had always known her parents would prefer that, and they had certainly spoken of it before, but she'd never heard of any plans to move in that direction. It had only ever been talk, never action.

Now a course had been set. Without her knowledge or consent, but that had never been in consideration anyway. She supposed she should be grateful that an engagement was not already in place, and that she was permitted to remain while they returned to the Continent. This Season would be her only chance to stay in England.

But for the life of her, she could not think of a single gentleman that she would wish to marry.

If they took gentlemen out of the requirements, she could think of one man who might serve her well...

She closed her eyes against the flash of pain and bit her lip. Her parents would never allow that sort of union. Even if she ruined herself with him, a rather intriguing thing to imagine, they would not follow British protocol and force a marriage. No, they would have only scuttled her away to Europe faster and arranged something with a man with less moral principle than British society would have.

Would she ever be able to forget him long enough to allow another man to capture her fancy?

It was a laughable thought, as she was too wrapped up in his mystery to even consider anyone else.

She would have to let him go to save herself. Not that she ever had him or anything of the sort, and it was a silly, girlish notion to pretend otherwise. But she could not deny that he did have a hold on her, and she had gleefully let him have it. Whatever she had built up in her own mind would have to fade into the background.

Falling in love was no longer an option.

A sensible, respectable marriage with congenial friendship would suffice. Love could grow. Good men could be found in Society, and a good man would make a far better husband than the rascal whose smile made her knees quiver. He probably had several ladies about town that he behaved similarly with. Why, he might even be married with six children, for all she knew.

Better to set her mind on a man who could keep her in England and give her a future.

Unfortunately, despite the best efforts of her parents and several governesses, tutors, and nannies, Margaret Easton had never been particularly adept at setting her mind on sensible things, and even worse at maintaining resolve, particularly where propriety was required. She'd always had a free spirit and independent will, no matter how prim and docile she appeared. Her parents had encouraged it, as several European families also did.

Could such an unconventional English girl snag a conventional, yet somehow still exciting English husband with only one Season to do so?

She swallowed and sipped her cold tea without tasting it.

It might be impossible.

But it was her only hope.

Rafe groaned and shoved his hands into his dark hair, disheveling it further than it already was, if that was possible. He hated the tedium of paperwork more than he hated anything in his life, and the mountains of information he had collected by conversation was now before him on parchment as proof.

And all of the pertinent details he needed for his current task lay within them.

Which meant he had to pore over them all with exactness.

He was a spy, a pickpocket, an actor, a jack of all trades, and on good days, a passable codebreaker. He possessed many skills, far more than anybody knew, and could pick up just about anything new in record time. He spoke six languages fluently and could mimic accents of seven more.

But he was no scholar, and he had limited patience.

He was going to die here in this dank office, buried in the papers that he had been tasked with investigating.

How long would it take for someone to find his body, he wondered as he moved his head to rest against the desk, closing his eyes.

"I doubt you are going to glean any information that way," Rogue's voice drawled from the doorway.

"If I am useless, so be it," Rafe returned, remaining as he was. "Then I will be dismissed and someone else will have to do this part."

Rogue gave a dry chuckle. "It's your own fault. If you would be more orderly in your interviews and structured in your reviews, this would all be much easier."

"Don't tell me how to do my job."

"I would never."

Something about his friend's tone gave Rafe pause as he considered beating his head against the aged wood of his desk. He raised his uninjured head and squinted at him. "What?"

Rogue leaned against the doorjamb with what could almost be considered a smile for him, which meant it was a vacant expression for any normal human being. "One of your vagrants came to report just now."

Rafe sighed in relief and satisfaction and avoided the urge to leap to his feet. "Excellent, I could use the distraction."

Rogue didn't move, but his mouth twitched, by some miracle, and Rafe stopped himself.

He sighed heavily. "You took the report already, didn't you?"

"I would never dream of interrupting your analysis," his friend replied with a mockingly respectful dip of his head. "I thought it my duty to see to the matter myself."

Rafe glared at him. "You must be exhausted after using so many words at one time. Have a lie down, why don't you?"

Rogue snorted and folded his arms, leaning more fully against his post. "If you would shut up for half a moment, you might find you are interested in what she had to say."

Sinking down into his chair, Rafe narrowed his eyes. "She? It was one of my girls?"

"It was."

"Which?"

"Daisy."

Rafe grinned and leaned back in his chair. "Daisy dearest. I hope you were kind to her, Rogue. She's only seven."

The almost smile flicked again. "Yes, so she told me. Repeatedly." He exhaled rather noisily. "And she kept clicking her tongue against those crooked teeth of hers."

That drew a chuckle from him and he shook his head. "You can't blame the child for her teeth. Besides, she's adorable, under all that dirt."

Rogue did not respond, which said mountains, and Rafe sat bolt upright.

"Good lord, you have no snide rebuttal," he gasped with a wild grin.

Rogue's pale eyes widened slightly.

"You like the child!" Rafe crowed, pointing a finger at him. "If you didn't, you would have said something callous and cynical, and I would have thought nothing of it, but you have nothing to say! You like Daisy!"

Rogue muttered something no doubt very foul under his breath, as the man did have a gift with profanity, and shoved off of the wall. "Well, let me know when you're going to read the banns for me, I'll make sure to say nothing then as well."

Rafe barked a laugh and waved a hand. "All right, I'm done, come back, come back."

Rogue sniffed and moved to the desk. "Impudent whelp. If you were still the youngest of us, I'd toss you out on your arse."

Rafe shrugged, still smiling. "Yes, well, feel free to wallop on Rook, then. He could use it, smarmy bloke."

They both fell silent at the mention of their newest colleague, who had been with them almost a year, and still had not managed to fill the void Trace had left. He was the best of any of the others that had been put forth by the Foreign Office, but it was not the same. The man had all the potential in the world, and was doing rather well, impressively at times, but...

"Daisy says her mark is having a meeting," Rogue said suddenly, his voice gruff as if he had been thinking along the same lines. "A maid in the house was overheard saying something about the master having gained a significant amount of money and having *another* meeting with some investors about it. Men of some importance, and when he returns from France..." He drew the silence out with emphasis, widening his eyes as if Rafe were dim-witted, "he would arrange matters."

Rafe gnawed on his lip for a moment. "Interesting..." He suddenly looked back at the files atop his desk and rifled through several, pulling out the specific file he needed quickly. "Yes, that is interesting. He should be drowning in debt, not gaining anything. Investitures middling..." He thought for a moment, then glanced back up. "When is he due back, did the child say?"

Rogue's expression was slightly aghast. "How did you... how did you know where that file was?"

He snorted and closed the file, tossing it back onto the desk. "Just because you don't understand my system does not mean I am also ignorant. When is the dirty cheat due back?"

"Next week. He's having a ball..." A ghost of a true smile appeared, and it alarmed Rafe slightly.

"Why do you look like that?" he asked warily, glancing out of the filthy window near him. "It's only a ball, I don't mind those."

"It's a very special occasion," Rogue replied, his mouth curving. "Select members of Society only. And he's promised his sister that her daughters may have full run of the bachelors in attendance, and invitation to the men of their choosing."

Horrified, Rafe returned his head to his desk with a moan of despair, tugging at his limp and faded cravat. "Do you think that Lord Marlowe would make that very exclusive list?" he asked aloud, squeezing his eyes shut against the vain hope of denial.

"I think Lord Marlowe already has," came the dry response.

He peered up at him suspiciously. "How do you know?"

Rogue rolled his eyes and went to the sideboard to pour himself a drink. "If you ever went to your own lodgings, Gent, you would know such things for yourself."

Rafe frowned and gestured for Rogue to pour him a glass as well. "Why do you know the workings of my house?"

The sardonic look he received answered his own question.

"Ah," he said knowingly with a nod. "Davis."

"For a man in his position, with a master in *his* position," Rogue muttered with a shake of his head, "that butler is not very good at his job. A servant is meant to keep his master's secrets, not spread them about for gossip."

Rafe smiled swiftly. "Davis keeps secrets better than anyone. Opinions, not so much. And you terrify him. I'm surprised he didn't bear his soul in confession."

Rogue shuddered visibly as he approached. "Lucky for me, I never venture to your house officially."

"Yes, I'd hate for you to set the place awry with all your doom and gloom."

Rogue stopped a few feet from him, holding his drink out of reach and raising a brow.

Rafe sighed and rolled his eyes. "Put off your affront and give that here. I need it to get through these damned financials, and now, apparently, a husband hunt."

They both shuddered at that and Rogue handed over the drink. "Fair enough." He glanced down at the stacks. "How is it going?

Finding anything?"

Rafe sipped cautiously, having never been a truly strong drinker. "I've narrowed the list down to a dozen, but it's not enough. I know at least half of the faction's money is coming from England, and most of that from fairly high up. Daisy's mark is a chief suspect, but as for the rest…" He shrugged and exhaled in frustration. "The trouble is most of this looks legitimate. I have a sense they may not be, but I can't prove anything." He glanced over at his colleague with a wince. "Financials and mathematics are not my strong suit. I was always more of a literature man."

Rogue made an irritated noise and muttered something suspiciously like "You would," under his breath. But his expression remained impassive, and he thought for a moment. "I know a man…" he said slowly.

"No," Rafe said at once, shaking his head. "None of your seedy gambling associates. I'll not let them run these through their grubby fingers."

Rogue's thick brows snapped down. "Says the man who gets his information from gypsies, pickpockets, urchins, and whores."

"Actresses," Rafe clarified with a faint finger in the air. "Tilda would be most put out to be reduced to such a level, considering all the effort she puts into those girls."

Rogue raised his hands in mock surrender. "Far be it from me to offend Mistress Tilda."

Rafe grinned slowly. "She would tear you limb from limb, my friend. And she's a most useful contact. Just ask Trick or Tumbler. Or Thistle."

"Really?" Rogue asked, sounding truly surprised, and no wonder, for the Foreign Office's deep-seated operatives rarely used any of their connections if they could help it.

He shrugged and tried for a nonchalant air, but couldn't hide the pride. "Unconfirmed, but…"

"Huh." Rogue sat back, a bit bemused. Then suddenly it was gone. "At any rate, I didn't mean to pass it off to one of my gamblers. I do have other connections, you know. Respectable ones."

Rafe tilted his head in concern. "And they know you personally? Do they know what that could do to their reputations?" He laughed at his own jest, mirth bubbling up within him.

"I mean to take it to Coin, you damned toff." He quirked a brow tauntingly when Rafe stopped chuckling at the suggestion. "Is that proper enough for you? Or is your pride too much to ask the man for his aid?"

"I forgot all about Coin," he breathed. He grinned in relief. "Please, take them to him. He likes you more than me."

"That's because I let him win when we play," Rogue said with a light shrug.

"You never let me win," Rafe pointed out without the indignation he ought to have had.

Rogue smiled darkly. "That is because you are a terrible card player, and your ego needs some deflating." He bowed politely, then ambled out of the room.

Rafe rolled his eyes and leaned back in his chair, his eyes aimlessly tracing the faded moldings on the ceiling. Coin would help, the rascally old codger. He'd make Rafe look like an idiot with whatever he missed, but not on any official reports. He might be high-handed in person, but he was the consummate professional in all else.

And he was shockingly good at his job.

What exactly that job was, Rafe wasn't exactly sure. Come to think of it, he didn't think anyone knew for certain.

Such was the mystery of Coin.

He spent a few minutes organizing the files he wanted examined most, and then pulled out the aged pocket watch in his weskit pocket.

It was Tuesday. She tended to shop on Tuesdays, in Bond Street, mostly. But she'd likely be finished by now, and on her way back to her home with that mother of hers.

She was a very proper sort of woman, and had no doubt once been a beauty, but she could not hold a candle to what her daughter was, and would be for eternity.

He couldn't leave the office to seek her out. Cap's warning rang in his head, and he was fairly certain his own people were being set to tail him.

He needed a reason.

A good one.

Something that…

A slow, smirking grin suddenly lit his features, and he rose from his chair. "Foster!" he bellowed.

"Sir?" came the reply from whatever his name was in the front.

"Send a message to my valet. Tell him we've a ball in two weeks, and an impression to make."

Swift footsteps came down the hall and the thin man looked rather unimpressed. "I'm not your errand boy, Gent."

"I know that, Vincent," he replied with a cheeky grin as he moved passed him. "But considering you do work here, you ought to do something to earn your keep."

"What, besides letting your costumes gather dust over my head?" came the answer as he followed.

"Keeper of the costumes," Rafe mused thoughtfully. "I like that. I'll find a name that sticks for you yet." He pulled his brown cap from the hook and perched it jauntily back, rolling his sleeves.

"I could tell you my real name," he said, folding his arms. "That makes it quite simple."

Rafe frowned at him as he moved to the door. "No names, Paul. We have rules."

"And those say you're not supposed to go out until you're done."

Rafe turned back, glowering. "Don't make me name you Snitch," he growled as he opened the door.

"And where are you going?" the snitch asked in hushed tones, given the open door.

Rafe turned and tipped his cap even more. "Tanks for the wages, guvnor," he called in his street Cockney. "I'll jus' be stoppin' into the market for a new coat, jus' like ye said!"

And with a boyish skip and a whistle, the Gent was back on the streets, wondering if it might be a ten second day after all.

Chapter Three

"*For* the husband hunt this is supposed to be, there are a shocking number of women here."

Margaret bit back a smile behind her fan, which was no trick of fashion for once, as the heat in the room was truly abominable. "There's a shocking number of *everyone* here," she replied. "I didn't think Lady Poole knew this many people."

The dark-haired beauty that was Rosalind Arden snorted softly and fidgeted with the green ribbon at her waist. "She doesn't. But as she's growing desperate to get the Poole pack married off, they invited everyone in London worth any sort of salt."

Margaret exchanged a quick, but surprised nod of acknowledgement to Lord and Lady Rothchild as the stunning couple passed by, wondering why the man who was one of the most popular dignitaries in Europe would have opted to come to an evening like this. She'd met him and his wife on several occasions on the Continent, and she knew his wife was certainly above the present company.

Lord Rothchild would probably enjoy this spectacle. He was full of good humor, as she recalled.

An overly exuberant dancer nearly crashed into Margaret and she backed up hastily, brushing off her cream muslin with a sigh. "Yes, and as the Season hasn't officially begun, this is the first chance to do anything of amusement. Who will be this Season's splash, hmm?"

"Why not you, Margaret?" Rosalind asked with a nudge. "Your fortune is admirable to the extreme, and you're quite pretty. Men should be falling over themselves to get to you."

Margaret shook her head. "See how they fall," she murmured, gesturing faintly to the lack of attendants. She glanced over at the taller girl, who was stunning and regal in appearance and nature, and whose lack of suitors was truly the most mysterious thing.

She followed Rosalind's gaze and saw where it was fixed, then smiled to herself.

Perhaps not so mysterious.

She cleared her throat a little. "What of you, Rosalind? I've heard some rather interesting things about a certain former captain of the Navy."

Rosalind's fan moved a bit more rapidly. "Will has no claim on me, and has not made any indication he wishes to."

Margaret grinned. "Oh, it's *Will*, now, is it?"

The fan snapped shut and a pair of dark eyes swung to hers. "Margaret Easton, spit out whatever ridiculous thought is swirling in your head, I've no patience for teasing."

Margaret shrugged one shoulder as daintily as she could. "Nothing at all, my dear. I only find it curious that this winter you couldn't stand him, and yet now he is Will."

Rosalind glowered and looked away. "Our families have become acquainted. My sister is close with the Blackmoors and they are Riverton cousins. Will and I took it upon ourselves to waltz improperly as a distraction last Season, and now everyone thinks there is an attachment."

"And what does Captain Riverton say?" Margaret asked, knowing the story already, having seen it for herself.

Rosalind's jaw tightened. "Nothing. The fool says nothing but expects the rest of us to know what he wants and what he thinks, and blasts the whole world if he doesn't get it."

Margaret raised a curious brow. "Why do you care what Captain Riverton wants and thinks and gets?"

Her friend sighed and looked suddenly irritated. "I don't. But he seems to think I do. We're at odds, Margaret, and always have been. I daresay we always will be."

Sensing the finality in her tone, Margaret let the conversation fade and looked around the overly elaborate ballroom with amusement. Sir Edgar Grimshaw was a socially ambitious man, and despite his comfortable house and fortune, it was never enough. Afraid of being found lacking, he overcompensated in an attempt to portray his estate and finances with all of the excesses and affluence that the highest circles did, though everyone knew the truth.

This evening, for example, rather than achieving the Grecian theme that was no doubt wished for, it rather looked as if one was mocking Greece, its rich history, and every legend, myth, and tale from its past. Ancient Greece might have died a rather painful death in this room. Additional Corinthian columns had been brought into the room and onto the terrace, each supporting overgrown ferns or badly formed busts of Grecian figures. Greenery adorned almost every sconce and open space of wall, wherever the swaths of white linen and what appeared to be green taffeta were gathered together, and, unless she was imagining it, atop the head of every footman in attendance. Sir Edgar and his male servants all wore a wreath of laurels.

Poor souls.

Sir Edgar also had the misfortune of having Lady Poole for a sister, and her three daughters each needed a match, and no one was asking. Lady Poole got more and more desperate every year, and her tastes ran from ridiculous to outlandish, and tonight she seemed to think that the London bachelors wished peacocks for brides, as they all bore gowns of rich blues and greens with the feathers of what could have been four of the birds in question on their persons.

And this was the select gathering that her companion had insisted she attend?

Margaret snorted. This was the most absurd event she'd ever attended, and she'd been to some rather inventive parties.

"Oh, look, someone is waltzing with a peacock," Rosalind said with barely restrained mirth.

Margaret bit her lip hard, watching Christian Harris waltz with Cressida Poole, and the feathers were quite in the way. "At least she's the sensible one."

Rosalind snorted delicately, then coughed when one of the old women looked at her in shock. "Compared to Geraldine and Fanny, Cressida is perfectly angelic," she muttered when she could. "Bless the dear Harris lad for taking pity on her."

"Don't call him a lad, he's our age," Margaret scolded with a snicker.

"So marry that one."

She rolled her eyes and saw her companion glaring at her, and lowered her gaze at once. Her parents had been gone two weeks, and the change in the house was as sudden as it was unpleasant. Miss Ritson was all angles and sharpness, in features and manner, and her age was far beyond her years. She disapproved of everything Margaret was and loved, and the crisp, clipped tones with which she spoke had a jolting effect on both Margaret and the servants.

Miss Ritson had been tasked with maintaining Margaret's social agenda, monitoring her behavior, and overseeing the courtships that were destined to follow this Season. She had been given explicit instructions to aid Margaret in securing a match with a suitable gentleman, be he peer or not, and had been assured of a reward if she would prove successful. A smaller reward would be administered if the Englishmen failed them and all she managed to do was prepare Margaret sufficiently for her marriage to a European suitor of her parents choosing. She reported biweekly to her parents via letter to Amsterdam, where they were beginning their tour, and the threat of including misbehaviors had already been weighing over Margaret's head. She felt as though she were twelve instead of twenty-two.

"Why did that bat have to be the one who impressed your parents?" Rosalind asked with a dark look. "She's a gargoyle. Any potential suitors would flee before her fire breath."

"You're confusing your creatures, Rosalind," Margaret murmured as her cheeks heated.

"But the sentiment stands," chirped another voice nearby.

Relief washed over Margaret as her cousin Helen came into view, looking like the picture of summer with her fair hair and pale blue muslin. Whatever plainness might have been ascribed to the Daltons, no one could deny that their daughter Helen was remarkably pretty.

"Thank you, Miss Dalton," Rosalind said triumphantly, beaming at her.

Helen inclined her head proudly, then took a glass of punch from a passing footman. "Lord, but it's hot. I hope they don't tamper with the drink here, I shall need quite a few, and I'd rather not be inebriated when Mr. Timmons tries to propose again." She sighed and smiled as she watched the dancing. "So, ladies, who are we ogling and how do we get him to come over here?"

Margaret laughed merrily, forgetting to hide the indelicacy behind her hand.

"All of them, Miss Dalton," Rosalind quipped, dark eyes dancing. "All of them at once."

Helen smiled mischievously. "Well, well, that should make things easier, don't you think?"

"Not for me," Margaret muttered, stifling a wince. "I can count my admirers without any fingers at all."

She suddenly found her knuckles rapped by an ebony and ivory fan and yelped, turning to her cousin with wide eyes.

Helen's delicate brows were lowered over her cobalt eyes and her jaw was tense. "Bite your tongue, Margaret Easton, and get out of the pity corner. Rickety Ritson might be charged with getting you a husband, but Rosalind and I are the ones to really see it done. I'm not letting you spend the rest of your life in Prussia."

"Hear, hear," Rosalind echoed, taking Margaret's hand.

Margaret smiled at them both. "I'm not desperate, you know," she informed them. "I want to love my husband, if I can."

Helen gave her an odd look. "Did you think we would throw you at Lord Viskin because 'any man will do'? Good lord, Margaret, with your generous heart and pretty face, we can find you a real suitor worth loving in no time at all."

"Whether you love him or not is up to you," Rosalind added, her gaze sliding to a woman sitting in a nearby chair, smiling sadly.

Margaret looked as well, and found herself sighing a little. It was a sad story, but Rosalind's sister Lily had married a few years ago to a man she had cared deeply for, but the circumstances of their marriage had been unpleasant and purely financial, and by all accounts, her husband had nothing to do with her. Lily Granger had once been a lively, vivacious, and stunning woman of admiration. Now she was withdrawn, reserved, and hauntingly beautiful in a tragic sort of way.

Perhaps love would not be so wonderful after all, if that was where it could lead.

"Is there anyone in particular you would like us to try for?"

Rosalind asked, the shadow passing as she smiled once more. "Who do you fancy, Margaret?"

An image of a dark and seductive pair of eyes and a devilish grin sprang to her mind, and she flushed a little as the full image of him rose before her. Heat coursed through her and her fan fluttered a little in her hold.

What would it be like to waltz in his arms? His hands on her body, properly placed and not so properly felt, his eyes on her face with the intensity of fire as his lithe and graceful movements led her around the floor. With his strength and heat and power, she would melt bonelessly into his embrace, letting him sweep her away, going breathless with the heady sensations he aroused, and she knew for a fact that the entire ballroom would be scandalized by only the look in her eyes as she boldly gazed back at her dashing partner, so familiar and so mysterious at once.

She swallowed hard against her suddenly parched throat and her hands shook once more.

Good heavens, it was hot.

"Lord, Margaret, no need to get so embarrassed," Helen laughed from her side. "Just give us an idea, then, no confessions."

She snapped out of her shocking reverie and cleared her throat. "It is just... Well... Who is the most dashing, do you think? Or desperate. Or both."

Rosalind chortled from her other side. "Dashing and desperate, it is. Come along, ladies, those fellows take up the Eastern wall. If we're lucky, Margaret, you might be asked to walk the gardens. Trap a man in the thorny hedges, and you might get somewhere."

Margaret blushed as Helen laughed, and the three of them traipsed delicately across the ballroom to attempt suitors and partners for the next dance, if not beyond.

Damnation, that was close.

Rafe leaned against the column that had become his hiding place, letting his heart and lungs settle as feeling returned to his legs.

What the devil was she doing here?

More to the point, what was she doing here looking like *that?*

She was utterly delicious, tempting saints beyond their piety and more worldly men beyond their sanity. How could a demure, modest little thing like her appeal to his most secret desires? She ought to have looked exactly like every other miss he had spent his entire life avoiding, cream muslin and pearls and all, but instead she looked like the goddess this very soiree would have worshipped. That *he* would have worshipped, and would very much like to.

He shook his head, desperate to rid the sudden scent of lavender and honey from his senses. She was a distraction, and one he certainly could not afford.

He'd been perfectly composed and focused, the utterly bored and forgettable Lord Marlowe in place and ignored, for the most part. He'd plotted every detail of the evening before him, contingency plans in place, every detail of the house memorized and secretly traipsed already in the dark nights past. He knew the schedules of the staff and their duties, the rooms most likely to be used for meeting, and the portion of the hallway where the floorboards creaked. He was ready for the gathering that was supposed to commence and only waited for his host to make the move from his current position as the apparent Dionysus of the evening.

Everything was ready.

And then he'd seen her, and suddenly his feet had moved in her direction, desperate to get closer, to hear her voice, to see the captivating azure of her eyes, to learn what made her smile so fetchingly. It wasn't until he had been almost close enough to touch that he'd realized what he was doing, and worst of all, that she would recognize him, and he'd hidden behind the pillar before she had seen him.

Why she should recognize him, he didn't know. There was very little similar between Lord Marlowe and the man who stared and winked so boldly at her whenever he could get a glimpse. That was the beauty of his appearance and his skills; he could be anyone and anywhere at any time and no one ever placed or recognized him. He was a master of disguise and a creature of stealth and mystery.

But somehow he had known, and still knew, down to his core,

that she would know him.

That was a terrifying thought.

This simple miss had the power to bring him down and she didn't even know it.

What was worse was that he wasn't sure he minded.

He swallowed harshly and leaned his head back against the column. It had been nearly a full week since he'd seen her. Her schedule was no longer the same, and his demands grew more and more inconvenient. He'd caught a glimpse of her sallow-faced chaperone the other day, and his instincts had kicked in, knowing she would not be so obtuse as the mother was. It had been miraculous they had managed a ten second look at all with her hovering about, but it had been managed, and Margaret had seemed both relieved and delighted by it.

It had never been so difficult to see her. She had always been there, like clockwork, and it had become part of his routine to include her in it. Now he had to trust in luck and creativity to see her, and he didn't trust luck in the least bit. He didn't like change, and he definitely didn't like the change that had come over Margaret.

Despite looking angelic and ethereal, she also seemed pale and worn, and there was an odd tension in her frame that did not belong. She was a free spirit, the kind of girl who would have tipped her head back to feel the rain more fully, and now she was somehow confined, no doubt chafing against the restraints placed upon her.

He would free her. He could revive her. He could…

He couldn't do anything here and now, hiding behind a pillar from the whole of Society.

But he couldn't very well move yet, either.

He had watched her for what felt like an eternity, feeling like an intruder, and yet thrilling at the chance. He'd caught every flicker of her features, every twinkle of her eye, and his heart had stopped at the music of her laugh. For all he knew of her from observation, he'd never heard her laugh, and it seemed his chief regret in life now. She laughed frequently, he decided, but not usually with such freedom. He shook his head at the thought. How could he know her so well and yet not at all?

His breath had caught when he'd seen that faraway look, the

blush creeping into her cheeks as if by a lover's whisper, the change in her breathing, the faint tremor in her hand... She'd never been so attractive to him, and yet so tender. What were those thoughts that brought her to such a state? Could he have stirred her to it if given a chance?

He craved the opportunity to try.

Rafe winced and tapped his head back against the column once. He needed to find control. He was no lovesick puppy, and this was not the time to be entertaining the pleasant and increasingly addictive thoughts of her.

He wasn't even alone in tonight's activities, he'd just seen Weaver come in, and having one of England's most accomplished covert operatives in attendance, knowing what was at stake, gave him additional confidence. Granted, he was here as his public persona of Lord Rothchild, and wasn't supposed to be engaging in covert operations himself anymore, and was making a splash with his still-beautiful wife, but if it came down to it, Weaver would step in. He was second in command of all the covert operatives in London, he could do whatever he liked.

Rafe doubted he would have to, but if he were distracted any further, he might have to ask Weaver for assistance.

He needed to focus on Sir Edgar Grimshaw and his ruddy meeting this evening.

Sir Edgar had likely been a supporter of Napoleon, and now of the small but willful faction that had been unsettled since the monarch had been placed back on the throne. Some suspected they supported Sieyés and what he had envisioned for France all along, others that they wanted Napoleon's son to return and take back his father's place. Whichever it was, they were unpredictable and dangerous, and the fact that much of their funding seemed to be coming from English fortunes was appalling and embarrassing.

This was his purpose tonight.

Not wondering how complicated his life would get if he indulged in a quadrille with Margaret Easton.

He'd rather a waltz, but he'd never let her out of his arms once she was in them.

"Marlowe, you look even more pained than usual," drawled a

low, feminine voice that he'd come to know well.

He glanced over at the welcome distraction of Marianne Gerrard, wife of one of his closest friends, and a former project of his, though she had never known it. Before her days as a wife, she had been the subject of many scandalous rumors and speculation, and she'd lived for such gossip.

Now she was only envied by all who knew her.

"Mrs. Gerrard," he said politely, straightening to bow.

She snorted softly, her dark curls bounding with the action. "Don't be so polite, Marlowe, it's only me."

"Marianne, I must at least pretend at politeness, you know that." He smiled evenly, reminding himself to be as boring as possible, but unable to resist teasing. He liked Marianne, which surprised him after all of the trouble he went to for her.

She returned his smile and raised a brow. "I know nothing of the sort. Now, before my husband finds you and interrogates you himself, I must ask when you are coming to see your godson again. He's got a fine set of teeth, and Kit seems to think you need to see them yourself." She folded her arms and smirked, though her eyes shone with pride and excitement.

Rafe forced his expression to remain devoid of either of those things, though he thrilled at the thought. "My namesake may be assured of my presence within a week, and his father need be reminded that I request the privilege of teaching the lad to ride when he is able."

"Do you now?"

"You don't wish Kit to teach him, do you? Not when I've beaten him in every race we've ever had."

Marianne's dubious expression amused him, and he bit back a grin. She, like everyone else, thought him a bit tiresome and utterly forgettable, but she also knew there was more to him than that. She would have made a fine operative if she weren't so notorious.

"You ride, Marlowe?" she asked with more than a hint of doubt.

He shrugged. "When I can be persuaded. Activity, you know, good for the health. Strenuous though."

She rolled her eyes and moved a bit closer, keeping her eyes fixed on the dancing behind him. "Pretend all you want, Marlowe," she whispered, her lips barely moving. "I know you're not as dull as you appear, and when you come to us at Glendare this summer, come as yourself."

He allowed a ghost of a smile to flick across his face and inclined his head. "As you wish, Marianne."

She gave him an amused look, then sauntered away, immediately gaining the attention of everyone around her.

Rafe exhaled and forced himself to focus. He stepped out from the pillar, blank expression in place, and began a slow, leisurely turn about the room, his eyes flicking repeatedly to Sir Edgar, still enjoying too much of his punch. Marianne and Kit made their way out to the dance floor, Kit giving him a serious nod, knowing better than to draw attention to him. He'd never told his friend what he did in any certain terms, but Kit had never asked. He seemed to know without any sort of information at all.

He noted the men circling Sir Edgar, studied the man himself with more care, and noted with some satisfaction, and grudging admiration, that he wasn't nearly as drunk as he appeared. His eyes were fixed and clear, and at a very slight nod, those men around him began to migrate.

Rafe looked at them all in turn, noting features and state of dress, if he did not know their names. A visit to Hal would help him with identities and then they would finally have some answers. It was long past time for progress to be made here.

He eased his way around the crush, glancing at the dance floor again, feeling his chest seize up at the sight of Margaret dancing with some fresh young lad with adoring eyes and a perfect cravat. His gaze narrowed and he willed fate to be on his side, then wrenched his attention back to the retreating forms of the traitors he would root out.

He frowned a little, his mind whirling with the plans and predictions he'd made. They were choosing to depart by the proper exits and entrances, thus staying in plain sight of the guests for much of the time. He'd expected them to slink off into the lesser known areas of the house where the safety of anonymity could guard them. It was a much cleverer, more daring plan to behave like this, but it would make his task more difficult.

There would be no easy way to follow them once they left the safety of the crowded ballroom, not when he was dressed as he was. He would stir up comment and draw attention to himself, no matter how careful he was. On a night such as this, the servants would be traipsing back and forth with trays and work and might take no notice of him, but he would certainly be in their way. He needed a way to blend in and allow him to move as freely as he might have done otherwise.

He paused at the side of a footman standing stock still with a tray of punch in his hands. They were of a height, similar in stature, and with the ridiculous leaves strewn in the powdered wig, no one would pay any attention to his true features. He smirked at the dark livery, and further still at the sudden wariness in the lad's eyes.

"My dear chap," he said in a very droll voice, "I am about to make your night. How would you like to earn a fiver?"

Chapter Four

"It's done. Should be easier from now on."

"Easier how? You've not done anything but gain a few extra pounds."

"Try a few extra *thousand* pounds."

Someone whistled low.

"How?"

"Prudent investments. The point is, it is enough."

Rafe pressed as close as he could to the door, holding himself as still as possible. It was beyond fortunate that they had chosen to meet in the second study, which was much smaller and much less conspicuous, and happened to have a connecting door to a small antechamber, where he currently waited. Ever the man to scrimp where he could, Sir Edgar had installed flimsy doors in the house, despite their ornate designs, and Rafe could hear every word.

He'd arrived in the antechamber moments before the men had entered the study and had lifted the latch of the door so it would be ever so slightly ajar without raising any suspicion.

The slightest noise from him, however, and they would know exactly where to look.

"Are we prepared to move forward then?" asked a rasping voice Rafe recognized.

He bit back a grim smile. Lord Viskin, it seemed. Well, well, that was one he hadn't expected.

"I've already got my pieces in place," an unfamiliar voice said.

"Do you?"

There was some slight shuffling and the light within the room suddenly increased. "See here, the profits will only increase once the contract is completed. I've given all I have of my own to the cause, but with this connection, the available support will be unending."

Another voice swore in a bit of awe. "And you're sure your contact can arrange this? It's not certain…"

"It *is* certain. It will happen."

"And then what?"

"My resources in Calais will provide us with the… inspiration we need to accomplish the next task."

The room rumbled with laughter, and Rafe frowned. His sources all spoke of Paris, not Calais, and Sieyès was in Brussels, young Napoleon in Austria, and the mysterious brothers of Napoleon, the former kings of Holland and Spain, remained clear of France. The Foreign Office hadn't given him any reason to think otherwise, not that they usually gave him much to go on anyway, considering he was a London operative.

The secret London-based coalition between Home and Foreign Office that had grown into the London League had begun as a small project at the height of trouble with Napoleon, and their successes had only made them more of an integral part of the covert operations realm. Despite complaints from other branches, they were a fixture now, and were not going anywhere.

If someone had neglected to inform them that their investigation into this as yet unnamed faction had greater ties than they'd previously anticipated, there would be hell to pay. Preferably from someone in the upper ranks.

Maybe the Eagle could put some pressure on… He might not be one of the Shopkeepers, but he could certainly have some influence. He'd saved the lives of each of the men in that group at least once, they certainly owed him something.

"Calais?" someone sputtered. "Why not Paris?"

"Munitions in Paris fall under more scrutiny, Terrence," Sir Edgar said without much patience. "Calais is safer and less conspicuous."

"So who is meeting with…?"

Rafe frowned, wondering if he'd missed a name.

"He will contact Grimshaw when he wants to meet," Lord

Viskin replied. "Until then, mind your business and keep to the plan. The last thing we need is for people to think we're doing business together."

"No one thinks you do business anyway."

Dark chuckles rumbled in the room and Rafe almost joined in. It was true, Viskin was known for his poor parties and excessive drink, not for anything productive. No one would believe him capable of concise thought, let alone treachery.

It was a perfect cover.

He heard the men shifting within the room and made to do so himself when he heard voices again.

"How certain are you of your plan?" Grimshaw muttered so low that Rafe had to strain to hear him.

There was a soft grunt. "Perfectly. It's too simple, really. My piece is in the perfect situation, and there is nothing to draw back to myself. The cover is foolproof, Grimshaw. No one will ever know."

"They'd better not. This is an opportunity here, Tobias, and you won't get a second one."

"From you or from him?"

"Whichever inspires you to succeed."

Their voices faded and the light in the room faded. Rafe sank against the floor, wincing as he set his head back against the wall.

Blast. This was getting more complicated all the time. Someone else was calling the shots, and thanks to their secrecy, he had no idea whom. He could get a fairly accurate detailing of the men who had gone into that room and thus were traitors to the British Crown, but it wouldn't get him the one pulling the strings.

But they had to start somewhere. Grimshaw was heavily involved, as he'd thought, and Viskin… Well, that was going to be a pleasure to bring to light.

Provided this came to light at all.

It might be prudent to let them alone for now. To disrupt their current plans would draw attention to their involvement, and ruin any chances at reaching the bigger fish.

The Shopkeepers loved the bigger fish.

He snorted softly as he picked himself up off of the floor. Shopkeepers, indeed. That was a point of pride for him. The heads of the Home, Foreign, and War Offices, as well as the spymaster and Prime Minister, had met for eons of time in secret about covert operations, and had kept themselves out of each other's hair for the most part. More recently, however, they'd been forced to mix and mingle their operations and meet more regularly, thus requiring reports to be more inclusive, and the need for secrecy only increased. Code names were usually earned rather than bestowed, but exceptions had to be made.

Inspiration had come when Bonaparte had so unwisely proclaimed that England was a country ruled by shopkeepers.

And then it suddenly was.

The Shopkeepers gleefully accepted the jab and had turned it into the greatest private joke in British history. No one knew of their covert dealings, and the boring lives they led as the most powerful political figures in Britain seemed to be task enough. Weaver, for example, was a Shopkeeper, but he was Lord Rothchild for the public, better than the official ambassadors to various nations, and more respected than the lot of them.

Of course, Weaver still dabbled in various operations, but the Fox, as he'd been when he was an operative, was officially retired.

Officially.

He wondered faintly if Lady Rothchild was aware of that...

Rafe sighed and brushed off the dark livery. This antechamber, however useful, was not well kept. He would have to pass that information on to his new friend, provided he could turn him. He usually could. Loyalty of servants was highly overrated.

He glared down at the ancient and stinking powdered wig, and the idiotic wreath currently tangled within it. If he'd been a footman in truth, he would have expected a great deal of bribery to remain in a house this mad.

But appearances must be kept, so he donned it once more and carefully made his way back through the halls.

"What are you doing there?" barked an older woman with a severe expression. She wore none of the finery of the guests, which placed her squarely with the household.

Perfect.

Long accustomed to being expressionless, Rafe adopted the

token placid face of a footman. "The master asked me to take something to the library for him. I'm returning to the ballroom."

She snorted and quirked fingers at him. "Not empty handed, you're not. You know better. Come with me."

Rafe fought a smile, but obediently followed. Either the woman had a miserable memory for her own staff, or Sir Edgar had hired out extra help for this ball.

Both options worked to his advantage quite well.

After being forced to bear another tray of whatever horrid concoction was supposed to represent Greece to the ballroom, and endure the inanity of the guests around him, he was at last able to slip away and meet the wigless and simply clad footman at the mews.

He shuddered as he removed the wig and tossed it at him. "I don't envy you that thing, lad."

The footman shrugged and set it atop his head, slightly askew. "Sad to say, sir, but you get used to it."

Rafe shucked the livery and brushed it off, giving him a frown. "You work at the house?"

As he thought, the footman shook his head. "No, sir, I work for Lady Poole. Sir Edgar needed extra hands for this soiree, so he brought us over. I made an extra five bob tonight." Again there came the shrug.

What a bizarre life, Rafe thought with a sad shake of his head. "You've made far more than that," he reminded him as he pulled out a bill from his trousers. "And more to come if you hear or notice anything of interest surrounding Sir Edgar. Understood?"

The footman's eyes widened as he took the note, then he swallowed and shoved it into his own.

Rafe bit back a smile. "And if you find that tending the Peacock Pooles or Sir Edgar is too much for you," he said, fumbling for the bit of pencil he always kept on him, "you can go here." He scribbled the address onto a spare bit of parchment and handed that over as well. "Ask for Horton. He'll help you out."

The footman took that as well, shaking his head. "Thank you, sir," he breathed.

Rafe shook his hand, then tapped his nose knowingly. "Your silence, remember. Not a word."

"About what, sir?" came the immediate reply.

"Exactly."

The footman shook his hand again and left, leaving Rafe to the silence, and his folded pile of finery.

He ought to rush off to Hal, or head back to the office, something significant after what he'd just heard.

But Margaret Easton was back at the house.

And blast it all if he didn't want to see her more than anything else.

Well, that was one event without success.

Margaret nibbled on her dry toast, without jam, and tried not to glare at her companion. She had no desire to be scolded this early in the morning, and she knew that she was due for it already.

The carriage ride last night was proof enough.

She'd been too forward with the men she had danced with, and her friend Miss Arden had been a bad influence. Her cousin was too wild and visits with her were to be curtailed, but not forbidden, as Miss Dalton could benefit from a good example. Events were now to be chosen by Miss Ritson alone, being the paragon of virtue and far more informed in Societal matters.

And, of course, fashion was to be addressed.

Margaret had no idea what there was to find fault about in her ensemble last night. She'd worn a simple cream muslin and pearls, hardly any additional adornments, and everything had been fitted according to the styles of the day.

But apparently, she was far more hopeless than she'd thought, and she was fortunate Miss Ritson had found her now before it was too late.

Such was her tirade, at any rate.

Margaret had actually enjoyed the night, had met some lovely gentlemen, though none that she truly thought she could marry, and had found the comfort in her friend and cousin that she had been seeking. But there would be less and less of that, and more suffering and enduring. If she managed to find a husband in truth with Miss Ritson prodding her along, it would be a miracle.

On the other hand, it might make her more desperate and less particular.

That was a rather terrifying thought.

She made a face as she bit into her toast again. She'd been forbidden jams and tarts, sweets of any kind, as she was apparently just as plump in the eyes of her companion as she was with her great aunt.

And she was starving.

"Mind your expression, Miss Easton," Miss Ritson barked in her chilling voice that was too low for her frame. "You must be refined at all times."

"Yes, Miss Ritson," she recited obediently.

"And sit up!"

She did so.

Miss Ritson frowned, the lines at her small mouth becoming more pronounced. "You have a willful spirit, Miss Easton, and that is unbecoming."

Margaret resisted the urge to sigh. It was not the first time she had heard about her independence as a flaw of massive proportions, and it would not be the last. Her parents had always allowed her a bit of leisure, and as such, she was, admittedly, freer than an average miss, but she was also unfailingly obedient, and surely that was something to be admired.

"Your expression indicates you are resentful," Miss Ritson said with a faint sniff. "Why are you determined to resist my efforts? Your parents have generously allowed you to remain for the Season, and I am to aid you in your attempts to find a suitable British husband, which is what you wish for yourself. How can I help you do so if you continue to remain unobliging?"

Despite her bristling at the implication that this was all her fault, Margaret lowered her chin in a demure submission. "I do not mean to be so," she murmured.

And she didn't. But really, how could she be faulted for not being admired as she was? She was not shocking or wild by any stretch, and she was no wallflower or spinster. Whatever was working against her, it had nothing to do with her being a pariah.

It was simply a matter of taste.

It had to be.

Miss Ritson shook her somehow lifeless brown hair and sighed, sipping her tea. "I don't know what to do with you, Miss Easton. Until you allow me to advise you in truth, you will not get anywhere."

Margaret chewed her lip, struggling within herself. Miss Ritson had an agenda, there was no question, but as she could not see to what end that would lead, she did not have much of a choice. Her chaperone was her key to going out at all, regardless of whether their plans would converge at any point. Could she let Miss Ritson take control of her without actually relinquishing control at all?

She had to. If she wanted any chance at a marriage of her own choice, she had to play along.

Miss Ritson had all the power to restrict her as she saw fit.

She could not let that happen.

"What would you suggest for my next social engagement, Miss Ritson?" she asked politely, pointedly taking much smaller bites.

The flash of victory in the pale eyes gave Margaret pause, but it was too late now.

"You have been invited to attend Lady Cavendish's card party," Miss Ritson reported, setting aside her silverware. "You will accept, and mingle with some ladies of high quality. They may open doors to you, and your impression must be favorable."

"Of course," Margaret murmured. "When is it?"

"Tomorrow, so we will not have time to find a suitable wardrobe for you."

Margaret frowned slightly. "No time? Why not today?"

Miss Ritson raised a brow at her. "It is Thursday, Miss Easton. We are to visit Mrs. Campbell."

The toast in her mouth suddenly felt drier. "Aunt Ada?" she squawked, her voice rising noticeably in pitch.

"Of course, you must maintain your family connections!" Miss Ritson shook her head in disappointment. "You cannot be so cruel as to ignore the dear lady while your parents are away."

Aunt Ada had never been considered a dear lady in her entire life, and certainly never in Margaret's, and she could not see any reason to go visit her without her mother as a buffer. The last two weeks had been lovely in that respect. Miss Ritson had never insisted on these visits before, and for that she was grateful.

Why now?

"I would never be so neglectful," Margaret replied with care. "I only… Well, we have not gone since my parents have left, so I was only clarifying."

Miss Ritson looked suspicious, narrowing her shrewd eyes and clearing her throat slightly. "That is because she has been unwell and sent a request that we not disturb her during her time of much needed rest. She is recovered now, and we shall maintain your usual schedule."

"Indeed?" Margaret asked, heart stuttering slightly, fingers beginning to tingle.

"Yes," her chaperone said absently, nodding and pulling a small book from somewhere Margaret could not see. "Thursdays to visit your great aunt, Tuesdays to Bond Street, returning calls on Mondays and Wednesdays, and Fridays for receiving."

Margaret fought the urge to bite her lip again, this time in delight. A return to her regular schedule would mean a return to seeing her mystery man, and she had been longing for ten second moments for what felt like an age. It made no difference that she could never have him, he made her come alive, and when she was feeling so very lost and adrift, she needed that steadying influence.

"Whatever you think is best, Miss Ritson," she murmured, hiding a smile.

Miss Ritson looked up at her, frowning slightly. "There shall be more things to your schedule than that, Miss Easton," she informed her in a tight voice. "I shall schedule as many events for you as I can, and we must work in fittings, elocution and etiquette lessons, dancing, music, French…"

"I am already fluent in French," Margaret interrupted, bewildered by the sudden addition of education to her tasks. "And I have completed my education at a finishing school in Switzerland."

"Do not interrupt, Miss Easton," came the quick reply. "It is very rude. And obviously your education and etiquette are lacking, for you are most certainly not finished, and not accomplished enough for

45

your fortune to tempt a man enough to wed you and bed you."

Margaret gasped a little and her fingers curled into a fist beneath the table.

Miss Ritson raised a brow at her. "I have not said anything you did not already know, do not act so surprised. Now, I must finish my report to your parents, who have sent their disappointment with your lack of success thus far, and you must practice your pianoforte."

Margaret blinked back an odd sense of tears and cleared her throat. "I do not play the pianoforte, Miss Ritson."

"You would if you practiced." Again came the sniff, and then her chaperone was off again, this time listing appropriate men for Margaret to try for, but she was no longer listening.

She ought to fight this prison of hers. It was confining her so much she would never be able to maneuver on her own when about. She would never find a husband worth his salt like this.

But fighting it would ensure she was married off to an Italian before Easter, and she couldn't give up so soon.

She would cling to the image of her mystery man, if she ever had freedom of her eyes to look for him, and hope that this would all prove worth it in the end.

She nodded once to herself, and to whatever Miss Ritson said, and bit into the last of her miserable toast again.

Chapter Five

One month. One whole blasted month and not a single moment with her.

He was going to go stark, raving mad.

He'd seen her, of course, and had done his part to make sure he was exactly where he should be at just the right moment, but she had never seen him. She was becoming a creature he did not recognize, and he was growing frantic. Where before she had looked fresh and clear and like the dawn now she was cool and pinched and pale, her dress was altered too much to the finery of the day, and her eyes held absolutely no expression to them. Worse than all of that, she no longer looked for him. She was as lifeless as any creature he had ever seen, yet she moved about in exactly the same way.

He knew the trouble lay with the bat that shadowed her, but surely that was not the only excuse. No one could hold that much power over a girl like Margaret.

Yet the proof was before him.

He'd be lying if he did not admit to thoughts and daydreams of storming the house and carrying her off, but he was a far more sensible creature than that.

Well, perhaps not *far* more, but just enough to avoid giving in to the impulse.

His work of late should have given him ample distraction, and yet…

It was hopeless. Not even the betrayal of the British upper class and the threat of Napoleonic sympathizers could scrub her out.

Rogue had given up. Rook laughed at him. Cap was bewildered.

Even Eagle had come down to have words with him, though he'd seemed amused by it.

He wasn't being neglectful in his work, he was just as efficient and accurate as he ever was. He was driven and active, thorough and focused, and his scouts were all very busy with leads and tips. All told, he was doing some of his best work.

But his heart wasn't in it.

He prided himself on not setting his people to tail her or give him updates on her, though he'd been more than tempted by that. He wanted Margaret Easton to remain a secret even to himself. He wanted to discover things about her himself. He wanted...

Well, he wanted a great many things he had no business wanting.

He strolled up the street now, heedless of the people surrounding him, tucked away in his careful ensemble of a nobody. He looked like everyone and no one at the same time, which was his greatest strength. Most of the time it was because he wanted to blend in and accomplish whatever his task or mission was, whether it was saving a lady from a rambling carriage or rooting out a traitor. Now, however, he only wanted to be ignored.

It was ridiculous, really. A young woman he knew nothing about, by his own omissions, and had only built up in his mind as the epitome of all, and all he could truly say was that he had not looked into her eyes in over a month.

Even the most romantic of fools would call him pathetic.

He knew that.

But he didn't mind being pathetic.

Not even the temptation of the Roma tribe on the outskirts of London seemed exciting, and he'd always had a way with the gypsies. He could have been one, for all anyone knew, though they'd never officially looked into it. He was all that remained of his family, and they'd been reserved and aloof for centuries. If someone had dallied with the Roma, it wouldn't surprise him.

He could have been a Roma in spirit, if not by birth. Roaming from place to place, finding home wherever your heart was, living by the Earth instead of by the profits... He could have done quite well in that life.

Not now, of course. Duty, honor, loyalty, and service to the

Crown were his life, not to mention his peerage duties, which he really did manage decently, if a bit absently. He ought to be seen in Parliament more, but considering his true duties, no one who knew the truth faulted him.

Come to think of it, there were only a very select few who actually knew the truth.

Everyone else just thought him one of the lazy lords of inherited titles and didn't expect much of him.

And those who had no idea of his birth only knew him as the Gent.

Gent who saw everything, knew everything, heard everything, and was the godfather of London itself.

Or so he'd heard.

He was quite infamous in certain circles, for better or worse, respected or hated.

He wished that actually helped him here.

Why couldn't Lord Marlowe take an interest in a young miss? He ought to have a bride, make some show of courtship, get on with his other duties; it would make perfect sense. Then he could call upon her and court her and…

He shook his head with a snort as he rounded a corner in Cheapside and slipped down a quiet lane.

No, Lord Marlowe wouldn't be doing that. Not when she was under guard and he had very little to recommend him.

And there was no saying that *she* would want him, if she knew how he'd misled her by his appearance, no matter how unintentional the slight.

He heaved a sigh as he mounted the stairs to the shabby building he'd been going to far too often of late.

Hal was getting very peeved with him.

The door was opened before he knocked, which was typical, and the surly faced servant that was once a street fighter and thief let him in without a word, which was also typical.

"Good morning, Tad," he greeted, smiling at the once-terrifying man.

The servant grunted. "Is it?" He turned without a bow or any sort of acknowledgement and disappeared down the dank corridor, leaving Rafe grinning behind him.

Tad didn't care who or what he was, and that was the most delightful part of it.

He made his way up the poky, narrow steps and avoided the creaky one near the top. "Hal!" he called jauntily, feeling a little uplifted just from being here. "Hal!"

He had no response, but he really hadn't expected one.

Hal's office was at the end of the hall, and he knocked twice, then pushed the door open without waiting for an answer. The "office" was really a library that had been made over into a workspace, and it looked as though a dervish had come through, as it usually did. Books and parchment were strewn all over the place, and easels were everywhere with drawings and paintings and sketches in various states of completion.

Hal was a method worker, and no one understood her method.

He doubted Hal understood either.

"Hal!" he called, looking around.

A blond head poked out from a wingback chair by the fire and spectacles glinted in the morning light from the windows. "What, Gent? For heaven's sake, I'm not deaf."

He grinned and stepped around the mess to approach. "No, you're not. But it's fun to pretend."

Hal scoffed and rose, dusting off a book and turning to face him. "What do you want? I'm not done with your maps, and you've already got your sketches from the card party. Don't tell me you've found more people…"

Rafe shook his head and shrugged. "No new ones, still working on the old. Can't seem to get a fix on those two men from Grimshaw's though."

Hal raised a brow at him. "You are having trouble with identification? You?"

Again, he shrugged. "I don't know everything."

"I've been telling you that for years."

Rafe snorted and grinned at the best sketch artist he had ever met in his years of work. "Yes, well, you've got a bit of attitude, Hal, and say all sorts of things you shouldn't."

That caused a smirk and the spectacles came down from their

perch as Hal folded them together. "True. What can I do for you? Is there something wrong with the sketches?"

Rafe sighed and sank into a nearby chair without invitation. "I don't know, Hal. It's that older man, the one I only glimpsed at the ball. His features keep changing in my mind, and brilliant as you are, I'm not sure the sketch is right."

Hal frowned and sat back down, hands folded. "You didn't see him at the card party?"

Rafe shook his head. "No, I've never seen him again, I'm sure of it. I purloined the list of people invited to Grimshaw's, but so many names are missing in general that it is impossible to identify him."

He glanced over at the girl beside him, spectacles still in her charcoal tinted fingers, looking at him with a furrowed brow. "Hmm. Well, let me pull out my versions of the sketches and we'll try again." She moved to a nearby desk with neatly stacked portfolios and pulled from the middle, then came back over, handing it to him.

He looked up in surprise. "You don't want to look?"

She shook her head at once, blond curls dancing wildly in their coif. "No, I don't want to be biased. So." She pulled out a pencil and a clean sheet, and looked at him expectantly. "Tell me again what he looks like, and take your time."

As he had done so often before, he recited everything he could remember, right down to the flapping jowls and flushed complexion. It wasn't the same as the first description he gave, but he suspected this man might be more like him than was comfortable.

Everyone and no one all at once.

And then something else popped up, something he'd forgotten in all of the fuss. "And he's got a pox scar above his left eyebrow! It's faint, but it's there."

Hal looked up with a half smile. "Really?"

He nodded proudly, then frowned at her dubious look. "What?"

She snorted softly and went back to her sketch, fingers flying across the page. "Long face, sagging skin, rotund in frame, beady eyes, high brow, fading hairline, and a pox scar? Gent…" She held up the paper and smiled a little. "I do believe you are speaking of Sir Vincent Castleton."

Rafe stared at the picture wide-eyed, heart pounding. A name!

But... "He's not been in London for decades, are you sure?"

Hal handed him the page and sat back, hands gripping the armrest. "I am. My family estate neighbored his in Sussex, and I could tell you some very intriguing stories about him."

Rafe sat back and smiled at her warmly. "My dear Hal, I had no idea you were a storyteller. Do please go on, I have all day."

She smiled, her chin dipping a little in pleasure. "For starters, he hates his name, and in his inner circles goes by his second name, Tobias."

Rafe stilled, his fingers tightening on the page. *Tobias.* That was it! He allowed himself a slow, predatory grin at the girl, somehow elfin in feature and statuesque in build, and at the moment, his favorite person on earth. "By Jove, Hal, you are a phenomenal woman. Why haven't I asked you to marry me yet?"

She threw her head back and laughed a throaty sort of laugh. "Because I like Rogue better than you, and you're too pretty. Now, do you want to hear the real stories or not?"

Margaret put a hand to her brow and tried not to look miserable. It was a herculean effort.

Why would anyone ask Lady Darlington to sing? The former Fanny Harville was the most horrific vocalist she had ever heard, and she'd endured Charlotte Truman for three Seasons.

But then, no one had ever said Miranda Ascott was an intelligent hostess. And from the looks of things, no one had taken the care to warn her of the dangers of Lady Darlington's voice.

Margaret winced as the lady in question attempted a note far out of her range. The desperate Lord Darlington had snatched up the only lady he could convince to have him, the equally desperate Miss Harville, and all of London had breathed a sigh of relief when they had married at the end of last Season.

Now they would not breathe so easily.

She glanced over and saw the tightness in Rosalind's features as she tried to maintain politeness, and the mirrored expression on her sister, Mrs. Granger. In fact, looking around, everyone looked that pained. Why, Lady Whitlock looked as though she were going to scream, and she was the most polite and composed lady in London.

She bit back a smile when she saw Lady Raeburn's expression. The eccentric woman, currently wrapped in plum silk and a matching turban, was wide eyed and tight about the mouth, and as she watched, she saw something twitch in her face.

As if she could sense when she was observed, Lady Raeburn met her gaze and blinked owlishly at her.

Margaret offered the smallest of smiles, fighting the urge to laugh.

Impossibly, Lady Raeburn's mouth quirked up slightly and she inclined her head a little.

A soft throat clearing beside her brought Margaret back around. Miss Ritson, her now almost constant companion, raised a scolding brow and shook her head slightly.

Margaret acknowledged the reprimand with a dip of her chin and applauded with the rest when Lady Darlington finished, and joined the rest in frantically looking around for another guest to avoid the horrors of an encore.

Blessedly, Mrs. Ascott rose and dismissed them all for refreshment, looking haggard now despite her overdone finery, which was designed to look simplistic, but fell short.

Margaret went to rise, but Miss Ritson clamped a hand on her arm. "Wait," she hissed beneath a polite smile. "Let the others rise, let them come to you."

That was a laughable thought.

"They don't come to me," she murmured back, smiling and nodding at Lady Blackmoor and her husband, who were fleeing with remarkable speed.

The hold on her arm clenched. "Just. Wait."

And so it had gone for the last five weeks. Everything Margaret did was wrong, no matter what her new tutors said. They all agreed she was accomplished and proficient in her endeavors, and saw no reason to be employed for her. But as the funds were coming from her parents and at Miss Ritson's discretion, there was nothing to be done about it.

Days upon endless days of correction and reprimand, social events that did very little to entertain or amuse her, and calls being paid and received to some of the most boring people she had ever met in her entire life. And she'd spent years in the company of her parents' European friends on the Continent. Miss Ritson rarely listened to her, and only did so if it involved her cousin, who had been Margaret's saving grace in all of this.

Helen had come to far more events than Margaret would have expected, always to ensure that it was not as horrible as Margaret feared. Rosalind, on the other hand, had apparently become the least favorite of all her associates in Miss Ritson's opinion, though why, she had no idea.

When she'd asked, Miss Ritson had only said that no one would look at Margaret if Rosalind were about, and she could not bear the competition for her.

That might have been a true statement, but Rosalind was also her key to attending the events that might actually prove fruitful to her. These parties and teas and carriage rides in Hyde Park were suffocating her, as they were starved for men with any sort of personality, or within a decade of her age, or that even remotely piqued her interest. All of the women she associated with, Helen aside, were remarkably plain, poor, or old. Or all of the above.

Was this what other girls had to deal with when the parents were not so lenient as hers? Or if their situations were truly desperate? The endless comparisons, the opportunistic ventures, ensuring attendance to events that would make her the most eligible woman there…

It was disgraceful and embarrassing.

She was ashamed of herself, and none of the plan was hers.

Would it really have been so bad to marry for comfort alone? This wasn't worth it, truly. Her heart could endure, so long as England was home.

Or… was the suffering so great that she would rather marry a European that might actually prove interesting and worthwhile?

No, she thought viciously. She'd had enough of that life, and she was set on England.

England was home.

"Margaret, will you take a turn about the room with me?" Helen asked from her side, having somehow approached her without Margaret noticing.

Miss Ritson stiffened beside her, but said nothing.

"I know that Lady Raeburn wishes to make your acquaintance," Helen continued, her voice as smooth as silk, as polite as was proper. "And once you meet her, I believe you will find several other people who will wish to do the same."

Margaret glanced up at her cousin, the very picture of an English miss, thin and fair and every feature perfectly situated. Miss Ritson ought to have hated her, but as the Daltons were not as wealthy as the Eastons, she was no competition. Apparently.

Miss Ritson nudged Margaret hard. "Go, Miss Easton," she urged, her eyes alight. "Your cousin is being very kind, and very astute. Go and meet those who can give you fairer prospects than your own dismal situation."

"Yes, Miss Ritson." Margaret rose as gracefully as she could and linked arms with her cousin, who led her away serenely.

"Lord, Margaret," Helen murmured when they were away, losing the polite air and speaking more like herself. "What has Rickety done to you?"

Margaret allowed herself to sigh and avoided looking behind her. "I cannot breathe," she replied in a low voice. "Everything is wrong, and if she sets my corsets any tighter…"

"She's making you wear corsets?" Helen interrupted quickly, eyes wide.

Margaret nodded morosely. "And restricting my food, and forcing me to walk Hyde Park every morning and evening… I had not thought myself quite so beyond a fashionable figure, but it seems to be the case."

Helen hissed between her teeth and pulled Margaret closer. "You are not even plump, darling. And even if you were, what is so very wrong with that? For heaven's sake, it is as though she thinks you the worst possible marriage candidate in London, which I know for a fact you are not."

Margaret sniffed in derision and nodded at Mrs. Granger, who smiled kindly. "Do you? How?"

Helen smiled and inclined her head towards a small gathering of men that were watching them. "The attention, dear. They aren't watching me, they know better. That is for you."

She glanced over and found one of them smiling at her. Encouraged, she allowed herself to smile in return, which made his smile grow.

"I'll never be able to make it over there," she whispered to Helen. "Miss Ritson would never…"

"Miss Ritson can eat my slippers," Helen snapped. "We're going to meet Lady Raeburn and Rosalind will speak with Captain Riverton, who will bring them over, it's all arranged. It is time you met some real prospects and not their portly uncles."

Margaret snorted a laugh and felt the tension leave her. Helen could always set her to rights, and whatever time she could spend away from Miss Ritson would be a blessing.

Rosalind swept to Helen's other side, knowing from experience that if she was too familiar with Margaret, Miss Ritson would intervene.

Truly, things were getting ridiculous.

Lady Raeburn was surrounded by admirers, as usual, including their hostess, and they all looked at the trio as they approached.

"Lady Raeburn," Helen began with a warm smile, "may I introduce my cousin, Miss Easton? Margaret, this is Lady Raeburn."

"A pleasure, my lady," Margaret said with a deep curtsey.

Lady Raeburn's painted lips quirked and she inclined her head regally. "Charming, Miss Easton. What a lovely picture you make. Tell me, do you really hunt for a husband just to keep yourself in England while your parents try for Europe?"

Someone nearby gasped, and Margaret felt her cheeks flush, but something within her prompted her to stare boldly back at this terrifying woman. "Yes, my lady," she answered as calmly as she could.

Lady Raeburn shook her head, the decorative beads of her turban clapping against the fabric. "European men make excellent lovers, but abysmal husbands. I should know, I've had my share of both."

Someone coughed in surprise, but Margaret found herself

smiling in spite of herself. "So what would you suggest, my lady?"

Lady Raeburn's eyes twinkled as she took in Margaret on the whole. "Find a British husband who can play the European lover," she finally replied, smiling slyly. "Best of both worlds, and nobody is shocked by it."

Margaret nodded sagely, fighting the urge to laugh. "I shall take that into advisement, my lady. Have you any suggestions for going about that?"

Now the company about them were beginning to warm to it, laughing softly and grinning at the exchange, but none so broadly as Lady Raeburn herself.

"Oh, my dear child," Lady Raeburn said as she smiled, "have I ever." She quirked her fingers and Captain Riverton, with the three men watching from before, sprang over to them, as well as a few others.

Feeling as though she had sold her soul somehow, Margaret greeted them all as they were introduced and smiled prettily, hoping no one would notice it was forced.

A British husband who could play the European lover. Well, there was one man she could picture in that role, but it was hardly suitable.

She had seen him every day, but had not been permitted to stare. Miss Ritson was like a hawk, and she'd never even had a five second moment with him, let alone ten. But she saw him, and fervently wished he would see her. She knew that if they could have their usual moment, he would see her distress and save her somehow. She knew that as well as she drew breath. He would save her, regardless of whether she could have him, and she could find a way to stay in England that satisfied her.

But if he never saw what was in her eyes, he couldn't know.

He couldn't save her.

How could a stranger, no matter how handsome, mean so much to her? She was a sensible girl, despite her imagination, and there was no reason for her to think him anything but a scoundrel and a roué.

Suddenly neither of those things seemed so much of a detriment.

Whoever he was, whatever he was, she missed him. She didn't even know him and she missed him. She still saw him everywhere and she missed him.

Her life was changing far too rapidly for her taste, and he was all that she could hold onto. He kept her steady, and despite the new reserve and hauteur forced on her by her chaperone, she would never be fully changed, not while the image of him was within her heart.

It was not good for her to think of him, she knew that, but her situation was so dismal she had to hold onto something. Her parents' letters held nothing but praise for Miss Ritson, which meant that her letters were not understood. Or perhaps they were misdirected. Whichever it was, she was running out of time and options, and her wistful imaginations, though delightful, were making things harder to accept. He could not be the bright shining hope of her life, even if he were as glorious in person as she imagined. However unlikely that was. He was sure to disappoint, if she ever did know him.

She smiled at the men around her, and prayed that one of them might be the one to save her, and make her forget him. She wanted so desperately to forget him, to be rid of him, to pretend they had never made eye contact at all. She would have been so much happier in ignorance.

But she doubted that was possible.

More than that, she knew she was lying.

Chapter Six

*T*wo weeks of investigation, and Rafe was convinced that Sir Vincent Castleton had been born out of hell itself.

That may have been a bit drastic, but he had very little to recommend him.

"Focusing on him so much is going to detract from the attention you ought to give to the rest," Rogue reminded him as they conversed on the subject yet again.

Rafe glared at him as he made further notes in the margins of his most recent reports. "The others are minor characters. Grimshaw is pulling strings, Viskin is full of hot air, but Castleton is the one with a plan. You should have heard Hal's stories."

Rogue remained unconvinced. "Hal doesn't know him that well. She's a gossiping child."

"She's twenty-four."

"When she knew Castleton, she was a child," Rogue corrected with a roll of his eyes.

"Most of what I've learned is gossip," Rafe replied, sitting back. "Most of what I gather is gossip, but that doesn't mean it isn't true."

Rogue acknowledged that with a nod. "Still, proceed with caution."

"Always do."

"No, you don't."

Rafe smiled tightly. "No, I don't. But you've seen the evidence, Rogue. Surely you see the patterns."

"Of course I see the patterns, I am not an infant." Rogue's pale eyes flicked to the papers. "He is involved, a key player, and by all accounts, the scum of the earth. I see that. All I am saying is there may be more here, so don't fixate."

Despite the inclination to bristle, Rafe saw the wisdom in that. He was aggravated at his inability to nail anything down, that everything seemed to be slipping through his fingers here, and with some plot in the works, that made him uneasy. Eagle wanted updates as fast as he could get them, which meant Cap was checking in more than usual, which meant they were all on their toes.

Even Rook had been pulled to help, and his talent for observation and memory had proven invaluable, despite his distracting persona.

Rafe's network was spread as thin as it had ever been, but all of the major suspects were covered, as well as some of his usual marks.

He was doing everything he could.

It never felt like enough.

His valet was starting to fret about his attire, mostly because Rafe no longer cared. Rogers had always taken pride in the variety of ensembles he sent Rafe out in, whether high standard or low, and when Rafe had begun returning everything in poor, tattered, worn conditions, Rogers nearly wept in distress.

Rafe didn't mean to upset him, he had simply been careless and was exhausted beyond measure. Last week he had only been home twice and only one of those times had involved him sleeping in his own bed.

Davis was used to expecting him randomly, if ever, but managed the household the same. The cook, whatever her name was, didn't even know him, and Callie, the maid he'd hired last year, was practically a housekeeper in her efficiency and orderliness, and never so much as batted an eye when he was at home. It made absolutely no difference to her, though her respect was impeccable and her actions prompt.

He'd have to keep an eye on that one. She'd make an excellent operative herself if she were half as intelligent as she appeared.

But his home had little meaning at the moment.

"What is it?" Rogue murmured, breaking his reverie.

Rafe looked over at him, suddenly fatigued. "What is what?"

Rogue simply waited, staring at him.

Rafe craned his neck, reluctant to let his friend in on his troubles, though they were practically brothers. Between this mess of Napoleonic supporters and his frustration over Margaret, he was a mass of quivering uncertainty, and for someone who had ever been steady in his life, it was worrisome.

Worrisome? It was terrifying!

He barely recognized himself anymore.

"For heaven's sake, do I need to go get Samuels to get you a drink?" Rogue barked.

Rafe raised a brow. "Who?"

"The clerk, you tiresome wretch. The one who answers to whatever we call him."

Rafe grunted and looked away. "Right. No, better not drink today."

There was a knock at the front door and they stilled, looking at the hallway. Very few people came to see them here, and if they did, it was only for reports. The average person would have no cause to seek them out. If they did, it was because someone knew something, and that was dangerous.

Rafe had to think hard to remember what the cover of their office even was. Investigators? Something like that. Cheaper than Bow Street and less official. Less formal. And less honorable, to boot.

But no one had tried for that yet, so they had no practice.

Did Taylor up front know that?

The unspoken questions were answered when Rook himself came into the room, looking like the dandy that he was, and very much out of place in their plain little office.

His dark hair fell over one green eye as he paused to look at them both, raising the one brow they could see. "Is there a problem, gentlemen?"

Rogue snorted and settled further into his seat. "Gent has several problems, but apparently cannot find words for them."

Rook looked at him in surprise, then slowly grinned the grin that he'd long ago learned to mistrust. "Indeed? Well..." He immediately dropped into the available chair without any of the grace someone dressed as finely as he should have employed and sobered. "I am all ears."

Rafe glared at them both, wishing there was someone here on his side.

Rook fought another smile as long as he could, then let it flash briefly across his face before turning to Rogue. "Part of the problem, I am sure, lies with his poor Miss Easton."

Rafe stiffened in his seat and his hands tightened into fists.

"Indeed?" Rogue said, crossing his legs and putting a finger to his lips. "You may be right. Any insight, Rook?"

Rook nodded, matching Rogue's pose. "A bit. I am quite the name in Society, you know. I have cultivated one very carefully. And Miss Easton is doing the same."

"Is she?"

"She is indeed."

Rafe was going to kill them both if they did not stop.

"What sort of name is she cultivating?"

"Oh, she is a husband hunter. Quite a shame, to be sure, as no one will have her."

"No one? Why not?"

"No one knows, so no one dares. She's very pretty, scandalously wealthy, and would certainly warm a fellow's bed right, but for some reason..."

"Enough!" Rafe snapped, banging his fist on the desk. "Enough!"

His colleagues looked surprised at him, no hint of amusement in either of their gazes.

Rook blinked, then looked over at Rogue. "I didn't expect that."

Rogue never took his eyes off of Rafe. "Nor did I. A bit much, in my opinion."

"Shut it," Rafe grumbled, sinking back into his chair and rubbing his hands over his eyes.

"Gladly, once you tell me what this is about," Rogue replied, folding his arms.

Rafe glanced at Rook, who shrugged. "I am here to help, believe it or not, and to report in on your marks, when you're of a mind."

He flicked his gaze between both of them, and sensed this was not a battle worth fighting. "Very well," he grumbled, rubbing at his brow, "since I know the pair of you won't leave me in peace until I tell you all."

And so he told them what he didn't dare put on paper, the inability to tie anything about the faction supporters down, seeing Castleton as a break in the struggle, but not knowing how to use him, the feeling that something was missing, the nagging sense of being one step behind...

They offered advice and counsel, helped him think through some of the more complicated matters that had been uncovered in the last several weeks, and shared what their own investigations had found. Ultimately, they had no answers for him, but he had not thought they would.

It was enough that they took his concerns seriously and could compare notes.

Whatever they were on the brink of, at least he was not alone in this.

"I don't want to miss anything," he said with a groan, grinding his hands into his eyes. "That's what cost us…"

"Trace," Rogue finished harshly. "I know."

Rafe glanced up and the two shared a look. Trace had died because somewhere, somehow, they had missed something, some connection they failed to make, some danger they had not seen. Nothing had been quite so complicated since then, but this felt eerily similar, and they could not lose another one of their group.

"I'll sniff around," Rook said, rising from the chair with a groan. "I doubt I'll be invited into the circle, but at least I can be annoyingly present. It's amazing what people say when they think you're not listening."

Rafe smiled, knowing from experience that was true. "I thought you were supposed to be a rake, not a peacock."

Rook gave him an utterly superior glare. "I am the only man on earth that can be both, Gent. You stick to avoiding attention and let me collect it."

"Gladly," he replied, waving him off with a laugh.

When he was gone, Rogue looked back at him knowingly. "You said nothing of Miss Easton."

"That is because I have nothing to say," Rafe informed him. "Unfortunately."

"Driving you to your wit's end?"

"Yes."

Rogue muttered something under his breath, then shifted in his chair. "How are the Roma? Anything useful there?"

Relieved at the change in topic, Rafe unfolded his experiences of late with the tribe, good and bad, and let his mind wander into other realms than the ones that occupied his mind too often these days.

"I don't know this shop," Margaret said for what had to be the fifth time this morning, confused as to why they were looking at a modiste shop on this side of London instead of in Bond Street, where they usually went. She'd lost track of the directions they had taken, but there were no familiar sights here, nor familiar faces. She had no idea where they were, but she did not like the looks of it.

"And that shows how unfortunate your experiences are," Miss Ritson replied, her tone crisp and final.

Margaret rolled her eyes behind her chaperone's back and followed into the dimly lit shop, wondering why a modiste would choose to keep the light so low. One could hardly get a fair estimate of the fabric if it could not be adequately seen.

Not that it mattered, as Margaret highly doubted her opinion would be consulted at all. They were finally having a proper session with someone who apparently could save her disastrous fashion sense, and all of this would undoubtedly lead her to finding a man in England to marry. Or simply be a waste of her parents' money and make Margaret feel ill about herself.

She suspected the latter was far more likely.

She never looked at herself in a mirror anymore. It was too distressing.

"Ah, Miss Ritson," called an older woman from the back. "Excellent, you are right on time." She came more fully into view, and Margaret felt more uneasy. She was a wiry woman with hard features and harder eyes, and she doubted the woman had smiled in her entire life. One smile might break her face entirely.

Miss Ritson nodded primly and stepped around a mannequin. "Mrs. Andrews, a pleasure to see you again." She turned and gestured to Margaret. "This is Miss Easton, whom I wrote to you about."

Mrs. Andrews looked her over from head to toe, and somehow seemed to frown further still. "You didn't tell me she was so poorly off, Ritson. This is going to cost you more."

"Her parents wish for her to make a good match," Miss Ritson explained with only enough sympathy to indicate that Margaret was pathetic. "They will pay whatever expenses necessary to make that happen."

Mrs. Andrews snorted and circled Margaret, tapping her mouth with a bony finger. "The figure is all wrong, far too simple in dress, and nothing at all to draw the eye."

"Exactly. I knew you could help us."

She suddenly grabbed Margaret's chin tightly and tilted her face from side to side, looking at her fiercely. "Bonnet off," she ordered briskly.

Margaret fumbled with the ribbons under her chin, trying not to touch the woman gripping her. She let it fall behind her and restrained a wince as the hold on her face tightened.

Mrs. Andrews clicked her tongue and gestured for them both to follow her. "This will take some time, I trust you have nowhere to be today."

Margaret was about to reply that she did, as she had arranged to have tea with Helen and Rosalind, but Miss Ritson overrode her quickly. "No, Mrs. Andrews, we are at your mercy."

Mrs. Andrews grunted without emotion and pointed at a pedestal for Margaret to stand upon, which she did, restraining a sigh.

This was how all her days had gone, and she was tired of it. Mute obedience in the face of degradation and humiliation, with being forced to endure tedium and boredom, nothing to brighten her days, and absolutely no prospects for marriage.

None of the gentlemen she had met at Mrs. Ascott's had called, and her parents had not written her about their ventures. They wrote to Miss Ritson regularly, but only told her to give her their love and affection. They'd never been regular at correspondence, even when she was at school, but this was too cruel. She had written them of her experiences, everything she could bear to, but she suspected her mail was being interfered with.

But why keep her from prospective gentlemen, if any were trying? Surely she wasn't so bad that *all* of the bachelors turned their nose up at her. Why, the ones she had met with Helen and Rosalind had been very charming, and Captain Riverton seemed fair enough friends with all of them, which ought to indicate good breeding and manners. Was she really as hopeless as everybody said?

Whatever it was, there was no excuse for this. She had not sinned to such a degree in her life to deserve this punishment.

She held her arms out as Mrs. Andrews and her very plain assistant stripped her to her unmentionables and began assessing her completely, with such disparagement that she wished she were deaf. There was apparently nothing of value to find in her, and she actually wished that Aunt Ada were here so she might have something to say on the subject. At least Aunt Ada thought she had potential.

Hours ticked by as she remained there, article after article being thrust upon her, measured and pressed and prodded, feeling utterly ridiculous. She knew the time had gone by, she could see the grandfather clock in the very back and watched the hands move. It couldn't be right, though; it was at least two days, not three hours. She was growing hungry, as her breakfasts were now miniscule, and her head was fuzzy with it.

She sputtered a little as feathers brushed by her nose and she barely avoided glaring at the assistant, whose vacant expression bode very ill for Margaret.

She glanced down at herself and wondered where in the world they expected her to go half dressed and wearing feathers. Good heavens, she looked like an underdressed Poole sister.

Rosalind and Helen would die of laughter if they saw her.

She saw Mrs. Andrews coming towards her with another bolt of fabric and pins, and nearly sighed in relief. At least she was about to be decently covered, if she had to endure feathers. For the present ensemble belonged on a woman with far less morals than she, and even then not outside of a boudoir.

Miss Ritson was nodding slowly, smiling in a way that Margaret did not appreciate one bit. She had long lost track of the conversation between her chaperone and her costumer, but she wished now that she had paid a bit more attention.

To her horror, Mrs. Andrews was looking at her and shaking her head. "No, that won't do. Take the bodice down further."

The assistant nodded, completely ignoring Margaret's squawk of protest. She was quite certain the only direction the bodice needed to go was up, and very much so at that.

Mrs. Andrews frowned further still, and shook her head harder. "It's the corset. Turn, child."

Wincing, Margaret did so and the corset about her was removed, much to her relief, and she exhaled heavily. But the reprieve was short lived as another was wrapped about her, and it took only a few moments for Margaret to realize that this was not only a smaller set than the previous one, but that it was absolutely not going to fit.

It couldn't.

She inhaled painfully as the laces were pulled tight, and then tighter still as she gasped. Apparently it could fit, but only if she did not breathe. Dots appeared before her eyes and certain rather crushed parts of her were going to expose themselves quite shamefully if one gave them the barest chance.

"Oh, that is perfect, Mrs. Andrews!" Miss Ritson gushed, sounding so unlike the creature Margaret lived with it was eerie.

"Not yet," Mrs. Andrews muttered, pulling somehow further still on the laces.

Margaret whimpered breathlessly in agony, pains beginning in her lower quarters, her ribs, her lungs, and an erratic pounding in her head made her sway.

"There. Now, replace the bodice, and add more ruffles to the skirt."

She couldn't even protest the atrocity, considering she could barely see or breathe. She managed a brief glimpse in the mirror and squeezed her eyes shut at once. Her figure was very pronounced now, but the gown looked like the worst version of her late aunt Mathilda in every other respect. Ruffles, feathers, far too much décolletage, and not a single aspect representing her at all.

Her right foot was lifted and a too-small heeled shoe was placed upon it, and then the other. She wobbled unsteadily in the unfamiliar shoes, and she focused on breathing in short bursts to avoid pain.

"Would you mind very much rouging her cheeks and her décolletage?" Miss Ritson murmured. "We are to pay a visit to Sir Vincent Castleton and his sister after this, and I should like Miss Easton to go as she is. Sir Vincent is *most* interested in making her better acquaintance, and I would like her to make an impression worth remembering."

Margaret's eyes flew open and she turned to look at her chaperone.

Mrs. Andrews was smiling and nodding, indicating that her assistant should do that. "That will be extra."

"As you wish."

"I can't..." Margaret gasped, gripping at her midsection as the assistant began rouging her. "I can't... meet with him."

Miss Ritson looked at her with derision. "Of course, you can. You have no other prospects."

"He is... a horrible man!" she protested weakly. A womanizer. A profligate. Vicious. At least thirty years older than her, and the rumors about him were too terrifying to comprehend.

Mrs. Andrews and Miss Ritson shook their heads. "Rumors are cruel, Miss Easton," Miss Ritson said with contempt. "I will be with you the entire time, and you need a husband. Accept the generosity of his invitation, and you may find you remain in England after all."

They turned to converse apart from her, but Margaret, whose hearing had grown in intensity with her breathlessness, heard the words "marriage" and "compromise" before they left her range.

She shook her head at herself and took in short rapid breaths, her mind whirling.

No. She would *not* be trussed up like a whore and laid before an evil man like a pagan sacrifice. She refused to let this happen. Miss Ritson did not control her as much as she wished, and she would not benefit from setting Margaret on this course.

She glanced down at the assistant, who blinked without expression, then vanished into a back room without a word.

Margaret followed her with her eyes, then glanced back towards the others, who were still deep in conversation. She looked up again towards the rear, where the back door was now free of obstacles.

She did not even pause for consideration.

She ran for it headlong, threw it open, and dashed out into the London streets.

Chapter Seven

*R*unning when one cannot breathe is not a wise course of action.

She did not have a choice, but the thought was a valid one.

Her corset seemed to grow tighter and tighter with every step, and her feet throbbed with the heeled monstrosities upon them. She hefted the heavy skirts in hand and ran as hard and as fast as she could through the unfamiliar streets, darting down as many side streets as she could, the fear of pursuit predominant in her mind.

She could only imagine the horrors Miss Ritson would unleash upon her if she were caught.

Oh, she was an idiot, she thought as she panted down another empty, filthy street. She was running through parts of London she did not know, less than half dressed, forced into a level of indecency she did not know she could attain, pins jabbing her at almost every point, and with absolutely no plan in her head but that of fleeing.

She cried out as her ankle turned, but didn't dare stop, somehow still running despite the throbbing.

She couldn't catch her breath, but that did not matter so much as putting as much distance between her and that place as she could. She felt safer fleeing in this state and in this distress than she had there, suffering under their attention and being part of their plans. Anywhere was better than there.

She tottered to a halt as she tried to get her bearings, her hair tumbling from the combs. She could only breathe in gasps, and her sides and her lower quarters ached from the pressure. Her dress felt heavier than the yards of ruffles and her arms ached with the weight of it. But she had run so many streets, was so turned around, surely no one could find her.

A faint whistling sent a chill up her spine and she glanced frantically around, seeing two men at the end of a nearby alley watching her with hooded eyes and knowing smirks. One of them whistled again, somehow making the sound evil and terrifying. They stared at her, and she stared back, trembling and horrified.

Then one of them took a step in her direction.

Somehow, she found more lung capacity to gasp and ran once again, turning to continue down the road she'd come in on. Ankles were forgotten, lungs were forgotten, it did not matter that she could not feel her face or anything below her neck, that she had no idea where she was, or that she was indecent. Now it was more than poor candidates for matrimony or the mortification of her appearance and demeanor. This was fleeing for her innocence, and her life, she was certain of it.

She had eavesdropped on enough conversations throughout her life to hear whispers of wicked things in dark places, and this was always how they went.

A woman in a place she should not be in, in a state she should not be in, and without any sense at all.

She was in exactly that predicament.

Street after street passed her, and she raced as fast as she could, limping and gasping pathetically. She could hear the men behind her, and her own clacking heels on the cobblestones gave them exact direction for her. She could not take the time to stop and remove them, or they would overtake her.

They would do so shortly as it was.

Odd sensations down her cheeks and burning in her eyes told her she was crying, but that seemed impossible. She could not do anything but run and panic, and she was not going to be able to do the former for very much longer.

In a last desperate attempt to throw off her pursuers, she wrenched down an alley suddenly, ignoring the dark and foreboding sense of it. She dodged crates and sludge, running headlong for the next street beyond.

Only to find that it ended around the next corner in a dank, filthy, sooty brick wall, and more wooden crates and scattered bits of rubbish.

She whimpered and swayed into the wall beside her, gripping it with her nails.

There was nowhere else to go.

She heard the footsteps come down the alley, and turned, sinking behind the nearest crates, hoping that the light was dim enough, and the men drunk enough, to somehow spare her.

And then she waited.

"'Ere, Precious," one of them called out. "Come to Papa."

The other chuckled darkly. "Give us a taste, poppet!"

Margaret bit her lip and squeezed her eyes shut.

Suddenly she heard shouts and scuffles, then other sounds, louder and echoing through the alley. A new voice, carrying above the others, rang out, followed by crashes and grunts, garbled exchanges, and the unmistakable sound of skin connecting with skin, as well as other things, and was that a snarl? She didn't dare move or look, and she felt no relief in hearing it. Things could always go from bad to worse, and until she knew for certain, she wasn't giving the newcomer any indication of her presence.

Her body shook and her limbs throbbed, her breath catching on each inhale and her vision swimming blearily before her. She was going to faint any moment, and that would not go well for her.

She reached behind her as her breath began to come faster, louder, and panic began to swell. She covered her mouth with her free hand while she desperately tried to pull the pinned fabric way and untangle the laces and knot, and only managed to mangle it and, somehow, pull even tighter.

Clamping down on a panicking whimper, she tried to use both hands to free herself, but nothing was happening except for making things much worse.

Tears sprang to her eyes again as the sounds in the alley were fading, or perhaps it was her hearing, as all she could make out now was the pounding of her heart and almost frantic pitch of her breath.

"Miss?" called the newer voice. He whistled a little and suddenly appeared in her portion of the alley. "Hey, miss, where are you?"

She ducked her head down further, which unfortunately made

her dress rustle and the ridiculous ruffles added to the sound in chorus.

He shifted in her direction. "Miss? You can come on out, I won't hurt you."

There was something about that voice, something warm and tingly that she ought to know. But everything was tingling right now, and she herself was both hot and cold, and wouldn't someone who wanted to trick her say exactly that?

But he didn't sound as coarse as her pursuers.

And she had no other options.

Ankles throbbing, head swimming, lungs and ribs screaming, she crawled out from her hiding spot and looked up at the man.

It was *him*.

She hiccupped a distressed sound of surprise and saw the recognition in his dark eyes as he looked at her. He was a glorious sight, dirty and rumpled and scruffy as he was, and somehow more handsome for not seeing him in ages. How long, she couldn't remember, but she could barely remember her name right now.

He shook his head as he looked at her, his expression softening. "Oh, pet. Not you."

She knew exactly what he meant. She didn't want to be found by him in this state, in this horrible place, with those men after her. She didn't want to see him like this.

But she was so relieved it *was* him that she couldn't do anything but choke out more sobs.

He came to her quickly and helped her to her feet, where she tottered for a moment on her weak angles and dratted heels, then collapsed again with a whimper of pain, grabbing at her ankles and her sides.

"Oh, sweetheart," he murmured, crouching down and wiping her tears from her cheeks. "It's all right, you're safe now."

Everything that had happened to her that day, that week, and longer, came crashing down around her, and suddenly she couldn't stop crying. Sob after sob wracked her frame, and her corset constricted tighter and tighter around her, cutting off her air and thought, and she clutched at his arms.

"I… can't… breathe…" she managed, gasping and panting, her

fingers clenching him.

He swore under his breath, his hands flying to her waist. "Why do you do this to yourselves?"

"I didn't!" she screeched, somehow managing to find some sort of indignation even like this. She swayed and hiccupped a wheezing breath, tearing at the barely pinned too-small bodice covering her corset. "They... made me. Get it... off!"

Dark eyes clashed with hers for an instant, and then he was nodding. "All right, pet. I will, I will, don't panic."

She shook her head frantically. "Already... panicking!"

She could have sworn she heard him laugh, and then there was a blade out and she shrieked a little.

"Easy," he ordered, his tone firm but his expression gentle. "Look at me."

She met his eyes and her breath snagged somewhere in her throat.

He held her gaze and she felt her panic begin to ebb back into only agitation.

A corner of his mouth curved up a little. "Breathe, sweetheart. If you can."

She bit her lip and whimpered with the pain tearing at her ribs. "I can't," she pleaded. "Please."

He dashed away another tear, and cupped her cheek softly. "Of course. I have to cut it, hence the blade, all right?"

She nodded frantically and turned to give him easier access.

His hands moved to the sides of the now exposed corset and she felt him tugging at them a little. "Just to be clear, you want me to cut the laces of your corset here in this alley?"

"Yes!" she gasped, her head pounding with her pulse. "Stop stalling!"

He chuckled softly and the sound sent ripples up her spine that had nothing to do with her lack of air. "I just wanted to clarify. I would hate to be compromised and forced into marriage."

The tension around her torso started to fade as he cut the laces and she found herself dragging in deep gulps of air with the release. "Is that... likely?"

He sighed heavily. "It would shock you how often it is

74

attempted. Women practically fall at my feet all the time, and I never go out into Society alone. I really am very sought after."

She managed a weak laugh and lowered her head as the air rushed back into her lungs. "Well, you are rather helpful. Probably would make a… most convenient husband."

"Oh, I am a perfect gentleman, I would be the ideal candidate, I am sure, if ever I was snatched up."

He cut away at the last of the laces and she felt the stiff fabric give way and fall against her arms, tightly pinned to her sides. His hand pressed lightly on her back, as if soothing her.

"Better?" he murmured, all teasing gone from his tone.

Slowly, Margaret nodded, letting her lungs remember how to function properly. "Never again," she whispered. "Never, ever again."

"What was that?" he asked, leaning forward. "Never what?"

"I am never wearing a corset ever again," she vowed. She sniffled once then sat back and turned to face him, suddenly aware of the precarious situation she was in with this man… this glorious, charming, heroic, absolutely perfect man who had just cut the laces of her corset and could see every inch of her disheveled undergarments and exposed skin. Her cheeks began to heat and she covered herself as best as she could without letting the shreds of her corset fall completely away.

He raised a brow at her, his eyes staying on hers. "You normally don't?"

She bit the inside of her lip, debating the propriety of having a conversation about undergarments with him, but considering her state, there was not much left to the imagination, and absolutely no propriety here. Slowly she shook her head and exhaled heavily, then winced at the sharp pain in her ribs.

"Interesting." He eyed her with concern. "You need a physician, I think. Can you stand?"

She started to nod and shifted her feet, then hissed as her ankles reminded her of their state and shook her head. "I don't think so."

He took one of her ankles in hand, his touch surprisingly warm and she squawked a little at the sensation. He turned her foot gently one way, then another, his eyes flicking between it and her face, noting her reactions and sounds. Then, without warning, he wrenched the horrid shoe from her foot, then did the same with the other.

"Bad corset *and* bad shoes?" he said as he rose, a hint of a scold in his voice. He clicked his tongue in disapproval. "Someone clearly does not like you very much. Or they have very poor fashion sense. Which is it?"

Margaret wriggled her now free toes with a sigh of relief and rubbed at her ankles. "Honestly, I think both."

He barked a laugh and stared down at her, looking her over with thoughtful attention.

Self-conscious and painfully aware of her indecency, she cowered a little. "What?"

He pursed his lips a little. "I'm trying to decide what to do about covering you. There's some material draping crates, but I wouldn't trust it to not be infested with things."

She shuddered and shook her head. "Thank you, no. What if we tear some of this horrid fabric off my skirts?"

He shook his head at once. "I think not. Ill-advised ruffles or not, it still leaves your legs covered, and I dare not tempt fate further by exposing them, fetching picture though it would make."

Margaret wondered if her cheeks would ever cool again and looked away, putting a hand to one. "Well, I suppose I shall go without, then."

He made no sound and she glanced up to see a thunderous expression that surprised her. "Not on your life," he said in a voice so low she felt it in her toes. "I've already fought off two blackguards for you, I'll not take on the rest of London too."

After she managed, eventually, to swallow, she found herself snorting in derision. "Hardly the whole of London, and I take no compliment in the attention, I assure you. It is not personal, merely a bit of female flesh, and that can be got anywhere, I expect. Nothing to do with me at all."

"You expect rightly, but I think you underestimate your charms." He snapped his fingers and pointed at her. "I have it. Don't go anywhere."

She gave him an incredulous look as he dashed back down the

alley. Where, exactly, did he think she was going to go?

He appeared a moment later with a gentleman's coat, poorly mended and hardly in good condition, but it was clean and it was large enough to cover her top half completely and entirely.

He grinned at her and her heart hammered against her ribs. "One of your admirers wore a coat, if you recall. As he is not currently in need of it, I thought it the least he could do to offer it up in recompense."

Ah, so not precisely a gentleman's coat then. No matter. "Rather thoughtful of him," she mused softly, smiling for the first time in what seemed to be years.

He nodded sagely and shook it out. "I thought so." He tilted his head at her, his smile softening into something that tickled her insides. "So you can smile. I thought perhaps you had lost that gift."

She thought about offering up a teasing quip, she thought about blushing and being demure, she thought about changing the subject... She thought of a hundred and three things she could, or should, have said in response that would have been appropriate and polite, and perfectly suitable to any such compliment from a man.

But he was different.

And with him, so was she.

She lowered her eyes and swallowed. "So did I."

For a moment, neither moved, and she could almost hear the measured breaths he took in the silence of the alley. Then he moved around her and the coat was gently placed across her shoulders.

Margaret slid her arms through the sleeves and pulled it tightly closed, buttoning it where she could, but still gripping it with one hand across her gaping bodice. "Thank you," she murmured.

In response, his arms came around her and she was hefted up in his hold. She gasped in a mixture of shock and pain, clamping down on her lips hard to keep from making a sound.

"Sorry," he said with a hiss, shifting her a little to move his arms to more comfortable places. "Is that better?"

She tucked her chin, mortification washing over her again. "It is fine."

He did not move, waiting, and she glanced up to find him pinning her with a hard look. "Fine is not exactly descriptive," he grunted, raising a brow rather imperiously.

She managed a weak smile. "To be perfectly frank, I am not sure any position would be comfortable at this moment. I hurt everywhere. Quite fiercely."

His shoulders dropped a little and his hold tightened, but not painfully. "I am so sorry. I'll take you somewhere to help. A friend of mine." He started out of the alley, his hold secure, yet gentle, and he carried her far too easily.

"Is he a physician?" she asked weakly, suddenly feeling fatigued and limp.

He made a noise of either amusement or derision, she couldn't tell. "He's something. Close enough, I expect. Less pompous, though."

Margaret gave up any idea of pretense and allowed herself to lay her head against his broad shoulder, tucked against his very firm, very warm, very impressive chest, and let herself feel the strength in his arms along her back and beneath her legs. She rather hoped he would carry her quite a long way, as this was all rather perfect. "It will do well enough," she replied, fighting the temptation to close her eyes.

The man of her dreams was carrying her through London and being a perfect gentleman about her horrid state. She was not going to miss a single second of staring at him or living in this moment, no matter how embarrassed she was.

He was so attractive it nearly hurt to look at him. Dark eyes that always seemed to laugh and could see everything a person might try to hide. The strong jaw that her fingers itched to touch and stroke. The scruff that she knew would scratch and tickle her skin, and she suspected even when he shaved the shadow of it remained. A profile that a sculptor would weep over.

She recalled his hands on her face, slightly calloused but somehow clean. Strong hands that held her tightly now, yet had been gentle enough to soothe her. Powerful legs that did not strain at lifting or carrying her, and, she had to admit, filled out his trousers sinfully well.

And if she did not stop recollecting every detail of his figure and appearance, she was going to become shamefully scandalous and her face would flush and he would know it.

If he did not already, the way her free hand had crept to rest on his chest, and would probably become permanently fixed there, as it was so perfect a place for it.

"So," he suddenly said, breaking through her thoughts of him with ease, his voice rumbling through his chest and consequently through her, "these friends of yours who don't like you and have no fashion sense... What exactly were they aiming for with this?"

Her hand on his chest stiffened and the rest of her followed. She closed her eyes and slowly inhaled through her nose, then exhaled much the same. "They wished me to be compromised and forced into marriage," she told him, keeping her voice low as she echoed his earlier words back to him.

His step faltered for a moment, and his hold on her flexed. It hurt a little, but she would die before saying so. It felt impossibly good, and the way his jaw tightened and his throat worked made her heart sing, just a little. A brief, but rough tremor coursed through him and she bit her lip as she felt it.

He cleared his throat lightly and shook his head a little. "Not to worry, pet. There will be no compromising here, unless you are doing it. I am a perfect gentleman at all times."

She snorted softly, but smiled.

He gave her an amused look. "I am," he insisted. "That is why they call me the Gent."

Margaret tilted her head back a little. "Who is 'they', exactly?"

He leaned closer and whispered, "Everyone. I am at once the best and worst kept secret in London."

She bit back another smile and let herself lean on him more.

He most certainly was.

And he was her secret as well.

Reading her attention as weariness, he sighed a little. "Just a few more blocks, sweetheart. Then you'll be set to rights."

She nodded against him, but said nothing.

She was already feeling more to rights.

But that, too, was a secret.

Chapter Eight

How ow Rafe was not exploding with the rage within him was a complete mystery.

Well, perhaps not, as he suspected it had everything to do with the delectable woman in his arms, but even he was impressed with the control he was managing, and he was almost never impressed with himself.

It was entirely too arrogant.

But now he very much wished that he had been far more brutal with those louts he had thrashed in the alley. Before he'd thought they were merely some lowlife scoundrels trying to make trouble for a poor girl in a sorry state, but he fully expected her to be a prostitute, or at the very least, some fool's wandering mistress.

Not his Margaret.

Not her.

He should have killed them.

He hadn't killed anybody in a long time, and only then had done so with good reason, and this seemed like a damned good reason to do it again. He would have been out of practice, but entirely justified.

He hadn't managed to ask her if she had actually been harmed, or if they had touched her, but he wasn't sure he could bear it. The haunted, terrified look in her eyes had shaken him, and his only thought had been to let her know she was safe, to chase the shadows away and bring back her smile.

That had been challenge enough.

Now that she was curled against him so trustingly, he was two seconds away from beaming like a fool. She fit perfectly in his arms, and despite her injuries, he was beyond delighted to hold her thus.

He did feel the slight twinge of guilt at the rather base recollection of how she had looked before, and he had done his utmost to remain respectful and polite, but…

He sent up a silent prayer for forgiveness, but she had been the most alluring sight he had ever seen, and every one of his more wicked fantasies had suddenly sprung to mind. He took no pleasure in the extremes she had been forced into, or the pain they had caused her, but her already lush figure on such display had triggered some impulses he'd had to fight hard to tamp down. Her hair had long fallen out of its hold and was tousled and tumbling all around her narrow shoulders, looking for all the world like a woman roused from her bed.

And that was a place he absolutely could *not* let his thoughts wander.

He'd distracted himself with reciting various philosophical musings in Latin in his mind, but the most perfect distraction of all, what had wrenched those thoughts almost completely away, had been her eyes.

Wide, translucent eyes of an almost violet shade, weary and worried and pleading.

He could have happily drowned in those eyes, and wanted, more than anything, for them to look at him with the trusting, teasing light from before. Those eyes would have driven him to ends of the earth on only the whisper of promise from her, and he would have thanked her for the privilege. He had to help her, fix her, save her from anything and everything.

No primal surge of masculine attention was going to let him do anything less. And he absolutely would not leave her exposed like that for more predatory eyes.

She was his, no matter what state she was in. His to protect, his to avenge, his to cherish.

He'd have her in any and all states, if only he could.

And she didn't even know his name.

Rafe found himself twisting his mouth a little, wondering if that was a good thing or a bad thing.

And blast it all if he didn't have the answer.

He rounded another corner, the streets more narrow and dank than before, and Margaret seemed to curl against him more.

He bit back the urge to smile and only patted her a little. "Steady on, pet. I've got you, you're safe."

"I know," she replied quietly, keeping her eyes averted.

Well, now, how was he to respond to that? He swallowed with difficulty and picked up his step, pretending that his heart wasn't racing just a little bit faster.

He sidestepped into a smaller street and stopped when he reached the thick, well-worn door with ancient hinges. He kicked it three times with his boot, and stepped back, glancing up and down the empty, cramped street.

"I could have knocked," Margaret offered in a very soft voice.

He looked down at her, letting one finger toy with a strand of hair near it, safely out of her sight. "And have you loosen your death grip on the coat shielding you? I think not, pet." He shook his head and set his mouth firmly. "Pritchard will already think he's died and gone to heaven when he sees you, best not to actually send him off to rapture before his time."

Margaret choked out a burst of surprised laughter, then covered her mouth with the hand that had been holding his heart in his chest for the last several minutes.

He grinned at the sound. He'd not heard her full laughter yet, but the hints of it were positively divine. He vowed to himself right then and there that he *would* make her laugh with enthusiasm and joy, naturally and completely.

"Are you trying to make me blush?" she asked, raising her eyes to his.

He shrugged, enjoying the brush of her body against his as he did so. "I might be."

Those eyes flickered with life and so did his heart. "I thought you were a gentleman," she replied, narrowing her eyes even as her mouth quirked.

He smiled and let himself look at her, long and hard. "I am," he told her, keeping his voice low. "But sometimes I like to pretend otherwise."

He saw her delicate throat work for a swallow and thought she might lower her eyes once more, as her cheeks flushed, but she surprised him by keeping her gaze on his. Her breathing grew unsettled, but her eyes were steady and clear.

And her lips…

Lord have mercy, those full lips would torment a saint.

And he was no saint.

He heard the faint rush of air pass through those parted lips and almost ducked his head to taste them when the door opened and he jerked like a guilty schoolboy.

Pritchard himself stood in the doorway, scratching his almost hairless head and peering up at him as though the sun shone directly into his eyes. His bushy greying brows shot up in surprise. "Gent? What sort of trouble have you gotten yourself into now?"

Rafe grinned at the wiry old man and ducked his head a little, hefting his precious bundle slightly. "It's not me, Suds. A damsel in distress this time."

Pritchard wheezed a chuckle even as he rolled his eyes. "Lord above, they're all damsels in distress, my boy." He cast a bawdy wink at Margaret. "No offense, milady."

"None taken," Margaret replied with a warm smile. "And I'm no milady, nor any sort of damsel in distress. Simply a bit unlucky, and out of sorts."

Now Pritchard grinned, his yellowing teeth on full display. "Fair maiden with real manners and no need of flattery? Oh, Gent, you shouldn't have!" He cackled another laugh and waved them in. "Come in, come in, and let's see what we have here."

Rafe ducked through the small door, taking care with Margaret in his arms, and followed Pritchard through the cramped apartments. Though the house should have been large enough for him, with his daughters having moved on in life, he seemed to collect odds and ends to such an extent that one could barely sit down on the faded furniture. The windows were smeared with dirt, as though someone tried to clean them and found the task too daunting, but light still managed to stream through, however tainted it was.

Rafe shook his head and bit back a smile. Suds had always been a bit bizarre, and his retirement hadn't changed that at all.

Towards the back of the house, things opened up quite a bit and there was space and light and air, in complete contrast to the front. It seemed that Suds wasn't quite so eccentric as he appeared.

As if he heard his thoughts, Pritchard turned to look at him over his shoulder. "I can't let people know what I do back here. Nobody bothers a man who hoards junk in his rooms, and only those who know me see beyond the front."

Rafe smiled and nodded in acknowledgement. "I should have known you had your faculties still, Suds."

Margaret tilted her head at them both. "Suds?" she repeated curiously. "I thought your name was Mr. Pritchard."

Pritchard wheezed a laugh. "I'm both, love. Suds was my name when I was a much younger man, able to do many more things."

"That was last year," Rafe snorted, taking care to duck under a low beam of a doorframe without infringing on Margaret's personal space. Much.

Pritchard ignored him and kept his gaze fixed on the young woman. "Pritchard is my correct and proper name, miss. And the only one that really suits me now. I am far too ancient to be anything else."

"It's only been a year," Rafe protested with a laugh.

The older man raised a brow. "You wait until your turn, Gent, and see how well retirement sits with you." He waved a hand at a cloth-covered table in the center of the surprisingly clean room, and set about working with an old and faded screen in the corner.

Rafe set Margaret down gently, and reluctantly, on the table, noting the faint blush on her cheeks as his arms slid out from her, brushing rather innocently against her as they did so. Well, well, this was an interesting development. His touch was stirring something, was it? That was most excellent to know. She looked even more fetching when she blushed, and the way she determinedly averted her eyes from him was quite charming.

A rather interesting development indeed.

"Retirement?" she asked softly, looking over at Pritchard even as she clutched that deuced coat more tightly across her. "From what?"

The men shared a sharp look, then Pritchard hefted the screen towards her. "Street life, my dear. Dangerous and dastardly and far too inappropriate to share with a sweet gel like you." He winked rather boldly at her.

Margaret cracked a smile and shrugged one shoulder. "I am not that sweet, Mr. Pritchard. Trust me."

He tossed his head back with a laugh and Rafe had to smile at her quip. After the day she'd had, she was tossing out wit like that? Remarkable creature.

"Sweet and spice are my favorite flavors, Miss," Pritchard told her, still laughing. "Especially when brought together."

Margaret giggled, then hissed a wince and grabbed at her left side, letting the coat gape a little.

Instantly, the amusement was gone, and Suds was back into play. "Ah, poor mouse. Let me have a look, shall we?"

She clamped down on her lip and nodded, her eyes casting over to Rafe, but not quite meeting his eyes.

Suds caught it, though, and grunted. "Gent, pull the screen. Pretend you are all that your name claims and give us privacy."

Rafe's fist formed a tight ball, but he saw the tension in Margaret, and the pain in her expression. He bit back a sharp retort and nodded firmly. But first... "Pet?"

She finally met his eyes and he saw the lingering fear there.

He kept his gaze steady. "I will be right here, if you need. Understand?"

Her lips wobbled and she nodded. "Thank you."

Struck by the sweetness of such a simple phrase, he found he could only nod in response, and pulled the screen out, shielding her from his view.

Silently, he exhaled, and sank into a rickety chair nearby, waiting.

"Does it hurt when I press here?"

Margaret gasped and nodded frantically, her eyes squeezing shut.

Pritchard made a noncommittal sound and shifted his hands a little lower on her left. "Here?"

"Not as much," she managed, shaking her head.

He chuckled softly. "But it still hurts."

She nodded, biting her lip.

Pritchard sighed a little. "I need to examine you more closely. It will not be pleasant, but it will not last long. Would you mind terribly if I…?" He gestured at her clothing and Margaret shook her head at once.

"If you must," she replied, removing the coat and revealing the remains of horrible dress beneath, trying to straighten up to remove the pins and sleeves.

"Allow me, miss," Pritchard said kindly, moving around her. "Three daughters and a wife gave me some skill with female dress, I believe I have seen and done it all."

Margaret laughed a little and felt more at ease. "I doubt you've seen anything quite like this monstrosity," she quipped, wheezing with the laugh.

Pritchard caught it but his fingers only briefly stilled. "No, I can't say that I have. Forgive the presumption, but your modiste ought to find a new line of work."

Now Margaret barked a laugh, which hurt a great deal, and grabbed at her side, still smiling. "Not *my* modiste, I can assure you."

He hummed a laugh behind her. "I thought not. It hurts to laugh, does it?"

She nodded and pulled her arms out of the tiny cap sleeves of the dress, letting the rest pool around her waist. "It hurts to do everything, Mr. Pritchard."

He clucked his tongue and came around to the front. "You can call me Suds, miss. Or Pritchard. I'm not about to stand on ceremony under the circumstances."

She offered him a shy smile, oddly comfortable despite being only in her chemise before him. "Then you may call me Margaret. Ceremony bores me."

She heard a low laugh from the other side of the screen and felt her cheeks heat. She'd almost forgotten he was there, that he could hear everything she said.

Suddenly she felt far more exposed than she was.

She looked up at Pritchard, who had noticed, and was now

smiling at her. But he said nothing except, "Now, can you lift your chemise just enough for me to see your ribs, Margaret? Keep yourself covered, by all means, but I really must see the skin."

She managed a snort. "I don't know how covered I am in this poor excuse for undergarments, but as you say."

It was painful, wriggling her hips and torso to tug her chemise up through the skirts, but she managed without making too much noise. And with the added fabric of the chemise at hand, she could cover her décolletage without any trouble. It might have been the most comfortable she had felt all day.

Pritchard eyed her sides with a knowing expression. "Slight bruising, but not bad," he muttered, laying his hands on her left side, fingers splaying the ribs as he pressed firmly, making her squeak. He did the same to the right side, with similar results. He laid one hand on each side and leaned back a little to get a better view. "Can you take a deep breath in, Margaret? And hold it?"

She did so, wincing and forcing herself not to exhale through her nose at the pain.

He frowned a little. "All right, you can release it."

She did so, in a harsh burst, which made him smile a little.

He pressed on both sides equally and she whimpered.

"What happened?" Gent called from the other side of the screen, his voice rising in pitch. "Are you all right?"

"She is perfectly well, Gent," Pritchard called, rolling his eyes. "Don't be a Mother Hen."

Gent muttered some very dark things that Margaret probably wasn't supposed to hear, but did, and she had to fight an insane desire to giggle madly at it.

"He's always been impertinent," Pritchard whispered with a twinkle in his eye. "I've known him for years, and he has never grown up."

Margaret clamped down on her lips, a slight laugh barely escaping.

Pritchard winked, then gave each of her sides another look. He moved around to the back of her and pressed against her lower back. "Pain there?"

"No," she replied. "Only stiff."

87

He moved up to her ribs along her back, but nothing elicited a response from her. "All right, love, you can pull that back down, and replace the coat if you like. Time to see to your ankles."

Margaret did so, tilting her head at a harsh mutter from the other side of the screen that sounded suspiciously like "Lucky," but she doubted that.

He was much quicker with her ankles, removing the stockings and pressing against the bones, moving her ankles in every direction and asking her the same sort of brisk questions. She felt a twinge in each ankle, and they were puffy, but they felt much better than they had before. She could probably walk on them, but she would certainly not be dancing.

She almost snorted. Dancing. Where in the world would she be dancing?

She was in some unknown corner of London with veritable strangers without a stitch of clothing and no idea what she was going to do. She ought to send a note to Helen, as Miss Ritson would probably inform them of her behavior, and while her aunt Dalton was more proper than her mother, she had no fondness for Miss Ritson.

It occurred to Margaret to wonder why her parents had found her a chaperone rather than let her stay with her cousins for a time, but, as with everything, she expected they rather hadn't thought of that. How fortunate she would be if they had thought a little more carefully about such things.

But there was no use in recriminations now. What was done was done, and she had run away.

Lord, but there would be much recompense to pay in the future.

Pritchard rose and put his hands on his hips. "Well, Miss Margaret, I think you will live."

She giggled and folded her arms over the borrowed coat. "That is indeed a relief. And what is your diagnosis, good physician?"

He barked a laugh. "Lord, child, I am no physician. I was trained in field medicine for the war, and dabble in it enough to be skilled, but I would never aspire to the intelligence of a trained physician."

She cocked her head with a teasing smile. "So I have been wasting my time with you and must find such a trained person to get the full measure of my state, is that it?"

He tapped her nose. "Cheeky. I like you." He shook his head. "No, you will be sore and bruised, but I think you are well and whole. No broken ribs and no breaks in your ankles, either. For all the dramatics you've endured, and others have employed," he jerked a thumb over his shoulder towards the screen, which made her cover her mouth to avoid laughing, "you are really not so badly off. Disappointed?"

She nodded soberly. "Terribly so. I was hoping for a grand story to tell with some dastardly injuries." She heaved a sigh that hurt, but she did not care. "Alas, I am to be found lacking even in my attempts at adventures."

Pritchard shook his head, smiling. "Oh, Miss Margaret, I don't think a single person in this room finds you lacking in any respect at all." He winked, which made her blush furiously, and then chuckled. "Well, let me fetch some fresh clothes for you from upstairs. My youngest gel is about your size, and she left enough things to start a shop in the front." He glanced down at her ankles, and said, "And something for your feet, I should think." He stepped outside and began conversing with Gent in tones too low for her to hear.

"Thank you, Pritchard," Margaret murmured with real gratitude.

She had not expected to find some fresh garments. She rather thought she would have to go on like this until they could find a way to purchase more, though what money Gent had would have been a mystery, and Margaret had none on her person herself. And she dared not venture out into shops that knew her where she had accounts, that would put her in danger of seeing someone who might alert Miss Ritson, and she had absolutely no desire to see her again.

Margaret sighed a little and began pulling the pins out of her hair, which was quite ruined as it was, and ill-suited for the situation as it was. She would much rather just let her hair down naturally, without any of the refinement that ladies of her station were expected to portray. She was no fine lady now, and after her actions today, she doubted she ever would be again.

"Don't sigh so, pet," Gent said from his side of the screen. "It's not so bad, is it?"

She closed her eyes and bit the inside of her lip. "I do not know.

It might be."

"Tell me."

She swallowed with difficulty. "I have behaved foolishly. At the time, I was certain it was my only alternative, but acting on impulse only proved my downfall. I cannot say what will happen after this, but I feel certain that everything will be changed. I feel quite ruined, though I am nothing of the sort. I will never be the girl I was and I do not even know what to wish for anymore."

He made a noise of disgruntlement, and she heard him shifting a little. "You sound so forlorn," he murmured. "I don't like it one bit."

She smiled, loving the sound of his voice and the way it made her feel. Despite her situation, hearing his voice made everything seem rather wonderful. She hadn't meant to sound so, nor to reveal so much, but it was so easy, too natural with him. "You don't know me well enough to like or not like it," she pointed out, smiling a little.

"I know you perfectly well enough," he replied, the teasing tone back once more. "Don't pretend that all of those days of seeing each other didn't give us a certain knowledge."

She bit her lip on a smile and looked up at the ceiling. "Well, I suppose it did enlighten me a little."

"Really?" he mused. "Do tell."

"I shouldn't."

"You should."

"A lady would never."

"So don't be a lady for the moment."

She laughed merrily and lay back on the table as though it were a bed. "You somehow blend in and stand out at the same time. I suspect that is part of your nature, and not only with me."

"You suspect rightly," he replied, sounding a bit surprised. "Very good."

She nodded to herself, feeling rather pleased. "Your eyes are quite remarkable, you know. I felt that from the very beginning. You must notice quite a lot, and probably remember everything."

He snorted. "Not everything, I leave that for Rook."

She turned her head as if she could see him. "Rook?"

She could feel the sudden tension in the room. "Another

colleague. And a bloody annoying one." He hissed a little. "Apologies, a blasted annoying one."

Margaret grinned. "No apology necessary. I find natural language rather refreshing. You may curse all you like, but I draw the line at blaspheming."

He laughed once. "Duly noted. Anything else enlighten you?"

She sighed a bit dreamily. "Oh, several things. Somehow you draw me out when I am naturally more inclined to reserve, and I've never minded it even once. It was quite exhilarating from the start, and you're the only one that has ever truly managed that. My friends have some success, but nothing quite like you." Her throat began to close up on emotion and she willed them all back with a nearly silent sigh. "And that is all I am going to say on the subject, for all other enlightenment is quite secret until I know you better."

Gent was silent for a long time, so long that Margaret's fingers began to itch and she had to ball them into fists to avoid drumming them on the table. "Gent?"

"You are the perfect English miss," he began, his voice low and warm, "but only on the exterior. From the very first, I saw in your eyes a desire to fly, and I wondered why you did not. You must have had a degree of freedom in your youth, no doubt your parents encouraged it?"

She smiled fondly and folded her fingers on her stomach. "They did. I was never without discipline or completely wild, but I was not exactly restricted either."

"I can see that," he replied, and she could hear the smile he must have worn and imagined the glorious sight it must have been. He cleared his throat a little. "You see the world with a sort of wide-eyed innocence, as if everything is new and fresh, and yet something in your eyes tells me that you are not ignorant, nor surprised, about much of what you see. I should like to see the world as you do. To smile about it. To have such wonder."

There was a note of longing in his voice and her heart clenched a little at the sound. "I do not deserve such inspirational thoughts," she managed, smiling. "I can assure you, I am a very regular sort of girl with very regular sorts of thoughts."

He seemed to laugh at that. "I highly doubt that. Don't tell me more, I rather like my delusions of you."

"Oh, well, if you insist," Margaret said with a wave of her hand. "If you'd rather think me a superior creature, I'll not naysay it. By all means, please go on."

Now he laughed in earnest and she did with him, and it felt charming and delightful and so natural. It was remarkable how they could converse in this manner, though they truly knew little about each other. And yet she had known it would be like this. Exactly like this.

"You are the most refreshing woman I have ever known," Gent said, still laughing. "Refreshing to the eyes, to the ears, and now to the mind as well. Truly, pet, you are beyond anything in this world."

Well, how was she to respond to that?

She was prevented from having to do so by Pritchard reappearing around the screen. "So sorry to keep you waiting, love," he said as he shook out a simple blue day dress. "My Annie had far more than I thought she did up there, and it took a moment to find everything."

Margaret sat up, smiling. "Not at all, Pritchard. I am so very grateful."

He winked and handed her the undergarments and stockings, laying the dress on the table behind her. "You go ahead and change, and let me know if you need me to play ladies' maid." He leaned close and whispered, "In my past, I may have actually played that role once or twice, as duty called." He put a finger to his lips, which only made her giggle more.

He disappeared, and Margaret divested herself of the horrid clothing she currently wore. She tossed both the remains of the dress and the sorry excuse for a shift on top of the screen and called, "Gent?"

"Yes?" he replied at once, sounding a bit odd.

She grinned. "Burn those wretched things, will you? They will be far kinder as ashes than clothes."

He barked a laugh and tugged the garments off the screen. "As you wish."

She slid the new chemise and petticoats on, which were lesser quality than she was used to, but fit her well enough. The stockings were worn, but clean, and she was hardly going to complain about it. She managed the dress on her own, the buttons easy enough to reach and though it was a trifle large in the waist, but as it fit her perfectly elsewhere, she was rather content with it. Her waist and ribs needed a reprieve as it was.

She was rather desperate for a mirror, but ran her fingers through her now loose tresses, praying the curl from this morning's styling would remain in place, and then, holding her breath, stepped out from behind the screen.

Gent and Pritchard turned to see her, both looking surprised. Pritchard smiled, and Gent simply stared, rather frankly, and seemed without thought.

Margaret smiled softly and, keeping her eyes on Gent, murmured, "Pritchard, would you introduce us properly, please?"

Pritchard chuckled and came to her side, patting her hand. "Miss Margaret, might I present my good friend, the Gent? Gent, this is Miss Margaret, who wishes to make your better acquaintance."

"And I hers," Gent finally managed, stepping forward. He took her free hand, bowed over it more perfectly than any gentlemen she'd ever met, and then brought it to his lips, his dark eyes searing hers with their intensity "A pleasure, Miss Margaret, and a long awaited one."

He kissed her hand, and Margaret was rather pleased she didn't swoon.

"The pleasure's all mine," she replied, too breathless.

He grinned at her in a slow, wicked way. "No, Miss Margaret, truly I believe it is all *mine*."

Chapter Nine

"*B*oots, my dear!" Pritchard said, clapping loudly and breaking the moment.

Margaret jerked, her hand still in Gent's heated grasp. "Wh-what?"

Pritchard moved just inside the room beyond and reappeared with some very fine-looking ankle boots certainly sturdy enough to support her and not give her much grief with her present injuries. She took them from him wordlessly, stroking the fine leather and admiring the soft, buttery color. Even with all of her admittedly considerable pairs of footwear, she did not think she'd owned a pair of boots this fine.

"Pritchard," she breathed, her eyes fixed on the boots, "I couldn't possibly…"

Pritchard chuckled. "I'd like to hear you say that as if you mean it, and then perhaps I would consider believing you." He pressed them more firmly into her hands. "Take them, love. My Annie wore them once, and did not care for the fit. A pity, that, as they were made by the finest cobbler in Venice as a gift." He shrugged and grinned at her, the lines near his eyes more pronounced. "Someone ought to wear them, don't you agree?"

"I do," Margaret said swiftly, moving to a chair faster than she thought she could on her unsteady ankles and sliding her feet into the boots. She bit back a squeal and looked up at Pritchard. "They fit perfectly!"

"Of course they do," he laughed. "Now lace them before you injure yourself further."

Margaret bent to do so, only to find Gent already there, lifting one ankle gently. "Allow me," he murmured with a crooked grin that made her stomach turn over several times.

She managed, somehow, to swallow. "If you like."

"Oh, I do like," he replied in the same low tone. "I very much do."

Instinct told Margaret he was not speaking of tying her laces for her, and she suddenly forgot how to breathe.

She clamped down on her lips hard as he finished, then nearly hiccupped when his warm hands encircled her now booted ankles.

"How do they feel now?" he asked softly.

"Perfect," she breathed, her words catching in her throat.

He grinned and sat back. "Let's see you walk then, pet."

She shook her head a little, wondering where her mind had gone. He was perfectly composed, while she was near to swooning. She ought to be more collected than this. She focused her energy on rising without faltering and found that, although she was rather sore, she could indeed walk. An occasional twinge of pain, but nothing like the weakness and agony from before.

She flashed a smile at Gent and Pritchard, watching her with pride. "I can walk so well I daresay I could dance."

Gent barked a laugh and shook his head. "Don't overtax yourself yet. We still must decide what to do with you."

Ah, yes. The small matter of her being in parts of London that no gently bred woman ought to be in after running away from her chaperone with no proper stitch of clothing to her name.

She swallowed harshly. "Well?" she prodded, folding her hands neatly before her.

Gent's eyes twinkled, and he crossed his arms over his chest. "Well…?" he echoed in much the same tone.

"Oh, Gent, don't tease the gel so," Pritchard scolded with a laugh.

Gent didn't even spare a glance for the old man. "Do you want me to take you home, Margaret?"

Her stomach clenched at the thought. To face Miss Ritson would be a horrible punishment, beyond anything she could comprehend, and she knew for a fact that she would have no freedom of any kind until her parents returned, which would mean she would never see Gent again.

She was not willing to take that chance.

"No," she said fiercely, her hands forming tight fists at her sides. "No, I don't want to go back there at all."

Gent's smile warmed her so completely her apprehensions about the future positively melted away. "Fine by me. I can entertain you well enough for a day or two. Perhaps longer."

The words were innocent enough, but suddenly she sensed a deeper meaning. She might have run away and been rash and impulsive, but she did have a reputation to consider.

"How?" she asked with suspicion.

His smile spread and crinkled his dark eyes. "Come with me and find out."

She wet her lips and her fingers rubbed against each other anxiously. "And how can I trust you, sir? I ran away from being compromised once, I would rather not do so again."

He sobered at once, his face tightening and his eyes deadly serious. "Margaret, I am called the Gent not only as a joke, but in sincerity. I may not have a proper chaperone for you, but you will not suffer any mistreatment at my hands, nor will I treat you with so little respect. You have my word of honor."

Well, that was enough to make the heart flutter, but how much honor did a man such as him have? He was no gentleman in truth, though he spoke well enough for one, and there was kindness in his eyes, and he had already been very protective and respectful.

She might not know him, but she had a sense about him.

And who would see her to find ruin within her anyway?

Only him.

And he saw no ruin.

She felt her lips part on a wide smile. "Then lead me away, Master Gent, and show me the sights."

Pritchard hooted a laugh and clapped Gent on the back. "Then you would be with the wrong sort, Margaret. Gent here knows London, sure enough, but not the sort of sights you would wish to see."

She softened her smile and tilted her head at Gent. "I have seen my sights. Now I wish to see his."

She might have imagined it, but she thought the steady breathing he had been doing so naturally might have faltered in his broad chest as he stared at her in surprise. Then it all melted away into a smile, warm and soft, his eyes twinkled at her, and suddenly she felt as though she would have followed him to France if he'd been so inclined. Which was just a further sign of how very far she had fallen. Pathetic creature, what in the world would become of her?

"Is there anyone you need to reassure of your safety?" Gent asked as she picked up a thick, cream-colored shawl that Pritchard had brought for her.

Margaret paused as she adjusted the shawl around her. There was a thought. She would never want to advertise her unchaperoned and ruined-by-association state, but neither could she let Helen or her aunt worry when word reached them of her escape. She had already missed her appointed tea time with Helen and Rosalind, without any sort of note or excuse. They would know something was wrong.

But how would they respond? Her uncle Dalton was a well-respected man, and he had always liked Margaret a great deal. She couldn't bear to wound him, but she could not bear the thought of him sending Bow Street or some other men to find her. They might injure Gent, and she would be returned to Miss Ritson.

She was not in danger, but no one would know that.

And if she were honest, she probably was in danger.

Not from Gent. But perhaps because of him.

And it was London.

She found herself nodding before she was aware of it. "Yes," she murmured. "I need to send word to my cousin." She looked up at Gent with a bit of an apology, perhaps not quite the free and refreshing woman he had once thought her.

He smiled fondly. "Of course, pet."

"She won't say anything," Margaret reassured him as Gent led her to a small writing desk.

"I wasn't worried."

"Why not?"

His look was a trifle difficult to decipher, some mixture of amusement and pride and chagrin. "Because I have long since learned that I have nothing to worry or fear where the general populace is concerned. And beyond that, Miss Margaret, I trust you implicitly. If you have faith and trust in your cousin, then so do I." He shrugged and gestured towards the desk.

She went to it, frowning in thought. Well that was the most absurd thing she had ever heard. How could he possibly trust her at all when they had known each other all of two hours, at most?

His words from only moments ago echoed in her mind. *Don't tell me that all of those moments didn't give us a certain knowledge of each other.*

He was right. She trusted him, though she had no reason to and probably ought not. Why should he feel any less for her?

Because she was simple, plain, rather unassuming Margaret Easton, who couldn't drum up an admirer even for her fortune, and did not fit anywhere.

Except, it seemed, for here.

She felt her cheeks blushing as she jotted down the vaguest sort of reassurance to Helen, her eyes barely reading the words. She would go mad with the complete lack of information the note contained, but it would suffice, and Helen hated Miss Ritson as much as Margaret did, so there would be no chance of betrayal.

She folded the note and rose from the desk, pinching the letter between her fingers. "There, I am ready now."

Gent and Pritchard had been talking in low voices, and both turned to look at her in midsentence.

She fought a smile, despite her nerves. "That is, if you are."

Gent smiled easily. "I am."

She looked down at the note in her hand, frowning slightly. "I am not sure how we will... That is..." She looked up at Gent for the words.

"We'll take it to some friends of mine," he assured her, still smiling. "They will see it safely delivered."

Margaret released a small sigh of relief. "Thank you." She smiled as he gestured for her to lead the way towards the door. She turned back as they reached it. "Thank you, Mr. Pritchard," she murmured, kissing his cheek fondly. "I will never forget your kindness."

The grizzled man seemed to blush and kissed her hand quickly. "Think nothing of it, Miss Margaret." He winked at her. "You let me know if Gent here misbehaves at all, you hear?"

She giggled as Gent groaned, and nodded. "To be sure, I shall." She cast a suspicious glance at Gent, then back to Pritchard. "Is that likely?"

Pritchard shrugged. "Never known it to happen, but I don't know how he behaves without adult supervision."

Margaret choked a laugh and could barely manage a farewell as Gent took her elbow and turned her out of the house, muttering under his breath.

He closed the door behind them, then gave her a long, searching look.

"What?" she finally asked, squirming under his intensity.

"If you come with me now," he murmured softly, "and we are seen by anyone of your acquaintance, you will likely be ruined. I can't do anything about that. There is still time for you to avoid such things, if you wish."

She tilted her head at him, giving his words some thought, but not precisely feeling warned off. "I have no wish to be ruined," she said simply, "and I don't exactly feel as though that is a danger."

"Margaret…"

She swallowed back the flash of delight at hearing her name from his lips. "Are you planning on parading me on Bond Street or in Mayfair?"

He looked faintly startled. "No."

She shrugged a shoulder. "Then I do not see the problem. No one looks twice at me, so even if I am seen, it shall not be marked."

His brow furrowed and his jaw tightened. "I did."

Margaret folded her arms, confused. "Did what?"

"Looked twice." He looked away quickly. "I looked a great deal more than twice."

She did not even try to hide her smile, even as her heart raced. "And that is why I am coming with you."

"It's probably why you shouldn't."

She huffed and put her hands on her hips, amused and exasperated by whatever he was trying to do. "Well, are you the Gent, or aren't you?"

He laughed and looked back at her, matching her pose. "Aye, I am," he told her, taking on a more common accent. "For my sins, Miss Margaret, I have the honor of two toffs, and if you're sure of yourself, I'll take you along."

Margaret beamed. "I am always sure of myself, Master Gent. Let's be off. Unless you wish to try and talk me out of it again?"

He chuckled. "No, I am done."

"Good. I was beginning to think you wanted to be rid of me."

His gaze became warmer and his smile softer. "No, pet. Not in the least."

Goodness, the day was suddenly warm. She exhaled a rush of air without shame. "Right, then. Lead on."

Gent looked amused by something or other, but he gestured towards their path, and fell into step beside her, letting his arm brush hers, despite keeping his hands clasped politely behind his back. He prodded her into conversation and no matter what she said, he listened, smiled, and responded as though she had said something important or interesting. She had no idea how her various escapades as a child could entertain, but she never saw any indication that he tired of her.

He most certainly was a gentleman, despite whatever common breeding he had, and it was the sweetest thing. She tired of her own voice and attempted as best as she could to turn the tables on him, but he was far too evasive and always managed to turn the conversation back to her.

She might not follow all of the usual behaviors of proper misses, but she did adhere to the rule that one should not monopolize conversation, and certainly not about one's self.

But talking with him was far too easy and comfortable, so talk she did.

Eventually, they came to a very small alley that she would have missed but for turning down it, and then it opened up into a narrow cobblestone street with the sort of dank corners that reminded her of the first alley of her day, except this one had less filth and clutter. It was empty for the moment, but the sounds of rattling carriages just beyond echoed off of the walls of the buildings, giving the impression that things were happening, despite the vacancy.

Gent took her hand in his almost absently and strode forward to one of the doors, rather plain and simple, and the building had no sign or indication that anyone lived or did business there.

"What is this?" she asked quietly, shifting her fingers slightly in his hold.

He looked down at her with a smile. "This, pet, is where I work."

She knew she did not hide her surprise well at all. "You have employment?"

He laughed once and squeezed her hand. "Sort of." He did not knock, just opened the door and pulled her along behind him.

A wiry young man sat at a desk, barely looking up when they entered. "Gent, you missed your passel."

"I thought I might have." He sighed and rubbed his free hand over his face. "I'll deal with them later."

The young man shrugged. "Makes no difference to me, so long as they don't come inside. Have you seen them lately?"

"Don't be a ninny, Hawkins. Children play, children get dirty."

That drew a shudder and he looked back up at Gent, shaking his head. "Not like that." His eyes landed on Margaret and his mouth fell open, quite literally, eyes wide.

Margaret was not used to reactions quite like that, so she blushed far too much and murmured, "Good day."

He looked at Gent, then back at her, his mouth working absently now.

Well, this was awkward. "Mr. Hawkins, was it?"

He shook himself and rose. "No, ma'am, it's…"

"Don't tell me!" Gent squawked, covering his ears.

The young man rolled his eyes and leaned against his desk. "Gent and the others don't want to know my real name," he explained patiently to Margaret. "They call me whatever strikes their fancy."

Margaret looked at Gent in disapproval. "Why would you do that?" she scolded.

He grinned without apology. "Because he answers to whatever we call him, so why bother with politeness?"

She shouldn't have laughed, she really shouldn't, but there was no help for it. She giggled and covered her mouth, looking back over at the other man, who was smiling himself.

"It's my own fault," he sighed, shrugging one shoulder. "I know they're talking to or about me, so why bother correcting? Until I earn a street name, whatever they call me is fine."

"You don't have one?" she asked sympathetically.

"He has to earn it," Gent informed her, folding his arms and giving the younger man a look.

Margaret slid her glance to him. "Working with you, I am surprised he has not already done so."

Gent put a hand to his chest, staggering backwards as if wounded, while the other man laughed loudly. "My lady doth wound me," Gent moaned, gripping the wall.

"I doubt it," Margaret quipped, rolling her eyes. She turned to face the other man with a polite smile. "What shall I call you, then, if politeness is ignored and you have no street name?"

He looked embarrassed and scratched at the back of his head, the freckles across his nose scrunching up. "Well, you might as well call me Sharp, miss. It's what Rogue's been calling me all day."

"Rogue?" She looked at Gent questioningly. "Is he another man here?"

Gent had stopped his dramatics and looked serious. "Yes," he said slowly, his eyes on Sharp. "I didn't know he would be here, I thought he was..." He trailed off, his eyes flicking to Margaret uneasily.

"If it is trouble for me to be here," she said, twisting her fingers, "I can wait outside. I don't mind."

"No," Gent and Sharp said at the same time, very firmly.

She clamped down on her lips hard, feeling awkward and conspicuous and in the way.

Gent sighed and came over to her, taking a hand. "We're just unused to having anybody here that isn't one of us. You are no trouble."

"Sure of that, are you?" drawled a cool voice in dangerous tones that Margaret did not care for.

They all turned to face two men entering the room from further in the building, one with icy blue eyes and dark curls, whose scowl told her he had spoken. The other was taller, older, fair haired, and very serious.

Neither looked pleased to see her.

Oh dear.

Gent, however, didn't seem perturbed in the least. "Lovely. Margaret, might I introduce Cap and Rogue?" He gestured to the tall one respectfully, the other with only a wave.

She dipped a brief curtsey that seemed to amuse Cap. Rogue only scowled more. She restrained the urge to duck behind Gent and forced herself to smile. "Good day, gentlemen," she murmured politely. "I am sorry to intrude."

Cap shook his head. "It's not an intrusion if Gent brought you." His look turned severe as he turned to his comrade. "A word, Gent?"

Gent shrugged. "If you like. I only came to get a few things, we'll be off soon." He gestured for Cap to precede him from the room, then turned to look at Margaret, giving her a wink. "I'll be right back, Margaret. Don't run off with Rogue."

She glanced at the obviously irritated man who was now skewering Gent with his eyes. "I don't think that will be an issue," she murmured. "He's going to follow you out of the room anyway, and probably eviscerate you. I'll just wait here to clear the mess away."

Rogue looked back at her in surprise, and Gent looked ready to laugh.

"I don't make messes," Rogue muttered reluctantly. "Too much work."

Margaret could have crumpled in relief. She covered it with a prim nod, taking the chair that Sharp had pulled out for her. "Best to be efficient and capitalize on effort. You are very wise, Mr. Rogue. Perhaps I will run off with you after all."

Gent did laugh now, a rough barking sound that made her smile. Rogue eyed her carefully, his eyes not quite so frosty anymore. "If I thought you would do for me, Miss Margaret, you wouldn't have much say in the matter," Rogue told her, his tone vastly different than before.

She sighed heavily and sat back without manners, surprising them. "Yes, that is what they all say, I'm afraid. Go on with your work, Rogue, I'll wait here for no one else to want me either."

Impossibly, he smiled, just a little. "All I said was *if* you would do for me. Nothing about wanting, especially the lack of it, was mentioned."

Margaret gave him a sly smile of her own. "Why, Rogue, I do believe I see where your name came from."

He sobered, but his eyes no longer chilled her. "No, Miss Margaret, you don't. Not yet."

Gent rolled his eyes and turned from the room. "Come on, Rogue! Cap's got a lot of yelling to do, and you never miss those moments."

Rogue followed without looking back at her, and Margaret let her smile fade. She glanced over at Sharp, who was back working at his desk, paying her no mind. She took in the plain room, the offices beyond, and the complete lack of anything resembling décor or personalization. There was no indication of what anybody did for work here, and nothing that signified they did whatever it was often. Aside from a collection of coats and hats on the wall behind her, there was nothing but the desks and the books and papers upon them.

And she couldn't see anything beyond this room from her present spot.

So, she would sit here and wait, with no answers and no indication of how long they would be.

She let the silence of the room fill her for a moment, then shook her head. "Mr. Sharp, have you all a maid here? The room is in shocking need of a good cleaning."

Chapter Ten

"*A*re you out of your mind?" Rogue snapped once they were ensconced in Rafe's office with the door closed.

Rafe scoffed as he looked through his things, collecting what he could take along with him while gadding about London with Margaret in tow. Nothing of critical importance, obviously, but a few things to make whatever he did accomplish worthwhile, if possible.

"Not lately, no," he replied calmly, scanning the latest reports that had come in.

"He's completely gone 'round the bend," Rogue said to Cap, who leaned against the wall, watching Rafe without a word.

"Have not."

"You brought that woman here!"

Rafe paused in his perusal and gave his friend a very calm look. "That woman being Miss Easton, with whom you were just flirting?"

Rogue sputtered and turned redder with rage. "I was doing no such thing!" he finally managed.

That was a ridiculous assertion. "Please. She took the wind right out of your sails," Rafe told him, smiling with understanding and pity. "You were your usual caustic self, and she melted you down with a smile."

Rogue opened his mouth, then closed it again. "She took me by surprise," he grumbled. "I expected a shy, retreating miss, not an impudent..."

"Careful," Cap said softly, speaking for the first time.

Rafe looked at him in gratitude, then went back to his papers.

"She's very pleasant and very quick-witted, I'll grant you that,"

Rogue went on, his tone reluctant to say anything nice if he could help it. "But that does not explain why you are with her and why she is here."

"That is what I would like to know as well," Cap added in his usual calm. "It is obvious that you trust her enough to bring her here, but we don't. So, if you would, explain please."

It sounded polite, but Rafe knew full well that the underlying steel of Cap's tone meant he was not particularly pleased either. He just possessed an unnerving reserve of composure and strength and he usually employed it in his emotions when they were not engaged in something tending towards the dangerous.

And there was no request in his tone, despite its apparent politeness.

It was a command.

He probably spoke to his four children that way, and they implicitly obeyed.

Rafe sighed to himself and quickly related what he could about the day's adventures thus far, watching with satisfaction as his colleagues' features hardened with the telling of Margaret's state and situation. They had no other expression, except for a snort of derision when Suds was mentioned, but he really didn't expect anything.

Stories were wasted on these two.

"You and your damned hero complex," Rogue muttered with a shake of his head, folding his arms.

Rafe frowned at him. "If you had seen her as I did then, even you would have found some small untarnished portion of your soul that had some honor, Rogue."

He glowered, but made no response except to grind his teeth.

Rafe took that as an unspoken agreement. Rogue would never admit it, but Rafe knew that he possessed some honor still, despite what he portrayed and claimed. He would have helped her too, and taken the responsibility of her safety on himself. He might not have been as pleased about it as Rafe was, but there was no accounting for taste.

"Why bring her here?" Cap asked as if Rogue had made no complaint.

"You object?" Rafe's tone was too defensive, but he did not

check it.

Cap gave him a sardonic look. "Of course I do not object to your actions, and if you have a good reason for her being here, I do not object to that either. I am not particularly pleased about you feeling the need to bring the object of your desires into our highly secretive place of work, but if it was necessary, so be it."

Rafe fought a heavy sigh and stopped fidgeting with whatever he could find on his desk. "I don't know that it *was* necessary," he admitted, "but I wasn't quite sure what else to do. Once I saw to her health and care, knowing she would not be safe if returned home, I was so tossed about that I couldn't think straight. So, I brought her here to find something to do with myself, some way to do my job with her and not compromise her or me or any of this."

"Then she doesn't know…?" Cap trailed off with a questioning tilt of his head.

Rafe shook his head. "She doesn't know anything. Hasn't even asked." He shrugged and gripped the back of his neck. "I was going to tell her the cover, if that's all right by you."

Cap nodded once, but Rogue looked unconvinced.

"What?" Rafe all but barked, tired of his friend's irascible behavior.

Rogue looked at him for a long moment, clear blue eyes almost eerie in their solemnity. "Should Margaret really be going around London with you?"

He chuckled a little. "Are you concerned for her virtue, Rogue?"

Rogue did not smile. "I might be."

Rafe straightened up fully, all traces of humor gone. "I don't think you are accusing me of lacking in morals," he said slowly, anger seeping through his tone. "I don't *think* you're suggesting that I would compromise her, now that she is finally at my fingertips…"

"Stand down, Rafe!" Cap barked, forgoing their absolute directive of only using code names.

Rafe and Rogue stared at Cap in horror, then at each other, unable to believe the most controlled of them had breached that particular barrier.

"Get over that, too," Cap muttered, his tone returning to normal. "And to be perfectly honest, Gent, I have the same concerns. Not that you would ruin her, but considering your feelings for her, is it really in her best interest to be with you?"

Rafe did not take offense this time, for some reason. He understood their concerns, and had had the same himself. But he knew himself, and he knew what he was doing. "I care about her," he admitted, surprising no one. "More than even I thought, and that is only growing the more I get to know her. But more than that, I want to protect her. She will not go home, and I very much fear she would run away again if I tried, and what if I cannot save her then?"

"You can't be with her all the time," Rogue reminded him. "Eventually, she will have to return home."

"I know." He was already dreading that. "But until she is ready, would she not be best suited to be with someone who would protect her above all others?"

"Even from yourself?"

He nodded once. "Especially from myself."

Cap was looking at him strangely, his mouth almost forming a smile. "Perhaps she ought to go with Rogue, since he is so very concerned about her and has no such ties to her."

Rogue laughed once, a bit roughly. "No, thank you. She's already won me over, three more minutes in her company and I'll be on one knee or headed for Gretna."

Rafe glowered at him, which only made him laugh more. "That's not funny," he muttered.

Rogue grinned, which was rare. "No, and neither is it true. But I can see your reasons for wanting her, and she'll be under my care as well, should she ever need it."

"And mine," Cap murmured, glancing towards the front of the building as if he could see through the walls. "With all she has been through today, she ought to be terrified, and yet she is teasing Rogue, of all people, and smiling." He shook his head. "A rare woman, Gent. Mind her well."

Rafe looked between the two of them, torn between elation and amusement. "For heaven's sake, I haven't married her," he said with a laugh at last. "I haven't promised anything at all but her safety. I've only taken her under my wing for the day, perhaps for a few of them. There is no... I haven't..."

Both of them looked at him steadily, and his words simply faltered off.

They knew what he knew.

Margaret was his.

Promises or no promises.

No matter what happened today, tomorrow, or beyond.

"Weaver likes her, for whatever that's worth," Cap said with a curious smile.

Rafe stared at Cap in a mixture of horror and amazement. "What? How does Weaver…?"

Cap almost grinned. "He's met her on several occasions on the Continent. Says he approves."

Rogue barked a laugh while Rafe glared at his superior. "I don't need his approval!"

"I'll be sure to tell him."

"Careful, Gent," Rogue told him, still chuckling, "you may get reassigned to Parliament note-taking if you disparage Weaver."

"I'd risk it for Margaret," Rafe heard himself say. All of the breath fled his lungs and he shook his head. "What am I to do?" he murmured, almost to himself.

"Visit the gypsies," Cap suggested, pushing off of the wall. "You're due to check in with them anyway."

There was a thought. Away from the city, among people who respected him and would treat her well, so long as she was with him… And there was a warmth and energy to the Rom that he thought she would find most appealing.

Yes, that would work rather well.

He glanced at Rogue. "You'll mind my traitors?"

Rogue snorted. "They've been silent for weeks, you think they'll exact a coup while you are distracted?"

"With my luck, probably." Rafe sighed and shook his head. "You know, there is one bright spot in all of this."

"Yes, we know, and she is sitting in the front office with Jones," Cap said with a faint smile.

Rogue snorted with derision as he picked up some of Rafe's reports to examine.

"Besides that," Rafe corrected, rolling his eyes.

"Oh?"

He nodded once. "She hasn't met Rook. You two are fairly immune to her, but Rook?"

The other two nodded with smiles. "And she would know Rook, more than likely," Rogue pointed out. "He moves in her circles."

Rafe shuddered at the thought.

They heard footsteps approaching and a knock at the door. Cap opened it and stepped back as their unnamed young associate entered. "Sorry to interrupt, but we may have a... situation."

All three men were instantly on alert. "What is it?" Rogue demanded.

"Where's Margaret?" Rafe barked.

The man looked at him first. "She's out front cataloguing things a maid could help with here. Don't ask." He looked at the others. "And... Rook just got here."

They all looked at each other, swore in various colors, then headed for the front.

Margaret was staring at Rook in bewilderment and Rook, to his credit, was still the peacock of Society.

"What," she asked with pointed curiosity, "is he doing here? I saw him last evening, and he was speaking with my cousin, *what* is he doing here?"

Rafe didn't even know how to respond. "I..."

"Miss Easton," Rook simpered with what was probably his trademark smile, "I am only just arrived, the poor chaps won't have any idea why I am here."

She folded her arms, crushing the paper in her hand as she did so. "Mr. Pratt, you are wandering in parts of London that no one of your reputation and character would."

"As are you, Miss Easton."

She frowned, but Rafe could see amusement in her features. And worry.

Rook sighed dramatically. "Very well, I shall confess, but only because I cannot bear your poor opinion. I require the services of these fellows in a matter of some delicacy. Nothing nefarious, I can assure you, but I cannot go to Bow Street for it. The rumor is that there are those in coarser circles that are just as efficient, but less official and less conspicuous." He gestured flippantly to Gent and the rest. "So I have come to see if they will take up my case and keep it quiet."

Margaret glanced at Rafe. "Is that what you all do here?"

He shrugged. "More or less."

"Sometimes less," Rogue muttered, looking very much like he wanted to murder Rook on the spot.

Rook ignored him and was looking rather imploringly at Margaret. "Do say you will keep my secret, Miss Easton," he pleaded, somehow sounding like a desperate man without being pathetic.

She cocked her head. "Will you keep mine, Mr. Pratt?"

He placed a hand over his heart. "I swear on my honor, I never saw you today."

Margaret's full lips quirked and she held out a hand. "You keep my secret, I will keep yours."

Rook grinned a surprisingly devilish grin and took her hand, kissing it gently, without any of the gallantry a peacock would have done. "I like that sentiment," he mused quietly. "Perhaps we might discuss where else it might apply?"

Rafe almost growled but Rogue pushed him aside. "Mr. Pratt, is it?" he intoned with the barest hint of politeness. "Come with me to discuss your... situation."

Rook nodded, bowing deeply to Margaret, then following as Rogue led him from the room. Rook barely glanced at Rafe, giving him a faint wink that tempted Rafe beyond belief to blacken both of the idiot's eyes for good measure.

Margaret watched him go, shaking her head, then looked down at her paper. "There is really so much to be done." She looked at Cap with a measure of pity. "You ought to consider a maid, sir. Or a housekeeper. A servant of any kind, really, and sooner rather than later. I am surprised that Mr. Sharp here hasn't developed a layer of dust himself, but I suspect the three of you keep him busy enough to avoid the settling."

Sharp tugged at his limp cravat restlessly.

Cap stared at Margaret without expression, which was usually how Cap stared at everybody, and then, to Rafe's astonishment, he nodded. "It is a good thought," he said quietly. "If we can find the funds, I will undertake the hiring myself."

Margaret blushed a little, which made her look all the more fetching. "Forgive me," she murmured. "I ought not to pry into affairs that are not mine."

Now Cap looked sympathetic. "Miss Easton, is it?"

She nodded, keeping her chin a bit lower.

"I do not consider an earnest concern prying," Cap told her, his voice surprisingly kind. "I daresay having a woman of your observation and determination here with us would turn this place on its head and have it in better working order in no time at all."

Margaret smiled shyly and looked up at him. "I'm an interfering busybody with little tact," she said bluntly. "It is a horrid flaw, and probably my chief reason for remaining unmarried at my age."

Rafe bit back a laugh at her quip and wished he were closer so he could squeeze her hand.

Cap smiled with more warmth than Rafe had ever seen him do since the death of his wife. "I doubt your age is that shocking, Miss Easton, and your interference comes with such charm that the so-called tactlessness is irrelevant."

Margaret grinned outright. "Well. Maybe I ought to run off with *you*, Cap."

Sharp hooted a laugh that Rafe echoed, and Cap's smile turned teasing. "I would only be so fortunate." He nodded to her, then to Rafe, and returned back to the offices behind them.

Rafe shook his head, coming closer to Margaret at last. "Well, now that you have charmed all of my colleagues, perhaps we should go and find other people to fall at your feet."

Margaret laughed and handed Sharp her list of chores. "If we step foot out that door, I think everyone will fall at *yours*."

Rafe switched his cap for another on the wall and picked up a satchel from the floor beneath it. "They just might," he replied without concern. "In which case, we will walk over everyone at our feet and have a merry time of it."

He opened the door for her, let her precede him, then was quick to offer his arm once they were out.

She took it at once, smiling brightly. "Where to, Master Gent?"

"Wherever the road may lead, Miss Margaret," he replied with a cheeky grin. "But first... You need to meet my children."

Before she could respond, he whistled three short bursts of sound, and then led her along out of the street and to the meeting place long ago set for his best group of informants.

Children?

Margaret could barely swallow as he led her along, blissfully unaware of her torment.

How could he have children? That positively ruined everything. Did he also have a wife who had borne him those children?

Oh lord, was she running off on an adventure with a disenchanted husband and father?

Her face flamed with the shame now filling her.

Gent was saying something jolly and bright, but she could barely listen at all when she wondered how she was going to disengage herself from such a person. How could she have been so totally mistaken in him?

"And then Daisy's mother passed away, and her father drinks his days away when he isn't at the docks, so there really wasn't an alternative but to take her in," Gent said on a heavy sigh. "She's a bit young, but her details are unmatched by any of the others."

Margaret perked up at that. Mother *and* father? She traced back the conversation as far as she could recall, trying to fixate on what he had been saying while she had worried herself into a frenzy.

She wet her lips hesitantly. "H-how many are like her?" she asked shakily.

If he heard her nerves, he gave no indication. "Most of them, sadly," he told her with a slow shake of his head. "A few are complete orphans, but they look out for each other so well, and having them tied to us gives them some security."

"And what do they do for you?" Margaret asked, warming to his conversation more and more. He may speak of them as a loving father would, but he was obviously not biologically their father.

She ought to have known that from the start. She knew him, after all, despite their lack of interpersonal association, and he would never have betrayed his own family by being so familiar with her. As he had said, he had the honor of two toffs. She'd seen it for herself.

But honor aside, she was fiercely glad, and desperately relieved, to have been such a ninny.

Gent slid his dark glance to her, his cap lower on his face than it had been all day. "Whatever we ask," he said, his tone too stiff. "Run errands, gather information, keep an eye on certain individuals…"

"Spy?" she asked before she could help herself.

He smiled at her. "More like pay attention. No one thinks much of a child, so they can gain access in very useful ways. And if there is an individual I wish to protect, for one reason or another, I can easily have a child tail them."

Margaret frowned at him. "How would a child keep them from danger? They would be at just as much of a risk."

His smile grew slightly cocky. "Not these children. But besides that, we have several other associates that can intervene if needed. But the children can inform us of changes or anything untoward, and they love sneaking around."

Margaret thought back to her own childhood and the number of times she had thought herself so very sly. She had to smile; she'd loved doing that too.

Gent stopped and stared at her, his smile gone, his eyes unreadable.

"What?" Margaret asked, tilting her head, still smiling.

He reached out and gently touched the corner of her lips. "That smile," he murmured. "You have no idea what it does to me."

His tone sent a shiver down her spine and it was all she could do to avoid actually leaning into his touch. "I can't help but smile," she managed to squeak. "You're speaking of children so warmly, and I thought of when I was a child myself, and…"

He pressed that same finger to her mouth, silencing her. "I didn't say I minded," he said gently, his mouth curving slightly. "I don't. Not at all."

Margaret inhaled a rough gasp, sure that she was going to expire on the spot.

Gent heard the sound and his eyes trained on her lips, where his finger still rested.

"Gent!"

Margaret jerked at the chorus of voices and the scampering sounds of little feet and took a step back, breaking the contact between them in favor of gathering her wits. And if these children saw and remembered as much as Gent said they did, she dared not give them an excuse to include her in their reports.

Gent had turned at the first sound and now swept two girls into his arms, nearly over his shoulders, while three boys grinned up at him as though he were their hero. The girls giggled madly and tried to get away, but he held them fast. A trickle of more children, some nearly adults, joined them and all held the same apparent adoration for him.

Margaret hung back, afraid that if she joined the throng, she would wear a similar expression, but without their reasoning.

He spoke to them all, somehow paying attention to each individual child, even the squirming ones in front and the ones who scuffled with each other. They did not take turns speaking, but he seemed to catch all of it, every interruption, every stammer, and every wrong word. The older children had a measure of reserve that she assumed meant that they had been given more stringent duties and felt the responsibility of it, but he treated them with no less concern and enthusiasm than he had the younger ones.

Margaret watched the entire interlude, her heart growing and expanding at what seemed to be an impossible rate. Was this what a woman with a husband and children witnessed on a regular basis? How did any female stand to see something so sweet and tender and attractive?

She was near to swooning once more, and it had nothing to do with a corset, or lack thereof.

As if he could hear her thoughts, Gent turned slightly and smiled warmly at her, winking a little, which did nothing for the state of her knees.

"Do you all see that woman over there?" Gent said to his gathering, his eyes still on Margaret.

Several heads nodded without any sort of synchronization.

"That is Miss Margaret," he told them with a smile that sent her toes tingling. "She is a very special friend of mine, and ought to be minded with care."

"Not too much care," she muttered as her cheeks flamed, tucking a loose strand of hair behind her ear.

He grinned rather boyishly. "Right, not as though she would break into pieces, but rather like a treasure. As if she were something precious." His smiled turned tender and soft. "For she truly is."

Lord, how was she to breathe properly after that?

She could not have looked away from him if she had wanted to. And she could not imagine ever wanting to do anything so ridiculous.

He said nothing as he, and the children, stared at her, but his smile told her he knew exactly what he was doing to her. And by the change in his breathing, she had the sense he was not so unmoved either.

She felt a tug at her dress and managed to wrench her gaze from him to the dark-haired urchin in a poorly patched dress. "Yes?" she asked primly, smiling.

The girl gave a shy smile, revealing a few missing teeth. "Are you Gent's lady?" she asked in a very rough and lisping voice.

Margaret could almost hear Gent's groan, but chose not to look at him. "What do you think?"

Her little friend grinned widely. "Yes. He has us watch ladies sometimes, but he don't say such nice things." She clicked her tongue against her teeth in a distinctive way. "I think you mus' be his favorite."

Enchanted, Margaret leaned down and cupped her hand around the girl's ear. "I certainly hope so," she whispered, making the girl giggle.

"Daisy, don't get the lady's dress dirty," one of the others called, coming over. He put his hands on Daisy's shoulders and gave Margaret an apologetic look. "Sorry, miss. Daisy don't mean to smudge."

The boy was obviously protective, but respectful. He seemed the oldest by a few years, and was without any of the rudeness that seemed prevalent in boys his age. Margaret smiled at him, feeling a surge of tenderness for a lad who could somehow be more gentlemanly than many gentlemen she knew. But with Gent as his mentor, that should not have surprised her one bit.

"I don't mind a bit of smudge," Margaret admitted, winking at Daisy, which made her grin. "I am not so fine as to be fussy, and certainly not if the smudge came from a sweet girl like Daisy."

Several of the other children giggled and a few more girls came over, eying her dress with awe and appreciation, though it was simple and ill-fitting.

The lad still holding to Daisy smiled a little, and she had the sense he did not do it often. "You ain't like other women, Miss Margaret."

She smirked. "I should hope not. What is your name?"

"Jamie."

She held out her hand. "Very nice to meet you, Jamie. Now perhaps you might introduce me to the rest of your friends, as Gent seems to be stuck in his present location without manners?" She tossed a teasing grin his way, loving the way he returned it, and how the children whooped in delight.

Jamie made a noise she took for a laugh. "With pleasure, Miss Margaret. This one here is Sarah, and mind you don't get between her and sweets, or your shins will feel it…"

Chapter Eleven

$\mathcal{T}$hey walked in silence, not touching, but the air between them somehow filled with words and emotions and thoughts that neither could bring to light.

Margaret, for her part, could not think how to tell him what she had thought of their brief interlude with the children. She had never thought much of motherhood, as she had always been more fixated on the idea of being a wife and finding love. That was not to say that she was opposed to the idea or that she disliked children, she had just never been particularly exposed to them.

Seeing Gent's tenderness with them, and spending a bit of time with them, knowing how little attention they received in their own life, she was moved beyond expression.

And her heart was on a very precarious slope as it was.

She had met all of the children present, though she had been repeatedly told that not all of them were there, and once she had done that, Gent reminded the children that they had business to attend to, and he really must be getting on with Miss Margaret. They had all rushed off at that, and in a few moments, the street was as empty as it had been before, with no sign that anything had disturbed it.

Gent had not said more than three words to her since then, but an echo of his look from before remained.

Silence was not something that made Margaret particularly uncomfortable, and even with Gent it seemed to feel rather nice, but with the way she felt now, she would have preferred he speak. Otherwise, she was likely to say or do something she might have cause to regret. Like throwing herself on him and kissing him with all of the inexperience and innocence she possessed.

It might not amount to very much for a man such as him, but she was feeling excessively passionate right now, and untried as she was, there was no way to know what to expect.

She bit down on her lip as they slowly walked; no doubt he was taking special care because of her ankles. He had never said a word, but his eyes were raking over her with enough frequency that she suspected he was analyzing her for injury. She walked perfectly, however, and gave him no cause for concern.

Her heart was racing within her, but that had nothing to do with this morning's excursions.

"You were perfect with the children," Gent suddenly said, making her jump as his arm brushed against hers gently. She hadn't known he was so close...

She managed to swallow. "Was I?"

He made a low humming sound that did nothing for her current state. "Yes, perfect. They don't have much exposure with fine ladies, only the whores and fishwives of the streets. And Tilda, I suppose, but she doesn't count."

Margaret smiled at the offhand manner he suddenly used. "Why doesn't Tilda count?"

He gave her a grin. "Tilda could pass for a queen if she wanted. But she works in the theaters at Covent Garden, mostly. Costumer and former actress. Loud and demanding, will do just about anything for crumpets, and does not take kindly to patronization. Quite a character. You'd like her."

She laughed merrily and looped her arm through his, taking the liberty of leaning against him a little. "I'm sure I would."

"Are you tired?" he asked immediately. "We can rest."

She shook her head, smiling. "No, I am not tired." She looked up at him with a bit of a dreamy expression. "If we stop to rest, I may realize this is all a dream and I am back with Miss Ritson, listening to her horrid plans for me. I much prefer being here with you."

His dark eyes searched hers, a peculiar light in them. "Oh, Margaret," he murmured, his look a caress. "You are here with me. This is no dream. I should know, I've dreamed often enough, and nothing was ever so pleasant."

"Of what were you dreaming, then, that this should be so pleasant?"

"You."

She blushed furiously and averted her eyes, her throat tight. There was the kissing impulse again, and her stomach seemed to pound furiously with some agitated fire. "Pleasant, is it, to have your day disrupted by a simpering female in shocking garments who is unwilling to return home?"

Gent chuckled and took her hand in his, pressing it to his lips. "Pleasant to be with *you*, Margaret, however the situation arose."

Margaret sighed a rather pathetic and swoony sigh that she ought to have been embarrassed about. "Gent, you really must stop saying such things. I might believe you."

He stopped them suddenly and turned to face her. "You ought to believe me," he told her with a fervent squeeze of her hands. "I've never meant anything more than the things I've said to you. Everything about you is different for me, Margaret, and I would never say or do anything where you were concerned that I did not mean to my core."

Her lips parted in surprise and she stared at him rather stupidly while her sense went to pieces. "Oh," she finally managed. "I... didn't know. I'm not used to such things."

He snorted softly. "That is just ridiculous."

She swallowed and managed a shrug. "'Tis my reality, Gent."

"Ridiculous," he repeated, more firmly. He suddenly frowned, staring at her without speaking. Then there came the barest hint of a nod, as if he had come to some sort of decision. "Call me 'Rafe'," he said in a low voice.

Margaret tilted her head up at him, bewildered by the sudden suggestion. "Rafe? Why?"

"It's my name." His tone was simple, but the gravity in his eyes told her this was no trifle.

Her eyes widened. "Your... your *real* name?" she squeaked.

He nodded once, his gaze steady.

"Why not your street name?" she asked, wishing she didn't sound so wildly breathless.

He stepped closer, still holding her hands, though now they

could easily have slid to his chest, and she was beyond tempted to indulge in that image. "Because," he murmured, "I want to be Rafe to you."

Oh my.

Would have been too improper to beg him for a kiss at this moment? Likely yes, so she would have to settle for a very harsh swallow that wouldn't fool anyone.

Rafe. The name suited him perfectly, somehow encompassing the essence of him in one single syllable. She had a real name for the face and body and man that had become so important to her, more in the last few hours than she'd ever thought, considering the pedestal she had already held him on. He wasn't a stranger anymore, a man with an identity but no name.

Now he was somehow more real; warm and breathing and standing closer than propriety would have allowed.

Propriety could shove off.

"All right then," she replied in a tone to match his, smiling softly. "Rafe it is."

A ripple of pleasure rolled through her at the heat in his smile and he brought her hand to his lips, kissing so gently it almost tickled. To her utter embarrassment, she giggled at the sensation.

He smiled, chuckling himself, and lowering her hand, placing it back in the crook of his arm.

As he led her back down the cobblestone road, Margaret let herself exhale in a whoosh of air, shaking her head. He had to know what he was doing to her, so she was not going to pretend otherwise.

The question was… What exactly did he think of her?

"A question for you, Margaret," Rafe said, sounding amused by something.

She cleared her throat and looked over at him. "Yes, Rafe?"

He grinned without reserve. "Can you ride?"

Margaret frowned a little. "Yes," she said slowly. "Why?"

"Because we are nearly to the mews, and we need a horse. It will be much easier if you have no qualms about it."

She shook her head. "I've been riding for years." She blushed a little. "Sidesaddle and bareback." At his laugh, she found herself smiling more. "Why do we need a horse? Where are we going?"

Now he seemed truly amused as he looked at her, a rather mischievous light in his eyes. "We're going to see the gypsies."

She was utterly terrified.

He probably should have explained himself a little, but the completely aghast expression she'd worn had been the most adorable, not to mention hilarious, thing he'd seen in some time. And now that they rode towards the camp, she was stiff and somehow colder as she brushed up against his chest.

He was rather enjoying this ride. Poor Margaret could have been thinking all sorts of things. He really couldn't go into much detail, as everything would be clear once they arrived. Besides, he doubted anything would change her feelings about seeing gypsies. The stigma against them was deeply seated, and until she saw for herself, she would not change her opinion.

But she hadn't refused to come with him. She was riding towards it with him.

That sent a thrill of satisfaction into Rafe, and he felt himself leaning just a little closer to her as they rode.

If she noticed, she gave no indication.

If he survived this day, it would be a miracle.

They crossed the small creek just before the camp, and Rafe bit back a smirk as Margaret pressed back against him, seeing the children appearing from the trees and running around the green.

"Steady," he murmured against her ear, delighting in the shiver that coursed through them both. "They are only excited about the horse, and a pretty girl."

He heard a very soft snort of derision, and it pleased him. If she still had spirit, she would do very well.

The wagons of the caravan soon came into view, bright and colorful as ever, and at the sound of their approach, several heads turned with a marked air of suspicion. Music was playing, as music always seemed to be, and there was a great bustle about the camp. More than usual.

A large and imposing man stepped forward and the children dashed back to stand behind him or go to their waiting mothers. The man folded his arms and his expression would have terrified the most stoic of Englishmen.

Luckily for Rafe, he was quite used to this.

Margaret made a soft noise of fear or distress and he shushed her gently, tightening his hold around her briefly before swinging off of the horse.

He swept off his hat and nodded respectfully, taking a few steps forward and leading the horse. "Good day, Kem. I see you've fixed your *vardo* without my help."

Kem growled in his chest the same sound Rafe had learned to accept as both a laugh and a snort. "Yes," he rumbled, "and better than you could have done had you been here, Gent."

Rafe grinned. "No doubt of it. Might we enter the camp, my friend?"

Kem slid his dark eyes over to Margaret, watching with a remarkably composed expression for one so utterly terrified. He grunted softly. "Your *monisha?*"

Rafe's heart sputtered at the word, wishing she were his wife and his love in truth, but knowing he could not pretend any such thing. And yet...

"Something like that," he muttered, scratching at the back of his neck.

Kem smiled, which rarely happened, and the wide grin made him look almost human. "I see we have much to discuss. Come, join us. We are in the middle of a *pliashka*, so you have come just in time." He turned more completely to Margaret and bowed as any Englishman would have done. "*Droboy tume Romale*. Welcome."

"Thank you," Margaret murmured so softly Rafe wondered if Kem could even hear it.

"*Nais tuke*," Rafe replied with a half-smile, making at least three of the women giggle with his bad accent.

Kem gave him a scolding look, knowing full well that Rafe could have a more perfect accent than half of his tribe, if he chose.

Rafe turned to Margaret and helped her down, wrapping an arm around her shoulder protectively as they followed Kem and the others towards the encampment.

"What did he say to me?" Margaret asked him, still shaking slightly.

"Welcome," he teased.

She nudged him a little. "I mean before that, you dolt."

He grinned. "As I said. Welcome."

She looked up at him in surprise, then looked away quickly. "Oh."

He chuckled. "Did you expect something else?"

"Well, yes," she admitted, fidgeting with her long strands of hair over one shoulder. "The language sounds rather harsh and strident, rather as if he were cursing me."

He'd give her that, but the idea made him laugh all the same, and several pairs of eyes turned at the sound. "I can assure you that if Kem decided to curse anybody, it would sound much fouler than that. I've actually never seen him more pleasant, you should be flattered."

Margaret glanced around at the laughing and dancing children, a smile forming on her lips. "I shall attempt to be so."

He saw the way she took in the state of living in the encampment, the large tents and decorated wagons, simple toys, the fires around which pots and plates and tankards sat, the blankets and bedrolls that seemed strewn about... It was a very different sort of life than anything she would have experienced, and the lack of material possessions could be a very striking observation.

"What are you thinking, pet?" he asked her softly, handing his horse off to two older boys with a warning look and two coins.

He'd been the brunt of too many jokes where horses were concerned, and there was a little truth to the rumors about the Roma and horses. Not all of them, and not all of the rumors, but just enough that a warning was warranted.

Margaret cupped a hand around her mouth and went up on tiptoe, but still he had to stoop. "I expected them to be dirtier," she whispered.

He laughed and pulled her shoulder in more tightly against him. "Sometimes they are. Some tribes certainly are. But Kem, he's the *rom boro*..."

"The what?"

"The leader. He has some very strict opinions, cleanliness being one of them. They wouldn't pass muster with the ladies of London…"

Margaret snorted in derision, shaking her head. "Even I cannot manage that half of the time, one can hardly expect high energy children in a nomadic family to do so."

Rafe grinned at her. Her tone was scornful, but not of the children. She was taking everything in with the same sense of wonder she seemed to do everything else, and there was no judgment in her gaze.

Saints above, she was a fine woman.

"Such a simple, easy life," she said softly, smiling at the game a few nearby children played. "Rather peaceful, I imagine."

"Not so easy," Rafe assured her with a sigh. "You know the feelings about gypsies as a whole. They are almost never well treated, and prejudices run deep. They never forget an insult, and are not inclined to be tolerant of them."

Several people called out greetings to Rafe and he waved with a smile, ignoring some of the comments the men were making about the woman beside him, grateful they spoke in their native tongue so that Margaret would have no idea. They knew better than to be derogatory, but that did not mean they could not tease Rafe about her.

He prayed his face would not be noticeably flushed.

"What else does Kem insist upon?" Margaret asked, stepping lightly around a few puddles.

He was so charmed by her almost skipping that he nearly forgot to answer. "No thievery. Respect the land. Loyalty to family. And…"

"And always having fine drink at hand," Kem overrode as they approached the largest and most elaborate wagon in the camp.

Rafe grinned. "Well, yes, that goes without saying."

Kem nodded and gestured for them to enter the large *vardo*. "And we have been known to thieve from time to time," Kem admitted with a smile to Margaret. "But only when we gamble too much, or if the men in question can afford to lose it."

Margaret grinned brightly and let Kem help her into the wagon. "What have you taken from Gent, then?"

Rafe barked a laugh and followed her into the wagon. "Two times everything I have brought in offering, my best hat, and the very first horse I ever rode in on."

Kem chuckled good-naturedly as they all situated themselves. "It is not my fault that you were naïve enough to think an unprotected horse of such caliber would remain yours when you left no incentive for it."

Rafe rolled his eyes and looked at Margaret. "It was my first time here, and my experience with the Roma was sadly lacking. I was delighted to be admitted in at all, I didn't think they'd steal the horse."

"Borrow," Kem corrected, sitting back comfortably despite his large stature. "You weren't using it."

"It wasn't even mine."

"Nothing truly is."

"Oh, yes, I'd heard that," Margaret chimed in, nodding with a smile. "You don't believe a man can truly possess anything, yes? We own nothing, and accumulation of goods is not something to be desired."

Kem looked at Rafe in surprise, but Rafe was just as shocked. Where in the world had she learned that? Most people only thought of gypsies as thieving wanderers with no respect for anything but their own ends, but this… This was fairly accurate.

"Very good, yes," Kem told her with an approving nod. "You are quite a different sort of woman."

Margaret blushed in a way that made Rafe want to kiss her. "Thank you."

"Apologies," Rafe broke in with a laugh. "Kem, this is Margaret. Margaret, Kem, the *rom boro*."

"A pleasure," Margaret said, holding out her hand.

Kem looked bewildered now and took her hand in his massive one slowly. "Likewise." He looked at Rafe and shook his head, bemused. "What can we do for the two of you, Gent?"

Rafe sighed a little. "Well, I was due for a visit to check reports, if you have any to share, but also to assure myself that things are well here." He slid his glance to Margaret. "And Miss Margaret has injured her ankles today, so I thought something might be done for that."

Kem nodded slowly. "All of those things can be done, yes." He folded his arms and smiled at Gent. "But I want to hear the story first."

Rafe laughed, ready to tell him off, but Margaret surprised them both by launching right into their tale, leaving no detail out, and telling it with such vivacity that it all seemed rather exciting and hilarious instead of harrowing and dangerous. She spared herself no embarrassment and gave just enough context to leave listeners with no questions. Kem was enraptured, and Rafe could see a few others gathered around the *vardo* listening in, laughing at all of the right parts.

Margaret sat back when her story was over, grinning in delight. "So you see, Mr. Kem, I truly am a different sort of woman."

Kem laughed. "Just Kem, Margaret, and yes, you are." He kissed her hand playfully, then called out of the wagon and a very pretty woman of some years appeared. "Lela, this is Margaret, and she has injured her ankles. Would you see to them?"

Lela smiled at Margaret warmly. "Of course," she replied, her accented voice lilting a little.

"Lela is my wife," Kem explained to Margaret with a wink. "She'll set you to rights."

Margaret raised a brow. "Am I dismissed then?"

Rafe rolled his eyes heavenward. Some impudence was a good thing, but in this Roma culture, the men controlled all and cultivated great respect from all. If Kem were not in an accommodating mood, Margaret's eccentricities could get them into a spot of trouble.

Thankfully, Kem seemed entertained by her. "Temporarily, I'm afraid. The *pliashka* must go on and you will wish to be refreshed to take part."

"What is a... a...?" Margaret tried to ask, her delicate brow furrowing.

"*Pliashka*," Rafe repeated. "It's a betrothal celebration. They can go on for days."

"And usually do," Kem added with a nod. "We've only had one day, so we've hardly begun. There is music and dancing and feasting and we all make rather merry, as you *gadje* would say."

"And we're invited?" Margaret asked, smiling broadly in delight.

"You are now," Kem told her. He gestured to Lela again. "Provided you are well enough to dance."

Margaret grinned at him. "I would not miss it." She allowed Rafe to help her out and seized his hand tightly. "I cannot believe we are invited to stay!" she whispered excitedly. "Do you know how to do their dances?"

He smiled down at her and nodded. "Yes, I do."

"Teach me, will you? I want to dance with them." Her face flushed a little. "I want to dance with you."

His throat went dry and he touched her cheek gently, marveling at her again. "I'll teach you, pet," he somehow managed. "And we'll dance all night if you want."

She bit her plump lower lip, smiling at him. "I just might."

Lela stepped forward and took Margaret's arm, giving Rafe a rather knowing look, and then steered Margaret away, speaking in a friendly mix of English and Romani that he hoped Margaret could translate. He didn't like her being away from him for a moment, but Lela was the most respected woman in the *kumpania*, and the Gent was an ally of the *rom boro*. No one would trifle with her.

He heard the rough laughing sound behind him and turned with a sardonic look to face Kem.

Kem inclined his head towards Margaret's retreating form. "*Monisha?*" he asked again.

Rafe sighed in defeat, knowing it was fruitless. "I certainly hope so, *Kako.*"

Kem chuckled and waved him back in. "Down to business, my friend, so we might get on to the drink you so obviously need."

Chapter Twelve

*M*argaret had no idea what Lela was saying to her, nor the two other women who were helping her, but she got on well enough. Lela was a stunning woman, despite being somewhere closer to her mother's age than her own, and the other two women just a bit older. The lines on their dark faces told of sleepless nights and laughter, of hard times and of joyous ones.

She had understood enough that the other two women, Emanaia and Drina, had some sort of experience with medicine, while Lela was more of a matron, if such a thing existed. They all served at the pleasure of the *rom boro*, but for the good of the camp.

And they were really very sweet.

She did not need to speak their language to know that they envied her hair and her figure, and she blushed as Drina gave her a frank look, patting her hips.

"Good for having babies," Drina said in her thick accent, smiling and showing fairly straight, if a bit dirty, teeth.

Emanaia cackled at Margaret's discomfort and gestured for her to sit down on the small stool in the colorful wagon. The canvas itself was simple enough, and rather like every other canvas she had ever seen, but the wagon itself was painted brightly and adorned with various designs in equally bright colors. Each wagon was different, she'd noticed that as she'd come into camp with Rafe. And despite the initial wariness in the eyes of everyone who looked at her, they had been warm and friendly.

Hardly the criminals that the world had made them out to be.

The women tending her were warm and kind, and they dressed

rather simply, but with as much color as they could, though it was all faded with use and wear. Lela was in a rich blue skirt and a simple linen shirt, Drina in emerald, and Emanaia in a rich purple with a gold-embroidered shawl tied about her. All three wore a considerable amount of jewelry, and smelled of jasmine and sandalwood.

Drina untied her boots and set them aside, speaking rapidly with the others. Then she smiled up at Margaret. "I will make a poultice for your ankles, *chavi*. It will help with the pain."

"I'm not in that much pain," Margaret protested, even as she winced with a certain motion Drina made.

Drina chuckled. "So I see. You are a stubborn *gadji*, no?"

"Does that mean a woman?" Margaret asked with a smile. "Because yes, I am."

"It means a woman who is not a Roma," Lela told her as she began to brush out Margaret's hair.

"And what about the other thing you called me?" Margaret asked. "*Chavi* was it?"

Emanaia smiled as she crushed a few things and prepared to make a poultice. "It is a term of endearment for a young girl."

Margaret frowned a little. "I'm not young at all. I am twenty-two."

Drina laughed a hoarse, throaty sort of laugh. "*Chavi*," she said again. "So young. Very pretty, you must mind that. A pretty face hides many sins."

"I know," Margaret said on a sigh, loving how Drina rubbed at her ankles. "And I have a fortune as well."

All three women tsked sadly, which amused her. In any other world, she would have been lauded for both of those things. Here they were not something to be envied.

She rather liked that.

"Why are you all being nice to me?" she asked as Emanaia brought the poultices over. "If I'm a… a *gadji*… shouldn't you be questioning me or intimidating me or something?"

Lela began to plait sections of her hair. "If you had come alone, Margaret, we certainly would have. We are a very cautious group, and our *kumpania* has had some less savory experiences of late."

All three women muttered something very dark sounding under

their breath, and she shivered at the sudden chill in the air.

Then, somehow, it was gone.

Lela resumed her plaiting as if nothing had happened. "But you came with the Gent today, and that makes all the difference."

"Does it?" she murmured with a smile, not entirely surprised.

Drina and Emanaia wrapped the poultices around her ankles, giggling in a manner entirely too young for their ages. Lela spared them an amused look, then turned Margaret so she could see her better, taking a damp cloth to her face. "Gent is what we call *poshram*, half-Rom." Her smile grew a little. "We cannot be sure, he has no knowledge of any Roma blood in him, but one only has to look at him to know. He is probably only slightly Rom, but we'll take him."

Drina muttered something under her breath that had Emanaia cackling as she finished wrapping the poultices.

Margaret had a fairly good idea what was being said, despite the language barrier. She flushed, but giggled, and twisted her ankles a little. "What have you wrapped on me, then?" she asked.

"*Panishok*," Drina told her, her face innocent as ever. "Watercress. Very good for injuries. You will dance tonight without pain."

"Excellent!" Margaret beamed at her and sighed. She looked over at Lela, who was smiling at her in a knowing way she did not particularly care for. "What... um... what brought Gent to your attention the first time?"

Lela sat back on her heels and pushed an ebony and silver lock of hair behind her ear. "Miri."

"Pardon?" Margaret asked, tilting her head. Perhaps that was another Romani word that she would have to learn or have explained.

"Miri," she said again. "She is the girl we celebrate with the *pliashka*. Four years ago, we were in this area, and she wandered too far, and some *gadjos* were not happy to see a Rom child in their vicinity. They chased her with their horses, terrifying her and threatening many things. We are so close to London here, and had been closer then, and she became lost in her attempts to hide. The Gent found her and brought her safely back to us." Lela smirked a little. "He also took care of those *gadjos* who abused her so. For that, he is always welcome. As are his friends." She gave Margaret a tilt of her head, indicating she was part of that group.

Margaret certainly hoped she was one of his friends. She would dearly love to be that and more. "That sounds like something he would do," she mused, covering her desire to sigh and swoon over him. "He is very much a hero."

"It is not only that," Emanaia said in her higher voice, settling a bright yellow shawl around Margaret's shoulders, making Drina hum in approval. "He does not see us as others do. He ensures that we are protected, that we may wander as we choose, and that we need not resort to the desperate tactics that some other *kumpaniyi* might. We come back to this area every year just for him, you know."

"Do you really?" That was intriguing. She'd never thought of a group of gypsies as having particular ties to an area.

All three women nodded. "He and Kem are allies, and meet as often as Kem permits," Lela told her, tying a small ribbon at the bottom of Margaret's delicate plait, the rest of her hair loose around her shoulders.

That was curious. "About what?" Margaret asked, fingering the plait and loving that ribbon had also been woven into it.

Lela smirked and shrugged. "Only Kem and Gent know, and they do not tell."

Margaret sat back in defeat, making a face, which made the others laugh. Drina patted at her ankles. "There is energy in you, Margaret," she said. "Much spirit."

"Yes, I know," Margaret sighed heavily. "Apparently, that is the problem."

Drina smiled, shaking her head. "No, it is a good thing. Let me show you." She gestured for Margaret's hand, and turned it palm up. She hummed as she ran her wrinkled, ring-strewn fingers over it, spreading her hand open and nodding to herself.

"This line here," she murmured, tracing one finger from the side of her palm across the middle, where it ended, "means that you think quickly, and make decisions without trouble. You know your mind."

Margaret grinned at her. "Yes, so my mother says."

Lela shushed her, but laughed. Emanaia said nothing, but began rummaging through a trunk nearby.

Drina moved her finger to a line near Margaret's small finger and traced it across her hand. "Here it says that you are a passionate creature, and your emotions and desires guide your actions. You are independent, and it makes no difference to you if that is known."

Now Margaret had to bite her lip to keep from laughing. That was true, by all accounts. Fleeing a dastardly situation, determined to marry a British man to stay in England, gallivanting off with the unsuitable man of her dreams… Margaret was remarkably willful, and it was going to get her into trouble.

"And this line," Drina continued in her low voice, tracing a bold line curving around Margaret's thumb, "tells me you are strong when life is hard. Difficulties do not upset you, but challenge you."

Margaret watched in fascination, smiling to herself at the woman's words.

Drina traced the faint broken line down the center of her palm. "You have had many changes in your life, and they were not of your making." Drina tilted her hand, smiling. "Your hands are delicate, *chavi.*"

"And what does that mean?" Margaret found herself whispering.

Drina chuckled, cupping her cheek fondly. "It means you are precious, and Gent ought to take care."

Margaret blushed furiously. "No, no, you misunderstand," she stammered, wringing her now tingling hands together. "He and I… That is, we are not…"

Emanaia draped a delicate gold chain with tinkling coins around one of Margaret's ankles, fastening the clasp. "Look in his eyes, *chavi*, and you will see it. And when you dance tonight, you will feel it."

Margaret twisted her poultice-covered ankle, loving the faint chiming sound it made. "Will I?" she whispered.

Emanaia smiled and nodded. "Dance is the music of the heart, Margaret. And when you hear his heart singing, you will make music together."

It was suddenly far too hot in this wagon, spacious though it was. She cleared her throat awkwardly, and turned to Drina. "Can you teach me how to read a palm, Drina? Can a *gadji* learn such a thing?"

Drina smiled at her. "Most likely no. But you have the heart of a Rom, *chavi*, so perhaps you can."

"What do you mean you've lost track of him?"

Kem gave Rafe a sharp and very pointed look, which scolded Rafe soundly. Kem was doing Rafe a great favor by being his contact, but he could hardly treat him as though he was one of his typical assets. Kem was a greatly respected leader who could very easily have Rafe torn apart bit by bit without anyone in London having any idea of trouble at all.

"Sorry," he mumbled, sitting back moodily and looking away. "I'm only anxious about the situation getting out of hand."

"As are we."

That brought Rafe's head around. Generally, the Rom didn't get anxious about much of anything. Why should they? They were nomads, living off of the land, and the affairs of the *gadje* as a whole were not something they were generally concerned with.

Kem sat forward and rubbed his hands together slowly. "Tensions between nations cause trouble for all of us. Suspicions are higher and the heart of the *gadje* is colder. Too many of our men become involved, and we suffer as much as the rest."

"If not more," Rafe pointed out, knowing the suffering the Rom endured during peaceful times.

Kem acknowledged this with a nod. "I tried to keep Pov within the *vitsa*, for his own safety, but he was straying too far out of our way. The *chorodies* have gotten into his soul, and his behavior made it impossible for him stay."

Rafe sighed and rubbed his head. Pov was a willful, hot-tempered Rom who never trusted Rafe, nor, it seemed, any *gadjo* who did not have a pocket of coins for him. He had been suspicious for years, and Rafe had seen him in the city on several occasions during that time, always in the company of people Rafe could tie to various crimes.

Reaching out to Kem had been a brilliant move on Rafe's part, as Kem would have far more sway over Pov than anyone else, and Kem did not approve of behavior considered "beneath one's dignity."

There was some debate as to what exactly that meant, but the sentiment stood.

Pov had been tied to the faction of rebels and traitors that the London League had been tracing, but as yet, Rafe had left him alone. He could prove useful, and as his loyalties only rested with himself, sufficient funds from their end might sway him to divulge sensitive information.

But if Pov was no longer with the *kumpania*, and cast out of the *vitsa*, then they had a dangerous and mercenary Rom with no moral compass roaming about with traitors and scum.

That was a sobering thought.

"Will he come back?" Rafe asked quietly.

Kem's wide jaw tightened and he shook his head. "No. He is now a *mahrime*."

Rafe hissed as if in pain. There could hardly be a stronger punishment for his betrayal than to be labeled an outcast, as a Rom unworthy of trust. Word tended to spread of that sort of thing, and any other encampments would have seen him the same, not wanting to bring such a man into their tribe. And there would be no evidence of any of his activities within the tribe, as they did not have personal belongings that he could search.

Perhaps he could ask for some of Pov's associates to be questioned, but he could not be the one to do it. Despite his ability to move freely about the camp, he was not a Rom. He might look like one, but he was fairly certain there was no Rom in his blood anywhere.

Which was probably why Pov hated him so much.

"If he makes his home with another *kumpania*, so be it," Kem said with a shrug. "Unless they have no scruples, I cannot see it."

"But it happens," Rafe pointed out.

Kem shrugged again.

"Well, what about everything else?" Rafe asked, trying not to be disappointed. While Pov and his activities were his prime concern, he also frequently used Kem and his tribe as sources of information for whatever else he could. They had the ability to be ingrained in a society without taking part, and observed far more than they were given credit for. He had been able to act on their tips more often than not with great success and without causing too much fuss and bother.

Kem told him what he knew, which seemed to be the same sort of reports he always received, nothing out of the ordinary or needing his attention.

All told, it was not a particularly useful excursion out here.

With the loss of Pov as a point of interest, he wasn't sure what else he could do. He would always have the interest of the Rom as one of his concerns, and certainly they were convenient allies, but with the looming threat of the traitors and faction, it was difficult to consider anything else.

"I will speak with Pov's brothers," Kem said suddenly, interrupting Rafe's dismal thoughts.

Rafe looked at him in surprise. "Really?"

Kem snorted in derision. "Not sure it will do any good. They do not share his temper, but perhaps they know something." He shrugged his broad shoulders and folded his arms. "I cannot see him reaching out to them, but you never know."

"Thank you." Rafe felt a little humbled by this large, powerful man who was willing to indulge him so. He doubted any other *rom boro* would have been so tolerant or understanding.

Fate was sometimes rather fond of him.

"So," Rafe drawled with a smile, "who are we celebrating this time?"

"Miri and Danior," Kem returned, smiling himself.

"Really?" Rafe laughed. "I didn't think a man alive would ever be permitted to have your niece."

"Nor I, but Danior loves her, and has proven himself. There is no one in the tribe I trust more." His grin was swift and ironic. "And there was Miri's opinion as well. I may be *rom boro*, but have you ever faced the power of a willful woman who knows her value?"

Rafe threw his head back on a hearty laugh. "Sweet little Miri stood her ground? Not very Roma at all! I should have married her when I had the chance."

Kem grunted, still smiling. "Not a chance. I like you, Gent, but *Gadje Gadjensa, Rom Romensa.*"

Rafe nodded in understanding, his smile fading only just. He knew that well; Gadje with Gadje, Rom with Rom. Anything else was unthinkable, and certainly frowned upon. "Don't you always tell me that I am *poshram*?" he teased.

"It is a courtesy title," Kem assured him. "Not enough to qualify you."

There was a bit of noise outside, and Kem indicated he wait while he got out to check. Rafe hid a smile, wondering what sort of scuffle might have ensued during their interview.

He heard the low rumble of male voices, then a brusque order of "*Avree!*" that had several sets of feet pounding away. Kem stuck his head back in with a mischievous glint that Rafe was instantly wary of. "What?" he asked, leaning away from his friend.

"The men of the camp wish to continue *pliashka*," Kem reported, still almost smiling. "And you have been selected."

"For what?"

"I believe you *gadje* would call it 'a bit of sport'," he replied with a mocking British accent.

Rafe groaned and helped himself out of the wagon, tugging off his cap and untucking his shirt. "Not again. Who am I to thrash, then?"

Kem put a heavy hand on his shoulder, laughing a deep, rumbling laugh. "Camlo. And I warn you, he has been training hard."

Rafe looked over to the center of the camp where the circle of onlookers was forming, a muscular and dangerous looking Rom standing in the middle, staring at him with an almost hungry look. Perfect, a motivated Rom with an agenda.

"So have I," Rafe growled, tugging off his shirt and tossing it at the nearest lad as he strode forward.

Chapter Thirteen

"*W*hat is that noise?"

Lela cocked her head, listening, then groaned. "A fight."

Drina and Emanaia muttered in obvious irritation, glancing out of the wagon.

Margaret frowned. "What sort of a fight? Is something wrong?"

"Probably not," Lela said, lifting a shoulder. "It is most likely something the men have arranged for *pliashka*. Fighting because they find it amusing."

"So it should not be very bad?" Margaret asked, not sure why anybody would find fighting amusing, or want to do such a thing. She'd never even understood the draw of gentleman's boxing that she'd heard about in London and other great cities of the world.

All three women laughed. "You don't know the Rom very well, *chavi*," Drina said, still laughing. "It will be quite brutal."

She shivered a little. "And who is fighting?"

A loud roar of the crowd reached them and she bit her lip, half tempted to dash out of the wagon to watch, half tempted to cower.

Lela smiled tightly, giving Margaret a pitying look. "I think we all know who would be fighting if the *vitsa* is so invested already."

Margaret felt the blood drain from her face, and probably the rest of her body as well. "No…"

"More than likely yes," Emanaia simpered with a pat to her hand. "Camlo is always threatening to beat him, he probably grew tired of waiting."

Margaret scrambled free of them and clambered forward. "I must see him," she gasped. "I must stop this!"

Lela helped her out and took her arm as the others followed. "You will make it worse if you stop it," Lela told her firmly. "They must settle it themselves. You may watch and cheer with the rest, but you must not interfere."

"He could be hurt!" Margaret protested.

"But he will not be dead."

That was not a comfort.

Margaret hurried forward as fast as her wrapped ankles would let her, and was pleased that Lela and the other women, now joined by four more, were helping her along. Rafe would never be so foolish as to take on a Rom in a fight for sport, would he? Had his meeting with Kem about whatever it was gone so poorly that they were making him fight? *Could* Rafe fight?

That was a bit of a stupid question, considering he had fought off her would-be attackers in the alley only this morning. But this was something entirely different. The Rom were known for their fighting, and it was never used in a complimentary way. Could he compete with that?

She would never forgive him if he died in a stupid bout for amusement, no matter how Lela assured her he would survive.

And she would have quite a bit of trouble getting out of the camp if he were dead.

"Do they do this often?" she asked as they hurried towards the gathered crowd.

"Like this?" Lela gestured to the group, then shook her head. "This is for special occasions."

"Lovely," Margaret muttered under her breath. She would never understand men.

They reached the edge of the group and Drina barked at several people, who moved aside for them, then pressed in behind them. Kem was a few people down from her and smiled when he saw her, looking rather like one of the little boys cheering them on. She gave him an exasperated look that he laughed at before returning to bellow at the men inside the circle.

Margaret gasped when she looked as well.

Rafe was circling the largest man she had ever seen in her entire life, and the man had more muscles and ridges to his body than seemed possible. More than that, the Rom bore a scar on his chest that spoke of other, more vicious fights from which he had obviously emerged victorious.

"Is that Camlo?" she asked Emanaia faintly, though her voice was almost lost in the din.

The older woman nodded, her earrings dancing with the movement. "Our best fighter. He was brought up fighting and does not lose."

Margaret swallowed. "Ever?"

"Not in recent memory," she replied, her eyes fixed on the fight, her body radiating excitement.

Margaret nearly swooned where she stood as she looked back into the circle, her body going cold.

Rafe was focused on Camlo, and didn't even look concerned about the fact that the man was twice his size. He was shirtless and gleaming in the light, and though he was a remarkable sight usually, in this state he was a thing of pure masculine beauty. His body was hard and sculpted, with a striking scar on his left side just below his ribs, and moved with a sort of feline grace that captivated her.

Her mouth went dry as she watched him, and the day suddenly seemed much warmer.

Camlo suddenly cuffed Rafe sharply on the ear in a way that made most of them wince, and Margaret was brought back to the urgency of the fight.

She had to admit it, despite her fear and horror for the fight itself, Rafe had remarkable skill, and she did not mind at all watching the way his muscles twisted and bent with every move he made. Her breath caught so often she felt as though *she* were fighting half of the time. She couldn't look away, both in appreciation and in anticipation. It would have been enough to draw anyone's attention, but with such a personal connection, it was sheer torment.

She'd never seen anything like this. Their hands were lightning quick, and every slap or punch that landed on skin created a loud crack that made her wince.

Rafe was a good fighter, quick and efficient, and very fluid in his movements. Somehow, he seemed to know what Camlo would do as soon as he decided to do it. But Camlo was a massive, terrifying Rom, and he was no less skilled. His blows had power to them, making Rafe stagger when they landed, and what he may have comparatively lacked in the smoothness of his moves, he more than made up for in his strength and agility.

It seemed impossible to tell who would win.

Margaret wondered to herself just how long they had been fighting, and how much longer they could possibly last. Their skin glistened with perspiration, and every now and then, she caught sight of a stray bead of sweat flying off in one direction or another, and to her horror, blood was now joining it. But yet, neither of them seemed to be tiring or slowing at all. Instead, they seemed to gain more energy as the fight went on.

The energy of the crowd was continually growing, and if one of the men reached those forming the circle, they were thrust back in with encouraging shouts and pats on the back. Several bottles were passed around the group, which Lela pointedly made sure Margaret never touched, though all else but the children seemed to partake.

Margaret barely noticed any of that as she watched the fight progress.

Rafe had a cut to his lip that bled, and another near his ear, while Camlo sported one high on his left cheek. She could see other injuries to their faces and bodies, but nothing to limit their momentum.

She clamped down on her lip, biting back a worried sound as Camlo delivered a powerful blow to Rafe's ribs that made the entire crowd hiss sympathetically, even the ones cheering Camlo on.

Rafe somehow seemed to hear her whimper and whipped his head around to see her. She met his eyes, still chewing on her lip, knowing she probably looked as terrified as she felt, if not more so.

Rafe grinned swiftly, winking at her, and then, somehow sensing Camlo barreling towards him, dodged a powerful punch and delivered one of his own to Camlo's exposed lower back, earning a grunt of pain that had onlookers whooping in delight.

Neither took notice of the crowd as they fought, swinging and kicking and punching away at each other. It was an impressive display of agility and strength, and Margaret felt herself getting caught up in it. The speed with which they fought was incredible, and at times impossible to comprehend. Yet she could see every move as it happened, and the intensity from the fight was leaving her dizzy.

And this was supposed to be a friendly bout for sport? She shuddered a little. What would these two be like against enemies and not each other?

It was a terrifying thought.

A mixture of Romani and English shouts of encouragement and energy rang through the air as the fight continued, as Camlo railed against Rafe's ribs, as Rafe wrapped an arm around Camlo's head and repeatedly drove his knee into Camlo's stomach...

Margaret could not take her eyes off of Rafe, her heart in her throat. He was fiercer than she would have ever thought, and yet she had always sensed a vibrant energy to him, an edge of danger that had captivated her from the beginning.

Camlo suddenly wrenched Rafe's arm behind him, then drove him into the ground. Rafe struggled under the weight, thrashing and grunting against it. The crowd roared, urging him on, and Margaret found herself doing the same, the women surrounding her yelling louder than most of the men.

Suddenly, Rafe hooked his leg around Camlo's and sent him crashing to the ground. Rafe sprang to his feet, wiping the blood, sweat, and dirt from his face, and circled slowly, waiting for Camlo to attack again.

They circled each other slowly, and the volume of the crowd lessened with the sudden tension.

Both men breathed heavily, muscular chests heaving with every pant. Their bodies were fatigued, but their eyes still had an intense fire that held no trace of surrender or weakness.

Camlo offered a slow, devious smirk, then charged like a raging bull. Rafe swiped him aside, shoving his elbow into the top of his opponent's back as he passed. Camlo turned with a savage growl and came at him again. Rafe ducked and wrapped his arms about Camlo's hips, tossing him over his back and sending him crashing to the ground with a deafening thud.

The crowd held its breath for a moment, then broke into thunderous applause as Camlo coughed a surprisingly weak laugh and closed his eyes. Rafe bent over, hands on his knees, finally showing his fatigue even as he smiled, murmuring something to Camlo, who responded with something that made Rafe laugh.

Kem moved between them and announced something in Romani to the effect of an official declaration of Rafe as the winner, which sent the crowd cheering to somehow unreached levels.

Rafe reached down to help Camlo up, and the two clapped each other on the back, grinning despite their injuries. Both were swarmed by people, and took their attentions with good graces, as well as the bottles that were passed to them.

Margaret felt herself nudged and turned to look at Drina, grinning beside her. "Aren't you going to go congratulate your gentleman?" Drina asked with a throaty laugh.

Margaret felt her brows rise, and turned to look at Rafe again.

Gentleman? He certainly was no gentleman, if her experience had taught her anything. No gentleman would have teased her as he had done. No gentleman would have lifted her skirts to inspect her ankles. No gentleman would have fought with such energy for sport. And no gentleman would look at her as directly as he did, nor with such fire.

Perhaps that was it, then. She'd been looking for a gentleman when what she really wanted was... him.

As if he felt her gaze, Rafe looked up and stared at her. He fought a smile, still almost vibrating with the energy and exhilaration of his fight, which she had felt herself as it had finished. Her breath had raced, her cheers had matched the others, and her heart had pounded furiously in her chest.

Now it was doing so again, and she felt the rush of every exhale pass her lips. Breathless and unsteady, and delirious with pride, she smiled at him, letting it spread until she was positively beaming.

Rafe suddenly moved towards her, stealing a bottle from a nearby Rom and taking a deep swig, his corded throat moving on a swallow. Then the bottle was thrust back, and he was to her.

Without any hint of hesitation, he hauled her up against him and kissed her with the same energy and fervor with which he had fought, with all of the intensity and focus she had ever felt from him.

Gasping against his mouth, thrilling with the contact, Margaret latched her fingers into his damp hair and opened to him, clinging and wild and soaring, her feet leaving the ground as he pulled her closer still.

The crowd erupted into delighted cheers, but nothing could drown out the joyous sounds of her own heart.

The *pliashka* was quite the event amongst the Rom usually, and this one was no exception.

Miri was glowing and beautiful in her traditional raiment, and her smile, though enchanting for the rest of them, was only for Danior, who would look nowhere else. They circled each other near the fire, torches pitched in the ground around them to add more light, and the stark shadows of the evening and firelight only added to the magic of the night.

Rafe, now recovered from his fight, and its victory, and properly dressed, was slightly less recovered from his victory celebration with Margaret. Standing next to her, murmuring an explanation of what was happening, having her so close to him... It was all he could do to keep from carrying her off like an actual Rom was known to do with his woman.

Watching the betrothal ceremony was far more moving than it should have been. Danior draped the necklace of coins about Miri's neck, signifying that she was now betrothed. Rafe relayed this to Margaret, who sighed happily and leaned against him.

Rafe looked heavenward in a silent plea for strength.

After having tasted the sweetness of her lips once, he could not imagine never doing so again. Her response to him had been eager and willing, as if she had been waiting for it, which made him wonder what the hell he'd been doing all this time. It unmanned him how much he needed her now, somehow more than he had before.

It would have been terrifying if he weren't so damned thrilled about it.

He ought not to have kissed her, but he was not about to regret it.

True to tradition, the gathered Rom shouted in jubilation of the betrothal.

"What did they say?" Margaret asked, turning to him, the light flickering off of her cheeks.

He smiled warmly. "*Sastismos*," he told her, his voice more of a growl.

She cocked her head with a smile. "And that means?"

"Good health."

She nodded and turned back, adding her voice to the rest.

Rafe shook his head, amused and enchanted. Mere hours with these people, and Margaret was actively participating, joining with them in every way she could. She had lost any fear and trepidation she'd had at the beginning, and seemed somehow to belong here with these warm, free, caring people.

Yet she was the very picture of an English miss.

What a contradiction his little Margaret was.

His heart jerked as he realized he'd identified her as his. She was nothing of the kind, he knew that well, but he was as possessive and protective of her as if they were bound together.

A surge of longing rose within him and he was quick to shove it aside. Now was not the time, and the future stretched before them with too many unknowns.

The group started to dance as the music picked up, and Margaret watched in fascination, her eyes tracking every movement and sway. It was very unlike the dancing in an English ballroom, and far less refined. But there was something very alive about the dance here, something almost elemental that was quite moving. He'd always been impressed with the emotion within it, and he was a man who did not particularly enjoy dancing.

Margaret whirled to face him, her eyes alight. "Teach me!" she demanded. "Teach me to dance!"

He looked down at her ankles, now free of the wraps and back in her boots. "Can you?"

She thumped him on the arm firmly. "Rafe, I will dance a quadrille on your head if you don't teach me to dance with them now!"

He threw his head back and laughed, delighted beyond words by her threat. "Steady on, pet," he told her, still laughing, reaching out to rub her arms. "I'll teach you."

Rafe urged her backward, turning her back to face the dance, but keeping her close to him, almost touching. "You see how they move?" he murmured near her ear. "There is no need for space, only for feeling." He began to sway a little behind her, feeling the beat and energy of the vibrant music. "Do you feel that?"

Margaret nodded without speaking, starting to move herself, mimicking the motions of the others in a much more reserved way.

"Let go, Margaret," he murmured, wrapping an arm around her waist and showing her the movement. "Let go."

She surprised him by dropping her head back against him and covering his hand with her own.

His throat clogged and his hand clenched against her as they moved, still not flush, but feeling somehow far closer. They swayed together silently, a pulse thrumming through them both as the movements grew and changed.

"Circle me," Rafe finally managed, watching as the others did so. He moved his hand and gently pressed her around, and she followed.

"Eyes on me," he ordered. "Always eyes on me."

She did so, her eyes bright and her cheeks flushed. "Why?" she asked. "Is it bad luck otherwise?"

"Yes," he lied without hesitation, clapping his hands in time with the music. It wasn't entirely a lie. It *would* be bad luck for him if she didn't look at him. He needed her eyes on him, he needed to feel that connection.

She dutifully kept her gaze fixed on his, a small smile on her full lips. "Now what?" she asked as she completed her second circle.

"My turn," he said, moving himself. She smiled more fully at him, watching his progress. "Raise your arms." He helped her to lift them to the sky, taking a selfish moment to run his hands down her arms as he circled her once, twice, three times. He felt her shiver, even as she swayed, and the tension between them hummed to life again.

"Leave them there," he whispered as she started to lower them. "Now stomp your feet. In time with the music."

He showed her how, and she repeated it, something jingling musically as she did so.

Margaret's eyes widened and she looked down at her feet, then laughed. "I'd forgotten about that!" She lifted her foot and placed it into his hand, boldly revealing her boots and ankles, around one of which was tied a small circle of coins.

Rafe grinned and touched the chain, and the hint of leg exposed above it. "Well," he mused, dipping his finger under the chain, "it is a pity your ankles are not strong enough to take the boots off."

"Yes," Margaret breathed, her eyes flicking between him and his hand.

"But…" He hooked his finger around the chain and made it jingle again. "This means you and I must do something just as shocking."

Margaret stilled. "What is that?"

Her stillness undid him and he grinned at her. "Dance to something a little more lively." He turned to whistle and the crowd whooped as the music turned jaunty.

Rafe took Margaret's hand and pulled her along to dance with the rest, clapping, stomping, and swaying, moving with the rest without pattern or order. They stayed close, and met eyes often, laughing and touching and twirling, dancing with the tribe long into the night.

Eventually, the dancing faded, and the others wandered sleepily, or drunkenly, off to their *vardos*, tents, or bedrolls, as the case may have been. Some had rolled them near the fire, others had picked a space beneath the stars.

Rafe had done both.

He wished there would be a more comfortable place for Margaret, a spot in a *vardo*, at least, but there was not. And if he were being perfectly honest, he wanted to be close to her, and he wanted them both beneath the stars.

Kem gave him a hard look as he and Lela entered their tent, and Rafe nodded with obedience and respect. It seemed that Margaret had earned herself a tribe of her own, and any slight against her would be avenged.

As if Rafe would do any such thing.

Rogue, on the other hand, couldn't be trusted in any circumstances.

But Rafe was the Gent. He would never behave as anything less.

Margaret sat down on the blankets and bedrolls that had been prepared for them, leaning back on her hands with an exhausted, but exuberant smile. "I don't think I have ever danced so much in my entire life," she told him as he approached. "I will be so sore tomorrow."

He shook his head as he sat down next to her. "You ought to have told me," he scolded. "Your ankles…"

She was shaking her head vigorously before he finished. "Absolutely not." She shook her head once more for effect. "You would have made me stop, and I didn't want to." She laughed breathlessly and let her head fall back with a sigh. "I have never known a night like this, Rafe. It was magical."

She transfixed him, entirely and completely, and coherent thought seemed far too difficult to manage. "I'm glad you enjoyed it."

"Enjoyed it?" she laughed, lifting her head to look at him. "I don't know how I will go back to life as it was before."

Rafe was suffering from the same affliction, but hardly for the same reason. "The Rom have a special view of life," he said carefully, looking up at the stars. "Of creation. Of being. Of everything." He shrugged a little. "It is not for everyone."

"I like it," Margaret replied bluntly. She was watching him, he could tell, but he forced himself to not look at her. "Are you really a *poshram*? Are you part Roma?"

He chuckled now and glanced over at her. "Promise not to tell?"

She nodded at once. "Of course."

He smiled. "No. Half Italian." He snorted and laid back on the bedroll, resting one hand on his chest. "I almost wish I was, but I think the Italian in me suffices, don't you?"

"Certainly does." She tilted to lean on one arm, looking at him closely. "That fight with you and Camlo…"

He made a face, hissing a little. "I'm sorry you had to see that. Not very gentlemanly of me."

"I'm not sorry."

He cocked his head a little, his body stilling. "You're not?"

She slowly shook her head. "I was worried," she said softly. "I was actually rather scared."

Rafe moved to comfort her, but she wasn't finished, so he waited, hating that he'd made her feel that way just for entertainment. If he'd refused, he would have received a ribbing from Camlo and the others, but nothing more would have happened. Wasn't Margaret's state more important than that?

"But then, when I saw you fight…" She trailed off, biting her lip once more. "I was so proud."

The breath in his lungs vanished.

"You were so powerful, Rafe," she told him, her eyes unfocused and not seeing him at all. "I forgot all about being afraid, and just wanted to watch, to see what you would do next, and… I just knew that you would win. I don't know how, Camlo was so strong and so much bigger than you, and he *should* have won… but I knew you would."

Rafe stared at her in awe, absently counting the heartbeats that pounded against his ribs.

Margaret's eyes suddenly focused on him again and she smiled a bit shyly. "What a thing to admit." She shook her head, laughing a little and looking away. "I cannot believe I told you that. As if I could truly know anything about you." She frowned a little and looked up at the stars. "And yet I do. Does that make any sense at all?"

"Yes," Rafe breathed, unable to take his eyes off of her. "It makes all the sense in the world."

She smiled up at the sky. "Of course you would say that. You, who stares at me for ten seconds at a time and hardly says a word."

He laughed a little, feeling returning to his body. "You stared back," he reminded her.

A soft giggle escaped her. "Yes, I did, didn't I?"

The sudden desire to know more about her rose within him, and he couldn't resist the impulse. He knew her by instinct, but not by fact. He knew her temperament, but not her story. He knew who she was, but not why.

And he wanted to know it all. "Tell me about yourself. Tell me anything."

Margaret looked over at him, smiling curiously. "Anything?"

He nodded. "Anything at all."

Her brow furrowed a little as she thought, apparently at a loss. "I never take milk in my tea. Only sugar," she began, sounding hesitant and still confused.

He smiled in encouragement and closed his eyes, listening to her voice and the sounds of the night.

"I wanted to play the harp, but I could never convince my parents to purchase one." She laughed a little, and he felt her settle in a little more beside him.

"I love to waltz," she said, her voice filled with suddenly longing. "Before I had permission, I learned on my own and waltzed in my bedroom at night. I could never marry a man who could not waltz." Her voice was very firm by the end, and he could almost see the stubborn set of her jaw in his mind's eye.

"Keep going," he encouraged. "Tell me more."

"When I was a child, I used to sneak out of my bedroom and creep into the library to read by the fire. The only person who knows that is the maid who would put out the fires every night, and she made sure to do the library last so I could read as long as possible."

He opened his eyes, looking up at her. "And then?"

She looked down at him, almost as if she had forgotten he was there. "Then what?"

"Surely it doesn't end there. Did she force you to go right to bed? Did she tell you further stories of her own?"

She smiled and he felt the warmth of it course through him. "She took me down to the kitchens for warm milk and honey."

He laughed and closed his eyes again. "One more. Tell me one more."

To his surprise, he felt her fingers suddenly touching his hair, running through it in long, even strokes.

"I love the rain," Margaret whispered, her fingers stroking along his scalp.

His breath caught at her words, and he opened his eyes to watch her, waiting, wondering if it was possible...

"Sometimes I go out into it without bonnet or hat and stand there, letting the rain fall upon me." Margaret's voice dipped lower, softer, lost in memory. "I tilt my head back and feel the drops as they hit my cheek, and I stay there as long as possible, until my mother

comes and forces me to go in, always asking if I mean to catch cold."
She smiled down at him. "I've never once caught cold from standing
out in the rain, but I always thought it would be a lovely reason to do
so."

Stunned, he propped himself up on one elbow, staring at her
now. "I knew it," he breathed.

"Knew what?" she replied in the same tone.

He slowly shook his head, reaching out to touch her cheek. "I
knew you would love the rain. I imagined it. I could see you standing
there, your faced tipped back as the drops fell upon your cheeks..."
His fingers traced her features, memorizing every facet of them.
"Your nose... your lips... those perfect, tempting, sweet lips..." He
held his breath as his fingers grazed her lips, and he couldn't look
away from them.

Margaret inhaled shakily, her breath tickling his finger as it
danced past. "Rather... rather too full, I've been told."

Again, he shook his head. "No..." he told her. "No, they are
perfect. Absolute perfection..."

And then he was kissing her, slowly, sweetly, with tenderness and
longing, drugging his senses and drowning his thoughts. She sighed
into him, and her delicate hands slid around his neck, searing his skin
and leaving a permanent mark on his heart.

She *was* his.

More than that, he was hers.

Chapter Fourteen

$\mathcal{M}$orning dawned early for Margaret, and though she had slept quite soundly, she could not say that she would be recommending the bedroll as a preferred accommodation for sleeping. It was far more comfortable than sleeping on a slab of wood might have been, but she could feel several stiff and aching parts of her that were crying for a more forgiving surface.

Still, it was the most pleasant night of her existence.

Dancing the night away with a group of gypsies, eating until she felt positively stuffed… and that had been with Rafe stealing food from her plate, claiming it was a Rom tradition. She'd checked, and it was, in fact, but it had still been something rather intimate, if amusing. Watching the betrothal ceremony, seeing how Rafe interacted with Miri and the rest, it had all been so magical and she had found herself more drawn to him than ever before.

He was so warm and kind, yet he'd been so fierce and powerful before. He danced with energy, he listened with intensity, and his smile stole the breath from her lungs and the feelings from her knees. More than any of that, he was protective of her, and so caring where she was concerned that it constantly surprised her.

Had they really only been together for one day? Less than that, even!

She looked over at the man sleeping next to her, who had not moved all night, and would have been a very polite distance away had she not curled up against him for warmth. She'd felt a slight amount of trepidation after their conversation last evening, and even more after that kiss.

Lord, what a kiss!

She'd been rather fond of that kiss after his fight, so thrilling and wild and breathless, somehow both taking from her and giving her everything. She'd been caught up against him like the heroine in a sensational novel she'd hide from her parents, and she had never felt anything like it.

And then he'd kissed her again last night, and she had felt it to her soul. He had worshipped her with his lips, and she would have cried at the tenderness if she'd been anything but overjoyed. What feelings she'd had; what sensations! Her lips still tingled in memory, and she was suddenly anxious to repeat the experience.

But Rafe had been a perfect gentleman, breaking the kiss before it became anything more, and informed her that Camlo would be sleeping just a few paces down, and if they needed any additional protection in the night, he would be more than happy to aid them.

Which was a silly, sweet thought. She needed no more protection than the man beside her, who seemed so bent on protecting and preserving her that she wondered what he thought about the rest of the time. He had seen that she had several blankets, he had put distance between them, had positioned them closer to the *rom boro*'s sleeping quarters, had made sure the scariest Rom she could have imagined was nearby... Truly, one would have had to be a truly dastardly villain with some evil skill and dark resources to accomplish any sort of wickedness under those circumstances.

Or simply have a willing female.

That was a bizarre thought.

Would she have been such a woman? She would never have imagined it of herself, but her feelings last night gave her pause.

Suddenly, seduction seemed like a much scarier thought, because now she had an inkling of how it could feel, and what if her strength of character failed her?

She shivered, and was not entirely sure if she wanted to move closer to Rafe or further away from him.

She settled for sitting up, wrapping the gold shawl from the night before and a blanket around her. The fire was still flickering a little, but was mostly coals. She could feel the faintest bit of heat from it, but hardly enough to signify. Still, she stared at it openly, her thoughts racing fast ahead of her.

What in the world was she doing? She had run away from home, from society, from her very life, in the company of the man who knew her better than any other person in the world. She had associated with gypsies, danced in their celebrations, accepted their hospitality. She had spent the night on the ground with the man she wanted above all others, wrapped in blankets and completely separate from him, but she had rested her head against him, and he had not pushed her away.

She had let herself be kissed senseless… twice!

Worse than that, she would let him do so again, should it occur.

Her parents would be told of her running away, which was shocking enough, but no one save she and Rafe would know of what transpired after that. The rumors would work their destructive powers, and it would make no difference that she had endured a remarkably innocent time, she would be ruined. Assuming the word ever got out. She was not so sought after that she would be missed, and Miss Ritson would never announce her disappearance. She cared about her own reputation too much.

But it could get out.

She would be ruined.

The question was… would she care so very much?

Would it be so bad to be a scandal in Society? Her cousins would still accept her, they would just not be able to do so publicly. She had never been one for the ceremony and pomp of Society, and she would not miss the forced activity of the Season.

Her parents would never dismiss her; they didn't care about England and its statutes of propriety. They wished to live abroad as it was, and would only come back to visit Margaret, should she remain there.

She would lose the association of her friends, most likely. But she had so few of those, it might not be such a sacrifice. Rosalind would find a way to see her somehow, and she was the one who mattered most.

She could do it.

She could be ruined.

And yet…

"Don't you think it is about time for you to tell me what you are running away from?"

Margaret turned to face Rafe, now sitting up beside her, watching her steadily. She wondered how long he had been doing so, what emotions he had seen flickering across her face. He did not look as sleep-deprived as she felt, and in fact, looked rather too appealing for a man who had just spent the night on the ground. His hair was more tousled than normal and his voice was rough from sleep, his eyes were a little bleary, but they were clear and focused. He had a thick morning's growth on his jaw, which only made him more attractive than before.

He tilted his head at her a little, waiting for a response, smiling gently.

She swallowed and looked down at his hand, dangling from where his arm rested on his knees. She took it in her own hand, tracing his palm faintly with a finger. "Drina taught me how to read palms," she murmured, letting the warmth from him seep into her chilled skin.

"Did she?"

Margaret nodded, looking at the lines. She traced the longest one that ran down the center of his palm. "This means you have a creative mind, and think quickly."

Rafe shifted closer to her, and though she could not see his face, she could feel that his eyes stayed on her.

She moved her finger to the short line near his fingers. "This means you require freedom, perhaps you are a man of action rather than words."

"I can use my words as well as anyone else," he said, his voice rumbling between them.

She smiled and nodded. "Yes, but you are more demonstrative. Particularly with…" Her cheeks flushed, and she couldn't get the words out.

"With…?" he prodded.

Her throat suddenly clogged, and she swallowed with difficulty. "Matters of the heart."

"Ah," he murmured, sounding amused, "that is good to know. Go on."

Sensing he was teasing her, she ducked her face a little more, and moved to the short line around his thumb. "This says that when life is difficult, you keep going. But the breaks…" She tilted her head to count two of them. "These are traumatic experiences, something that affected your choices in life."

She looked up at him, ready to ask him, but his suddenly vacant expression silenced her. Obviously, he did not wish to share if there were such experiences, let alone what they were, and she would not press him.

Her fingers absently moved about his hand, stroking the skin softly as if they wished to comfort him for the wounds he would not share. She forced herself to focus on the last line, the deep crease that divided his hand down the center. "This one," she managed, finding speaking a trifle more difficult, "means you are strongly controlled by fate." She frowned. "I don't know if I believe that."

"What?" he whispered. "Fate?"

She nodded, keeping her eyes on the line. "Are we not controlled by our own actions?"

"Who is to say that fate does not have a hand in our actions?" he countered. "Opportunities present themselves to us, and we react how we will. Why cannot fate have a hand in all of that?"

His fingers were suddenly at her chin, tilting her face up to look at him, and her breath caught at the intensity swirling in their dark depths.

"I believe in fate," Rafe murmured, stroking the underside of her jaw. "I believe it was fate that brought me to you that first day all those months ago. How else could I explain being so inexplicably drawn to you? The light caught your eyes as they fell in my direction, and I couldn't move." His fingers moved up to touch her cheek, grazing over the skin there. "I couldn't breathe. You could have been an angel for all I knew, with your white dress and flowers, the way you tilted your face back to feel the sun… You laughed at something your mother said, and at that moment, I knew."

"Knew what?" Margaret asked, hardly breathing for the feelings she felt.

Rafe ran a soft hand over her hair, fingering the now loosened plaits from the night before. "I didn't know. Still don't. But… I know."

Margaret shivered at his words, somehow disappointed by his answer, but warmed by it all the same. Wasn't that how it had been for her? She didn't know what she felt, only that she felt it. It had been as powerful as it was sudden.

Could she blame him for not knowing what this thing between them was when she did not know herself?

She smiled a little as he laced their fingers.

"Tell me what you're running from, Margaret," Rafe urged quietly, covering their hands with his free one.

Well, she supposed she would never be ready to confess everything, so she might as well get on with it.

She found herself nodding without thinking about it. "All right."

Rafe listened patiently as she recounted the last few weeks. Her parents wanting her to marry, worrying it would never happen in England, Margaret's unwillingness to consider Europe for finding her a husband, and the deal they had struck that she could remain behind to try for another Season. She told him all about Miss Ritson taking over her life, and he had shared some observations on the woman, as he'd seen her a few times. Though Margaret had never considered Miss Ritson as a pinched and hairless cat, once Rafe described her that way, she could not deny that it was a rather apt description for her.

She told him about her dietary restrictions, clothing alterations, being forced to mingle with men of Miss Ritson's choosing, and rarely seeing her friends. She told him of all the additional unnecessary lessons she'd been forced to undertake, the modifications she'd had to make in behavior, and the criticisms of her person at almost every turn. Why, she'd even told him of visits to Aunt Ada, who seemed to regard Miss Ritson as a sort of peculiar insect, almost entirely ignoring Margaret, which was a pleasant reprieve from her normal attacks.

When Margaret reached the events of the day before in the modiste shop, and spoke of Miss Ritson's plans for her and Sir Vincent Castleton, Rafe suddenly wrenched away from her with a strange snarl of anger and distress, his face full of revulsion. He shook his head and got to his feet, striding a short distance from her.

She felt strangely bereft without his touch, and watched him carefully as he moved, rubbing his hands over his face, pacing in agitation, crossing and uncrossing his arms as he muttered rapidly in languages that Margaret did not understand.

He turned to face her, his expression cold and furious. "You are to have nothing to do with that man, do you understand me? Not a thing!"

Margaret felt tears rising and she bit her lip. "She wants me to make a match with him."

His mouth dropped open, then snapped shut, a muscle ticking ominously in his jaw. "No," he said in a dark tone. He shook his head furiously. "No, no, no!" he bellowed, not bothering to keep his voice down. "Absolutely not!"

"I don't want to!" Margaret cried, the tears making their way down her cheeks. "Don't yell at me!"

"I'm not yelling at you, I'm just yelling!"

A voice from one of the *vardos* yelled something back in Romani, and Rafe responded with something rather harsh and snarling, then looked back at Margaret, his eyes wild and unhinged.

She clamped down on a hiccup, swiping at her face. "I don't want to," she managed.

Rafe sighed heavily and ran his hands through his hair, then set them on his hips. "You can't marry him," he growled.

Margaret looked up at him, her heart breaking as she did so. "Can you stop it?" she asked mournfully. "He is the only one making any offers. If I don't marry him, my parents will have me promised to some European and I'll never live in England again."

He looked as if he'd been struck. "They'd take you away?"

She nodded, brushing another tear from her cheek. "My parents are not fond of England, and unless I give them a reason to stay…" She looked at him for a long moment, her words simply fading away.

"What?" he said softly, looking back at her with longing that her heart echoed.

A soft sob escaped her. "I don't think I could bear not seeing you anymore," she whispered, as a tear ran down her cheek.

He came to her with a soft groan, kneeling on the blankets and brushing away her tear with his thumb.

"All the people I know, every person I see, and you are the only one I thought could really see me. And after yesterday…" She sniffed and shook her head. "I don't know what to do."

He swallowed with difficulty, taking her hand in his. "I don't want you to leave," he rasped. "I love seeing you so often. I did that on purpose. I knew your usual patterns and I'd wait for you to come." Some days I'd follow, just to keep seeing you. It sounds ridiculous, even to me, but I couldn't..." He shook his head, then reached out a hand to cup her cheek, stroking it softly. "I couldn't imagine not seeing your face. It killed me when you didn't look for me anymore. I could see the change in you, but you stopped looking. And now, after all we've been through?" He exhaled harshly. "Now it would be impossible to go a day without you, Margaret." He leaned forward and kissed her softly.

Margaret leaned into his caress, whimpering at his words, at his lips, and she brought her hands to his face. He kissed her slowly, reverently, tender and gentle, with none of the frantic energy nor the searing passion of the night before. This was a kiss that said so much more.

Rafe pulled away, leaving Margaret weak and somehow more wanting. "Stay with me," he whispered, touching his forehead to hers. "Stay here and stay with me. We could do it, we could live here, and let the rest of the world go to hell. We could go anywhere, be anyone we want. Stay with me."

Do *what?*

Margaret reared back, staring at him, breathless with anticipation. And shockingly enough, considering it.

Could she? Could she leave everything she knew and be with him? Where would they live? Who would they be? Did it matter as long as she was with him?

She wanted to say yes. She wanted to go with him and forget the rest of it. She wanted everything with him.

Yet something held her back, prevented her from jumping into his arms forever.

Rafe ran a hand over her hair slowly. "You can't," he said after a long moment, sounding sad, but understanding.

She swallowed and shook her head.

He sighed and gave her a kind smile. "Your parents?"

She nodded, a tear rolling down her cheek. "I couldn't bear not seeing them either. I love them, in spite of everything."

"As you should, pet," he murmured, smoothing away her tear. "As you should."

"It's not their fault I'm in this mess," she reminded him with a sniff. "It's my fault. I am the one who cannot manage to secure a husband."

He gave her a look. "Did I or did I not just ask you to stay with me? What exactly did you think I meant by that?"

Margaret's breath caught in her throat and she laid a hand on his face. "You know what I mean," she whispered, the words hurting.

He looked at her for a long moment, and she could see that he did know. "I would if I could," he told her in a voice so soft she almost missed it.

She leaned forward and pressed her lips to his softly, then wrapped her arms around him, snuggling close.

Rafe enveloped her, holding her tightly and running his hands over her. He ran his fingers slowly through her loose hair, and then sighed again. "All right, we'll figure something out. Let's get you out of here."

She nodded against him, mostly because she couldn't do anything else.

The man she loved… *loved?*… more than she could express had asked her to stay with him, and she had said no.

What sort of fool was she?

Rafe held her so long she wondered if he'd forgotten he wanted to get her out of the camp. But then he kissed her hair and helped her up, going to speak softly with Kem and Lela.

Lela came over to Margaret then, wrapping the shawl more securely around her, then smiling. "A gift for you, *chavi*," she murmured, indicating the shawl.

"Oh, I couldn't!" Margaret protested, trying to take it off.

Lela seized her arms. "Yes, you can." She smiled as if that settled matters. She looked into Margaret's eyes and seemed to see far more than Margaret wanted her to. "*Ov ilo isi?*" she murmured.

Margaret shook her head. "I don't know what that means."

Lela smiled. "I know, but sometimes the meaning comes through. It means 'is there heart here.' To translate, it means 'Are you

160

well?' or 'is all well?'"

Margaret bit her lip hard, and shook her head once more. "No," she whispered. "No, it isn't."

Lela wrapped her arms around her with a soft tutting noise, then murmured in Romani, the words somehow comforting her despite not knowing their meaning.

Eventually, Margaret pulled back and smiled. "Tell Emanaia and Drina thank you."

Lela nodded, tapping her on the chin.

Kem and Rafe approached and Kem smiled fondly at Margaret. "So you will not stay, Margaret?"

She laughed, the sound seeming strange, given how she ached. "I didn't know I had been invited."

Kem inclined his head politely. "Always, Margaret. We are never here for long, but you are always welcome at our fire."

Margaret was touched and clamped down on her lips to keep from crying again. She was never so teary! She managed to smile. "I had a lovely time, Kem."

He smiled. "*O manusha khelevan tut*," he replied, bowing this time.

Margaret raised a brow and looked at Rafe, who grinned at her. "He said 'The people make you dance.' It means yes, this place is nice." He shrugged a little. "More or less. I think he's complimenting England, actually."

Kem glowered at him. "Something like that. Now you had better leave, Gent, before Camlo wants a rematch."

Rafe held up his hands in surrender. "Yes, sir, you won't hear argument from me." He offered his arm to Margaret, which she took, waving at Kem and Lela as they headed for the edge of the camp.

They fetched Rafe's horse from a rather sleepy looking lad, then rode back to London in silence, Margaret taking the opportunity to lean more fully against Rafe as they rode.

He did not speak, and she did not feel the need to make him.

They were going back to London. Who knew what could happen there?

She ought to have accepted his offer to remain, to run away.

Even as she thought it, she knew it was wrong. They needed to find another way.

They arrived at the mews without having said a word. Rafe helped Margaret down from the horse, kissing her brow and dusting his lips across her face.

She arched up to him, a sudden sense of foreboding surrounding her now that they were in London.

He captured her lips in a fierce kiss, tilting her head back a little and tangling his fingers within her loose hair. Margaret gripped the back of his neck, clinging as if for her very life.

"Rafe, I'm afraid," she whispered against his lips.

He groaned and kissed her softly once more. "We will figure something out, Margaret. Trust me."

She nodded, lowering herself back to the ground, gnawing at her lip.

Rafe smiled and ran his thumb along her lower lip slowly. "That mouth," he murmured, shaking his head.

Margaret managed to snort, despite the tingling of her lips. "I know, it will get me into trouble one of these days."

His eyes flashed and his smile turned devious. "Yes, and you have no idea how much."

Oh my.

Margaret swallowed and put a hand to her chest, wondering where her breath had gone.

Rafe chuckled and pulled her along behind him as they started their path through London again.

People were not yet milling about, but some of the poorer citizens were setting up their wares, or begging for coin, and some called out to Gent by name, waving and smiling at him.

"Do you know everybody?" Margaret asked with a half-smile.

Rafe looked a bit embarrassed. "No... but I do know quite a number of people."

She shook her head, grinning to herself.

Rafe suddenly stiffened and Margaret instinctively did the same. But then the tension was gone and Rafe pulled her into a clean and well-lit alley, a far cry from their forays into the city yesterday.

He cupped her cheek and peered into her eyes with the sort of intensity that robbed her of thought. "I need to see to something," he murmured seriously. "Nothing dangerous, nothing out of sorts, but something important. I won't be more than a few minutes. Can you wait here for me?"

Margaret nodded, but her heart seized up. He was leaving her? Alone and in the city? She was away from anything she knew, anything she was familiar with, and he was abandoning her?

"Margaret."

She focused on him again, realizing that her breathing had become erratic. "Wh-what?"

"You are in no danger here," he told her firmly. "I have a contact whose shop is right across the way. He can see us right now. He will keep an eye on you until I return."

"Why can I not wait in there?" she asked in a small voice. "Or come with you?"

He smiled a little. "Because, pet, it is not a shop that you should enter, and he cannot vouch for his clientele, nor his employees. Trust me, you are safer here. And as for me…" He stroked her cheek gently. "This is something that I cannot have you tangled up in. Understand?"

She didn't, not really. But if he was comfortable with this, knowing how uncomfortable she was, and with his protective instincts, she would trust him in this.

She really had no other option.

Margaret nodded slowly, feeling a resigned sigh escape her.

Rafe touched his forehead to hers, nuzzling his nose against her. "Thank you." He kissed her softly, and she could feel him smile as he did so. Then he pulled away and winked. "I'll jus' be takin' a walk, pet. You wait 'ere, and I'll bring you somefink nice."

Margaret laughed and waved him on, then leaned against the wall once he'd left, closing her eyes. London smelled far worse on this side of town, but there was none of the presumption of Mayfair, no false airs, nothing but honesty and earnestness. Criminals and depravity as well, she supposed, but one could clearly see those in this area. In the finer circles, they simply hid better.

She heard some bawdy singing from the street, whistling from the windows above her, and the laughter and indignant screeches of children. It was a busy, bustling day, and the city was alive with it.

Would this be the sort of world she would have to live in if she married Rafe? She had a fortune, it was true, but he had nothing of consequence. He worked in a shabby office and had no prospects. How could they live? What would they do?

Surely, he could be trained in propriety. He was a talented mimic, and a very quick mind. He would be able to pass himself off as anything.

They could do this.

Couldn't they?

Margaret's arm was suddenly seized and she was hauled out of the alley, pulled towards a dark hack. She looked up at the man holding her, a stone-faced, clean-shaven man with no sympathy in his demeanor, much taller than her, and clenching her arm tightly.

"Let go of me!" she yelled, struggling and flailing.

It had no effect on him. "Stop that," he barked, pulling her more. "I've told you trollops again and again, you are not to set up in these parts."

"I am *not...*" she started protest.

His grip tightened and he gave her a look. "That is not my concern. Take it up with the office. Now shut up and get in the hack."

Without waiting for her to do anything, he wrenched open the door and shoved her in, bellowing at the driver, who snapped the reins and had the hack barreling off before Margaret could say anything else.

In the dark, windowless hack, Margaret covered her face with a whimper.

How was Rafe going to save her now?

Chapter Fifteen

$\mathcal{T}$he moment Rafe left Margaret's side, he knew it was a bad idea.

He didn't have a choice, but he felt uneasy no matter which way he went.

It was an easy decision to make. The moment he'd caught glimpse of Sir Vincent Castleton strolling down this east side of London early in the morning, without any of the finery of his class, all of Rafe's senses had gone on the alert. He could not let him see Margaret, and he could not let Margaret see him.

And he could not let Castleton go about his business without any action on his part.

The conflict between protecting Margaret and loyalty to his mission combatted fiercely within him for a few heartbeats, and then his decision was made.

She would be well looked after if she remained in view of Cooke's store. He was used to Rafe's comings and goings, and when Rafe had given him the signal, he'd nodded in response. He knew what to do, and Margaret would be as safe as if she had been with him the entire time.

So why did he feel so uneasy as he shadowed Castleton down these narrow and crooked alleys?

He shook his head at himself, forcing himself to focus. This was a rare opportunity and could make up for the months of no information.

His mind worked quickly, tracking where they were and what businesses were nearby, any contacts he had, and the likelihood of any connection he might have to whatever it was Castleton had planned. None of the prospects were encouraging, but he had been in his position long enough to have cultivated many useful associates, and if none of his were unsavory enough for Castleton's plans, Rogue would certainly be able to fill in for him. His connections were always rather dark and varied.

Rafe traced Castleton for several streets, wondering where exactly the devil was taking him, knowing there was no chance he'd been discovered, but also clueless now as to the end goal.

A sudden twist of his stomach pulled him up short, and he looked behind him, feeling as though something was now shadowing *him*... or that danger lurked. He'd always had a sense about that as well, which had saved him at school and in his work more than once, and he was never wrong.

But there was nothing in the streets or area around him that posed any sort of threat.

An uneasy feeling rose and he felt his neck begin to perspire. He needed to get out of here and get back to Margaret. But he couldn't let Castleton go, not when so much could rest on his task.

To his relief, he saw one of his men coming down a nearby alley towards him. He signaled for him to take over, which was received with a curt nod, and then Rafe turned and bolted back the way he had come, grateful that he knew London well enough to take three shortcuts to get back to Cooke's.

Each step felt slow and sluggish, despite his haste, and his sense of foreboding only grew more and more intense the closer he got. He needed to get Margaret somewhere safe, somewhere he knew she would be protected and away from danger or strife.

He could take her to his home and let Davis and Callie mind her. They wouldn't like it, but Margaret would win them over the way she did everyone. Perhaps they could write to her parents and convince them of the horrors of her Miss Ritson, tell them the truth, and encourage their return.

Perhaps Margaret ought to leave England, despite her feelings.

Pain slashed through him at the thought and he forced it back. He couldn't give her up.

But what sort of life would she have with him?

He was getting ahead of himself. He quickened his step and made his way through the last few streets.

His heart was in his throat and he turned to the alley where he'd left Margaret, an apology on his tongue.

It died before passing his lips.

The alley was empty.

Rafe stared for a couple of heartbeats, then whirled around, glancing up and down the main street, no sign of a woman in a blue dress with a gold shawl, no cries of distress, no sign that anything was out of the ordinary at all.

His vision began to spot before him and he shook away the panic gripping him. He was a spy, for pity's sake, he had been in far more harrowing spots than this on a regular basis.

But this was different.

This was Margaret.

He snarled a low sound and went around to the back door of Cooke's shop, forcing his way in.

Cooke was already headed back towards him, hands up. "I swear on my life, Gent, I had my eyes on her."

Rafe gripped his friend by the shirt and slammed him against the wall. "Where is she, then?"

Cooke's large hands encircled his wrists, trying to pull him off. "I couldn't get to her, Gent. And even if I could, I can't fight Bow Street."

Rafe pulled back a little, his eyes wide. "Bow Street? A damned Runner has her?"

Cooke nodded, pushing at his wrists again.

Rafe swore and released him, turning away to mutter to himself, yanking his cap off of his head and throwing it against the wall viciously. A Runner might have been worse than a criminal taking her. He could storm any criminal holding, thrash whoever he wanted, and make any sort of fuss he wished about it.

Bow Street was proper law enforcement, and he could not actually defy them. Technically, he could order them about and do as he pleased, but not as the Gent, and not to the extent of breaking down their doors and pulling Margaret out of whatever office or drawing room they had ensconced her in.

Oh, lord, they would take her back to Ritson!

And she would try for Castleton.

Damn.

"Where did they take her?" Rafe asked, grinding his hands into his eyes.

"Dunno, Gent. Large bloke hauled her off like a strumpet and forced her into one of those dark hacks wif no windows." He heard Cooke shrug, and turned to look at the rotund man. "I couldn't leave to follow, but they left somefink quick."

That wasn't good. He hated the thought of Margaret barreling off to parts unknown in a completely dark carriage.

They would probably take her to the main office in Bow Street, and he would risk everything he and his associates had spent years building, and the wrath of the Shopkeepers, if he set foot in there.

He nodded at Cooke, picked up his cap, and left the building, a lethal glower forming.

It only grew darker the further he went, and people began avoiding him and his path. It occurred to him that this was a very rare occurrence, as no one was ever really skittish around him. He was congenial and open, under usual circumstances.

Now he would rather have a reputation for ruthlessness and the demeanor to match.

He had no patience for niceties. Margaret was gone, and he needed help to get her back.

The only people he knew that could do that were the same ones who had warned him about taking her on anyway. But their loyalties were infallible and they would be by his side. They would help him find the best solution and give him clearer sight, as his emotions were clouding his judgment and his vision was so tinged with red fury he was growing lightheaded.

He would find out who had taken Margaret and why.

And there would be hell to pay when he did.

He spoke with a few of his contacts along the way, sending them out for more information, anything that could give him leads on what happened, what was said, or where Margaret might have gone. He needed something, anything, not just the basic notation that Bow Street had her.

He couldn't help her until he knew more.

Rafe stormed into the office without warning, ignoring Simmons' inane protests and exclamations, and headed directly for the back of the building where Cap and Rogue would be.

He stopped short at the sight of Tilda sitting in one of Cap's chairs, looking properly demure and buttoned up, despite her usual outlandish dress. Her dark hair was pulled tightly back, surprisingly elegant, and her complexion free and clear of any stage makeup that she tended to don. She could have been any other lady in London, and one of high caliber for her appearance.

It was almost eerie.

She never called at the offices, and it faintly registered to be curious about that, but he was too frantic to think much of it.

Cap and Tilda looked up at him in surprise, and Cap's eyes narrowed a little. "Gent."

He nodded at him, then at Tilda. "Tilda, lovely to see you."

She smiled softly, her eyes twinkling. "And you, dear. You look quite done for, care to share?"

Cap looked at her in surprise, then back at him. "Yes, by all means, Gent."

Rafe shook his head. "Can't. Not in front of Tilda."

That was not the correct thing to say and he almost winced as the words escaped him.

"You can't *what?*" she demanded, her voice rising as she pushed herself out of her chair. "Might I remind you, Gent, of all your secrets that I have kept? All of the valuable information that I have helped you attain through my position and my connections, not to mention letting you use my props and wares for your needs without ever asking any questions, and *then* all that I do for your children that no one else does…"

"Tilda," Cap and Rafe said together, trying to soothe her as she marched towards Rafe.

"After all of that," Tilda bellowed with all the majesty she held herself with, "you *still* don't trust me? How dare you, Gent!"

She moved to strike him, but Rafe gripped her wrist in his hand and gave her a hard look. "Don't hit me, Tilda, I've had a hard enough day as it is."

She gave him a long, dubious look, then sniffed and stepped back, brushing off her prim dress and sitting herself back in her chair.

Cap looked almost amused as he watched her, then turned back to Rafe with a more serious expression. "As I was saying, Gent, please proceed."

Rafe opened his mouth to begin, when there was a brief commotion behind him.

"Who the bloody hell set Tilda off?" Rogue demanded from the doorway. "My ears are going to bleed." He stopped at Rafe's side, pretending to be surprised at the woman's presence. "Ah, Tilda, my fine flower, what a pleasant…"

"Shove it, Rogue," Tilda replied with a smile that would not have been out of place outside of a boudoir. "And shouldn't you mind your language in front of a lady?"

Rogue snorted. "Not when that lady is you."

"Save your flirtation for another time, Rogue," Cap ordered, waving him into the room. "Rook! Stop lurking outside to eavesdrop and make your presence known."

Rook grumbled loudly and pushed passed Rafe, going to lean against the desk as Rogue settled himself on the arm of Tilda's chair, triggering Tilda to rub his back soothingly as a sister, mother, or lover might have. Cap kept his gaze squarely on Rafe, as if he could dismantle him through his eyes alone.

He probably could, under other circumstances.

"Gent," Rook drawled, folding his arms and smirking. "Where's Margaret? I would love to see what she looks like after a full day with you."

Tilda perked up, slapping Rogue on the back. "What?" she practically squawked. "Who is Margaret? Gent, do you have a woman?"

Rogue chuckled darkly. "Oh, he's got something, all right."

"Shut up, all of you!" Rafe barked, in no mood for anyone's games.

They did so, looking at him with suddenly alert eyes, all traces of humor gone.

Rafe felt his arms begin to tingle with an odd warmth, now that he was faced with admitting his worst fear, and currently reality, aloud.

He cleared his throat and forced himself to look directly at his superior and mentor. "Margaret is gone," he said, his voice weaker than he'd meant it to be.

Cap straightened up slowly, his gaze focusing even more. "What do you mean, gone?"

Rafe rubbed a hand over her face. "She was taken."

"By who?" Rogue demanded sharply.

"Whom," Rook corrected.

"Shut up."

"Where?" Tilda asked, her still-young face hard with determination.

"Just outside of Cooke's shop," Rafe told her. "Cooke saw the whole thing. Says it was Bow Street."

Rook pushed off of the desk and left the room, his face suddenly furious and set.

Rafe looked after him, then glanced at Cap. "What is that all about?"

"His brother is at Bow Street," Cap told him. "Works for us, though."

Rogue groaned. "There are two of them? God save me."

Cap gave him a sardonic look. "His brother is Sphinx."

Rogue coughed in surprise and Rafe would have to consider Rook in a whole new light. Sphinx was the most brilliant code breaker, cypher, and linguist they'd ever seen, and were he not one of the deepest seated assets they had, Rafe would have hunted him down to learn from him.

And he was related to Rook? That was mind boggling.

Tilda brought him back to attention with a click of her tongue. "Cooke's shop is not a good area for a miss to be alone in. My girls have had some trouble there."

Rafe looked at her sharply. "How so?"

Tilda lifted an elegant shoulder. "Confusing my chicks for common street whores, picking up the less than honest working woman for minding her own business, poor treatment by the high and mighty..." She smirked a little. "It has not been pretty. Bow Street is fine enough, I have no issue with them as a body, but certain individuals…" She shook her head. "I would rather thieves took your lovely instead of them."

Rafe swore under his breath and turned to the window in the back wall, far too dirty to actually be used as such, but light enough streamed through.

"Where would Bow Street take her?" Rogue asked, his voice clipped. "And why?"

"My contacts are spreading out to get information," Rafe said with a sigh, pinching the bridge of his nose. "I don't know how long that will take, but Margaret won't have that much time."

He told them what he could about her situation, which didn't sound dire at all until he told them about Castleton being in the mix. Then Rogue and Cap sprang into action, each having their own network they could tap into. Cap issued several orders, none of which Rafe heard as he sank into a chair, weary and worried and desperately needing a drink.

"Gent," Tilda said quietly, coming over to him and taking his hand.

"Leave it alone, Tilda," he replied, shaking his head. "I can't…"

"If she got picked up at Cooke's, they probably thought she was a whore." Tilda squeezed his hand hard. "And I can talk to my girls, but I'm fairly certain when they pick them up, they don't take them to Bow Street."

Rafe looked at her, feeling hope flare to life. "Where do they go?"

"The Bounty."

That brought a frown to his face. He'd heard of the place, but it wasn't part of his usual haunts, nor had he ever had any reason to explore it.

"What is that place, exactly?" he asked, fearing the answer.

Tilda gave him a thin smile. "A holding place, more than anything else. Common drunks and trollops go there, as do missing children. Someone comes to claim them, or they stay for a day, and then are released with a warning. It's fairly innocent, all told, but…"

"It won't be for Margaret," Rafe groaned. "It might as well be a prison for all she's experienced. She's not nearly as bold as she thinks she is, and seeing a place like that…" He shuddered and covered his face with his hands. "I shouldn't have left her, Tilda. I shouldn't have left her."

He felt his shoulder being squeezed and heard Tilda tell him she would talk to her girls, then he was left alone again.

What had he been thinking?

He knew the answer easily enough, and it was not such an easy thing. He'd been thinking of duty and loyalty, and that had driven him his entire life. The thrill of the chase, the energy of being on a trail of something particularly exciting, the satisfaction of knowing he had the upper hand… All of those instincts had taken over, and even his burning passions and emotions for Margaret had been pushed to the background in favor of what he knew.

He didn't deserve her if that was his inclination. She deserved a man who would cherish her and put her above all else.

And yet…

He hadn't forgotten her entirely. He'd thought of her first when he'd seen Castleton. His instinct had been to hide Margaret from his sight, and *then* to investigate what the traitor was up to. What else could he have done? He would have never been able to forgive himself if he'd let Castleton go without setting someone on him.

But how would he ever forgive himself for letting Margaret be snatched up? And now she would be served up to Castleton anyway, because he couldn't storm into the Bounty and thrash Bow Street.

Or could he?

Something inside him snapped and he surged to his feet, overturning his chair with his fury. He stormed out of the office, down the hall, ignored Johnson's warning calls, and wrenched open the door, only to be pulled back in and have the door slammed in his face. He was whirled around and shoved back against the door, and an irate Rogue was in his face.

"Are you outside of your ever-bleeding mind?" he bellowed, gripping Rafe's shirt in his fists.

Rafe's vision turned red and he shoved Rogue off of him, the shorter man being stockier, but Rafe's rage was enough to unbalance him. "Shove off!"

Rogue rolled up his sleeves, shaking his head. "Not a chance. You aren't setting foot out of that door until you've got a clear head,

I'll not have you ruining everything we have worked so hard for over some impudent, wandering, spoiled chit."

Rafe released a roar of some dark anger and charged at his friend, finding himself swept aside as easily as he had done to Camlo only the day before. He was still sore and ached in various places, but that was nothing in the face of his crazed emotions now. He spun back and punched Rogue quickly in the face, then swung his left fist into his jaw, sending Rogue stumbling back.

Pearce squawked again, something about the office and the desks, but Rafe ignored him. The scrawny fellow was pressing himself back against the far wall, out of the way as it was, there was no cause to even acknowledge him.

Rogue wiped at the blood that streamed from one corner of his mouth, his brow furrowing darkly. "That is one shot I've let you get in," he growled. "You won't get another."

Rafe smirked at him. "That was two shots, Rogue, and I've got a few more for you."

Rogue's lip curled in a sneer. "Come on then, Gent."

Never one to refuse such a kind invitation, Rafe came again, only to have Rogue slam his elbow into his still-tender ribs, wringing a pained grunt from him as he tossed Rogue off of him and into the wall.

Rogue laughed darkly and gestured for him to come again, and that laugh irritated Rafe so much that he snarled and started forward once more.

"Enough!" Cap barked as he wrapped an arm around Rafe and hauled him away with surprising strength. "What the hell is the matter with you, Gent?"

Rafe seethed, exhaling noisily, a buzzing sound in his head, and feeling as though he had fought three of Camlo. He couldn't see straight and he wanted to tear the room apart. "I have to get Margaret," he managed. "I have to save her, I can't leave her there, I can't…"

Cap grabbed his shirt and yanked hard. "Pull yourself together, Gent! You are *not* going to Bow Street, you are *not* going to come at Rogue again, and you are *not* going to tear this office apart because your blood is boiling, am I understood?"

Cap's firm, no-nonsense commands were enough to break through his haze, and he wondered how he'd been able to pinpoint his chief desires so easily. But then, Rafe wasn't that complicated a man. It was probably written across his face.

He nodded slowly, and felt his limbs shaking as the fight left him. He grabbed Cap's arms as he inhaled sharply. "I love her," he managed. "I can't… I love her, Cap."

Cap met his eyes, and gripped his forearms back, hard. "I know, Gent. I know." He shook him slightly. "We will do what we can, but you need to collect yourself and let us handle this."

"You want me to stand aside?" Rafe cried, releasing his mentor and feeling betrayed.

Cap gave him a sardonic look. "Of course not, I'm not that idiotic. But you do need a clear head and some semblance of sense."

Rafe made a face. "That might not happen."

"Then pretend." Cap patted his shoulder, then left the room, apparently satisfied.

Rafe looked over at Rogue, who had watched the whole exchange calmly, and now regarded him with bland interest.

"Rogue…"

He held up a hand. "I don't actually think any of those things about Margaret, I was goading you." He shrugged. "I figured you needed to let off some steam before you tore apart the more respectable parts of London looking for her."

Rafe exhaled a laugh. "Thank you."

Rogue nodded, then straightened. "Come with me, we'll see what we can do until Rook and Tilda come back with reports, and then we can act."

Rafe followed, his anger simmering beneath the surface, wondering if he was going to be able to last that long.

But his words to Cap kept rising to the surface. *I love her.*

It was that simple… and that complicated.

Love.

Despite everything, his anger, his worry, his desire to storm into the streets, he found himself smiling a little. But only a little.

Chapter Sixteen

" '*E*re, you let me go, I ain't done nuffin'! You dirty crock, I'm respectable, I am!"

"Of course you are, now shut up."

Margaret winced at the volley of vulgarities the underdressed woman unleashed at the poor officer who had deposited her into the cell.

A very rough-looking, buxom woman next to her snorted loudly. "Respectable me arse," she muttered. "Mollie Grover ain't a respectable nuffin 'cepting a pain in the royal…" She looked over at Margaret with a knowing nod, and Margaret swallowed, not entirely sure where she was going with the expression, but also not wanting to know.

She had been here for a couple of hours, and only recently she actually been interviewed by one of the officers. There weren't very many of them who seemed capable and intelligent, let alone appearing to have authority. The building appeared to be a house from the exterior, but once within, it could not be more different.

There were large cells with bars, not unlike pictures she had seen of prisons, and there was cheap, uncomfortable furniture within, as each cell had space for several people. Each room in the house was a cell or two, and there were guards at every turn, large and silent men who looked as dangerous as the room of men she had glimpsed upon her arrival. She did have to admit, the eyes of the guards were not as frightening as those men had been, who had eyed her with a very dark sort of appreciation, while the guards only viewed her as an irritation.

She'd learned that this was an operation of the Bow Street

Runners, who were obviously spread far too thin and ought to be dealing with more serious issues than picking up stray females from the street. But she suspected that now was not the time to inform anyone of her opinions on the subject.

Her interview with one of the better dressed men in the building, a stern but kind-looking gentleman with manners and an expression that told her he had been in this position far too long. He listened to her very brief story, and her name had sparked a flicker of recognition, but then he'd returned her to the cell with an apology, as he had nothing else to offer her, and until he checked into her story, he could not make other arrangements for her.

It was the only apology she'd received, and one more than she had expected.

Once or twice it had occurred to her to lie, to give them a false name and story, but lying had never been Margaret's strong suit. Even with her parents, she had never been able to manage it convincingly. A stranger might possibly believe her lies, but without any sort of plan, or assurances that her deceptions might work, she couldn't manage anything conceivable in her mind. She hadn't mentioned Miss Ritson or any of the troubles she'd faced, as no one would want to hear that sordid tale, but she'd had the fortitude to tell him to contact her aunt when asked if there was someone he could contact for her.

Perhaps she could resolve something of this situation after all.

She sighed a little to herself, forgetting that she was in a room filled with ill-mannered women who were no better dressed than she had been yesterday.

The one next to her was covered enough, but only just, and certainly not politely. Two others were rail thin, the rest all excessively buxom, which led her to believe all wore corsets far too tight for their natural figures. All were over-painted, over-trimmed, and overly familiar with the guards, the male cell occupants across the hall, and each other.

The language was crass, but with the exception of Mollie, none of them had any airs.

One across the room was watching her with a tilt of her head, her filthy, matted hair slowly unraveling. "What are you doing in 'ere, poppet?" she asked, lifting her chin at her. "Yer not one of us."

Margaret wrapped her shawl around her as tightly as she could. "No," she said in a small voice. "I was brought in by mistake."

A dark-haired woman with pox scars laughed in a low, throaty voice. "Tha's what we all say, dearie."

The blonde one threw a dark look at her. "Bessie, bite yer tongue. She's proper, look at her, she's tellin' the truth!"

Bessie rolled her eyes. "Anyone can see that, Rose. I'm jus' sayin' we all say it."

Another brunette in the corner snorted. "I said it meself this morning. Can't a gel walk a decent street without the toffs suspecting somefink of her?"

"Not when it's you, Fern."

Most of the women laughed, but Margaret only retreated further into herself, biting her lip and trying not to whimper. She'd lost all of her bravery without Rafe, and what she wanted above all else was to go home.

"Polly, shut yer gob. You ain't had a man in so long it's a wonder ye still call yourself a whore."

"I've 'ad more than you, Annie Wells, and at least I've 'ad no babies from 'em."

The women in the cell tittered and laughed, and Margaret wanted to clap her hands over her ears.

"Oh, stop it, gels," Rose said with a wave of her hand. "Yer frightening the thing."

"Serves 'er right for not 'aving a proper escort."

"It's a pity the Gent weren't about to save 'er. He's the best at protecting reputations."

At least three of the women sighed loudly, and Margaret lifted her head to look around with interest, in spite of herself.

The largest woman in the room was fanning herself. "Oh, the Gent could save me any day o' the week, and twice on a Sunday."

"He'd need to save you twice on Sundays, Millie."

Millie cackled and winked, which made the others laugh.

Margaret looked around at the women, wondering how any of them knew Rafe, or how well. She knew Rafe was a bit of a hero, as evidenced by his saving of her before he knew her identity, but had he saved these women?

Bessie caught her interest and smiled indulgently. "Oh, you know him, do you? I'm not surprised at all. Did he play the errant knight?" She chuckled and sat back with a sigh. "He's very good at it. More than one young lady has found herself swoony over those dark eyes of his."

"No, it's his strength that gets them. Lifts them with such ease," Rose argued, shaking her head.

Polly snorted. "No, no, you imbecile, it's his sense of adventure. Captivating it is."

Millie folded her arms and gave Polly a withering look. "Oh, and what adventures has he taken you on lately?"

Margaret watched and listened as the rest added in things about the Gent, different aspects of his nature and behavior, all of which she had witnessed. They really had interacted with him, probably more than once, based on their descriptions. She could see Rafe doing everything they described, all manners and politeness, treating these women as properly as fine ladies, but with a smile and a wink.

Her cheeks began to heat and she wished she could unhear what she had heard, forget what she now knew, and go back to her ignorance. Humiliation coursed through her, burning and twisting her up in knots. Why should hearing about his good deeds hurt so much?

Because it meant she wasn't special. He would have done the same for anyone else, and had done. What if she had imagined the special treatment all for her? What if she was just another female that he could save?

What if she wasn't as different as he'd said?

These women around her were worldly, experienced women. They had no reputation to ruin, no family to care, nothing left in the world to surprise them. They could just as easily be a woman that he could love, and would more easily be a woman he could be with.

Had any of them gone to see Suds? Or visited a gypsy camp? Had they spent a night under the stars with him?

Suddenly, she didn't know anything at all.

What if she'd imagined Rafe and all his glory, and he was only a figment of her romantic imaginations? What if he was just like every other man she had ever known, only interested in what he could gain and the entertainment to be had by it? What if...? What if...?

"Don't let them bother you, sweet," said the woman beside her, her scratching voice matching her expression perfectly. She patted her hand with surprising gentleness. "I've known the Gent for years, and there's not a better man in the world. I should know. I've met most of them." She chuckled with an understanding that made Margaret want to recoil, but there was a degree of warmth in her eyes that settled her. "What are you here for, dearie? Don't get your kind here."

Margaret's eyes filled with tears and she bit her lip. "I don't know," she sniffed. "I don't know what happened. I was just... standing there, just waiting, and they took me..."

At least two of the women clucked sympathetically, the rest still going on about the Gent's virtues.

"Aggie, give her your kerchief!" one of them suggested.

Aggie shushed her, giving Margaret a half smile. "I would, poppet, but trust me, you don't want to dab your pretty eyes with my kerchief."

Margaret managed a smile. "Thank you for the offer all the same."

Aggie nodded, giving her a serious look. "Where did they take you from, then?"

Tears burned again as Margaret shook her head. "I don't know. I don't know where I was or where I am, I don't know anything..." She paused for a surprisingly dry sob, then looked at Aggie with pleading eyes. "But he'll come for me... won't he?"

The large woman sighed heavily, taking her hand again. "I don't think so, love. He can't come 'round here, he'd be caught."

"Caught?" Margaret choked. It had never occurred to her that Rafe... or was he just the Gent?... could ever be any kind of criminal, or ever have to avoid something for his own safety.

"Oh, there's a great many people who wants him," Aggie said with a sage nod. "No one comes here who hasn't been caught for something or someone."

"I'd like to catch the Gent," Polly mused in a dark tone that made Margaret shudder.

"Shut it, Polly!" three women said at once, as if the Gent somehow belonged to them.

Aggie clucked her tongue, shaking her head. "No, dearie, he must stay far away from here. Least of all to keep away from them." She lifted her chin in the direction of the others, who couldn't hear her. She snorted and shook her greying hair. "He can't come here, not even for a fair maiden like yerself. It would be the end of him."

Margaret had felt that, wondered it, but now it seemed to sink in. And oh, how it hurt. "But he saved me before…" she protested weakly.

"I'm sure he did," Aggie said with another pat to her hand. "He saves a lot of people. He may play the knight, but deep down he is just as human as the rest of us. Self-preservation reigns supreme, even in the best. No, my dear, best to forget him. You're on your own now."

She was on her own. She had run away from her chaperone. She had spent the night in a gypsy camp with a complete stranger. She was ruined, absolutely and completely. Worse than that, her heart was broken, ruined, and she had nothing to cling to now. She put her face in her hands and cried.

"Oh, love, don't take on so," Aggie soothed, rubbing her back gently. "Aggie'll look out for you, see if I won't."

Two of the girls came over to Margaret's other side, and tried to settle her, telling her more stories of the Gent to try and entertain her.

They had no idea they were only making things infinitely worse.

In the end, the Runners did not contact her aunt at all, but Miss Ritson. It seemed that Miss Ritson had filed her complaint with their main office, and they were to contact her when Margaret was found again, despite any protest Margaret might have made. As she was Margaret's chaperone, and had been entrusted with her care, they agreed to it.

What was the point of a young woman reaching her majority if no one considered her any sort of responsible adult?

All told, it was much worse than she thought it would be when she saw Miss Ritson again. Margaret had been taken from the cell, waved farewell to Aggie and the rest, and was escorted out of the building to a waiting carriage. Inside, unwilling to come into the building at all, was Miss Ritson. She gave Margaret a cold look, taking in her appearance from head to toe, without any change in her expression. No false claims of relief or concern, no raging exclamations of fear or distress, and no hint of warmth. She merely tilted her chin at Margaret to indicate she should be seated, then nodded at the escort to close the door, and they were off.

She said nothing as they drove on but stared at Margaret as though she could turn her to ice.

Margaret squirmed under the steady, haughty gaze. Her instincts told her to apologize for her behavior, but her emotions and pride bristled at the very thought. She settled for avoiding looking at her chaperone and being sullen and cross.

Miss Ritson demanded no explanation, asked no questions, and left no doubt in Margaret's mind that her life was about to get even more miserable. Various scenarios formed in her mind, and each was more horrifying than the last. Miss Ritson didn't even have to say anything, Margaret was taking care of terrifying herself into a panic all on her own.

When they arrived at the house, Miss Ritson exited and led Margaret inside, and it took only a moment for Margaret to realize that something was different.

She looked around the house, and then back at her chaperone. "Where are the maids?"

Miss Ritson raised one thin brow imperiously. "They are working, of course. Elsewhere. I did not think any of them should come to greet you, as you have behaved without respect or decency. And until you prove that you are capable of making your own decisions, you will not be permitted to do so."

Margaret folded her arms, looking at the other woman in disbelief. "I beg your pardon?"

Miss Ritson blinked slowly. "It is about time you did."

"That is not what I meant."

"Yes, your tone implied such, but I am choosing to put you in a better light than you deserve." She cleared her throat and clasped her hands before her. "You are to be restricted to your room. You will have no callers or social occasions but what I dictate, and you will have no correspondence, not even to your parents. You will be permitted meals, naturally, but portions will be diminished, as we had been doing previously to help your figure. We will be visiting your aunt Campbell tomorrow, and you will behave with perfection. I have no idea what folly persuaded you to behave in such a way as you did yesterday, but I attribute it to a lack of discipline and a want of propriety, and no doubt it is the influence of that Miss Arden. She is not to be welcomed here, and you will be very fortunate to ever see her again."

Margaret stared at Miss Ritson in horror. "Rosalind is a perfectly behaved woman."

"Then she would be appalled to be seen with you as it is."

Margaret looked back at the front door, wondering if it would be possible for her to return out into the streets. Then she considered the layout of her room and wondered if she were daring enough to risk escape through her window.

"Let me make one thing perfectly clear, Miss Easton," the older woman said in the coldest, most chilling voice Margaret had ever heard. "Should you attempt any sort of escape again, I will see to it that not only will you leave England, but you will have absolutely no ties or associations to allow you back to these shores in any sort of polite company." Her face was set as if in stone, and the sharp angles somehow looked more pronounced and stark with the fury radiating off of her.

Margaret stared at the woman in horror.

"And just in case you think the middle of the night might be an easy time for it," Miss Ritson continued, "I have a footman posted at your door at all times. And not one of yours, as they would all be far too loyal, but of my own. You see, in their haste to be gone to Europe, your parents allowed me to staff the house with any additional servants I thought were necessary, should the need arise. Well, it has arisen, so your footmen are no longer with us, I am sorry to say. And neither is your maid. You will have someone to dress your hair when it is called for, but I shall determine that." She tilted her head as if considering Margaret with kindness. "Is that understood?"

Margaret's mouth worked on an answer, and several new words she had learned in the Bounty that day were springing to mind, but nothing seemed willing to come out.

"Very good," Miss Ritson said with a nod, as if that were answer enough. "Go upstairs now, you need a bath. Dinner will be brought to you when it is appropriate, and the upstairs maids will see to the bath."

Summarily dismissed, Margaret turned and slowly made her way up the stairs, fearing that she had been all too hasty in her desire for home.

Several hours later, Margaret was dejected and forlorn, but clean.

She had thought of everything she could possibly think of to get out of her situation, had tried to convince the maids to have a letter delivered to Helen, but they had all been threatened with sacking, and they knew that Margaret's family was a very fortunate situation for them, no matter how horrid Miss Ritson was for the time being.

Her dinner had been sparse, her supper palatable, but she could honestly say she had barely tasted it. Her guard at the door for the moment was Horace, who looked exactly like a man with that name should, and the livery was ill-suited to him. He was clearly loyal to Miss Ritson, and therefore no friend of hers.

She was trapped. And even as her heart yearned for Rafe to come find her, to rescue her, she wished him far away. She couldn't believe in the man she had met and spent so little time with, by all accounts. He was a delightful imagination, but how could she trust in him? He could save her, but he could destroy her.

And Lord help her, she was not sure she was brave enough to risk it.

But he would never see her again, unless they managed a ten second moment the next time they saw Aunt Ada. Even then, she was not inclined to look.

Had any of it been real? The night before seemed like a lifetime ago, when they had danced beneath the stars with their gypsy friends, celebrating life and happiness, no worries or concerns to plague them. She'd come alive under his tutelage, and opened herself to him completely. She trusted him so easily, thought that somehow they knew each other despite their lack of verbal communication.

He had never been hers, he belonged to every woman. Any woman. Oh, he was the perfect gentleman, it was true. No one would ever accuse him of taking advantage of her or being any sort of scoundrel. But his solicitation was less sweet when it was shared among many.

Margaret moved to the window, which she had opened earlier to let in fresh air, and now the night sky beckoned her. The stars twinkled just as brightly as they had the night before, but there was much less magic now. They seemed to be dim, distant, and cold. She shivered and recalled the almost unbearable warmth from the night before, with the fire they danced around and the fire within her, rising and burning the closer Rafe had been, and when he had kissed her... She moaned softly at the memory.

That, at least, had felt real.

But she was an innocent, and he a man of the world. He acted for a living, in a way, and she had no deception about her.

She would be the easiest woman in the world to fool.

Silly, stupid fool.

She ought to have known better, playing with fire when her heart was so vulnerable.

She sighed as she closed her eyes, letting the memories flood her.

And then came the tears. Soft, painful tears that slowly moved down her cheeks. No frenzy, no sobs, just silent agony that leaked through every tear.

"Don't cry, pet," begged a warm voice, breaking through her reminiscing.

She jerked with a sniff and looked down in the darkness.

Rafe stepped into a sliver of light under her window, tilting his face up to her, looking earnest.

She bristled and hissed at the slash of pain she felt. "What are you doing here?" she whispered.

His face turned incredulous. "Seeing you, of course. Step back, I'm coming up."

Margaret stared down in shock. There was no way he could possibly do such a thing. "No, don't..." she protested, but he was already on his way up.

He easily navigated the nooks and crannies of the walls,

somehow finding a way up with ease.

Against her better judgment, she stepped back and let him come.

He climbed into the room and grinned rakishly in her direction, at which point she turned away, arms folded.

How could he be here? How could he do this to her? Couldn't he see she was not another woman for him to play with?

It was all she could do to avoid bursting into angry, painful tears.

"What's the matter?" he asked, coming over.

She sniffed in disbelief. "What's the matter?" she repeated. "What is the matter?" She whirled to face him, fury rising rapidly. "Where were you?"

He fell back a step, hands raised. "What do you mean where was I? I was looking for you!"

She laughed harshly. "Can't have looked very hard. I was easy enough for others to find."

Rafe shook his head, apparently confused. "I have been searching all day for you!" he insisted, taking her arms. "I have been frantic, all day. Then I found out Bow Street had taken you to the Bounty, and I felt..."

"Don't talk to me about that place!" she cried, turning away. "Do you have any idea what that was like for me? To be sitting like a criminal in a place filled with ruffians and whores, to be treated like a common woman of no influence or standing, to be patronized by people who wouldn't be able to go two hours without a strong drink! To be forced to wait for someone to fetch me home like a disobedient child, knowing they would bring me back to her and her plans for me... I have never been so humiliated! Or so frightened." Her resistance crumbled and she burst into those tears, gripping her bedpost and leaning against it for support.

"Oh, pet," he said in a rough voice, coming towards her. "Sweet love, I am so..."

"Stop." She turned back to him, shaking and furious through her tears. "Do not play the knight with me, Gent. I'll not be another one of your ladies to fall at your feet."

He stilled and his brows rose slowly at her words, and she saw his jaw tighten at the name she used. "Excuse me?"

She strode towards him with fire in her step. "What a fool I was to think a man like you was real. That I was special."

His eyes widened. "You are."

"No more lying!" she cried. "I know about the others! Aggie and Rose and Bessie, Millie and Polly and Annie… That is what happened at the Bounty, I learned all about you. How you play the knight and show grand adventures, how you make all women fall in love with you at an impossible speed, but how in your heart you care only for yourself."

"I…"

Margaret shook her head frantically, jabbing a finger into his chest. "You left me there! Alone! And now I am to be trapped in this room until she decides I am fit to come out, at which time I shall probably be forced to marry Sir Vincent because my parents will be told all the lies! And then you'll have your wish, Gent, I shall remain in England, and you may comfort yourself with the knowledge that I shall hate you more and more every day of my life."

"It's Rafe," he pleaded softly. "Margaret…"

She fought tears, and shook her head. "Get out."

He stared at her in agony, his hand outstretched.

"Get out," she said again, the words catching on a sob.

Slowly he lowered his hand. "I love you," he murmured.

She closed her eyes, tears leaking out, even as her heart fluttered. "Get out."

She heard him murmur his love again, then she heard the sounds of him climbing back out of the window, the faint scraping as he started down the wall, and then nothing at all. She opened her eyes, saw the empty room, and moved to the window to close it, taking care not to look down and see if he remained.

And then, after all of that, she sank to the floor and buried her head in her knees, sobbing silently.

Chapter Seventeen

$\mathcal{T}$he carriage ride to Aunt Ada's the next morning was silent, and Margaret avoided looking out of any of the windows, for fear of seeing Rafe.

Her sleep last night had been blessedly dreamless, but it had also been highly unsatisfying. She woke with as much fatigue as she had gone to sleep with, and her heart was heavier than before.

Miss Ritson had allowed one of the maids to come help Margaret with her hair and dress, as Aunt Ada was considered high Society, and it would not do to offend her sensibilities by being underdressed.

To be perfectly honest, Margaret was rather looking forward to Aunt Ada. She was harsh to Margaret, but at least she was honest, and she was familiar. This was something upon which she could rely, and she could nearly predict the weather by Aunt Ada's behavior. This, at least, would not change.

"Now behave yourself, Miss Easton," Miss Ritson said, as if Margaret were all of eight years old. "And not a word of your recklessness to your aunt."

"Yes, Miss Ritson," Margaret said automatically, wondering what would happen if she did not respond at all.

They were shown into the drawing room, which somehow seemed to have gained more lace since the last time she was here, and waited for Aunt Ada to appear.

She heard her before she saw her.

"Good gracious, why do I let myself be talked into these things? What sort of generous soul willingly takes tea with her ungrateful relations?"

"I am sure I do not know, Ada," chimed another voice that rang with sympathy. This voice was familiar, but Margaret could not identify it.

Miss Ritson frowned. "I did not know your aunt would be having company." Disapproval was etched on her face, but Margaret was almost beside herself with glee.

Someone else who would have to see this ridiculous spectacle? It was more than she could have hoped for.

She fixed a properly demure expression on her face and straightened up in her olive-colored monstrosity of a dress.

Aunt Ada entered the room first, looking as though someone had tried to dress her for the grave but had grown tired of the exercise. Lace flowed over and around her as if sprung from a fountain within her, and her frilled cap was slightly askew. The lace had no doubt been white at one point, but now was a cream with yellowed edges, rather like Aunt Ada herself, and the whole thing looked rather like Margaret's morning porridge had.

"Ridiculous business," Aunt Ada muttered. She glanced behind her out into the hall. "Don't dawdle, Tibby, this is interminable as it is."

Margaret gaped as Lady Raeburn followed her aunt into the room, shocking in her ensemble of pink and black, which so differed from Aunt Ada's blandness. Lady Raeburn was always one for making a statement, and this was no different. The fabric shimmered and tightened about her pristine figure as she glided, and it was impossible to look anywhere else.

Belatedly, Margaret remembered to rise and curtsey, and felt a brief stab of satisfaction that Miss Ritson had forgotten as well.

Aunt Ada tsked as she looked over Margaret. "That is a horrible color for you, Margaret. Who is dressing you these days?"

Margaret choked a little, biting back a laugh. "I am sure I do not know, Aunt," she replied perfectly, knowing better than to besmirch Miss Ritson.

Aunt Ada shook her head. "Tell me at least that you did not choose it yourself."

"I did not."

"Hmm." She sat and offered up her cheek, which Margaret

189

dutifully kissed. "I presume you know Lady Raeburn?"

Margaret nodded and turned to the vibrant woman. "I do. A pleasure to see you again, my lady."

Lady Raeburn inclined her head and sat, her emerald eyes clashing with her red hair in a surprisingly charming way. "Yes, it is always a pleasure to see me, Miss Easton. But I am delighted to see you as well, though I fear you are looking a bit thin. Are you well?"

Margaret heard Miss Ritson faintly clear her throat, and turned. "I am quite well, my lady, thank you. May I introduce my companion, Miss Ritson?"

Lady Raeburn looked at Miss Ritson with an upraised brow. "If you must, I suppose. Is she companion or chaperone?" She glanced up at Margaret with a daring tilt to her chin.

"Both, I imagine," Margaret admitted, smiling.

"I have been charged with aiding Miss Easton this Season," Miss Ritson said in her most polite voice.

"In her husband hunt?" Lady Raeburn asked bluntly, as she poured tea for them. "One lump or two, Ada?"

"Two," Aunt Ada grunted, sitting back.

Miss Ritson looked perplexed by the question. "If you mean in her desire to make a good match, then yes, I am aiding her in that, but also in her navigation of society."

"Can't have done a very good job of that," Aunt Ada replied as she took her tea. "The girl is still as much of a spinster as she was before."

"And I've always thought Miss Easton navigated society quite well," Lady Raeburn mused, handing tea to Margaret. "She is sensible and lively, has excellent manners, and she dances with grace and spirit."

"Thank you, my lady." Margaret beamed at her before sipping her tea.

"Miss Easton, be demure," Miss Ritson snapped.

Aunt Ada cleared her throat. "I thought that was demure, Ritson. She didn't misstep. I'm inclined to believe that monstrosity she is wearing is of your choosing, the way you order her about."

Margaret took another quick sip of tea to avoid laughing at Miss Ritson's expression.

"I advise Miss Easton on many things," Miss Ritson replied as calmly as she could manage, her voice shaking a touch.

"Of course, you do," Lady Raeburn soothed, "and it does you credit. This dress, however…" She sighed and shook her head. "I have so many gowns that would suit her better. I wonder if I might have them sent over? They will only require a bit of alteration, nothing extravagant."

Miss Ritson stared at Lady Raeburn in horror. "Oh, I don't think…"

"Yes, that is obvious," Aunt Ada interrupted, "but that doesn't mean you cannot start now. Take the dresses, Ritson, Margaret needs to look appealing if she is to land a husband."

Caught between two powerful women, Miss Ritson had no choice but to nod and allow it.

"Margaret, eat a tart," Aunt Ada ordered when Margaret let the plate pass her.

"Miss Easton is watching her figure, Mrs. Campbell," Miss Ritson informed her with a prim sniff as she took a tart herself.

Aunt Ada snorted loudly. "Yes, so am I. Watching it fade away. No man wants a waif for a wife, Margaret. Eat a tart."

Chastened yet again, Miss Ritson handed the plate of tarts back to Margaret, fuming.

Margaret somehow managed to remain composed as she took one, then gave her aunt a look. "I thought you wanted me to be thinner, Aunt."

Aunt Ada gave her a very serious and almost warm look. "I wanted you to have a figure, Margaret, not to become one. Eat two tarts or I will cut you off."

"Yes, Aunt," she dutifully replied, taking two tarts and earning herself a wink from Lady Raeburn.

Thankfully, Miss Ritson had a reprieve from being attacked as Lady Raeburn and Aunt Ada spoke of the gossip surrounding ladies of their generation, though Margaret was quite sure Lady Raeburn was twenty years younger than Aunt Ada, and Margaret was able to focus on her tarts. She made sure to take small bites, and sip her tea carefully, so that Miss Ritson would have nothing at all to find fault in. She was watching Margaret very closely, no doubt cataloguing her faults for a later berating.

They went on about it for so long that Margaret had quite lost track of the conversation, and would have upended her teacup, had there been anything in it, when Lady Raeburn asked, "What say you, Miss Easton?"

Margaret managed to not look too startled, despite her suddenly racing heart. "About what, my lady?"

Lady Raeburn smiled a little. "I knew you were not marking me, but Ada thought you were. I insist upon having you attend an evening at my home on Wednesday. My niece and her husband are to attend, as are Lord and Lady Blackmoor, and I believe your charming cousin Miss Dalton as well."

Margaret thought back on family connections, and if the Blackmoors and the Gerrards were attending, it was a fair bet that the Grangers would attend, which would mean that Rosalind would be there as well.

A chance to be with Rosalind and Helen in a setting that Miss Ritson could not control? It was too good to be true.

She had to play this carefully. She turned cautiously to Miss Ritson, fixing her expression into one of polite deference. "Miss Ritson, do I have your permission to attend the evening at Lady Raeburn's?"

Miss Ritson looked suspicious, and obviously did not want her to go, but she could not refuse a kind invitation from a lady of such standing, and she did so love Helen. "Of course, Miss Easton, it would be a lovely evening for you, and with such guests? You must attend!"

Margaret looked back at Lady Raeburn with a smile. "Then I shall attend, my lady."

Lady Raeburn looked between her and Miss Ritson with a frown. "I was not aware that a woman of twenty-two must ask permission before attending a simple evening, but that is neither here nor there. You are to come, and I will be sure to invite several eligible gentlemen that will meet the requirements we have discussed previously."

Margaret choked a laugh that she turned into a cough, and pointedly ignored Miss Ritson's curious look.

"And for pity's sake, Ritson," Aunt Ada chimed in, sounding

disgusted, "let Margaret pick her own dress. Your selection is atrocious. In fact, have Tibby send the dress. Anything is better than that."

They left shortly after that, with Lady Raeburn taking a private moment with Margaret to whisper that her "dear friend Mrs. Dalton" would be delighted to know that she had seen her today, which made Margaret want to hug the woman. Her aunt would be told of the situation, and perhaps Lady Raeburn would be an ally for her.

Aunt Ada squeezed Margaret's hands as they left, and winked, which was the most bizarre thing she had ever seen, but then, she was fairly certain she had imagined this entire day. Aunt Ada actually *liked* Margaret? That was a bewildering thought. But if her great aunt was friends with Lady Raeburn, there was hope for the old crone after all.

Margaret smiled to herself as she and Miss Ritson made their way out to the carriage, and something made Margaret pause.

She turned to look down the street, wondering…

A familiar figure leaned against a building nearby, dark eyes intent on her.

She ought to look away. She ought to sniff and turn back. She ought to frown or glare or something to show him she was still angry and he was not forgiven.

But she didn't.

She stared back, breathlessly counting in her mind.

At five he straightened up. At seven he tilted his head. At nine his lips quirked.

And at ten…

She smiled.

Then Miss Ritson barked at her, and she loaded herself into the carriage, and when they drove passed, she looked out of the window.

But he was gone.

That smile…

He could have taken on the entire French army and Napoleon himself for the promise of that smile.

What amused him, and made him wildly curious, was the fact that she had exited her aunt's home with a smile, which had never happened in all the time he had known her. The fact that she had smiled more broadly at him, particularly after their last exchange, was beyond encouraging.

But he would not presume anything. Not yet.

He didn't mean to follow her, not this time. He'd actually been minding his own business when he'd realized the day and his proximity to her aunt's, and wondered if Miss Ritson might have kept Margaret's schedule the same on certain things, and he was right.

Seeing Margaret smile again was a breath of fresh air.

He'd spoken with Tilda as well as with Rook and he now had a fairly good idea of what had happened yesterday, and he shouldn't have been surprised that Margaret would hear a version of his story and reputation tinged by the women of the streets. Truth be told, he rarely spent any time with them, and certainly never in the regard that they were prone to suggest. At least three of the women had been Tilda's girls, who were slightly more reputable than the average woman one might see there, but they were actresses, and sometimes even Rafe forgot their true profession.

But they made valuable contacts and never missed details.

Aggie had been invaluable this morning, once Tilda had brought her over to see him. Rose had added in some fine details as well, and the two of them led Rafe to believe that Margaret's outburst was one borne of embarrassment and shock rather than her own true emotions.

He thanked them for their insight, but doubted it was that simple.

There was some truth to Margaret's words. He had left her there alone, and he'd had his reasons. And Cap and Rogue would have shot him before letting him do what he wanted to, but he couldn't explain any of that. There would never be an explanation for why he'd had to leave her there. He did have a healthy sense of self-preservation, but not in the way she thought. He had to preserve himself in some regards because it was highly dangerous for him to do otherwise.

There were other women in his life. Dozens of them. Hundreds, if he were to count every single incident, and some of them were now in very significant positions in London's society. Some were at the very lowest, and some, he was sad to admit, were now dead. But they weren't romantic attachments, none of them. He hadn't actually thought he was capable of romantic attachments before Margaret. He'd always just done his duty and looked out for those he could help. Then she had crossed his path, and his entire world had changed.

There were a lot of women that he had helped.

But there were also a number of children.

And plenty of men.

There were people who did not even know he had helped them, some of whom were at very high levels.

But Margaret couldn't know any of that.

All she knew was that there was more to him than she knew, and it probably terrified her.

He had to prove to her that there was only her. But he failed to see how he could accomplish that while things stood as they were.

Her smile was the promise of what was to come, and he would keep that in his mind.

And now that he had seen her well and whole, he had business to attend to.

He slid his hands into his pockets and whistled as he walked the streets, turning a corner and seeing two of his children standing there. He tilted his head and headed in their direction.

"Sarah, Arthur, what brings you out here?" he asked, leaning against the wall beside them.

Arthur shrugged and thumbed his nose. "Me mark's inside, Gent. I tried the kitchens, but the cook walloped me somefink fierce."

Rafe tsked and looked the boy over. "Are you all right?"

Arthur gave him a withering look. "She ain't me mam, Gent. I can take worse, and 'ave done."

Rafe smiled at him and nodded, knowing it was true, and also knowing that Arthur would be mortally offended if he suggested he was not strong enough to receive some cook's punishment.

He looked down at the dark-haired girl tapping her shoe. "Sarah, your turn."

Sarah looked up at him with a strange look. "Mine's inside, too,

Gent."

He looked between them both, his thoughts spinning fast. Their marks should not be connected at all. One was on Rafe's traitor list, but a fairly mild character, and the other was simply an unpleasant fellow with some less than savory ties, and...

Rafe nearly slapped his forehead. Why wouldn't they be connected? But if it was getting to be more of a problem, he needed more stealth and could not let the children be so involved.

He glanced back down at them, thinking fast. "Sarah, see if the cook will let you inside. She might be more sympathetic to girls. Can you cry?"

Immediately the girl's big brown eyes welled up and Rafe grinned. "Perfect. Go and see what you can do. Ears open."

Sarah nodded and dashed around the back of the building.

Rafe turned to Arthur, who thumbed his cap back a little. "Arthur, run down the lane and give the signal. See if Kip comes around, and have him take over. If he doesn't, any of the others will do. Then you mark the movements of yours and report to him, all right?"

Arthur saluted and dashed off.

Rafe exhaled, his heart pounding. Between Castleton's odd maneuvering in darker sides of London and the suspicious meetings of others, something was in the works, and the familiar excitement of his profession stirred within him. The thrill of the chase never got old.

He waited across the street unobtrusively until Kip and Arthur returned, exchanged nods, and then Rafe went on, heading towards finer parts of London than he usually visited as the Gent, but he had an appointment with Rook and his brother, and it had to be done with the utmost caution.

Sphinx had his own intelligence on the situation, and rarely reported in person, but this was a special situation with far too many players.

So they had chosen a fairly neutral and safe location for them all to meet.

Rafe's home.

Usually, this was a very frowned upon idea, but Rook had

insisted that he and his brother could absolutely call upon Lord Marlowe, as they had all gone to Eton, and had even offered to schedule a duel for later, if he was so inclined.

He might have taken him up on it, if he thought they wouldn't be hanged by the Shopkeepers for making a spectacle of themselves unnecessarily.

Rook didn't know how good Rafe was with weaponry.

Then again, he didn't know how good Rook was, either.

He shook his head as he went in the back servant's entrance of his house, as per usual when he was dressed like this. The narrow, pokey hall opened up to the servants' stair, and Rafe glanced up as something creaked above him.

"My lord," greeted Rogers, his ginger-haired valet, who looked over his ensemble with a wrinkled up nose as he descended.

Rafe grinned and inclined his head. "Rogers."

"Have we been scuttling coal this morning, my lord?" Rogers asked, his voice slightly nasal as if he were holding his breath.

"No, just the usual." He shrugged and brushed at his sleeves. "Perhaps a little more than the usual, but no coal. You wouldn't believe how filthy one can get in my profession."

As he expected, Rogers stiffened and shook his head.

"I don't know," Rogers muttered, walking away. "I don't know, and I don't want to know."

Rafe followed into the main of the house, grinning like a fool. "You sure, Rogers? I trust you, I could tell you."

His valet completely ignored him. "I could have worked for the Lord Mayor," he muttered. "I could have gone into theater. Mother always said my talents were wasted on the mundane."

Rafe bit back a laugh and turned the opposite way from his dramatic valet, grateful he had so few servants, but such entertaining ones. It made coming home such a pleasure, when he was able to.

"Sir, you have guests in the library."

Rafe turned to see his long-faced butler, who was neither surprised at his ensemble nor ruffled by his sudden appearance. Davis was used to his comings and goings, and had learned to never expect anything of him.

"Excellent, Davis," Rafe answered with a clipped nod. He took two steps, then glanced over at the greying man. "Remind me where the library is."

Davis exhaled noisily, which made Rafe smile with sympathy. Poor Davis, it was such a trial working for him.

"I know where it is, Davis," he assured him, wondering if he would respond well to a patting on the shoulder. "I was only having a laugh."

His butler's expression never changed. "Very amusing, my lord."

Rafe shook his head to himself, and started towards the library.

"My lord?"

He turned back with a raised brow.

Davis kept his gaze firmly over Rafe's left shoulder. "Your ensemble, sir. Perhaps you should change."

Rafe looked down at himself, then back up at his butler, hands on his hips. "Are you trying to replace Rogers?"

Davis seemed to shudder. "No, my lord."

Rafe hummed a little in thought, then shook his head. "No, I'll go in as I am. This won't take long."

He turned for the library, wondering just what Davis was muttering to himself, and grinned as he pushed open the library door.

Rook looked like his usual peacock self in a sapphire waistcoat and silvery coat, his hair perfection, his face clean-shaven. The other man in the room was an older, darker, more reserved version of him. Their eyes were the same shade of green, and he could see the similar features, but they could not have been more different. The brother wore grey as well, but a very subdued version, far more typical of the men of London, and he looked as though life had not been kind to him.

If Rafe didn't know better, he would say that this older brother was a dullard and more inclined to sleep than think. But that was the genius of Sphinx. He was brilliant, and not a soul would suspect it.

Both men rose and bowed in unison, and Rafe reciprocated. "Thank you for coming," he said simply, gesturing for them to be seated and then taking a seat as well.

Rook nodded, then gestured at his brother. "You know Sphinx?"

"Only by reputation," Rafe replied, inclining his head respectfully. "A privilege, sir."

Sphinx waved his hand dismissively. "Not a sir," he told him in a surprisingly deep voice. "And you know full well you two have the more dangerous tasks."

Rafe smiled, looking at Rook, who was regarding his brother with a sort of amused irritation. Rook was a dandy, but he was a damned fine operative, and it was obvious he and his brother were close, despite their differences in personality and skills.

"That may be," Rafe allowed, crossing his ankles, "but only in the physical sense. Now, am I to understand you have some information I need?"

Sphinx nodded slowly. "I do. But first, I believe Rook has an idea to tell you, which will make what I am to tell you more interesting."

Rafe turned to his colleague expectantly. "Do I want to know?"

Rook smiled a little. "Your Castleton is a slimy fellow, which you will soon know more about, but based on Sphinx's information, you will want an operative within his home."

Rafe sat back heavily. "We don't have anyone available. I've asked Cap and Eagle. And Milliner. There is no one."

"There is no one *trained*," Rook corrected, smiling a little. "Which is easy enough to fix, given she won't need much."

Rafe stared at Rook for a long moment, putting the pieces together. "You have someone in mind."

Rook nodded once. "I do. Well, Weaver did, anyway. Come!" he called.

The door to the library opened and in strode Tilda, looking too pleased with herself, Hal, looking suspicious, and oddly enough, Callie, the one maid he employed here.

The men rose as they entered, which made Hal snort and roll her eyes, and Callie looked bewildered by it.

"What's all this?" Rafe asked, though he suspected he knew already.

Rook didn't say anything, and Sphinx was staring at Hal with a little too much interest. Not that Hal noticed, she was already sitting down and sketching away, spectacles perched on her head.

Tilda sat next to Rook, draping herself on him, and waved Callie into a seat. "Sit down, love, you'll need to hear this."

"Hear what?" Rafe asked of anyone.

Rook cleared his throat, and Hal looked up at Rafe. "Sir Vincent likes blondes."

Rafe glanced at Callie, who, it seemed, had already been briefed on this, and then back at Hal. "So you want to send Callie to work for him in the hopes he bites?"

Rook chortled and Tilda tittered, while Sphinx just shook his head. "He won't do anything, and Callie can handle herself, I presume."

"How's that? You just met her," Hal retorted, obviously not in favor of the plan.

Sphinx looked at her with one imperious brow raised. "She works for Gent."

That made the whole room laugh, even Callie.

"I can handle it, my lord," Callie told him, her diction as perfect as a London miss. "He'll be wanting a new maid, and I can manage myself. He's interested in your lady for her money, but it'll be me he chases. I can get close without raising suspicions and hear everything that goes on in the house."

Rafe smiled at his spunky maid, wondering who had tapped her for this. "You have been fully briefed, haven't you, Callie?"

She smiled back, ducking her chin. "I'm an old friend of Trick, my lord. I got this post on purpose."

Rafe looked at Hal in surprise, but his friend gave nothing away. Not many people in the world knew about Trick, let alone that Hal was his sister. But if that was Callie's connection, this could all work out quite brilliantly.

He began to slowly nod and turned back to Sphinx. "What is the mission, then?"

Chapter Eighteen

$\mathcal{I}$t had been a week from hell itself. Margaret had not thought things could get any worse than they'd already been, but every time she had the thought, it always got worse.

From not eating, to no social agenda, to no entertainment of any sort, and the only thing to come from the good behavior that she had exhibited was that now she was able to leave her room for two hours a day without cause.

Lady Raeburn had called three times since their tea with Aunt Ada, and she was always permitted to see her. Each time, Lady Raeburn had devised an excuse for Miss Ritson to leave the room and she had given Margaret a note from her cousin, and Margaret could respond. After the first time, Margaret had a letter ready to give, and Lady Raeburn had a very serious talk with her about what was going on, and let it be known that her parents had been sent for, but there had been no word from them.

It was the only bright spot in her days, knowing now that she had individuals on whom she could rely for a good account of what was happening.

Somehow, the servant situation was getting worse. The numbers were dwindling, and she could see it. Miss Ritson denied any issues, claiming they were all simply too busy to stand for Margaret's inspection.

There was something wrong about the house and way Miss Ritson was controlling everything. Everything felt wrong, and as she was so limited in her activities and abilities, she could not investigate the feeling. She felt as though she were living in someone else's house, a prisoner in some unfamiliar place with only strangers for company. It was unnerving and eerie, and Margaret found herself wishing there was a way to get word to Rafe somehow.

Her anger had abated, and now she wanted him more desperately than ever, which undoubtedly made her a fool and a coward. He may not be the man she thought he was, but he was a good man all the same, and she could see how he had not set out to make her fall in love with him. She had done that all to herself. All he had done was be there. And stir up thoughts. And dreams. And save her from ruin.

He was the Gent, just as he had always said, and he had never pretended anything else.

She had pretended and imagined quite enough for them both.

But could she have imagined the way he looked at her? Could he really have treated anyone else with the same gentleness and warmth? Did he kiss another woman the way he had kissed her?

She couldn't believe it. He was too good for that.

Don't pretend that all of those days of seeing each other didn't give us a certain knowledge.

Rafe's words to her echoed in her mind again, warming her and confusing her all at once. She thought she knew him, but could she be sure? He had not come again, but she had not given him reason to. She had no way to get word to him as it was, and she knew, somehow, that if she sent for him, he would appear.

And she greatly feared that if he did, she would know in an instant if she loved him still.

She rather suspected she did.

He had been there at Aunt Ada's, just as he had been so many times before, and the comfort that had brought her had surprised her. It was so natural for him to be there, so easy and familiar.

And she was positive that he did not do *that* for all those other women.

She shivered now, waiting in her room for Miss Ritson to allow her out. They were to go out and pay calls today, but she had not been informed as to whom. She doubted she would enjoy the experience.

For one thing, the gown she was wearing was an uglier rendition of the ensemble from Mrs. Andrews' shop, and the only thing to recommend it was the fact that the neckline was higher than that particular gown. But only just. It was a deep red, which she did not mind, except when combined with the black lace emphasizing certain parts of her, she felt like one of the women sitting in the Bounty. Her corset had been laced too tight, but not as tightly as that horrible day, so at least she could breathe without pain.

She could not move, but she could breathe.

Small mercies.

A knock on her door sounded. "Miss Easton?" called a low male voice. "Are you ready?"

She snorted softly and rose from her chair. "Yes, Horace, I am ready."

The door opened, and the burly man stood at the threshold. "Miss Ritson is waiting for you downstairs."

"Of course, she is," Margaret replied, sighing heavily. She twisted her lips, then looked at her guard. "Horace, do I look as ridiculous as I think I do?"

He glanced her over, then looked away, face flushing. "It's not my place, miss."

She glowered at him. "That's all right. You just did." She shook her head and strode past him, heading down the stairs and trying not to notice how the few maids about the house stared at her.

She looked like a Cyprian off to meet her protector.

Which meant she had a fair idea of where they were going.

Miss Ritson was properly dressed and waiting for her at the door, and looked her over with a bizarre sort of pride. "Yes, that will do nicely," she told her, almost praising. "Sir Vincent will be most pleased with you."

Margaret gave her a disgusted look. "Would it not be more efficient for you if I went in my undergarments? Then we could claim myself compromised within five minutes of entry, and the whole thing will be over, and much less expensively done."

Miss Ritson's eyes flashed and she flicked her wrist at the maids waiting with Margaret's bonnet and cloak. "Mind your tongue, or there will be no meals at all for the rest of the day."

"That would be a change," Margaret muttered as she tied her bonnet ribbons, feeling a jolt of satisfaction at the way Sally made a choking sound behind her as she adjusted the cloak.

Her chaperone's jaw tensed so much that Margaret was positive her face was going to break into a thousand pieces. "You are dismissed!" Miss Ritson barked.

The maids bobbed and vanished quickly, and Margaret folded her hands primly before her, waiting for the fury to unleash upon her.

Miss Ritson stared at her for a moment, her breathing erratic and unsteady, her eyes wild. She took two steps closer to Margaret, and exhaled shortly. "Let me make something perfectly clear to you. Whatever airs and authority you think you have, you do not. Whatever choice you think you have, you do not. You and your impudent quips have no influence on what is about to happen."

Margaret felt the first twinges of fear as she watched her composed chaperone grow colder and crueler in expression and being than ever before.

The lines on Miss Ritson's face became more pronounced somehow. "We are going to take tea with Sir Vincent Castleton, who has an interest in you. A very marked interest. You will behave yourself with all of the training that your parents and I have instilled in you. To his credit, Sir Vincent knows of your escapade and somehow still has an interest, perhaps even more now than before. He is being very generous. And when he offers for you, you will accept."

Margaret lifted her chin and swallowed, despite her suddenly quivering insides. "I will not."

"You will," Miss Ritson reiterated, taking another step closer. "You will marry Sir Vincent, because after your parents hear the story, and after I tell them all of Sir Vincent's virtues and how he still will have you after such shocking behavior, they will jump at the chance." She smiled tightly, her face stretching with the effort. "And they will pay me handsomely for my efforts, which is why I took up this ridiculous endeavor in the first place. Imagine a woman unable to secure a husband with a fortune like yours. Not that anyone would suspect it is so grand, which is the most ridiculous part of it. Your family has wealth beyond measure and they don't even act like it. Nothing at all to show for it, and it is offensive to witness."

Margaret stared at Miss Ritson in horror, not that the other woman would notice. She seemed to be staring through Margaret rather than at her, and appeared to not even notice the words she spoke.

"Your parents are fools, but they will learn. And when they see the match I have settled for you, they will be so grateful." Her smiled turned whimsical, and it was a frightening sight. "I cannot imagine the gratitude they might bestow upon me."

The foyer remained silent after her speech, and Margaret waited for her to collect herself, her mind whirling. This was all about money, and plenty of it. Margaret knew they were different in their lifestyle, how their finery was not extravagant or elaborate, and how she did not behave as an heiress might, but she had never seen that as any sort of detriment. Miss Ritson was fixated on the reward she expected, and on Margaret's match with Sir Vincent, and those two things drove her.

Control, money, and the match.

It made no sense, Margaret thought as Miss Ritson came to herself and led her into the coach. Why would an older, plain woman of no means herself be so concerned with things of such a nature? There were more profitable ways of earning an income, and it was not as though the Eastons would settle an annuity on her after all of this. What, precisely, did Miss Ritson expect?

As they drove through Mayfair, Margaret pondered the situation with care. She suspected that if she'd had a brother, Miss Ritson might have tried to marry him in order to gain the fortune she apparently desired. It was a disturbing thought, but Margaret had an inkling that any brother of hers would have been appalled by the thought and never so idiotic.

And no brother of hers would have allowed her to consider Sir Vincent as any sort of prospect.

Before she could reach any conclusion about anything, they had arrived at the respectable residence of the man in question, though she knew full well that what occurred inside was not at all respectable.

Rumors sprang into her mind and she could not suppress the shudder that coursed through her.

"Get up there, girl, or I will drag you. In public." Miss Ritson jabbed her in the back, and Margaret moved forward, determined to be perfectly behaved as any proper London miss would be. Calm, collected, and cold.

Perhaps she could put him off with her demeanor.

They were let into the house directly after the first knock, and a wiry old butler showed them into a sparsely decorated drawing room, then departed without a word.

"Lovely decorating, even for a man," Miss Ritson praised as she looked about. "This would do nicely for you."

Margaret stared around at the pale pink walls, the paper faded and peeling in places, and the furniture scattered about, looking as though it had come from the last century and had not been used since. There were no paintings, no cushions, and the ceilings bore so many cobwebs that she wondered where the details of the crown moldings actually began.

This was not lovely. This was disgusting.

The door to the room opened and in came Sir Vincent, his hair greying but for the top, where there was none, his cheeks sagging almost below his jawline, and his stomach so paunchy it was evidence of his tendency to drink, particularly when combined with his overly ruddy complexion. His dark eyes held no warmth and seemed to be in a constant leer, made more uncomfortable by the pox scar above one brow. His half smile was directed at her and he bowed so that his eyes would line up perfectly with her neckline, which was where his eyes focused.

"Miss Easton, it is a pleasure to make your acquaintance at last. Thank you for calling upon me."

He took her hand in his and pressed cold lips to her knuckles, lingering far too long, and tickling against her glove in an uncomfortable way.

"Thank you for the invitation," she said, with as much politeness as she could.

He smiled at her décolletage again, and sat himself beside her. "Not at all, not at all. I have sent for some tea, will you take some?"

"Of course." She introduced him to Miss Ritson quickly, but he never looked anywhere but at her.

"You are such a lovely woman," he murmured, interrupting some polite conversation she was attempting, his voice dipping as his eyes raked her with dark appreciation. "Such a perfect picture of everything an English girl ought to be. Beautiful beyond compare, and tempting… So tempting…"

Margaret's eyes widened and she flicked her eyes to Miss Ritson, who was watching with satisfaction.

"Sir Vincent," Margaret protested as he scooted closer to her. "Really, I do not know you well, and I think such flattery might be premature."

And unwelcome. And disgraceful. And…

His hand was suddenly tracing her neckline, the fingers grazing the skin a little, making her jump. "I think we could know each other much better, my dear," he told her, his eyes widening as his fingers moved. "I think prematurity can be a blessing in disguise. And I also think I need to taste you, my flower, before I go mad with wanting."

He leaned forward and Margaret reared back with a squeal. "Sir Vincent, no!"

The door opened suddenly and a tall maid entered, eyes low, apparently distracted. "Windows, shelves, draperies," she whispered to herself firmly, as if from memory. "Windows, shelves…"

Sir Vincent sat back, his hand dropping from Margaret's dress, which Margaret adjusted quickly, yanking it higher than it was meant to be, popping a few threads, and earning her a throat clearing from Miss Ritson, which she pointedly ignored.

"Callie," Sir Vincent called out, his voice tinged with a new interest that Margaret was grateful for.

The maid jerked and looked at him, eyes wide and horrified. "Sir! I didna mean… I didna know the room was in use…" She turned and went to leave.

"No, no, Callie, stay," Sir Vincent told her, his large head moving as he eyed her entire figure. "Stay and see to your tasks. The work must be completed, after all."

Callie nodded obediently, then moved to the shelves behind Margaret and began to clean them.

Sir Vincent looked at Margaret once more, but his eyes kept moving back to Callie. "Now, my dear Miss Easton, where were we?"

Margaret swallowed and barely avoided wringing her hands together. "You were about to tell me more of yourself, sir, so that I might know you better."

"Was I?" he mused distractedly, watching Callie. "How remiss. I come from Dorset, my dove, and have a fine estate there…"

Thankfully, Sir Vincent enjoyed talking as much as he enjoyed leering, and his conversation was longwinded and one-sided, allowing Margaret to take her bland tea in silence. Callie continued about her work, and Sir Vincent frequently lost his train of thought, which Margaret was only too glad to assist with resetting.

Miss Ritson was growing more and more disgruntled by the minute, and Margaret caught her glaring at the maid more than seemed appropriate, but as it was not her home, she could not very well order Callie out, particularly when her master had indicated his wish that she stay.

Margaret was considering hiring Callie for herself when her parents and sanity returned to her life. Her arrival had saved her, and she was not about to forget it. And as she watched the maid herself, she suspected she was not quite so simple-minded as she seemed. She had moved on to the windows, and had washed the same pane three times now, lingering as if her life depended upon that window, which probably had not been clean in twenty years.

Callie apparently heard nothing of their conversation, as she continually hummed or spoke softly to herself, but once or twice, Margaret swore the girl looked at her, and that was certainly not a maid's usual behavior.

A knock came at the door and Sir Vincent, pulled from his view of Callie's backside or Margaret's neckline, looked towards it.

The butler entered and came to him, speaking softly, and Sir Vincent's entire demeanor changed. Gone was the leering profligate of a man, and a cold, calculated anger appeared. She saw him look at Miss Ritson, whose expression did not change, and then back to his butler, nodding.

The butler vanished, and a tall, dark Rom appeared in the door, a jagged scar on his cheek, and a glittering earring in one ear. He folded his arms, which became more muscled than one might have thought, and a dagger on his belt came into view. He looked at Sir Vincent with an impatient air, and Sir Vincent glared in return.

Then he turned to Margaret with a heavy sigh that did not fool her for a moment. "My dear Margaret, I fear business has come up and I must end our interlude." He slid her glove off of one hand and rained wet kisses upon her hand, palm, and wrist. "But I trust I may receive you again? Perhaps… more privately?"

Bile rose in Margaret's throat and she pulled her hand away firmly. "Perhaps," she said in a tone that indicated she rather thought hell would freeze over before that occurred.

He missed the tone and smiled indulgently. "Ah, my dove, you are a spirited one. I love a woman with spirit. It is so… invigorating."

He leaned in and pressed an equally wet kiss to her earlobe, inhaling sharply. "I so look forward to our private time, Margaret," he whispered against her skin.

Callie let loose with an expletive of shocking nature as she dropped the tea tray she had suddenly decided to move, and Margaret took the opportunity to spring from her seat, as if to avoid the remains of the tea.

"Clumsy fool!" Miss Ritson shrieked, whirling on the girl. "How dare you…"

"Ritson," Sir Vincent snapped, "do shut up. Callie is my maid, and I will not see her maligned by you for finding misstep." He came to Callie and ran a soothing hand too far down her back. "Not to worry, Callie. Just clean it up, and we will forget it ever happened."

Callie sniffled and wiped at her eyes with the rag from the windows. "Y-yes, sir," she stammered. She flicked her eyes to Margaret, standing a bit away, and winked.

Margaret hid a smile, and tipped her chin in the barest hint of a nod.

"Come, Miss Easton," Miss Ritson ordered, her tone clipped. "We must leave Sir Vincent to his business." She swept from the room, moving past the Rom without any trepidation at all.

Margaret hurried after her, wishing to avoid any further attentions from Sir Vincent, and found the Rom standing too close to the door for her to move easily.

"Excuse me," she murmured, daring to look up at him.

His eyes were hard and unfeeling, but he took half a step back for her, his eyes speculative, and then moved into the room that she had vacated and closed the door sharply.

Margaret exhaled slowly as a repulsed shudder rang through her. The butler brought her cloak and bonnet, and she hurriedly fixed them, then followed Miss Ritson out.

"That went well," Miss Ritson said, almost to herself. "But for the stupid maid, we might have gotten somewhere."

Margaret said nothing, tears welling as she glanced down the street.

Her eyes trained on a boy leaning against the wall of Sir Vincent's house just a few feet to her right. His cap was lowered, but he tilted his head up to look at her for a moment, and she recognized him at once.

Jamie.

She glanced at Miss Ritson, now climbing into the carriage. Margaret leaned closer to Jamie, pretending to adjust her gloves. "Something is wrong, Jamie," she whispered. "Tell him something is terribly, terribly wrong."

She moved on into the carriage, but she heard the soft, short whistle from behind her, and felt a little more at ease.

Rafe would be told of her warning, and perhaps he would do something. Save her, kill him, have Miss Ritson abducted, any of the alternatives were good ones. She only needed him to know, and perhaps in the warning, he would know she trusted him.

"Your behavior was not at all encouraging," Miss Ritson scolded as the carriage moved. "You might have offended Sir Vincent the way you acted."

Margaret kept her eyes lowered and her jaw locked. She would not respond beyond what she had to, and she was only grateful Lady Raeburn's evening tomorrow night was still on the agenda. She was running out of time.

"He *kissed* her?"

"Gent, sit down."

He whirled to face Rogue, wondering where his friend had gone and why he was so calm. "Are you hearing the same report I am, Rogue?"

Rogue met his look calmly. "Yes. Callie saved Margaret from being ruined and from anything truly damaging twice, and managed to distract Sir Vincent enough to keep the visit relatively painless. I'd say that deserves a commendation, and you are focused on some flabby codger taking a small liberty with your woman?" He shook his head slowly and looked over at Callie, who stood before them both. "I'm sorry, Callie, Gent's a bit single-minded."

Rafe looked at Callie, feeling a little ashamed. "I'm sorry, Callie. Thank you for intervening."

She smiled back, shrugging. "It was nothing, really. Sir Vincent doesn't get involved with servants, finds it beneath his dignity. He might have roving hands, but they don't go nowhere in particular. He can look, but he can't touch. Your Miss Margaret handled herself beautifully. Nary a tremor, my lord, and that's the truth."

Rogue snorted. "Don't call him 'my lord' here. He's got airs enough as it is."

Rafe shook his head, still filled with furious rage about the whole situation and what Margaret had endured at the hands of that blackguard, but he could see that Rogue was right. It could have been so much worse but for Callie.

"I'd best be getting back," Callie said, straightening up. "There's another meeting tonight, probably like the one two days ago."

Rafe nodded, focusing his mind on the task at hand. Installing Callie into the house had been a brilliant move, and he hated that he hadn't thought of something like that before. Sir Vincent was not the ringleader of their traitors, but he was highly placed. He frequently met with some of the others, and only Callie had been able to tell them details of those meetings, as she was permitted absolutely everywhere in the house.

The men wanted to overthrow the French government with someone else, and it was sounding more and more like Sieyès was their candidate. Whether the old man knew that or not was not known, and he hardly seemed the type to bring about an uprising. But he was in Brussels, and no one spoke of Belgium at all. What they did know was that each man entering a meeting of this kind repeated

Sieyès' famed phrase from the Revolution deposition: *"J'ai vécu."* I lived.

If that did not show their indication, he didn't know what else would.

The Shopkeepers had been informed, and the decision had come to let the group continue to meet without intervention until they could get more information about actual activities or events. This was only one small group of British supporters, who knew what else lay in wait?

And as no one had been harmed by their actions yet, they were not giving them reason to act quickly.

Rafe disagreed, but he followed direct orders. He might take opportunity to have some of their less than reputable contacts thrash Sir Vincent to within an inch of his life, but he would let him continue to meet with the traitors until the day they could take them all down and bring them to justice.

But if he touched Margaret one more time, he was going to take matters into his own hands. Literally.

Callie left the room, and before Rafe could sit down, Jamie entered, looking dirtier than normal.

Rogue lifted a brow. "Chimney sweep today, Jamie?"

Jamie shrugged. "Got me in, didn't it?"

Rogue nodded his acceptance, and waved for him to go on.

Jamie looked at Rafe with serious eyes. "I followed your Miss Margaret, Gent, and I was wif her this morning at Sir Vincent's."

Rafe sank into a chair and groaned, not sure he could bear hearing more. "What is it now?"

"She saw me, and says I'm to tell you somefink is 'terribly, terribly wrong'." Jamie shrugged and scratched his nose. "She seemed a mite upset, sir, and I 'ung around to see what might be the trouble, and Miss Callie got sent from the room when the Rom went in…"

Rafe's head snapped up and he stared at Jamie for a long moment, then glanced at Rogue briefly. "What Rom?" he asked slowly.

"Big bloke. Got a knife mark on his face and a dagger on his belt. 'ands that could wring chickens by themselves. Spoke 'arshly to Sir Vincent, but listened and obeyed 'im all the same." Jamie wrinkled up his nose a little. "Seems strange to me. I stayed for a while, then went back to minding Miss Margaret, like you said. She don't do much, Gent. The maid says she's in her room all the time, and aside from the silver gone missing, there's not much to tell."

Rafe nodded slowly, processing this new information. The Rom was obviously Pov, from this account, and Jamie's cleverness might have saved them more trouble. If Pov were working with Sir Vincent, things were dire indeed, and it sounded as though Margaret was more trapped than he'd realized. He'd wondered if she might be avoiding going out because of him, but it seemed her Miss Ritson was playing jailkeeper now as well.

This was not good.

Jamie left to find something to eat, and Rafe looked at Rogue with resignation. "Something's got to give, Rogue," he told him.

Rouge nodded slowly, for once not arguing. "I agree. Probably time to tap into your more respectable resources."

He groaned. "I hate doing that."

Rogue smiled briefly, then waved him out with a dismissive flick of his fingers. "Yes, but you are so good at it, and they can give you the information you need. Go on, be a good lord and do your duty."

"Shut up."

Chapter Nineteen

"*I* am so sorry, my dear Margaret, I had a particular gentleman all set for you to meet this evening, but something came up and he had to refuse me." Lady Raeburn pursed her lips in displeasure. "I do so hate being refused."

Margaret smiled, grateful that Miss Ritson had not followed when Lady Raeburn had taken her for a stroll about the room. "It is no matter, my lady. I will meet anyone you would like me to."

"Yes, but Marlowe would have been a fine match for you. A bit dull, but quite proper. My niece's husband knows him well, he recommended him, in fact, and I always trust Kit's word. I don't know Lord Marlowe well, but he is pretty to look at, and one must always appreciate that." Lady Raeburn sighed heavily and shook her bronze turbaned head. "No matter. I suppose someone else will have to do. I hope you are not disappointed."

"How can I be?" Margaret laughed. "I don't know him myself, my lady, so it makes no difference on my account."

Lady Raeburn tsked. "Call me Tibby, Margaret. I insist."

"I couldn't."

"You will."

"I couldn't!"

"Margaret, protesting once is demure, twice annoying. I am to be Tibby or nothing else." She gave Margaret a look so severe she nodded out of fear, swallowing harshly.

The evening was a glorious reprieve from her captivity, and Lady Raeburn… Tibby… had a home that made one weep with envy. The rooms held all of the elegance of the lady herself and just a hint of the eccentricities she bore, all melding together into something that was truly a spectacular sight. She had seen gold trimming on the ceiling, bold splashes of color in nearly every room, and antiquities that could only have come from the Indies and other exotic places. The furniture was clean, classic, and elegant, and so fine it was leaving her with no doubt that the woman in question was wealthier than anybody might have guessed.

What would it be like to live in such splendor?

Each room was alight with dozens of candles, chandeliers twinkling in the light, and everywhere she looked, there were servants with trays of food and drink. People she had only seen in the finer ballrooms of London were milling about, mingling with each other and looking very fine and important. And the house was rapidly filling with more.

And this was a quiet evening?

"I never do anything by halves," Tibby told Margaret as she patted her hand, reading her thoughts with ease. "It is much more fun to be bold and daring."

Margaret glanced at the woman, whose entire ensemble directed all attention to her. "I can see that," she said drily. "I am neither bold nor daring, and I could not manage an evening like this if I tried."

Tibby gave her a sharp look. "Self-pity? Oh no, my dear, we cannot have that. It would clash horribly with that lavender gown you wear, and you wear it so well, just as I knew you would."

That drew a grin from Margaret. "Yes, thank you, my lady."

"Tibby," she scolded, her lips quirking.

"Tibby," Margaret corrected with a slight roll of her eyes, which made the other woman laugh. "It is a lovely gown, and suits me and my tastes well." She looked down at the skirt, then up at Tibby with a wry brow lift. "Are the skirts supposed to be that full?"

Tibby snorted. "Darling, just because it does not cling to you does not make it full. Now…" She glanced about the room, which was filling with people. "…if we are out of sight of that horrid woman, I can introduce you to some more entertaining people."

Margaret glanced back and could not even see Miss Ritson for the guests between them.

"Don't worry, my dear," Tibby said rather smugly. "I've asked

215

Lady Darlington to pay special attention to your Miss Ritson this evening. She may be rather cantankerous when you leave, but that will not be your fault." She smirked and steered Margaret along the outside of the columns in her music room. "Now, I believe you need to meet my niece and her darling husband."

Marianne Gerrard and her husband were pleasant and warm, and Margaret was adopted by Mrs. Gerrard at once, and introduced to so many people her head was spinning. Mr. Gerrard followed along behind them, seeming disinclined to leave his wife's side, which was quite touching. She met Mr. Gerrard's twin brother, who made her and several others laugh easily, and introduced her to several other couples, among whom were Lord and Lady Whitlock, whom she had met before, but was hardly on speaking terms with.

They were all pleasant and refined, and Margaret felt distinctly out of her element. Oh, by all accounts she belonged in this circle, by her fortune and standing, but by her nature, personality, and prospects, this was all too much.

Not that Mrs. Gerrard or Tibby cared, for they continued to tote Margaret along with them, ensuring that she was always surrounded by people, introducing her to scads more, and finding every eligible bachelor in the room to meet her.

Some of them she already knew, and they had not expressed any interest in her at all, but in the company of these women, she was suddenly worthy of attention.

It was quite a bewildering thing.

Eventually, something caught Mrs. Gerrard's eye, and she tugged Margaret away from a rather nice man whose name she could not recall. "I think I see something more to your interest than worthless suitors who are not truly interested in you or anything you have to say."

Margaret laughed in surprise. "Is it so obvious?" she asked as Mrs. Gerrard weaved through the people, her majestic blue silk swirling around her feet.

Mrs. Gerrard gave her a pointed look. "Dear Miss Easton, if it requires my interest to make them interested, they are highly unintelligent and not worth your time. You need a man who wants you regardless of what anybody else thinks of you."

Rafe's face flashed in Margaret's mind and she felt her cheeks heat.

Mrs. Gerrard caught the flush and smiled a bit deviously. "Oh my, there is a telltale sign. But I will not ask, much as it might kill me. Do not let Tibby see that, she has less control than I."

"Noted," Margaret remarked, raising a cool, gloved hand to her face. "Where did you say we were going?"

She heard a squeal and looked up just in time to see Helen and Rosalind descending on her, hugging and squeezing and rambling on like schoolgirls about everything under the sun.

Mrs. Gerrard chuckled and squeezed Margaret's arm. "I believe I can leave you to their care, Miss Easton. Rosalind, would you see to it that she meets the Blackmoors? And then the Rivertons, if the Blackmoors are up to it."

"Of course, Marianne," Rosalind said, her dark eyes dancing merrily. She looked at Margaret and grinned. "You must have stories to tell. Come on and meet the others so we can go and have a chat."

Helen and Rosalind took her over where Mrs. Gerrard had indicated, and while Lord Blackmoor scared her to death with his severe expression and solemn reserve, Lady Blackmoor was warm and vivacious, and insisted she be allowed to call upon her the next day. Lady Blackmoor introduced her to Lord Sheffield, who would be Lord Riverton when his father passed, and he expressed his condolences that she already knew his brother, Captain Riverton. She laughed at that, and Captain Riverton, much offended by his brother's insult, took Margaret away and insisted that there be dancing, which prompted Lily Granger to take up the pianoforte, and soon several others were lined up to dance.

Captain Riverton was charming and entertaining, and Margaret thought she could probably find herself in love with him in another time and place. But she suspected he held a *tendre* for Rosalind, despite her bristling at him, and was not convinced Rosalind did not feel the same.

When Captain Riverton returned her to Helen, he plucked Rosalind away to dance without even asking, which made Margaret and Helen choke back laughter. Rosalind looked infuriated, but she did not resist him, which was also telling.

"She really ought to just encourage him a little," Helen said with a fond smile. "He would make her a quite charming husband."

"You know Rosalind," Margaret sighed as she watched her friend dance. "She is determined to have her way, and nothing must come easily. And Captain Riverton's charm irritates her."

Helen snorted, her eyes twinkling. "Because it works, even on her. She cannot abide the flutterings he produces, and until she succumbs to the very great pleasure of it, she will resist every single one."

Margaret looked at her cousin in surprise. "When did you become such an expert on men and feelings?"

Helen gave her a sly look. "I have my ways."

Margaret rolled her eyes, and saw Mr. and Mrs. Gerrard dancing nearby, both of whom had their eyes on her, speaking softly to each other.

"Lord, Margaret," Helen murmured under her breath. "What did you do to become adopted by everyone of significance in this room?"

Margaret shook her head. "I have no idea. I met Lady Raeburn at Aunt Ada's and she seems to be my sponsor now."

"Or your protector," Helen added darkly, nodding her head towards a portion of the room as she sipped punch.

Margaret looked and saw Miss Ritson staring at her in an unmistakably hostile manner. "Oh lord," Margaret whispered. "I am going to be in so much trouble."

"Why? You've done nothing but go where you are led." Helen snorted and tossed her blonde curls, glinting like spun gold in the light of the room. "If she wanted you to be prisoner, she ought to have refused invitation."

Margaret shook her head, looking down at her new slippers. "I doubt even Ritson has fortitude enough to withstand Lady Raeburn."

Helen laughed and set aside her cup of punch. "No one has, not even Mama."

That prompted Margaret to glance up at her cousin, finding her smiling at Tibby fondly and receiving an equally warm look in return. "What is their connection, Helen? I did not know they were so acquainted."

"They've been friends for years," Helen said, craning her long neck as if looking for someone. "She happened to be visiting Mama when your first note came, and when we didn't hear more, she took it upon herself to visit Mrs. Campbell on the day when you usually visited." Helen made a soft tsking noise of disappointment. "You haven't seen Mr. Pratt this evening, have you?"

Margaret shook her head, chewing her lip a little. "So you know everything, then."

Helen smirked. "Not everything, Margaret. I still don't know where you were that day." Her look became prodding, her eyes teasing.

Margaret looked away quickly, not ready to speak of it, even to her cousin. "It makes no difference now. So long as I know you have received my notes and know…"

Her hand was seized and squeezed hard. "Margaret, come and stay with us. Surely Rickety will allow that."

Tears formed as she felt a surge of longing. "I don't think she will allow it," Margaret managed. "She does not want me out of her sight, and if I have to visit Sir Vincent again…"

Helen's eyes widened and she snapped her head around to look at Rosalind, who was nearing the end of her dance. Rosalind caught it, said something to Captain Riverton, who looked as well and seemed concerned, and both came to her.

"Margaret, what is it?" Rosalind asked, taking her hand.

She shook her head, exhaling slowly. "Nothing, continue your dancing. Really."

"It's over," Rosalind retorted with a wave of her hand. "And Will trod my toes."

Captain Riverton gave her a hard look. "I did not."

Rosalind didn't even look at him. "Don't be childish. Margaret, we need to talk."

Helen cursed under her breath, making Captain Riverton cough a surprised laugh. "Rickety is coming." She glanced around, then tugged Margaret towards the door, Rosalind trailing behind.

"She'll follow us," Margaret warned.

"She can try," Rosalind said with a smile. "Will is very good at distractions and diversions."

Helen and Margaret shared a look, avoiding smiles as much as they could.

Once out in the hall, Margaret told them everything of her last week at home, and her prospects for the future.

They were appropriately appalled.

"I am going to tell Papa about this!" Helen snapped, her delicate brows lowered. "He would not tolerate it."

"Climb out of the window," Rosalind suggested. "You can use the bedsheets."

Margaret shook her head. "It's too far, and I don't think I could manage it."

"I think you could." Rosalind tapped her chin, brow furrowed in thought "What would it take to get you down safely? There is no point in escape if your legs are broken."

"I am going to insist that Papa invite you to stay!" Helen said again, not hearing them. "Let Rickety try to deny Edmund Dalton his niece's company!"

Margaret sighed softly. "She'd find a way. You did not see her, Helen. She is completely fixated on controlling me and on my being with Sir Vincent. She was disappointed that he did not get a chance to compromise me."

Both of her friends shrieked in outrage and began concocting all sorts of plans to break Margaret free of her prison, of preventing her from seeing Sir Vincent again, and various methods of harm to concoct for Miss Ritson. It was entertaining to hear, but Margaret felt a wave of sadness crash over her. No matter what they plotted and tried, nothing would be able to free her from Miss Ritson, or Sir Vincent. Even if she did manage to escape, she could not hide away forever.

Her parents were her only hope.

Her parents... and Rafe.

"Miss Easton," Captain Riverton said, coming down the hall quickly. "Your chaperone is asking for you. I think she is prepared to make a scene."

Margaret closed her eyes, suddenly ill. She was going to be forced to leave, and to never go anywhere or do anything again.

"Will, do something!" Rosalind pleaded, sounding more angry than distraught, though her voice was wavering.

"What would you like me to do, Roz?" He gave her a somber look. "I barely managed to escape to warn you all."

"She's going to make her wed Sir Vincent Castleton!" Rosalind cried.

"Oh, very discreet, Rosalind," Helen said with a roll of her eyes. "Excellent with secrets, very impressive."

Captain Riverton winced and shook his head. "No one in their right mind would pair her with him."

"Yes, well, apparently one can be a chaperone without being in their right minds," Helen snapped. "It's not a prerequisite."

"Can you pretend an engagement with her?" Rosalind asked Captain Riverton hopefully. "That would take care of things."

Captain Riverton's look was pitying. "No, Roz, I can't. It would harm Miss Easton's future chances, and it is possible that an actual wedding would be insisted upon, and not even my family's clout could prevent that."

"And he can't marry her in truth because he fancies someone else," Helen said dismissively.

Both Captain Riverton and Rosalind seemed startled by the statement, and flushed a little.

"I'll manage," Margaret murmured softly.

Captain Riverton shook himself and straightened. "I can't distract her any longer, and making a scene myself wouldn't help Miss Easton a bit." He looked at Margaret with an apologetic expression. "I don't know what else to do, Miss Easton, but I am at your service."

"I refuse to let you go back to her!" Helen raged, her hands tight fists. "I won't stand for it!"

"I'll speak to my brother-in-law," Rosalind vowed, tears glinting at the corners of her dark eyes. "Granger is a respected man, he won't tolerate it."

"And there is a room filled with important people who like you quite a bit, I think," Captain Riverton reminded her. "You would have no end of help there."

Margaret smiled wanly. "So many saviors, so little time." She looked down the hall towards the room, exhaling slowly. "I cannot let anyone fight my battles for me. I will see her, and I will find a way."

"We'll go with you," Rosalind said, taking her arm.

Margaret shook her head and moved out of her hold. "No, you will go and dance with Captain Riverton again. Helen, you will go back to looking for Mr. Pratt or whichever man you seem to be missing this evening. Let me see to my own problems."

Her friends stared at her in surprise, but Captain Riverton was grinning, a newfound respect in his eyes.

She smiled at them all. "I will manage, I promise. I have let myself be submissive long enough. I know I have you all with me, and that is going to carry me through."

Helen opened her mouth to reply, but Captain Riverton was quick to interject. "Well, we have our marching orders. Come along, Rosalind, Miss Dalton." His tone was firm and very authoritative, no doubt from his days with the navy, and there was no denying him.

Helen and Rosalind hugged her quickly, then returned to the party, and Margaret slowly followed, praying she could actually be as strong as she had just pretended for her friends.

Miss Ritson found her quickly, looking murderous. "Where have you been?" she demanded, seizing Margaret's forearm.

"Miss Dalton required some assistance with her dress, and I gave it," Margaret lied easily.

Miss Ritson snorted, tugging her towards the door. "This evening is a waste. You are claiming a headache and going home."

Margaret did not budge. "No, I will not."

Miss Ritson stopped and slowly turned to look at her, eyes flashing. "Excuse me?"

Margaret raised a brow. "Miss Ritson, you are under the impression that you actually have authority in my life. You are an employee of my family, and are meant to protect my reputation and person, not control me or dictate the manner in which I live my life. I have no qualms about leaving early if that is what I wish to do, but I will not disrespect our hostess by doing so abruptly and without explanation, and I will not allow you to tell me that I must do so."

If looks could harm a person, Margaret would have died three times over standing there. Miss Ritson was livid, bright splotches of color appearing on her cheeks, and there seemed to be a slight tremor to her frame. "Make your excuses," Miss Ritson hissed shakily.

"Now."

"Miss Easton, I believe this dance is mine," said a low voice nearby.

Margaret turned to see Lord Blackmoor and felt her stomach clench in apprehension. She knew she had not promised any dance to any man, let alone him, and his expression was not encouraging.

But he was not looking at her, he was looking at Miss Ritson. His hand was extended to Margaret, but the thunderous expression was all for her chaperone.

It seemed she had made an indelible impression upon the imposing man after all.

"Thank you, my lord," Margaret began, reaching for his hand.

"Miss Easton must decline, my lord," Miss Ritson interrupted, taking Margaret's hand and pulling her away. "She has a fearful headache, and must go home at once. She has a very important outing with her betrothed, Sir Vincent Castleton, in the morning, and must rest for it."

Margaret gasped, staring at her chaperone in horror.

Miss Ritson never looked at her, but kept her gaze on the viscount.

Lord Blackmoor's expression somehow darkened and he seemed to be fighting a battle within himself. "Very well, then," he murmured, causing Margaret's heart to sink. He turned to her with a slight bow. "If Miss Easton should require anything, I trust she might call upon me for assistance."

Margaret nodded glumly, knowing she would never do so.

"And you will both forgive me if I do not congratulate Miss Easton on her betrothal, should such a ludicrous connection actually exist," he went on smoothly, making Margaret jerk her head up to stare at him and Miss Ritson gape openly. "Sir Vincent is a disgusting, infectious plague upon society and human life, and I would not shake hands with him under any circumstances. And knowing my own reputation, you can only imagine how much more the villain I consider him to be. Miss Easton deserves a husband of far, far superior caliber than he."

He inclined his head to Miss Ritson, then took Margaret's hand and pressed a polite kiss to her glove, and she might have imagined it, but she thought she saw him wink briefly at her, and then he departed quickly.

Miss Ritson sputtered, knowing that people around them had heard her too loud declaration of Margaret's supposed engagement, and then Lord Blackmoor's response.

Margaret took the opportunity to thank Tibby for her invitation, and informed her that Miss Ritson had a fearful headache, and Margaret was going to see her home.

Tibby did not believe her for a second, but promised to call upon her soon.

Helen and Rosalind were deep in conversation with Mrs. Gerrard as Margaret left, but all three waved at her, looking worried.

Margaret was worried herself.

Gossip carried like a tide in London, and an engagement rumor carried like nothing else. She would need a miracle now, no matter how many allies she had gained this evening. Even they could not stave off ruination and consequences of them.

When they returned to the house, Miss Ritson hauled Margaret upstairs with surprising strength and forced her into her room. "You are remaining in here for the entire day tomorrow," she informed her. "I will be writing to Sir Vincent, and he is the only person you will be permitted to see."

Margaret raised her chin defiantly. "You can't forbid everyone else."

Miss Ritson snorted. "Watch me."

"You can't make me marry him," Margaret snarled, teeth grinding. "I won't do it."

A light of satisfaction game into her chaperone's beady eyes. "Yes, I can. And yes, you will."

She slammed the door, locked it, and barked some orders at the guard at the door that Margaret couldn't make out.

She raced to the window and wrenched it open, looking down the side of the building. Could she get out? Could she escape? She dashed to her bed and pulled off the blankets and coverlet, stripping the bed completely of sheets and all coverings. She tied the ends together and went back to the window.

There below, directly in her path, was another one of Ritson's new footmen, staring up and watching her, arms folded across his chest.

Margaret stared back at him for a long moment, then exhaled heavily and turned back into her room, dropping the makeshift rope onto the ground and then curling up against it, corset and new gown and all.

What was she going to do now?

Chapter Twenty

"Engaged? She's not engaged, she couldn't be."

"She's obviously not, but that is what is being said, thanks to that bat of a chaperone."

Rafe cursed and rubbed his eyes. He knew he shouldn't have had Kit and Blackmoor assist in this when he couldn't be involved himself. It was going to kill him to turn all of this over to them, but what else could he do? He could not pretend his dual life did not present risks, and he could not... *could* not reveal that side of him yet.

It was why he'd asked them to see to Margaret at Tibby's party, and why he would dare to rescind his acceptance of her invitation. It was why he had prompted Tibby to get involved in the first place, though she would never know him well enough to know he had manipulated everything through her niece and Kit. It was why they were here now, telling him the things he craved to know, but could not explain why.

"Marianne says things are awful for Margaret at home, she and Tibby talk about it all the time."

Rafe looked up at his friends, sitting in his library far too early for a man who worked himself into a frenzy at all hours and did not sleep well anymore. "I've heard, but what can I do about that? I can't storm the house and pull her out and ride off into the sunset."

"I don't see why not," Blackmoor said with a shrug. "I think that would be rather poetic of you."

Rafe glared at him, which did not have much effect, as Blackmoor was usually the one doling out the glares, and far more successfully. "I can't. You know I can't."

"Actually," Kit said as he sat back and watched Rafe carefully, "I don't see why not either. Lord Marlowe can do whatever he wants, you'd be a fine match for her, and it would solve all of your problems."

Rafe winced and looked away, his traitorous heart pounding harder at the thought.

"Wait…" Blackmoor said slowly. "Wait. Lord Marlowe isn't the one who wants her."

"Excuse me?" Kit barked, his pitch higher than normal. "But… Oh, Rafe, you didn't…"

Rafe sank further into his chair.

Blackmoor swore and Kit echoed it with a milder version.

"I met her as the Gent," he said softly, almost defensively. "No one in their right mind would have thought me a peer, and I couldn't very well reveal myself."

"And when was this?" Kit asked.

"Ages ago. Months. We've been… That is…" He sighed heavily and rubbed at his brow. "Our relationship is unusual. Less verbal."

Blackmoor snorted a loud laugh, which drew a scolding glare from Rafe. "That is *not* what I mean. I mean as the Gent, I move freely about London and I have seen her on a regular basis for months."

"Stalking?" Blackmoor suggested, a half smile on his face. That was a testament to his change, as Blackmoor never even managed that prior to his marriage. Gemma had changed him in more ways than one, but that was the most obvious.

"No!" Rafe insisted. Then he wrinkled up his nose in distaste. "Maybe. But not like that."

Kit looked at Blackmoor with a tame expression. "Well, that's making sense, isn't it?"

Blackmoor nodded. "Yes, I follow perfectly."

"Shove off."

"Gladly, once you actually explain yourself."

"Yes, Rafe, do explain."

He tried, he really did, but no matter how many times he tried to describe his relationship with Margaret, it always sounded strange and flat. There was no magic in the retelling, not in his following her, or her looking for him, or their ten-second moments. It would make no sense to anyone else, and he didn't see why it should.

But as these were his most trusted friends, he had nowhere else to go.

"Rafe, you're like a puppy, what is all of this?" Kit finally asked with a laugh. "You've never been like this in all the years we've known you."

"I'm beginning to wonder if you might be mad from your years of spying," Blackmoor added with a sage nod. "It wouldn't surprise me."

Rafe looked at them both, then leveled a serious look at Kit. "How do you explain how you felt the first time Marianne captivated you?"

Kit inhaled sharply, his amusement fading into surprise. "I... She..."

Rafe turned to Blackmoor. "How do you explain how Gemma makes you smile and laugh when thunder fled from you before?"

"Well..." Blackmoor began, looking uncomfortable. "She's... It's complicated."

"No. It's not." Rafe shook his head slowly. "I can't describe it. I don't know why things happened the way they did, or why it means so much when we've actually not had much time together at all. But I love her. As the Gent, as Lord Marlowe, as Raphael William Edward Thornton, and with everything that all three of them are. She doesn't know who I really am, and the person she knows me as is in no position to provide the solution to her problem. But I cannot sit idly by and let her be treated like this. And I will be damned to hell five times over before I will let Sir Vincent Castleton have her."

His friends sat there for a long moment, staring at him in wonder. Then Blackmoor turned to Kit with an innocent expression. "I think he loves Miss Easton, Gerrard. Just a thought."

"You might be right," Kit murmured, still watching Rafe.

Rafe slumped back in his chair, rubbing his hands over his face. "I am going mad with it, so please, tell me everything."

"First of all, Gent," Blackmoor said with a hint of mockery on his street name, "I think you might need to tell her that you love her."

"I have."

"And?"

"She told me to get out."

His friends made sympathetic noises, and he glared at them both. "I know! I climbed the wall of her house and into her bed chamber just to see her, and she rebuffs my declaration?"

Kit clicked his tongue. "Such disregard for your efforts."

Sensing he was being mocked, Rafe sniffed dismissively. "After all I've done for her, that wasn't proof enough that I wanted to be with her."

"And what exactly have you done?" Blackmoor asked, lacing his fingers around one of his knees and sitting back.

With a resigned sigh, Rafe told them the rest. He left out the parts that related to national security, naturally, but everything else he told, including the things Callie had told him about Margaret's visit with Sir Vincent. He told them about the Bounty and the rumors, everything Margaret would have heard there, and the change it had wrought in her.

They listened with interest, their faces darkening at the appropriate times, and then faint amusement settling in by the end. The more Rafe spoke, the more the tightening in his chest began to unravel, and the more he missed Margaret and all she meant to him. And the more confused he became about why he was sitting around and not taking her for himself.

"Well, that was enlightening," Kit said when the story was done, scratching at his jaw.

"Certainly was." Blackmoor nodded slowly, his eyes on Rafe the entire time.

Rafe rolled his eyes and folded his arms about his chest. "And?" he prodded without patience.

Blackmoor shrugged, and Kit smiled. "We're still of the opinion that you should storm the house and take her for yourself."

"What?" Rafe barked. "I already told you I can't." But it was sounding more like a good idea the more they repeated it.

"Indeed." Blackmoor's mouth twitched in an almost smile. "So, in light of that, the protection of several powerful members of Society might be your best bet."

"Which is why I had you all take her under your wings and

introduce her to everyone you could at Tibby's. Thank you for that, by the way." He looked between the two with a smile.

Blackmoor waved it off. "That was easy. I hadn't known much of Miss Easton before this, but I was impressed with her. She showed a lot of spirit, and I think that, given the chance, she will break off her restraints."

Rafe smiled before he was aware of it, a surge of pride swelling within him. "She is not quite the demure and proper miss she portrays."

Kit chuckled a little. "That explains why Tibby has taken such an interest in her."

"And Gemma," Blackmoor added.

"And it's why I love her," Rafe admitted. "One of the reasons, anyway."

There was so much to love about Margaret, so many pleasant surprises, even for him, who thought he knew her so well. She would never become dull, life with her would never be tame, and he knew that he would find more and more to love about her as time went on.

He needed her, and that was all there was to it.

"So what can we do?" Kit asked him. "You obviously love her, so why aren't you with her?"

"Are they preventing you from being with her?" Blackmoor's question was sharp and accusatory, and Rafe was torn between defending his colleagues and praising his friend's loyalty.

Thankfully, he didn't have to make the distinction.

He smiled wryly. "Actually, they are working on taking care of certain situations so that I can be with her while still maintaining my position."

Both men looked surprised by that, and exchanged a look. "You are going to have to reveal your real identity, you know," Kit told him carefully. "And what you are."

Rafe shrugged. "I am prepared to do so, as soon as it is safe."

Blackmoor nodded, but frowned. "And until then?"

The question was expected, but it didn't lessen the pain of it. "Until then," Rafe told them on a long exhale, "I am to continue as I am, focus on my task, and not cause any trouble."

"So you need me to cause trouble," Blackmoor said bluntly.

Rafe barked a laugh, tossing his head back. "Not at all. I just need you two to continue to mind her, if she manages to get out in Society. I have one of my scouts posted at her house and following her everywhere, and Callie is still in Sir Vincent's employ, but…" He shrugged uneasily. "I need to know she is protected at all times, as I am not in a position to do so."

Kit had been watching him closely, and now leaned forward, his eyes earnest. "Rafe, what else are you doing? You have dark shadows under your eyes and lines on your face, and you're not as sharp as you normally are. I know you well enough to know this is more than a poor night's sleep. What else?"

He had not expected any such accusations, nor had he thought that he showed so very much of his exhaustion. He couldn't bring himself to tell them everything, how he had spent his nights outside of her home, near her window, just to ensure that nothing happened. If his information was correct, Sir Vincent would stop at nothing to have Margaret, and her chaperone was somehow in favor of it, if not orchestrating the whole thing. He'd had visions of Sir Vincent coming to Margaret's bedchamber, and the horror of such scenes terrified him to his core.

He might not be able to be by Margaret's side, given her situation and her last words to him, but it was not about to keep him from ensuring her safety and well-being as much as he was able.

He was treading a fine line as it was, and if anything else happened, he would probably do something irrational.

A knock on his study door prevented him from having to answer Kit. Davis entered and raised a fluffy brow in greeting. "Sir, a message for you."

"From whom?" he asked, signaling for the butler to come over.

"The lad did not say, sir," Davis said, delivering the note, bowing, and departing the room.

Rafe's hands stilled on the note, and he glanced up at his friends to see them watching warily. He broke the seal and scanned the lines in Rogue's scratchy scrawl quickly.

Your Roman uncle is in the office. Says the renegade is recruiting. Damsel in distress. Details upon arrival.

He shot to his feet, his mind scrambling. He had no living

relatives, as Rogue knew, let alone ones from Rome, so he could only deduce that meant a Rom was in the office, and there was only one Rom that would seek him out through official straits. Kem had come into London, which had never happened in the years he had known him, and if that was true, the renegade would be Pov, and if Pov, working for Sir Vincent, was attempting to recruit...

And the only damsel that could be in distress would be Margaret.

Rafe was out of the study before his friends said a single word, and he gave them no apology or explanation. They were used to his comings and goings, and if they needed to know, he would have told them.

He slipped out of his house through the kitchens, and took the crooked back streets to the office at a fast clip, his mind spinning. Was Margaret in danger at this moment, or was it in the future? Was Pov inciting a riot with his brothers and other discontented Roms? Had Sir Vincent finally shown his hand?

It was a maddeningly complex situation, and it ought to have been very simple. Curse his life and its various aspects that were now all getting in the way of each other.

He pushed into the office when he arrived and tossed his cap at Gordon, who caught it and hung it on the wall automatically.

Rogue and Kem met him in the hall, both wearing serious expressions.

"What is it?" he demanded. "What's wrong?"

Kem shook his head slowly. "I am so sorry, Gent. I didn't know."

"Know what?" He was close to bellowing, but he was beyond caring.

"In here," Rogue ordered, gesturing with his head towards the empty office.

Rafe and Kem followed, and only when the door was closed did Kem look at Rafe again.

"Tell me," Rafe said darkly. "Tell me everything."

"Pov has been in contact with his brothers," Kem told him. "They communicate frequently, despite my dictates. He's been trying to convince them to come with him. He knows Margaret was in the camp, and that you are her protector."

Rafe swore and sank into a chair, putting his head into his hands.

"His brothers started to get suspicious when he wanted details of the girl," Kem went on, "and they brought their concerns to me. They liked Margaret and you know they respect you greatly. They have no interest in joining him, and are keeping others from doing so."

Rafe didn't respond to that. He rubbed his hands over his face and looked up. "What is Pov doing?"

Kem looked disgruntled, and folded his massive arms. "He works for a peer in London. I don't know who. It is not respectable work, that much I do know. He will do whatever is requested for an impressive sum of money, and it seems his employer has enough to keep him on."

"I know who it is," Rafe muttered darkly, "and I know what sort of a man he is."

"Then perhaps you would like to know that the man in question is asking more unusual things of Pov?" Kem suggested, his tone matching Rafe's. "Like procuring a carriage without windows and a driver to be on standby? Or that Pov has been examining Margaret's house and layout?"

The room went deathly still, and Rafe could only blink.

"Or that your urchin has seen Pov talking with the bat?" Rogue added in a low voice. "And another report came in about him talking with the bat's footmen?"

Rafe looked at Rogue, who leaned against the desk, watching him.

"Well?" Rogue said quietly. "What do we do about this?"

"He's going after her," Rafe said quietly. "That's what this is. The bat is in on it, if not working for him, and all of this is to get him Margaret."

"Why?" Rogue asked bluntly. "What does she have to offer?"

Kem growled darkly and Rafe held up a hand. "He's all right, he likes Margaret a great deal."

"Doesn't sound like it," Kem snarled.

Rogue looked mildly surprised. "You too?" He looked at Rafe in exasperation. "She's won over everyone, except for London Society. How did you manage to fall for the one woman in the world who actually suits your life?"

Rafe managed a smile. "I am that good." He pressed his hands against his temples. "Why Margaret? He doesn't even need to marry, and he's never had an inclination before. Of all the women in London, why...?" Realization dawned and he dropped his hands, eyes widening. "It's all about the money."

"What?" Rogue asked, having missed his muttering.

Rafe got to his feet, pacing the room. "It's money. He said at the beginning that he had a plan, something that would bring in unending profits, or some such. A contract, and pieces in place. Don't you see? They need money to fund the operations, and we couldn't figure out where it was going to come from. He doesn't have impressive financial ties, not like the others, and we could prove theirs. He's taking Margaret's money."

Rogue whistled low. "Is it a lot?"

Rafe nodded quickly. "She has her own inheritance, plus whatever her aunt has coming. She's an heiress, and if anybody knew just how much she is worth, she would not be nearly so ignored." He paced faster, his mind whirling. "He doesn't need to marry, he doesn't care about Margaret, he just needs the money. Her parents are gone, which makes it easy to compromise her, and..." He stopped and whirled to Rogue, who stared at him wide-eyed. "The chaperone is in on it, and he'd be able to compromise her without any resistance there. And the bat is just cruel enough to make sure it is a public spectacle with no recourse available but marriage."

Rogue moved quickly out of the room and barked something at Harrison that he couldn't make out.

Kem stared at Rafe without expression, then exhaled slowly. "I am sorry, Gent, for what Pov has done, and the part he plays."

Rafe shook his head and came over to shake Kem's hand. "No apologies needed, old friend. You are not responsible for Pov. Every man must make his own path."

"Well, if you see him again, feel free to kill him. *Te malavel les i menkiva.*" Kem spat on the floor, shaking his head.

May the malignant disease waste him. Rafe coughed a surprised laugh at the harsh insult, and allowed Kem to clamp him on the shoulder, then slip from the building without any fuss.

Rafe rather hoped a malignant disease would waste Pov. That would solve many problems. On the other hand, without Pov trying to recruit his brothers, they wouldn't have received this information, and now he thought he might be able to make a move. Now he could act.

Now he could save Margaret.

But first…

He jotted off a note on a slip of paper, folded it, and left the now empty office.

Out in the street, he whistled, and one of his little tykes, Frank, appeared.

He gave the sandy-haired boy a serious look. "Take this to Helen Dalton, tell her Tibby will vouch for it, and wait for a response."

Frank nodded, took the note, and dashed off.

Rafe stared after him for a long moment, then sighed softly. "Hold on, pet. Hold on."

Chapter Twenty-One

$\mathcal{T}$hree days of no callers, not even Sir Vincent, and no reprieve from her boredom, and Margaret was beginning to go mad.

The only thing that had brightened her time was that Helen had come to stay with her for a time. They were not to share a room, but she was permitted to spend time out of her room to see her. She had arrived that morning under strict instructions that Margaret was practically disturbed, not herself, and for her own protection, she was confined to her room most of the time.

Well, if that was how one wanted to describe being prisoner in one's own room and being locked in on a regular basis, so be it.

Helen had appeared full of concern, and the moment she had been let in Margaret's room she'd embraced her and cried in such a dramatic display that Margaret had been almost convinced that it was Helen that was disturbed.

Then the door had closed and Helen's tears had miraculously vanished.

"Lord, that took a lot of work," she'd groaned, flinging off her bonnet and cloak. "I thought Ritson might actually toss me out when I showed up."

Margaret had hugged her cousin again, no longer in danger of being collapsed on by a fountain of tears. "How did you manage it?"

Helen had pulled back and given her a look. "Didn't you wonder why after such a party no one had come to see you?"

"Well, yes, actually," Margaret had said, sinking onto her tidy bed.

Helen went to the bed and sprawled on it in a very unladylike fashion. "They were all told that you were very ill. The Whitlocks sent a physician over, but he was told you'd already seen one. Tibby tried everything, but she could not get through. Marianne Gerrard was going mad with worry, fearing you'd actually been killed or something." Helen had rolled her eyes for effect.

Margaret had snorted and sat back on her elbows. "How is Rosalind?"

"Beside herself. She knows there is no way that Ritson would let her anywhere near you even if you were well." She shrugged a shoulder nonchalantly. "I think Will is helping her through it." She smiled at Margaret deviously. "When all of this is over, they might have you to thank for getting Rosalind to fall for him."

That made Margaret laugh, and she felt lighter than she had in ages for it. "But how did you get in here today, Helen? I haven't even seen Ritson in days, she won't come up here."

Helen smirked, her cobalt eyes twinkling. "Well, when I heard that my beloved cousin was so very unwell for the third day in a row, and even her supposed betrothed was not permitted to see her, despite his ardent attentions…"

"My *what?*" Margaret interrupted, rolling onto her side.

"Betrothed. You're going to marry Sir Vincent as soon as your parents' permission is secured." Helen mimicked retching and shuddered. "When I imagine that man taking his husbandly rights…"

"Why would you do that?" Margaret shrieked, feeling sick to her stomach in truth.

Helen gave her a hard look. "He is very vocal in his praises of your person. Disturbingly so."

Margaret flung an arm over her eyes and lay back on the bed. "Oh, lord…"

"Anyway, I showed up on the doorstep today with my eyes filled with tears and begged to stay with my poor cousin and tend to her in her hour of need." Helen had nestled closer to Margaret and sighed. "Ritson couldn't refuse me. Particularly when I barged my way in and only got more hysterical." She'd reached down and taken Margaret's hand. "I don't know what is going to happen, Margaret, but I am here with you now, and I'm not going anywhere."

Even now, hours later, Helen's fierce words brought tears to

Margaret's eyes. She knew that there was not much that Helen could do in truth, but knowing she was here brought a measure of comfort.

She knew she was beyond fortunate that Sir Vincent had not made an appearance yet, but it was only a matter of time. No doubt he was laying a foundation of ardency to their relationship so that when he truly did come to compromise her, it would not paint him in such a villainous light. And with her prim and proper chaperone as his ally, he would have all the access to her that he needed.

Where were her parents, and how could they go this long without hearing from her and not knowing something was wrong?

And what about Rafe? Had he left her to her fate? Or was he finding a way to fix all of this?

A low rumbling of thunder met her ears and she looked over at the window, hearing the rain beginning to patter on the glass lightly.

She opened the window a little, breathing in the fresh air of the storm, feeling the rain on her face. Each drop on her cheeks reminded her of Rafe, how he had imagined her out in the rain and letting it fall upon her face and hair, tracing each and every feature. She exhaled shakily, the sudden warmth filling her body contrasting sharply with the cold raindrops on her cheeks.

Someday, she would watch a storm roll in with his arms around her, pressed against his warm, strong chest, inhaling his scent. He would press feather-light kisses upon her skin, murmuring words of love and tenderness that would fill her soul with wanting, and then, just when she couldn't bear it, he would pull her out into the rain and dance with her, just as they had that night around the fire.

Margaret moaned softly with longing for that vision, and opened her eyes to the night sky.

A flash of lightning lit the world around her and she looked down, then gasped.

A man in dark clothing was sneaking around the side of her house, treading with familiarity and ease. She covered her mouth to keep from making too much noise, but gasped again when he found the side door and opened it, slipping into the house without a single creak or misstep.

Someone had left the door open for him, and he knew the layout of the house well enough to know where it was.

And now he was inside. With her. And Helen.

Margaret didn't hesitate. She screamed for help as loud as she could out of the window, her cries getting lost in the sounds of the storm. She raced to her bedroom door and pounded on it. "Horace! Martin! Somebody, help!"

Her guards, who had always responded to her before, even if it was not an answer she had wanted, were silent.

Or gone.

Margaret clapped her hands over her eyes, whimpering loudly as panic and fear warred within her. She turned to the window once more and opened it more widely. "Help!" she shrieked as loudly as she could. "Help! Help, oh somebody, help!"

"Margaret?"

She gasped and looked down to find Rafe jogging into view, the shadows of the night and of his stubble giving him a dark, mysterious look. He was damp with rain, in dirty clothing, and he was the most glorious sight she had ever seen.

"Rafe," she choked out, her throat clogging with emotion. Her eyes burned and she covered her mouth.

"What is it?" he called, his voice barely audible above the rain. "What's wrong? Are you all right?"

She shook her head quickly. "There's a man!"

He stiffened. "Where?" he asked, his voice suddenly harsh.

"In the house! He entered only a few minutes ago, and something is terribly wrong!"

Rafe stepped closer to the house, and even from her place, she could see the firm set of his jaw. "Did he break in?"

She shook her head frantically. "No! He opened the door and walked right in! Rafe, there are only maids in this house, hardly any men, and my cousin!"

"I'm coming up!"

"No, don't! The door is locked from the outside, and it will take too much time to break it down!"

He scowled, putting his hands on his hips. "How else do I get in, then?"

She leaned out and pointed to the door. "The side door. It is how he entered, so it ought to be open still. Take the corridor to the right.

239

It looks small and poorly lit, but it will get you to the main of the house faster."

He nodded and turned to go, then looked back up at her as he jogged towards it. "Don't go anywhere."

She frowned at his retreating back. "Where exactly would I go?" she mused aloud. "I just said my door is locked from the outside, and I am prevented from escaping out the window by the terrifyingly long drop to the ground."

She glanced down the wall, and saw that, to her surprise, it would not be so very difficult to manage. It would take some considerable effort, and she would be in danger of serious injury, but when faced with the alternatives of dying or being ruined, it was far preferable.

She paced around the room, waiting for some sign, some sound to indicate that Rafe was successful, or at least doing something. But there was nothing but the eerily silent house and her frantically pounding heart.

Margaret glanced at the window, then back at the door, then at the window again. She exhaled sharply. "Surely he meant only not to go far…"

She threw her bedcovers off and tugged the sheets, recreating the sheet rope she'd constructed days before. She tied it onto her bedpost and hoisted herself out of the window, letting her wrap drop to the floor. She tossed the rest of the rope down to the ground and began easing her way down the wall, holding her breath as her slippers slid a little on the wet stone.

"Steady, Margaret," she muttered to herself. "Steady…"

She gripped the sheets tightly, wishing she had thought about this more thoroughly before actually climbing out of the window. It was wet and raining, and she would be absolutely drenched before she got anywhere. She ought to have waited for Rafe, he could have told her what to do, and all would have gone smoothly. But no, she had to be impulsive, and…

Her breath caught as she felt the sheet start to give above her, and she tried to move faster down the wall, only for her feet to slip more in her haste. She scraped her knees and hands against the walls, wincing at the abrasions. Suddenly she found herself clinging to the sheets with her feet in the air, and a rapidly loosening sheet above her.

There was no time for anything else. She lowered herself with her arms a few more feet, and then shrieked softly when the knot gave way completely, sending her and the sheets tumbling to the ground, which thankfully was now only a few feet away.

More bruised in pride than in body, Margaret got to her feet and ran to the side door, which opened with ease for its third guest, and she found herself engulfed in the darkness of the servants' side hall. She felt her way along the wall, treading as lightly as she could in her sodden slippers and nightgown. She felt a gap in the wall and glanced down to see two of the maids cowering in a doorway.

"Miss!" one of them whimpered. "There are two strange men in the house! One came in after the other, and we hid ourselves!"

"Good," Margaret said firmly. "Stay hidden. It's going to be all right."

"Where?" the other whispered.

Margaret almost sighed in exasperation. "Go down to the kitchens. It will be quite safe there."

"Yes, Miss."

She paused in her motion, and glanced at them. "How should I go to the guest rooms if I do not want to be seen?"

"Take the servants' stair. It's a few paces behind you to the left."

Margaret nodded her thanks, and waved them away, waiting for them to move before she did so. She hurried on, taking the long and cramped servants' stair up to the third floor, then rushing down to the room Helen was in. She entered the room without knocking and found Helen sitting on the bed in her wrap, awake and confused.

"Lord, Margaret," she said faintly, looking her over. "Did you climb out of your window?"

"As a matter of fact, yes," Margaret retorted. She glanced down at herself, and found that her nightgown was filthy and in its current drenched state, left nothing to the imagination. She grabbed for one of Helen's wraps nearby and donned it, cinching the sash tightly around her. "Come with me."

Helen scrambled off of the bed. "What is going on?"

"Shh!" Margaret scolded, gesturing for silence, and for her cousin to follow.

They made their way down the stairs to the rest of the house, only to suddenly hear several thumps and crashes from her father's study. Margaret started to run towards the noises, but Helen grabbed her arm.

"Margaret!" she hissed, her eyes wide and terrified. "Let's go for help!"

Margaret tugged her arm free. "Help is in the study, and I am going after him." She dashed down the carpeted hall and pushed open the slightly ajar door.

Chest heaving, Rafe stood over a fallen body, the identity of which was hidden by her father's massive mahogany desk. He turned at the creak of the door and his eyes met hers, a fire in them.

"You're safe," he said simply.

"Yes," Margaret managed, heart pounding and fingers tingling.

He exhaled a shaking breath. "I went to your room first, the moment I could figure out how to get there. The door was locked from the outside, no protection in sight, and you were gone. Do you have any idea what I...?" He shuddered slightly and shook his head, striding around the desk. "Dammit, Margaret..."

Rafe came to her, his hands sliding into her damp tresses and pulling her towards him, his lips crashing down on hers. She wrapped her arms around him tightly, pressing herself as close as she could, arching up onto her tiptoes and returning his breathless kiss with all of the frantic passion and need coursing through her. He tilted her head for a deeper, more intimate kiss, and her knees shook with the intensity. He held her tightly, almost painfully so, but she thrilled with the pressure, the pleasure, the relief...

He broke off, kissing her cheeks, her nose, her brow. "I can't bear it, pet. I can't..."

"H-how did you hear me?" she asked, lowering herself down to the ground, her fingers gripping his damp shirt.

He grinned swiftly and kissed her nose again. "Providence. Fate. And the fact that I've been walking nearby every night since you sent me away, hoping for just a glimpse of you."

Margaret reared back as far as she could while he still held her face in his hands. "You were?"

He nodded, his eyes never leaving hers. "I told you I don't want to spend another day not seeing you. And I had to make sure you were safe. I had to protect you, even if you didn't want me anymore." He cupped her cheeks and stroked them softly. "I meant what I said. I love you."

All of the breath vanished from Margaret's lungs and she stared at Rafe in wonder. She pulled on his shirt and drew his mouth to hers, melting against him. His arms moved and encircled her, pulling her close, and she thought, very faintly, that she could die quite happily thusly. After he'd kissed her senseless, of course.

"Lord, Margaret…"

Margaret broke from Rafe's lips with a gasp and whirled, Rafe's arms still around her, and they pulled her against his body protectively.

Helen stood in the door with a raised brow and a curious half smile. "Help is in the study, you said. Clever girl."

Rafe chuckled and stepped away from Margaret, but only just. He bowed perfectly. "Miss Dalton, I presume."

"And you would be the man who sent me that rather cryptic note this week." She gave him a coy hint of a curtsey. "Much obliged." She glanced down the hall, and her playfulness faded. "Ritson is coming, and she is in a frenzy." Helen folded her arms and moved around the desk to look at the fallen man, wrinkling her nose up. "Oh, lord, it's a Rom. I thought they hated city life."

"They do," Rafe and Margaret said together.

Helen leaned down, then looked at Rafe in shock. "He is out cold."

"He ought to be," Rafe muttered darkly. "He had a good thrashing coming, and I was only too delighted to comply."

"Lord, Margaret," Helen murmured, smiling a little. "Find one for me, will you?"

Ignoring her, Rafe pulled Margaret to the side of the room. He glanced out of the door, then took her hands and squeezed tightly. "Margaret, listen to me," he said earnestly. "There is something I need to tell you."

Margaret opened her mouth to reply, but then a horrible screeching sound rent the air, and Miss Ritson, in all her terrifying fury, appeared in the doorway. "Thieves! Ruffians! They are after the master's fortune!"

"What?" Margaret cried, trying to stand between Rafe and her chaperone. "No!"

"Help!" Miss Ritson called, trying to sound concerned while she appeared irate. "Help! Seize him! Protect our sweet lambs!"

Horace and Martin entered, looking large and menacing, and they took Rafe easily, as he did not resist.

"No!" Margaret screamed, tugging at Martin's arms. "No, it wasn't him!"

"Miss Ritson." Helen tried to interject, her voice calmer.

"Miss Dalton, I don't know how I will face your parents after this horrible incident," Miss Ritson overrode, dripping an apology in every word. She turned to Margaret and moved to embrace her, which sent Margaret careening back into the bookshelf with a painful lurch. "My dear Margaret, you are safe!"

The footmen hauled Rafe out of the room, but he dragged his feet, keeping his eyes on her.

"You can't take him!" Margaret cried, trying to move past her.

Miss Ritson shook her head, her expression furious. "I've already sent for the magistrate, and he will be here shortly to take them both away."

"You knew he was coming!" Margaret accused, pointing at the fallen Rom. "You called the magistrate for him before he could do anything!"

"Such lies and falsehoods!" Miss Ritson scolded. "You poor, poor dear. The thief has been apprehended, and his accomplice there must have had a stroke of conscience that irritated him." She leaned closer and gripped Margaret's arm. "Did he take you from your room?"

"No," Margaret snapped, trying to wrench away.

The grip tightened. "Say that he did. Or would you like your parents to know that you aided in an attempted robbery?"

Margaret glowered. "I did no such…"

"What is all this?"

Margaret gasped as her father's voice met her ears and Miss Ritson's eyes widened. Margaret dashed around her and flung herself into her father's open arms, heedless of the damp greatcoat. Her mother tittered about Margaret's nightgown, and Miss Ritson started in on the story of the break in and the dangers they had been in, as the footmen returned for the unconscious Rom. Margaret recognized him at once as the one she had seen with Sir Vincent, and she shivered at the memory.

Her father patted her softly, then turned to listen to Miss Ritson's story, with Helen standing in the background, looking rather amused by the new tale.

Margaret took the opportunity to run to the front door and wrench it open, just in time to see Rafe being loaded into the magistrate's carriage, still not fighting anyone off. She shook her head and started to run out into the storm, but his eyes met hers, and he shook his head slowly.

She stopped on the stair and bit her lip, longing for one more touch of his lips, one more brush of his fingers, one more... something.

Rafe smiled a little as shackles were clamped around his hands. "It's all right," he mouthed.

It wouldn't be all right. He'd saved her, and now he was being blamed for the crime he had prevented. They would be separated, and that was most certainly *not* all right.

"I love you," she replied in kind, covering her heart with one hand, curling it tightly against her skin. The silent words spread between them, and she felt herself soaring with them, despite the agony that was pulsing through her with every beat of her heart.

His smile grew into a wild grin and he winked.

Then he was fully loaded into the carriage, and the footmen brushed passed her with the Rom, who was also loaded in, and then the carriage rolled away just as a sob escaped Margaret's throat.

"Margaret, what happened here?" her mother's voice chirped from inside the house.

Margaret shook her head, closed her eyes on tears, and ran back into the house, up the stairs, and into her room, flinging herself onto the bed and sobbing loudly into the pile of bedcovers. The sound was smothered, but it echoed within her, and she wished, just once, to feel nothing.

It was several minutes later when her father knocked on her

door, saying her name softly.

Not used to anyone asking for permission to enter, Margaret turned and stared at the door curiously. "Come in?"

He entered the room and looked much more himself, without greatcoat or coat, cravat limp, and his greying hair rumpled. He smiled fondly, his round face transforming. "Margaret, love, I've been speaking with your cousin, and she has told me a very interesting tale. Have you been locked in your room all this week and beyond?"

The strain of the last few weeks finally settled upon her and she felt unbearably weary. "Yes."

His brows lowered and he came over to the bed. "Because you ran away."

She nodded repeatedly. "Yes."

"Because Miss Ritson wanted you to marry this Sir Vincent person."

Margaret's eyes filled with tears. She wouldn't have to marry Sir Vincent anymore. She wouldn't be forced to do anything anymore. "Yes," she said again, her tears finding their way into the tiny word.

Her father sighed and took her hand. "I think you had better tell me why."

She did so, slowly and carefully, reliving the last few weeks for his benefit. She left out everything romantic about Rafe, everything that she would never want to tell her father, but all of the pertinent details remained. Her father remained very calm through the telling, only the growing furrows in his brow indicating his displeasure.

When she was done, he shook his head slowly. "And the man they took away just now. Your cousin said he saved you."

Margaret straightened, nodding. "Yes, he did. You've seen him, Father, he is often down by the grocers and is always so polite and considerate to Mama and me. He heard me calling for help and came to my rescue."

"Yes, I thought so," her father replied with a nod, his mouth curving in satisfaction. "We must repay him for his kindness. Do you know his name?"

She hesitated, wondering what she could say, how the magistrate would know him. "I believe he is called the Gent, Father."

He chuckled, shaking his head. "How very apt a name. I shall call on the magistrate at once and have him released and rewarded. And you need not worry, my dear. You don't have to marry Sir Vincent. Your mother and I shall find a proper European for you. We have a number in mind already, it was a most productive trip."

Margaret sighed heavily, discouragement and relief filling her. "And Miss Ritson?"

Her father snorted. "She will be dismissed, of course. We never would have hired her if we had known she would behave so cruelly."

He rose from the bed, and stroked Margaret's cheek as he had when she was a little girl. "Don't worry, duckie. I will take care of everything."

Margaret managed a smile for him, then tilted her head. "I did not expect you back. What happened?"

"Oh, we had word from Helen several days ago," he told her with a wave of his hand. "She said things were not at all well and we would do best by returning to you. I've always found Helen a touch dramatic, so we did not hasten back. I am sorry for it now, but you seem well enough."

He kissed her cheek and tapped her chin, then left the room.

One of the maids came up to help Margaret reset her room and change into fresh nightclothes, and then Margaret sat before her window, staring out into the night, the storm now passed.

She would have to find Rafe after he was released. She had to tell him that she would be leaving after all, forced to marry a foreigner. But at least he would be free. If she had to do it so he could be free, she would.

It might break her heart, but for him, she could do so.

It was her turn to save him now.

Chapter Twenty-Two

$\mathcal{M}$argaret raced down to breakfast almost the moment she awoke, seeing that it was far later than she normally slept, and knowing her father was a very early riser. He would have been about his business first thing, and she had to know what had happened.

She had to know Rafe was safe and well and whole and...

She passed the study with a shiver, but was gratified that her usual footmen had been returned to their posts, and they seemed pleased by it as well.

"Margaret," Helen called from the morning room, sitting on a sofa and embroidering with her mother.

"Not now!" she called, foregoing politeness.

She pushed into the library, knowing that was where her father would be, now that he was returned from his travels.

He sat by the fire, despite the warmth of the day, and his spectacles were perched on his long nose. He looked over them at her as she entered the room. "Good morning, my dear. Or is it afternoon yet?"

She smiled tightly. "Not yet, Father."

He grunted and went back to his book.

Margaret frowned, then cleared her throat softly. "Father, I wondered... Have you been to see the magistrate this morning?"

"Hmm?" he asked, looking up distractedly.

"The magistrate," she repeated firmly, losing her innocent daughter tone.

Her father missed the change. "Ah, yes, yes, of course." He pulled off his spectacles and tapped his mouth with them. "I went to see Lord Cartwright this morning, yes. I explained the situation and asked if the Gent could be released, as he had done us quite a service, and Lord Cartwright agreed that the circumstances were extenuating, and he thought there should be some leniency."

Margaret's heart swelled and she forced herself to calm, clasping her fingers in front of her. "That is wonderful," she managed to say without inflection.

"Unfortunately, his lordship had already been asked to turn the Gent over to the Home Office, for some reason." He shook his head as if the notion bewildered him. "He had no information on what had proceeded from that point on. It seemed that there was quite an interest in him, so I can only presume that he was not always such a gentleman, as it were."

Margaret clamped down on her lips hard, letting her eyes flutter shut. "I see."

"So I felt my only recourse was to venture down to the Home Office myself."

Her eyes sprang open and she gaped. "You did?"

He nodded, his eyes twinkling a little. "I know Sir Robert Peel a little from our younger years, so I thought I might be able to persuade him. But he was not in, and the whole venture proved fruitless."

Margaret's heart sank and she leaned against the chair nearest her. "Was it?"

"They flatly refused to help me," he grumbled, shaking his head. "Would not even confirm that they had him, or that the Gent even existed." He exhaled irritably. "I shall be writing to Sir Robert to express my disappointment, and I shall use some very strong words."

Margaret was fairly certain *she* was going to be using some very strong words momentarily. "So... that is it?" she asked faintly.

Her father's soft eyes met hers. "I am so sorry, duckie, I tried. I cannot do anything else."

Her throat worked on a swallow and a sob. "But he could die!" she managed to force out. "They wouldn't care about him, he's nothing and no one, he could die and no one would be the wiser!"

"He could," her father replied with a sad nod. "And that would be a tragedy. He deserves so much more. But my dear..." He gestured for her to come closer, and took her hand when she did so, kissing it fondly. "All will be sorted out in the end. One way or another. You are safe, and I thank him for it. Now that is that, and we must put it behind us."

Margaret resisted the urge to yank her hand away from her father's, and let it fall to her side limply. "Yes, Father."

She turned to leave the room, wondering where her heart had gone, and why it hurt to place one step in front of the other.

It was over. She would never see him again, and if Rafe's past was half as colorful as she thought it was, he would be dealt with quickly and without any fuss. As he had no standing, no family, and no one of consequence to care, they could avoid any of the entanglements of law.

She would move to Europe for her foreign husband, and he would be dead.

There was nothing else to do.

"Margaret?" her father called. "Don't forget, we are promised to Lord and Lady Smithfield's tomorrow. Wear something fetching, the ambassador from Austria is to attend, and I know his uncle."

She closed her eyes on tears, forcing herself to swallow. "Y-yes, Papa."

She winced as the childish name escaped her lips. She had not called him that since she was very little, and if he was listening at all, he would know she was distressed.

"Thank you, duckie. You are such a gentle love."

Margaret rolled her eyes and gave up the pretense of calm, as her father was not listening and thought she was eight years old as it was. She left the library and moved towards the back of the house, intending to go out into the gardens and walk in the morning sunshine.

"Margaret…"

Helen's soft voice stopped her, and Margaret half turned, her hands forming fists at her side. "I am going to cry, Helen," she said through gritted teeth. "If you cannot…"

She heard Helen hiccup and looked up in surprise.

Her cousin had tears streaming down her cheeks, staring at Margaret sadly.

"What's wrong?" she asked, her curiosity outweighing her pain for the moment.

Helen shook her head. "You!" She sniffled and came to Margaret, throwing her arms around her. "I was eavesdropping, of course, and I heard everything. Oh, Margaret…"

Margaret tensed for a moment, resisting the onslaught of emotion, and then released it in one loud, gasping sob, burying her face into her cousin's shoulder, and crying with her.

"He's a ruddy hero," Helen told her stubbornly, her words wavering. "He's a masterpiece of a man, and he… He…"

"He loved me," Margaret whimpered, shuddering with more tears.

Helen wailed more loudly. "He's not dead yet!" she protested, trying to slap Margaret's hand, but not managing.

"He is," Margaret insisted, pushing off of her cousin and moving to the window. "Whether he is in truth or not, to me, he might as well be dead."

Helen came to her and took her hand, dabbing at her own eyes. "Tell me about him, Margaret. Please. He sent me a note that told me you were in trouble, which is why I sent Tibby to see what Ritson was up to. He trusted me without ever knowing me, and he loved you with a passion that I did not believe any Englishman possessed. He deserves to be more than a name to us."

Margaret sniffed and smiled up at the ceiling, letting the morning light from the window warm her. "He was. Oh, he was."

Helen pulled her to the sofa and listened while Margaret told her all of the details that she had left out of every story, even the ones she had told to herself. She never said his real name, that was still hers alone, but everything else about him, she shared.

And it did not hurt as much as she thought it would.

But later that night, alone in her room, it hurt quite a good deal.

The Smithfields were not exactly intolerable people, but they were a bit tedious, if one were to be perfectly honest. They were fine company, it was true, but all that was required for fine company was decent conversation, respectability, and not desiring to escape.

And if Lady Smithfield attempted small talk with Margaret one more time, she just might scream.

She had not wanted to attend, waking up in more pain this morning than she had gone to bed with. Helen had gone home, and was undoubtedly here tonight somewhere, but she would not come to Margaret right away. She knew what torment this would be, and she would be the only one.

Margaret had begged to stay at home with a headache, but her mother had only brought out her usual remedies for such things, which had always worked in the past, and having them fail now would only increase the attention she received, when all she wanted was the opposite. She wanted to be left alone in her room, or to wander the house as she would. She wanted to wear black and play sad songs on the pianoforte, though she would play them badly. She wanted to think dismal thoughts and not be forced into the world of social gatherings.

But she could not tell her parents the truth.

She could not tell them she was in love with the intruder who was not a robber who was a nobody she saw on the street every day. She could not actually mourn a man to whom she had no ties or bindings. She could not turn recluse without raising suspicions.

So here she was, against the wall, hoping, for the first time, that she would be as invisible tonight as she had been every other night in London.

She watched the guests milling about, only truly seeing a few.

Lord Rothchild was there, along with his wife, and Margaret watched them for a long time, catching all of the looks and smiles they gave each other. The way her fingers brushed against his arm as he led her about the room. The way Lord Rothchild's eyes lingered on his wife long after she'd looked away. The way they stood so close together as though they couldn't bear to be further apart. They had been married for ages, and to still have that sort of love and passion... It was somehow both painful and beautiful.

Mr. Pratt was making a splash, as usual, his bright green waistcoat a thing of interest for many, and even Helen, dressed in a radiant white, had been seen taking notice. And if Margaret's observations told any tales, it would certainly tell of the repetition of Mr. Pratt's gaze straying towards her cousin's fine figure as she moved past, both in dance and in walk. And if that was a truth, it would also bear the repeating of Helen's soft smirk, acknowledging what Margaret strongly suspected: she knew he was looking, and she moved for that benefit alone.

Had that gone on all Season without her seeing it? She'd been so distracted by her own worries and cares that she had missed so many things.

She saw the way Rosalind lingered at the edge of Captain Riverton's circle, her back turned towards him, yet somehow the two met eyes more often than seemed possible. Rosalind was softer now, less inclined to bristle, and Captain Riverton spoke with less boisterousness, his smile a little less brash. They had both greeted her already, and fondly at that, which she had reciprocated. But even then, she had felt like an intruder in some private, ongoing conversation.

The Gerrards came to her and spoke for a bit, but did not linger, as did the Blackmoors. Tibby had not yet arrived, which was a blessing, as her intuition would never let Margaret alone in her present distress. All of the associations she had made while under Tibby's protection paid their due respects to her, but no one overstayed politeness, for which she was grateful.

She had a slight reprieve from the monotony when Mr. Pratt came to her, having broken free from his circle.

He bowed before her. "Miss Easton, that green you wear is most becoming, and compliments my own perfectly. Would you favor me with this dance?"

Margaret tilted her head, considering the foppish man with a bit of amusement. "I may prove a poor partner, Mr. Pratt. I am not particularly inclined to dance this evening."

The smile he offered was surprisingly gentle. "So I see, my dear, but one dance with me just might make you smile, and that is all I seek."

Now she did smile, and placed her hand in his. "Oh, very well, Mr. Pratt."

He clamped a hand over his heart. "Let the heavens rejoice!"

Margaret rolled her eyes. "Oh, lord."

He chuckled and led her into the line as the music struck up. "I must thank you, Miss Easton, for keeping my little secret."

She looked at him sharply, wondering that he should even bring it up. His expression was composed, but she saw a deeper intensity in his eyes. "It's nothing," she murmured, a little confused. "I promised I would, and so I shall."

He nodded, moving around her for the dance, his steps light and graceful. "A woman of your word, are you?"

"I try to be, yes," she replied as she mimicked his motions around him. She took his hand and allowed him to turn her. "Integrity is the key to honor, and I take it seriously."

"So you should, my dear." He parted from her to dance with the woman beside her, and she with her partner.

When they were reunited, he offered her a boyish grin. "You have not said anything of your secret, Miss Easton."

"No, and nor shall I." She gave him a severe look that only made him smile more. "There is no cause to let anyone have more to speak of when it comes to me."

"Truly?" he asked, moving around her once more. "I have only heard the most praiseworthy things of you."

She snorted softly as she took her turn. "Then you have not been listening to the right sources. I have it on good authority that a great many things were being said about me that I did not know."

He took her hand to lead her down the line, and leaned a little too close. "I never listen to the wrong sources, Miss Easton. I hear everything. And while there may have been some less than pleasant rumors, I can assure you that tonight all of it is behind you."

She glanced up at him as they finished their promenade. "How can you be sure?"

He raised a brow, the dandy expression completely gone. "I never mistake with gossip. And haven't you wondered why no one was whispering about you? Why everyone is behaving so normally?"

Margaret had wondered, actually. With everything that Ritson and Sir Vincent had brought about, and with all of the threats of exposure, she was sure that she would be nearly shunned, and yet she had not been. She looked up at Mr. Pratt, her mouth working silently.

He grinned swiftly and spun her around for the last movement. "Nothing but praises, Miss Easton. No harm done."

"How?" she managed to ask.

"By your own merits," he assured her.

She gave him a look, which made him chuckle.

"Very well, and by the efforts of your friends and mine." He bowed to her as the music finished. "And I might have said a few things myself. I do consider us the greatest of friends now, you know."

Margaret smirked a little as he led her back to her position by the wall. "Do you? How fortunate for me."

"Isn't it, though?" He winked and bowed once more, leaving her to her thoughts, wishing she felt any sort of attraction to Mr. Pratt or Captain Riverton or any of the men in this room. Oh, she could have married any one of them and had a perfectly acceptable marriage, by all accounts. But after feeling so much for Rafe, she had discovered what she was capable of, and settling for anything less just for convenience would have been a crime.

Perhaps she could actually fall in love with one of the European men her parents wanted. It was possible, she supposed, but not now, and not for some time. Everything hurt too much. Even watching the dancing now was painful.

She would have loved to dance with Rafe in public, as she'd once dreamed. To waltz in his arms, to laugh in a quadrille, to see his eyes dance more merrily than his feet... To steal away to secluded corner of the host's house to embrace freely... To rival the Rothchilds for most enviable couple...

Margaret closed her eyes, now burning with unshed tears. She could not cry here. She could not make a scene. She exhaled slowly and felt the tears subside, then forced her eyes open, keeping her expression calm and unaffected.

She could pretend for a while longer.

"Miss Easton, I have someone for you to meet!" Marianne Gerrard's cheerful voice chirped near her.

Margaret tried not to roll her eyes, wishing that her friends with good intentions would be a little less determined. She turned towards the approaching beauty, and bit back a gasp.

Standing next to Mrs. Gerrard's resplendent blue ensemble was a tall, perfectly formed man in a pristine set of formal wear. He was clean shaven, tanned, and in possession of a pair of very familiar dark eyes that were now alight with mirth.

Rafe.

"My dear Miss Easton, might I introduce Lord Marlowe?" Mrs. Gerrard said, her voice a faint humming in Margaret's ears. "He is a dear friend of my husband's, and godfather of my son. He would like to make your acquaintance."

Margaret stared at him in shock, her mind whirling. How... *how...?*

"A pleasure, Miss Easton," he intoned gravely. He took her hand and bowed over it, heat from his touch racing up her arm, making her breath catch in her throat.

"L-lord Marlowe," she squeaked, her fingers twitching in his hold.

Rafe's eyes met hers, and she could see the smile in them, despite his bored expression.

"Tibby was so angry with him for not coming to her evening," Mrs. Gerrard was saying beside them. "She wanted you both to meet then, but I suppose meeting now is as good a time as any."

"Marianne," Rafe murmured without looking at her, "do shut up and go away."

Margaret's eyes widened, but Mrs. Gerrard only laughed merrily. "Marlowe, you are the only one in the world who can speak to me like that and not have repercussions. Very well, I will leave you to it. Behave, Marlowe," she called as she wandered away, her skirts swishing audibly against the floor.

"Always," he replied, though Margaret did not believe him for a second.

She stared at him, afraid to blink. He still held her hand, and tightly, and she replayed the last few moments over and over. Lord Marlowe. Lord. Marlowe. He had a title. He was here.

He was alive.

Her chest began to tighten and squeeze, a deep ache forming. Her breathing turned unsteady and a tremor started in her hands.

A movement behind him caught her eye, and she saw her parents coming over to them, looking interested.

Rafe didn't even spare a glance to see what she saw, he only led her out to the dance floor, his steps swift and sure.

"Say something," he said softly, squeezing her hand.

Margaret tried to inhale, but it caught and hiccupped. "You're here…" she managed, too emotional for their situation at present. "You're alive?"

He smiled tenderly, setting his hand on her waist for the waltz, pulling her as close as he could without being scandalous. "Shhh, love. Dance with me for a bit, and we'll escape when your parents stop watching."

She nodded, her eyes filling as she let him move her through the waltz, his motions sure. She had no idea how they moved so gracefully, as she wasn't aware of moving her feet at all, and she could not look anywhere but at him. Her chest shook and gasping breaths were all she could manage, a tear escaping and coursing down one cheek.

"Don't cry," he said with a laugh. "I'll never make it if you cry."

"You're alive," she said, her voice choked with tears. She shook her head, wishing the tears away, but they only rose with a vengeance. "You're alive."

Rafe growled low in his throat and glanced around. "Oh, to hell with it." He turned her through the other couples, waltzing perfectly towards the back of the room, then ducking with her into a side hallway. He pulled her along quickly, moving almost soundlessly through the house until they reached a small terrace. He closed the doors behind them and turned to face her.

"Margaret…" he said simply, and she could hear an apology coming.

She didn't need one.

She threw herself into his arms, and he gathered her up, one hand latching around her, the other holding her head against him. "Oh, love, don't…"

Margaret sobbed against his chest, shaking with the force of her cries.

"I hope these aren't tears of fury," he teased, pulling her tighter, his lips dancing against her ear. "I can't bear your tears of any kind, but…"

"Shut up," she hiccupped, leaning back. "I thought you were dead! Father went to have you freed, and they said that…" She reached up and took his face in her hands, and pressed her lips to his frantically.

He gentled the kiss with a murmur, stroking the back of her neck soothingly. Over and over he kissed her, soft, feather-light kisses that reminded her that he was here, and she was in his arms.

"You're alive!" she whispered against his lips.

He groaned softly and pulled back, forcing her to look at him. "Oh, pet, I am so sorry, I wanted to tell you from the start. I work for the government. I'm a spy. You got wrapped up in all of this by sheer bad luck, and I will explain everything soon, but all you need to know is that you are out of danger now. I took care of Castleton and things should be calm for some time. I didn't want to lie to you, and I won't anymore, but…"

"I don't care," she interrupted, shaking her head. "I don't care! You're here and I'm here and I love you, and if you say yes, I won't have to move to Europe and marry an ambassador!"

He reared back, eyes wide. "What? No!"

"No?" she cried.

"I mean, yes!" he said at once, shaking his head, then nodding it. "Yes, yes. You're not marrying anybody but me, I'm not even going to ask." He kissed her hard, his fingers tangling in her hair.

"Good," she sighed with a smile, when he allowed her to break free.

He stroked her cheek softly. "My Margaret… You really don't mind? There are details and specifics, and you can never tell anyone…"

She shrugged, covering his hand with her own. "I don't mind. I love you, Rafe, and all I have ever wanted is to be with you. I would move heaven and earth to have you, and I felt all of that before I ever knew you had a title."

He smiled warmly, his eyes crinkling. "And I wanted you before I ever knew just how extensive your fortune was."

She giggled and kissed him again, then pulled back. "Is your name really Rafe?"

He nodded, folding his arms around her, tucking her against him. "It is. Raphael William Edward Thornton, seventh Lord Marlowe. But most people just call me Marlowe. Or Gent. Depends on the person in particular. Rogue calls me all sorts of things that I will never be able to repeat."

Margaret nuzzled against him, sighing. "And what shall I call you, my lord?"

"Yours, my love. Always and forever yours."

Epilogue

She was out in the rain again. It was the silliest thing, she was always doing it, and it was going to get her sick one of these days. She just stood there, head tilting back, breathing in the fresh air and soaking her skin and clothing with the raindrops.

An artist would have wept at the beauty in the scene, and begged for opportunity to capture it onto canvas.

But there were no artists here, and certainly no weeping.

"Helena Thornton, what do you think you are doing?"

The little dark-haired girl looked coyly over her shoulder and wrinkled her nose up. "Catching raindrops."

"Oh? What with?"

"My face."

Rafe chuckled and opened the door further. "Well, you've certainly caught enough for today. Come on inside and dry off now."

His daughter turned and put her hands on her hips, her brow furrowing in a frown. "You never force Mama to come inside when she does it."

"Your mama is a grown woman and I do not force her to do anything." He waved her in, his expression serious, despite his urge to laugh. "You, however, I can, because I am your father, and it is getting cold."

Helena grumbled under her breath and marched towards him.

He bit back a smile as he took the toweling from the maid and rubbed it through his daughter's long hair. She crossed her arms, shivering slightly.

"I told you it was cold," he teased, moving to wrap the towel around her shoulders.

"It wasn't cold until I came inside," she insisted firmly.

Rafe sighed a longsuffering sigh, knowing his daughter took after him in many ways, despite looking exactly like her mother. And her uncle Rogue was a horrible influence on her. "Well, we had better sit by the fire then, hadn't we, poppet?"

She grinned up at him and nodded.

He moved over to the large chair by the fire, and laughed when she jumped into his lap, snuggling close. She was almost too big to be doing this, and it would break his heart when she was. At a very precocious eight years old, she was growing more and more independent, with some rather mature moments, and her younger siblings followed her lead in all things.

It was one of the reasons Rafe rarely slept well anymore.

"What did you do today, poppet?" he asked her, running his hand over her damp head.

"Mama let Anna Riverton come to play," Helena replied, sounding sleepy. "She has the best dolls, and her papa is always giving her more."

Rafe laughed and looked down at his oldest child. "And your papa does not?"

"No," she said stubbornly. "You always say we must play with what we have until we can prove we deserve more."

"That's right," he replied with a sage nod, enjoying the petulant tone his daughter employed. "And have you?"

"I should say so!" she retorted, pushing back and looking at him with a fierce frown. "I am always letting the boys play with my things, and I tend them while Mama and Cousin Helen visit, even when she brings those awful twins."

"Don't say awful."

"AWE-FULL," she insisted, pronouncing each syllable emphatically.

Rafe leaned his head back against his chair. "They are not awful."

"Yes, they are."

"Oh, all right, yes they are, but you are sweet for tolerating them."

Helena sniffed with too much airs. "I know. But they do bring out the worst in Gabriel and Christopher. David behaves himself, but only just."

"And what about Lucy?"

Helena smiled at the mention of her youngest sibling and only sister, not yet two years in age. "Lucy is perfect, Papa, and you know it." She snuggled against him again, closing her eyes. "Why were you gone so long this time? It took *ages* for you to come back."

He sighed and hugged his little girl close. "I'm sorry, poppet. Business took far longer than I thought it would, but it is all settled now, and I won't be going away for a while."

"That's good," she replied, her words slurring a little with her drowsiness.

Within moments, she was asleep, and he was close to it himself.

"When did you get home?"

Rafe turned at the soft scold of his wife, now standing in the doorway, as beautiful now as the first day he'd seen her in the streets of London. He smiled fondly, momentarily without words. "Only just," he assured her.

She raised a brow and folded her arms, the motion emphasizing her swollen abdomen. "You know perfectly well you are supposed to come directly to me the moment you arrive from any trip, Rafe Thornton."

The rule had been instituted almost from the first moments of their marriage, and he had never broken it before now. He'd never even considered doing so, as he rather liked greeting his wife first after an absence, even if it was only after one day. Nothing was certain in his life but the love of his wife and children, and he refused to take a single moment with them for granted.

"I was about to do so," he told her, "when I saw our oldest out in the rain."

Margaret smiled, her violet eyes twinkling merrily. "What was she doing? Dancing?"

He shook his head. "She said she was catching the rain. With her face."

Margaret laughed, glancing out of the windows. "Well, it is a rather lovely rain today."

Rafe gave her a playful look. "Are you so inclined?"

She smirked a little. "You just scolded our daughter for going out into the rain, Lord Marlowe. Are you now encouraging your wife to do the same?"

"I might be." He shrugged as best as he could with his daughter sleeping in his lap. "There are far more benefits to my wife being out in the rain than my daughter."

Margaret watched him for a long moment, her eyes softening. "I missed you," she whispered.

Instantly, his teasing was gone. "Oh, pet…"

She waved a hand, the sheen of tears in her eyes now. "Stop."

He shook his head and rose from the chair carefully, then deposited Helena back into it, covering her with a nearby blanket. Then he moved to his wife and pulled her into his arms.

"I always miss you when you're away," Margaret whispered, her voice wavering. "It doesn't matter how many times you go, or how many years it has been, it always aches just as much as the first."

"I know, love," he murmured, kissing her hair and dusting his lips along her hairline. "It kills me to be away from you, each and every time. I hardly leave before I am yearning for home."

She arched up to kiss his lips softly, lingering a bit, then she sighed. "I'm sorry. I should not complain."

Rafe snorted and tucked her head under his chin. "My love, you are not complaining, and you never have. It is a hard thing I do, and you are an angel for putting up with it. Hush and let me hold you a while."

Margaret patted his chest softly. "How was it?"

"Challenging," he replied carefully. "But Kem and Lela send their regards, as well as gifts for the children."

"I would have loved to see them."

"Yes, I know. But not this time, sweetheart. Maybe next."

He never told her specifics of his missions, and she never asked. He never told her of the dangers, but she knew anyway. She knew when he was worried, stressed, or needed assistance, and his rare bursts of temper had never once upset her. She took his comings and goings with patience and tolerance, and loved him when he was at his most unlovable.

He had devoted his life to loving her with passion and

tenderness, to proving to her that he was worth the risk of loving him, but he still did not know why she had agreed to marry him after everything. Her parents had left England shortly after their marriage, and only returned for the occasional visits and to see the children, but Margaret had never expressed a moment of regret about their life.

She always teased that she'd wanted to remain in England, and he was her best alternative, but he'd never forgotten those harried days before their surprise betrothal, short as it had been. He'd never forgotten how close he came to losing her, and times like these, it felt closer than usual, and he held her a little tighter.

His one comfort in leaving her as often as he must was that she was never unprotected. Half of their servants were his operatives or part of the network, and extras were posted nearby when he was away. It might have seemed excessive, but he knew the others did the same.

"Are you well?" Margaret asked, bringing his thoughts back to his most recent mission.

"I am now," he told her, tipping her chin back to kiss her softly.

Margaret broke off the kiss before he expected, backing away with a sly smile.

"Where are you going, Lady Marlowe?" Rafe purred, smiling and following her slowly.

She started humming softly, and turned to the terrace doors, pushing them open once more, then striding out into the rain, tipping her head back, just as her daughter had.

"It is a lovely rain," she murmured in a throaty tone that drove him mad.

He stared at her for the longest time, his breath catching. He'd seen her do this before, hundreds of times, but it never felt any less stirring. This was the essence of his wife, and this was what had made him fall in love with her. Not her wit or her beauty, not her unconventional ways or stubborn will... It was this contentment, peace, and moving energy that encompassed everything she did and was.

She turned slightly to look at him, smiling as the rain dampened her hair and clothes further. "Come and dance with me, Rafe."

He stared at her, held her loving, violet gaze with his own.

"One," he murmured slowly, sliding his hands into his trouser pockets.

Margaret's full lips curved into a smile and she stared back at him.

At three she sighed.

At five her eyes turned a dusky, darker shade that almost undid him.

At eight his heart cried out for mercy.

At ten…

"Ten," she whispered, exhaling unsteadily and holding out a hand to him.

He was to her in an instant, cupping her dampened cheeks and staring deeply into those wondrous eyes of hers. "I love you," he choked out, his emotions completely beyond his control.

She kissed the palm of his hand. "I love you, too." Smiling gently, she nuzzled against him. "Dance with me, Rafe."

He chuckled and prepared to waltz, but she shook her head, turning her back to him. "Not like that," she whispered. She placed his hand on her waist, then drew the other around her middle, and began swaying, humming once more.

Rafe pulled his wife flush against him, closing his eyes as they danced in the rain, turning and stomping, staying close to each other, their hands running the familiar courses of each other as they swayed and moved together.

A soft jingling sound accompanied them, and Rafe grinned as Margaret flashed her ankle at him, where a small chain of coins danced against her skin.

He pulled her back to his front, wrapped his arms around her, and kissed her hungrily, almost smiling when one of her hands reached up to his hair, the other lacing with his fingers where they rested on her stomach, where their next child kicked in time with the dance.

"I love you so much, *monisha*," Rafe rasped, stroking her jaw with a free hand.

Margaret smiled, and it dazzled him. "Darling Gent, I know you do." And then she kissed him again.

Helena Thornton, now not so very asleep, watched her parents kiss in the rain, dancing in that rather strange way, and wondered where in the world her very proper mother had learned that, and how her slightly boring father had convinced her to marry him. And why in the world they were always counting to ten with each other…

They were a very unusual family, and she had far too many siblings for her taste, but they all loved each other, and she supposed there were worse things.

Besides, it was her mother who taught her to stand in the rain.

And someday, she had promised, some man will find that a very fine thing indeed.

Helena smiled now, and settled back down into her chair by the fire.

She did so love when her father came home.

Coming Soon

The London League
Book Two

"No honor among rogues."

by

Rebecca Connolly

Lightning Source UK Ltd.
Milton Keynes UK
UKHW020852250322
400611UK00010B/630

9 781943 048496